P9-DXJ-715

022

This gift
provided by:

NO LONGER PROPERTY OF
SEATTLE PUBLIC LIBRARY

SUPPORTSPL.ORG

The
Seattle
Public
Library
Foundation

ALSO BY DASHKA SLATER

The Book of Fatal Errors

DASHKA SLATER

FARRAR STRAUS GIROUX
NEW YORK

Farrar Straus Giroux Books for Young Readers
An imprint of Macmillan Publishing Group, LLC
120 Broadway, New York, NY 10271
mackids.com

Text copyright © 2022 by Dashka Slater
Map credit © Celia Krampien
All rights reserved.
Our books may be purchased in bulk for promotional, educational, or business use. Please
contact your local bookseller or the Macmillan Corporate and Premium Sales Department
at (800) 221-7945 ext. 5442 or by email at MacmillanSpecialMarkets@macmillan.com.

Library of Congress Cataloging-in-Publication Data is available.

First edition, 2022
Book design by Carol Ly
Printed in the United States of America by LSC Communications, Harrisonburg, Virginia

ISBN 978-0-374-30648-9 (hardcover)
1 3 5 7 9 10 8 6 4 2

For my mother

CONTENTS

1

CAMP BIZBUZZ

According to the sign on her tank, the chameleon's name was Kesha. Pale green, with a tail that curled like a fiddlehead fern, she was perched on a branch inside a glass terrarium in a classroom at Stormweather Prep, the fancy private school on the hill overlooking Galosh. It was a nice classroom—nicer than anything at Galosh Middle School—but Kesha didn't seem particularly enthusiastic about the inspirational posters or the hardwood floors or the floor-to-ceiling windows. She regarded Rufus with a baleful eye as he squatted in front of her, clearly wondering why she was in a classroom at all instead of scampering around the jungle catching flies or whatever it was that chameleons did in their free time.

Rufus could relate. It was the middle of July, and he felt as trapped in the classroom as Kesha probably did inside her tank. He should be at Feylawn, the rambling property where his grandfather lived. Feylawn was where, at the start of summer, he had first met a tiny winged feyling named Iris, who drew him and his cousin Abigail into a hunt for the feylings' missing train and a battle with their enemies, the goblins. Now the feylings had gone back home to the Green World. Rufus and Abigail had promised to take care of Feylawn in their absence.

But instead of being at Feylawn, he was at camp. Chess camp last week, Plumbing camp the week before that, and now Camp BizBuzz, a two-week summer program "for the leaders and entrepreneurs of the future," according to the brochure. Kids like the ones who were now entering the classroom and greeting each other with hugs and high fives. Smart kids. Ambitious kids. Kids who excelled. Not kids like Rufus, whose one and only unusual talent was being able to see creatures that no normal twelve-year-old believed existed.

He watched the other campers through the glass of Kesha's tank. They clustered in clumps, filling the room with their voices, comparing shoes and haircuts and smartphones, saving each other side-by-side seats at the long tables arranged in a U shape. He recognized a few from Galosh Middle School, but he guessed that most of them went to Stormweather Prep. It was clear they'd all known each other for years.

"We don't belong here," he whispered to Kesha.

Kesha moved farther up the branch, her color brightening to a chartreuse banded with brown stripes and spots.

Her message was clear: *If you want to survive, you're going to have to blend in.*

But Rufus didn't *want* to blend in. Camp BizBuzz had been his father's idea, not his. Every minute he was away from Feylawn was a minute lost. A minute in which he wasn't attacking the list of chores Iris had left. A minute in which he wasn't figuring out how to persuade his family not to go through with their plan to sell it.

He looked at Kesha, green and brown on a green and brown branch. "What are your *true* colors?" he asked. "Don't you get tired of just adapting?"

Kesha looked back at him with one unblinking eye. She puffed out her throat.

"Stop *staring* at her—she thinks you're going to eat her."

Rufus swiveled so fast he lost his balance and landed on his butt. Abigail stood looking down at him, her long black hair neatly braided, her hands in the pockets of her denim shorts.

"Fun fact: the whole camouflage thing about chameleons is kind of a myth," she said, pulling him to his feet. "They change colors to communicate, not to blend in. Right now she's telling you to back off."

Rufus grinned. Of course Abigail would turn out to be a chameleon expert. "What are you doing here? I thought you had Mandarin Camp."

"I did. But then my mom heard your dad snagged you a

spot at Camp BizBuzz and she somehow got me in as well. Opportunity to excel and all that."

"Where are you sitting?"

"Next to you, obviously." Abigail strode over to the table and Rufus followed. She had laid her turquoise hoodie across two chairs on the right side of the U, a little closer to the front than Rufus would have chosen on his own. Now she unzipped her backpack and began placing materials in neat piles in front of her seat: notebook, pencil case, a folder of printed documents.

"What's this?" He gestured to the folder.

"Research materials," she said. "Just some stuff I printed out last night."

"Research on *what*? We don't even know what we're going to be doing yet."

"*Preliminary* research," Abigail corrected. "Look around. Every one of these kids is a competitor. We have to be quick out of the starting gate if we want to win this thing."

Before Rufus could ask what thing they were trying to win, a skinny guy in his early twenties strode to the front of the room. He wore a novelty baseball cap in the shape of a bee with a long stinger.

"Good morning, BizBuzzers! I'm Mark Trang and I have the great honor of being your team leader for the next two weeks of entrepreneurial adventures! You kids are the entrepreneurs of tomorrow, but your future is created by what you do *today*." He gestured at the whiteboard beside him, on which he'd written, *Procrastination is the thief of time.—Edward Young.* "You don't have to *wait* to be successful. All of you have the power to be successful *right now*. Each day this week we'll meet some crazy-cool, crazy-smart businesspeople, and then you'll get to work creating your own business plans!"

Some of the Stormweather Prep kids actually cheered. Rufus glanced at Abigail, who was scanning the room like a photographer on safari. Outside, it had started to rain. The droplets pattered on the windows like tapping fingers. *Come out, come out, come out.*

Mark raised his hand as if he were a camper, and then he called on himself.

"Yes, Mark? Do you have a question?

"I *do* have a question, Mark! If we're doing all this fun stuff *this* week, what will we do *next* week?

"That's an excellent question, Mark—go to the head of the class. Oh, wait, you're already here!"

Chuckles from the other campers. Even Abigail laughed.

"Next week, you'll get to make a YouTube ad for your business!" Mark continued. "And then, on Thursday, we have our *grand-ay fee-nall-ay*: the Piranha Pitch Session."

"I guess that's our first business lesson," Rufus whispered. "Charge boatloads of money for a two-week camp and then end one day early."

Abigail shot him a warning look. *Pay attention*, she mouthed.

"What is the Piranha Pitch Session, you ask?" Mark was saying. "It's a chance to test your mettle. You'll pitch your business before a panel of three judges. The best pitch wins five hundred dollars in start-up money!"

"Five hundred dollars?" whispered Rufus. "That's snack money for these rich kids."

"But it's real money for *us*," Abigail replied. "One of us has to win it."

"That would be you," Rufus said. He had zero ideas for a business, and zero interest in coming up with one. What interested him was finding a way to get out of that room and up to Feylawn. Just before climbing on the train that would take her back to the Green World, Iris had told Rufus and Abigail that she'd left them a list of chores to do—chores that would keep Feylawn safe. Rufus had studied the list so often he had it memorized. He wrote it down now on the first page of his notebook, hoping the act of writing would make him look like he was paying attention.

1. Smuckle border
2. Ward scrygrass
3. Goblin patrol
4. Keep umbrals from house
5. Troll (lunch)
6. Daily the diarnuts
7. Janati nests

8. Spetch the nimbolichen
9. Weed wanderlust
10. Cotter counseling

Rufus knew some of the words on the list. *Smuckling* was what kept anyone outside the family from finding Feylawn, even though it was right in the middle of town. *Umbrals* looked like large flying manta rays and made the electricity go out if they got too close to the house. *Cotters* were tiny orange fur balls who lived inside apricots and fell in love with everyone they met, leading to more relationship drama than any soap opera. But what on earth was a *diarnut*? What did it mean to *spetch* or *ward* or *daily*? Where would he find *scrygrass* and *wanderlust*?

Abigail looked over at the page.

"I know you hate Nettle, but we're going to have to let him do some of that stuff," Abigail said in a low voice. "He's there, and he knows how to do it, and we're at camp. Plus, it's pouring."

Rufus shook his head. "Why would I trust him to do anything important? He nearly killed my dad! He's the *reason* they want to sell Feylawn."

"But now he can't hurt us," Abigail reminded him. "Iris made him swallow peony seed for a reason—so he could help us do the stuff on this list. If we want our parents to change their mind about selling it, we have to keep things from getting crazy over there."

"Just because he *can't* hurt us doesn't mean he doesn't *want* to."

"It's in his own best interest to help us," Abigail argued. They both knew that Nettle had to make amends for what he did, or he'd never return to the Green World. "At least let him explain what warding the scrygrass means. It's the second thing on this list. Seems like it might be important."

"I'll figure it out on my own," Rufus said. "We can sneak up there today, after camp."

"You've already spent three weeks trying to figure it out," Abigail said. "And I have swim practice after camp."

"Just come long enough to check on the cotters and the umbrals. You're the one who gets along with them."

"Fine." Abigail rolled her eyes. "Now stop talking and focus on the assignment. *Procrastination is the thief of time.*"

"What assignment?"

Abigail gestured at the instructions on the whiteboard. "'Brainstorm a list of possible businesses. Consider how to monetize your hobbies.'"

Rufus flipped to a blank sheet of paper and sighed.

Procrastination wasn't the thief of time. Summer camp was.

THE GATE OF A THOUSAND LOCKS

Rance Diggs had been trapped in the Place Between for a while, but it was impossible to say how long. There was nothing to measure it by. The silence sucked at his large piglike ears. The air was leaden, bearing down on him like the low ceilings of the tunnels at home. For a long time, he had shimmied around on his belly like a worm, but there were no places to go, no enticing corridors or caverns, and at last he'd simply lain on his back and yelled. He was a Very Important Goblin, Northwest Regional tunnel boss, eldest of thirty-seven brothers, and he'd had his hands on, literally *on*, the train that would gain him entrance to the Green World, enriching him beyond measure while also bestowing the not-inconsiderable side benefit of bringing the feylings, his long-standing enemies, to a final and brutal extinction.

And then the boy, Rufus Collins, had somehow awakened the train, which had struck Diggs head-on and knocked him here. The Place Between. Where no one could find him and where his guile, his craft, his wealth, and his authority had no power. And so he kicked his thin bird-like legs in the air, and yowled with frustration, tearing at the Nothing around him with the talons of his feet. Perhaps he did this for hours. Perhaps for days or even weeks.

Eventually he stopped and lay on his back. Then he saw it: a small rip in the air, with a hanging flap of gunmetal-gray sky dangling from it like a torn cuticle. Rolling to his knees, he yanked at the dangling sky-skin until it tore further. He pushed an arm through, and then his head, and then he dug his long nails into the dirt of the other place and levered his way through.

He rolled to his knees and wrinkled his nose. The air had a briny, grassy smell. Being a rock goblin, he preferred the dank scent of tunnels and pits, but even an unpleasant *something* was better than a neutral *nothing*. He was getting somewhere at least.

He began to walk.

⁘

The path was narrow. To his left, violet waves clawed a rocky shore. To his right stood a six-foot-high wall of deep-red brambles. He ignored them, keeping his eyes on the queasy, disorganized swells of the purple sea, scanning the horizon for any sign of a boat, a bay, or a distant shore. He had been walking for most of the afternoon when he came across the print of his own talons in the dirt. He had come full circle.

As Mr. Diggs inspected the talon-print, his neck prickled with the sensation of being watched. He straightened slowly and scanned the late-afternoon shadows: the shore, the brambles, the few stunted trees. Nothing. And yet he was certain that someone was there.

Seeking cover, he dropped to his belly and wormed his way into the bramble thicket as if through a tight passage. Insects and snakes scuttled and squirmed out of his way. Sharp-beaked birds wheeled over his head. Rats skittered and squeaked as they burrowed deeper into the undergrowth. He ignored them all, just as he ignored the thorns that tore his flesh. He paid attention only to one thing: the sensation that something was on his trail, silently tracking him.

At last he emerged into a clearing. In front of him was a fence made of tall metal bars positioned so close together that he could barely poke a fingernail between. He stood and craned his neck up at their length, calculating that they were about the height of a five-story building, then inspected the metalwork with professional interest. He found it to be without fault or fissure, uncorrupted by the salt air. Behind those bars was either something valuable or something dangerous.

But which was it, and how could he turn it to his advantage?

The fence extended some fifty yards in each direction, then turned a corner. He walked along the perimeter, tracing its rectangular shape, until he came to a pair of gates lashed tight with chains. Here he stopped, his jaw dropping in surprise. He had heard of this place, but only in stories: a gate fastened not just by one lock, not just by two, but by hundreds and hundreds of locks, all of them black, all of them round, all of them tightly closed.

"The Gate of a Thousand Locks," he said aloud.

"Do you want to count them to make sure?" said a voice on the other side of the fence. "You seem quite a thorough creature, tramping round and round like a dog on a chain."

Mr. Diggs didn't like being startled and he didn't like being spoken to by someone he couldn't see. The skin on his legs and arms had begun to sting and swell, and now it suddenly itched so viciously that he hunched over, trying to scratch himself with both his hands and one of his talons.

"Who speaks? Are you guard or prisoner?" he called.

"I could ask the same of you," said the voice. It was a female voice, and it had far too much of a smile in it for Diggs's taste.

Irritation wrinkled his throat. "I'm a free man," he said, hoping it was true. "And you're a prisoner."

"Genius," marveled the voice. "What was your first clue?" She laughed. "Here's what I know about you. You're short. You've either got a thick hide, a high tolerance for pain and itching, or a complete lack of sense. I'd guess all three. That combined with your bilious temper says *goblin* to me. Welcome to the island of Imura, goblin. Have you come to set me free?"

Diggs snorted. "Let's say for the sake of argument that I wanted to. And let's say that I somehow managed to unfasten the one thousand locks. Then what? We're on an island without a boat. How do you propose we escape?"

"Ah," said the voice. "I've had so much time to ponder this question, but I prefer thinking about what we'll do when the escape is accomplished."

"The meals you'll eat, you mean?" Mr. Diggs said this in a careless tone, but his stomach grumbled. Goblins could go quite a long time without eating, but he was starving.

The laugh squeezed through the bars and exploded in Diggs's ear. "The meals will be the same inside or out— stupendous. I've got the Horn of Plenty in my cell. Spits out anything I'd like."

Diggs sank to the ground in astonishment. "The Horn of Plenty? That's been missing for five hundred years."

"I don't see how it can be missing when it's right here," the voice said. "The only one of my prizes my captors allowed me to keep. Here, I'll waft the smell your way."

A moment later the scent of stewed hooves and antlers drifted through the bars. "Borlibganlan," sighed Mr. Diggs. "Like my mother used to make for Fortieth Feast. With beetles." He closed his eyes and let the acrid smell burn itself into his nasal passages. Then his eyes snapped open.

"You're the Thief of the Eight Worlds," he said. "The one they call the Calamand."

"I am," said the Calamand in a modest tone.

"You stole the Horn of Plenty and the Felling Ax and the Slicers."

"I did," said the Calamand. "And much, much more."

"And you're locked here till the end of time."

"Gosh, I hope not," said the Calamand. "I have other plans for the end of time."

Mr. Diggs got to his feet. "We have a lot to discuss," he said. "But first, breakfast."

3

SCRYGRASS

It wasn't supposed to rain in Galosh in the summer. It rained from October to May, and then it was supposed to *stop* raining, giving Galoshites the opportunity to dry their socks, scrub the mold from their ceilings, and enjoy the emerald-green days of summer. But this summer had featured the rainiest July that Rufus could ever remember. As he walked across Feylawn's meadow, the rain filled his ears and trickled down the bridge of his nose. Beside him, Abigail huddled under the hood of her sweatshirt, her braids dripping squiggles of water down the front like twin paintbrushes.

"This is dumb," she said. "It's too wet to do anything, and I have to be at swim practice in twenty minutes."

Rufus shoved his hands in his pockets. Feylawn wasn't supposed to be a place with a schedule. It was supposed to be a place where time slowed down, stretched its legs.

"Just check on the cotters and the umbrals," he said.

"I'll look for janati-goose nests." Rufus had figured out that janati geese were the white birds with copper-colored beaks that honked random words at you when you got close, but he had no idea where they were likely to build their nests or why he was supposed to care. Even so, he kept searching for them, just like he kept trying to patrol for goblins and figure out what scrygrass was.

"You know, you *could* ask Nettle," Abigail said.

As if summoned, a blue Steller's jay landed on a boulder beside them. "Pledge Lord. Pledge Lady." He nodded his black crest at each of them in turn. "How can I be of help?"

"We're fine," Rufus said, scowling at Abigail. Just the sight of Nettle made him want to punch something. He could still hear Nettle shrieking, "Death to glompers!" just after he snapped the rope swing and sent his father crashing into the ravine.

"If I could just remind you about the scrygrass—perhaps it's slipped your mind?" Nettle spread his wings and hopped down to a puddle at their feet.

"I'll get to it," Rufus said. He hunched his shoulders against the rain. "Anything else?"

"I've smuckled the border and chased the umbrals out of the garden. As for goblin patrol—"

"I'll take care of that." Rufus refused to meet the bird's eye. He knew Nettle had smuckled the border between Feylawn and the rest of Galosh, because Feylawn continued to be invisible—or at least not noticeable—to everyone outside the family. But he didn't trust Nettle to keep out the goblins.

"Anti-goblin measures aren't for amateurs, Pledge Lord," Nettle said. "The seedcraft is complicated: goblinsbane, turntwist, fill-mallow. Better if I take care of it. I'm the last feyling here; protecting Feylawn is my sacred obligation."

"Could you just *clarify* what we're supposed to do about the scrygrass?" Abigail said, ignoring Rufus's glare. "Like, what it looks like? And where to find it? And how to 'ward' it?"

Nettle examined his own reflection in the puddle. "It wouldn't take long for me to do it," he said. "Comes naturally, if you're a feyling rather than a glomper. And as I've mentioned several times, it's important to catch the scrygrass before it flowers—"

"Fine! Go ahead! Do it!" Rufus brushed his dripping bangs off his face. "I'll handle the goblins and the geese." He turned toward the creek, where the janati geese sometimes congregated. The rain began again in earnest, the drops pounding the ground like hooves.

Or were those actual hooves?

Rufus spun around just as a herd of white-tailed deer bounded toward them, tails flapping. He and Abigail stumbled backward to get out of the way.

"What the—?" he burst out as the deer thundered past.

The last doe in the herd stopped, locked eyes with Abigail, and stamped one spindly leg.

"Oh!" Abigail said. "Wait, what?"

The doe snorted loudly, a sound like air being forced out of a balloon. Then her tail flared and she darted into the trees.

"What the heck is going on?" Rufus asked.

The whole meadow seemed to be moving. A hare hopped wildly toward them, stamped its immense back legs, and then careened toward the creek. It was followed by a scurry of squirrels, two badgers, three slow-moving turtles, and a single, irritated-looking mole. Seven or eight fluffy apricot imps rolled by, each one tucked into a ball. Overhead, a committee of turkey vultures circled.

"Something's freaking out the animals," Abigail said as a fox catapulted past. "That doe—she thinks something horrible's going to happen!"

"Something horrible *is* going to happen, Abby-gell!" One of the cotters unfurled himself and scampered up Abigail's leg with suction-cup paws. "Bobalo has seen it!" His fur puffed into spikes as he pressed his nose to hers. "A badness is coming! A badness that will separate Bobalo from his sweet Loubella! A badness that wants to hurt Abby-gell and Cousin of Abby-gell. Do not, do not, do not let it!"

"What kind of badness?" Abigail asked. But Bobalo had already jumped down and rolled away.

From his perch on the boulder, Nettle cleared his throat. He'd retaken his feyling form: black hair swept up in a top-knot, green lizard-skin suit dotted with drops of rain.

"About that scrygrass, Pledge Lady. It seems to have flowered."

"What does it *do*?" Abigail asked. "Everyone's so upset. Except those guys." She looked up at the circling turkey vultures. "They seem kind of happy."

"The scent of scrygrass flowers shows you the future," Nettle said. "Or a glimpse of it, anyway. I wouldn't be too alarmed: deer and rabbits are prey animals, and they are going to be preyed upon. Some of them will be eaten. You know it, and I know it, but these stupid creatures *didn't* know it, which is how they were able to enjoy their lives. I did try to warn you." He folded his arms and gave Rufus a significant look.

"Instead of rubbing my face in it, just tell me what to do," Rufus snapped as several dozen mice scampered over his foot.

"You'll need wardweed—" Nettle began.

He was interrupted by a horrible scream.

Three figures hurtled toward them, half running, half floating—or maybe swimming? They were shaped like women, but they had a greenish tinge, and their limbs were draped in mossy sheets of water plants. "Take heed! Take heed!"

Nettle groaned. "The Crinnyeyes! What are they doing out of the well?"

"Destruction!" the Crinnyeyes cried. "Sorrow! Time is running out!"

One of the women grasped Rufus's hands with clammy urgency. As she spoke, water dripped from her mouth. "Click go the locks. Tick go the clocks. The leopard comes with his spots undone."

Rufus tried to pull his hands away. "Wh-who?" he stammered. "What?"

"It appears that the women of the well have gotten into the scrygrass," Nettle interjected. "I'd ignore them if I were you."

"The women of the well?" Rufus repeated. The pale-green figure tightened her grip on his hands. "Are you talking about the old well in the garden? Why are there women in there?"

"The Crinnyeyes are a kind of water spirit," Nettle said. "Usually they stay in the well, but I suppose the scent of scrygrass drew them out." He smirked. "Too bad we didn't get to it earlier."

Rufus tried to speak, but found he could only stare. A second Crinnyeye put an arm around Abigail's shoulders. "Splat go the trees. Flat goes the ground. Feylawn is gone, gone, *gone!*"

"Gone?" Abigail repeated. "What do you mean, *gone?*"

"Save it! Save us!" cried the third Crinnyeye. She seemed the wettest and greenest of the bunch, her limbs and hair streaming with water and weeds. She sidled up behind Rufus and whispered wetly in his ear, "You must give up all that you love for all that you are."

"Hold on." Abigail twisted free of the Crinnyeye who held her shoulders and shrugged off her backpack. She shook her hair out of her face as she scrambled to undo the zipper. "Just a sec."

"Tick! Tock! Click! Lock!" the Crinnyeyes chorused. "Feylawn falls. Feylawn fails!"

A cascade of water from the Crinnyeye's hair trickled down Rufus's neck, just as a chill ran up his spine.

"What's going to happen to it?" he whispered.

The third Crinnyeye gave a bubbling laugh, water streaming from her lips. "He takes their blood! He takes their bones! Little pills for every ill! All of them dead, dead, dead!"

Abigail had wrestled a notebook from her backpack and was trying to find a pen. "Just tell us what to do," she said. "How do we save Feylawn?"

The first Crinnyeye bowed her dripping head until her cold forehead pressed against Rufus's. "What to do? What to do?" she murmured. "Four impossible tasks. Just four, no more."

"Thank you, ladies," Nettle interjected. "We'll take all that under consideration. Now back to the well with you!"

The three Crinnyeyes swiveled to look at him. "The feyling with two faces!" they chorused. "We see your deeds. We see! We see!"

Nettle gave a squawk, and in a moment he was a jay again, his black topknot flaring into a black crest and his thin leafy wings fanning into feathered ones. With a grating cry, he rose into the air and dive-bombed the dripping women, pecking at their shoulders. They covered their heads with their hands, still talking.

"Read the tale to unwrite the story! *Ow!*" the first one cried.

"Recover the moment that was lost!" added the second. She swirled away, her dripping hair snaking behind her.

"Crack the nut that has no meat!" yelled the third.

They began to run—or at least float—at an impressive speed, with Nettle cawing and flapping behind them.

"Sunder the bond that cannot break!" the Crinnyeyes shrieked as they ran. "It's up to you! To you! To yoooooooooo-ooouuuuuuuuu!"

When the three Crinnyeyes were out of sight, Rufus and Abigail turned to look at each other. They were both soaked through and smeared with green slime.

"Did any of that make any sense to you?" Rufus asked. "I mean, aside from the fact that we're doomed?"

"We *might* be doomed. But we're also supposed to save Feylawn." Abigail sat down in the muddy grass and scribbled frantically in her notebook. "Prognostication isn't an exact science."

"You pick really weird times to be scientific," Rufus said. He took a deep breath and tried to slow the skittering of his heart. "You're acting like it's totally normal for three wet lunatics to shriek at us about the future."

"*Possible* future," Abigail said. She counted something on her fingers, added a few words to the soggy page of her notebook, and got to her feet. "We already knew our parents wanted to sell Feylawn. Now we have some idea what to do about it."

Rufus stared at her. "We do?"

"Yes," Abigail said, tapping her notebook. "I wrote it down right here."

4

MR. GNEISS GUY

When Rufus got home, his father was asleep on the couch, his legs draped over the armrest. One arm was flung over his eyes to shield them from the light. On the coffee table beside him was his laptop and a stack of papers.

"Dad," Rufus whispered after he'd changed out of his wet clothes. He touched his father's shoulder.

His father shifted. The arm shielding his eyes flailed outward and landed on Rufus's knee.

"Hey, buddy. How was your first day at Camp BizBuzz?"

"Great," Rufus said, doing his best to sound enthusiastic. "We're learning how to monetize our hobbies. And the CFO from Buckett Brand Windshield Wipers gave a presentation about the exciting world of corporate finance."

Rufus's father sat up. "My old boss," he said, rubbing his eyes with his thumb and forefinger. "The guy who fired me."

"He was kind of boring," Rufus said hastily. This, at least, was true.

It was not, however, the right thing to say. "It might seem boring to *you*, Rufus, but accounting can be pretty fascinating when you really understand it. You do a lot of problem-solving. It's crucial work for determining future investing." He sounded wistful.

"It's just that the *guy* was boring," Rufus clarified. "You would have been a better speaker."

That was true as well. His dad was passionate about math. He was goofy, but he wasn't boring. Or at least, not at the beginning. Sometimes he did go on for a while.

His father didn't acknowledge the compliment. He rubbed his temples. "It wasn't easy to get you into BizBuzz. It's very exclusive. *And* expensive. I hope you're finding it worthwhile."

"Definitely," Rufus said. He was done fighting with his dad. He'd made a bargain with the universe. It went like this:

I, Rufus, will make my dad happy. I won't argue with him. I will go to summer camp without complaint and try to be the kind of high-achieving son he wants. And, in exchange, you, the universe, will make sure that my dad stays safe, and finds a job, and stops worrying about money all the time.

Rufus looked around for a new topic. "Where's Mom?"

"At the hospital. Extra shift. She won't be home for dinner." His dad blinked sleepily.

After his father's accident, Rufus's mom had given up her temporary nursing job in Phoenix, the one she'd taken for the summer because his father was out of work. Nursing jobs in Galosh didn't pay as well as the Phoenix one did, so now she was back working as many extra shifts as she could.

"Do you want me to check your email?" Rufus asked, reaching for his dad's laptop. His father wasn't supposed to stare at a computer screen too much while his brain was healing from the fall. At first Rufus had hoped that meant his dad would go for walks with him at Feylawn, maybe visit the osprey nest or help collect seeds or go fishing in the creek. But his father never seemed to be in the mood for any of that, particularly not since it had started raining. So he'd been trying to help his Dad with his job search instead.

"Sure." Rufus's father slumped back down on the couch with his eyes closed. "Hey, I saw a bird today."

"You went outside?" Rufus fumbled with the lid of the laptop.

"Had to get the mail." His father stretched out his arms and examined them. He'd been doing this a lot since the accident—surveying his body as if it belonged to someone else. "That bird you like, the blue one, hopped right up to say hi."

"Say *hi*?" Rufus turned to look his father full in the face. "Birds don't talk."

His father laughed. "Good point! But this one has

become quite my little companion. The other day he gave me a peanut. First time I've ever gotten a present from a bird."

Rufus's heart began to pound. "Steller's jays carry diseases," he said.

"I'm not going to *eat* it, Rufus," his father said. "But I *have* started a little collection. He brought me a bottle cap today. Just dropped it at my feet and then flew up to a tree, squawking. What a character!"

"Don't let him get too close to you," Rufus said. "Jays are unpredictable."

His father shrugged. "You once told me they steal stuff—somebody's probably missing the top to their beer." He patted Rufus's leg. "Read me my email."

Rufus scrolled through the messages, looking for anything that might be a response to a job application. "It all looks like spam. And something from Aunt Chrissy." He paused, his already-thumping heart suddenly diving into the pit of his stomach. "Subject line 'Possible Buyer.'"

His father's eyes flashed open. "Read it. Maybe that was a lucky bottle cap."

Rufus swallowed. "'Adam—see below,'" he read. "'Spoke by phone with Mr.—' I'm not sure how you say this name. 'Guh-neiss'? 'He wants to set up appointment to view.'"

Rufus started to scan the forwarded email, but his father lifted the laptop from his hands and read it himself.

"Nice," his father said. "That's how you say it. Mr. Gneiss. The G is silent. He says he represents a large, vertically integrated development company—did you learn that term at BizBuzz? It means they do everything themselves, from planning to construction."

Rufus could barely hear him over the roaring in his ears. So *this* was what the Crinnyeyes had meant. They were doomed. The shrieks echoed in his ear. *Splat go the trees. Flat goes the ground. Feylawn is gone, gone,* gone!

He peered over his father's shoulder. The language was formal, but a few key sentences jumped out. *Interested in acquiring the large undeveloped property adjacent to Flood-town Burrito. Would like to view with our acquisition manager and surveyor to assess for several high-value projects.*

"But they won't be able to find it," he said. That was the thing he and Abigail had been counting on: the fact that Feylawn was almost impossible to find.

"Not a problem—Chrissy and I can take them there." Rufus's father was smiling for what seemed like the first time in weeks. "A buyer, Rufus! This could mean a whole new start for us. What do you say we go out for ice cream after dinner?"

"I don't want—" Rufus began. Then he remembered his bargain and took a deep breath. "Sure," he said. "That sounds great."

✺✺✺

Rufus's phone buzzed in his pocket. He'd only had it a week, and it was a weird sensation—like having a new pet. Phones didn't work at Feylawn, so there had never been much point in getting him one, but now that he was going to summer camp instead of spending his days with Grandpa Jack, his parents had decided he should have it for emergencies.

He unlocked the screen. There was a text from Abigail.

Mom says there's a possible buyer!

Rufus slid away from his father, who was tapping eagerly at his keyboard. He could barely think enough to type a response.

I know. What do we do?!?!

He watched the three dots that signaled that Abigail was typing a response. A long response.

Four impossible tasks.
1. Read the tale to unwrite the story.
2. Recover the moment that was lost.
3. Crack the nut that has no meat.
4. Sunder the bond that cannot break.

Rufus read them over and shook his head.

Four *incomprehensible* tasks, more like it. It wasn't a lot to go on.

A BUSINESS
PROPOSITION

M r. Diggs did not have borlibganlan for dinner. He ate
a selection of the small gray crabs that patrolled the
beach and tasted like moldy towel. As he crunched mis-
erably through their shells, he again felt himself being
watched. He was pretty sure that the Calamand couldn't
see him, even when he was close to the fence, which meant
that there was someone else. Or some*thing* else. The top
of his spine prickled. He had never liked being seen, and
he liked being watched even less. He considered cloaking
himself in the glamour that made him appear human, but
he suspected that it wouldn't do much good.

Instead he chewed through one last crab, walked to the
edge of the bramble wood, and began to dig. Within an
hour, the hole was large enough to hide inside. By the next
afternoon, he had lengthened the hole into a tunnel that
led from the shoreline to the spot by the fence where he
had first spoken to the Calamand.

"There's something watching me," he announced.

"Of course there is," said the Calamand. "Frankly, I'm surprised he hasn't eaten you yet."

"I pride myself on being indigestible," Mr. Diggs boasted. "But it's clearly time for me to go."

"Ah," said the Calamand. "What will you do when you get back to the Sunless World?"

"I'm not going there," said Mr. Diggs. "I have business in the Blue World."

"Of course," said the Calamand. "You have the voice of an Important Person."

"Rance Diggs, tunnel boss for the Northwest Region." Mr. Diggs made no effort to disguise his pride in the title.

"Well you've tunneled into the wrong place, boss. No handy path or passage back to the Northwest Region. Not unless you're a strong swimmer."

Mr. Diggs was silent. He was a rock goblin. His kind avoided water whenever possible.

The Calamand laughed. "Didn't think so. Tell me, what would you do if you *could* get home?"

Mr. Diggs clasped his bony hands. He'd had ample time to consider this question while lying on his back in the Place Between. "Get revenge on the child who sent me here. Once I've killed him, I'll find a new business partner and get back to work."

"What happened to your last business partner?"

"Disintegrated."

"Sorry to hear it."

"He'd been dead for years. It was only a matter of time."

"So, a living partner would be an upgrade." There was a skipping quality to the voice that Diggs disliked, a kind of perpetual merriment.

"Are you applying for the job?"

The Calamand laughed. "Jobs have never been my style. I don't dig digging, Mr. Diggs."

Mr. Diggs tore at his itching shoulder. "Tunneling's played out. Before I came here, I was in the process of diversifying. Real estate. Pharmaceuticals. I have big plans. Tunnel boss for the entire US, then for all of North America. After that—"

"I like a man who's forward-thinking," interrupted the Calamand. "Forward, full-bore-ward, and when I say *bore*, I mean talking a bit more than will interest the average listener."

"The Northwest Region," a second voice interjected. "Tell me, does that include the town of Galosh, California, by any chance?"

"Who's that?" demanded Mr. Diggs, startled by the intrusion. He looked around. "Is there someone else here?"

"Just my sister, Mandolyn," said the Calamand. "She goes where I go. You might say we're inseparable."

"Why hasn't she spoken before?" asked Mr. Diggs. He didn't like being taken by surprise.

"Why haven't you answered my question?" retorted

Mandolyn. Her voice was quieter and sadder than her sister's. "I was asking about Galosh."

"I was there quite recently," Mr. Diggs said, trying to keep the bitterness out of his voice. How he wished he knew how to get back there.

"We have some unfinished business in Galosh," said the Calamand. "A little something that slipped through our fingers. And once we're there, we can reward you for freeing us."

"Tell me more," said Mr. Diggs.

"All in good time," said the Calamand. "How are you at picking locks?"

Mr. Diggs glanced up at the chain-lashed gates and the hundreds of dangling locks.

"If only my wife were here," he muttered. "My little lozenge can talk to locks."

There was an unusual silence on the other side of the bars. At last, the Calamand spoke. "You're married to a feyling?"

"The queen of the feylings, actually. Queen Queen-Anne's-Lace." Mr. Diggs puffed his chest.

"I thought feylings and goblins were mortal enemies. Have we missed the forging of an alliance?"

"A temporary one. She gave herself to me in exchange for a service I performed for the feylings. We combined seedcraft and metalcraft to build a train together. One that crosses between the worlds."

"So she loves you?"

"No."

"But she's bound to you."

"She is mine until death." Mr. Diggs grinned. The feyling queen had been foolish enough to agree to a goblin marriage, which bound her to him forever.

"Interesting. Let's say I could tell you how to get home to her. Would you come back for me?"

"I'd need a reason."

"Gratitude. I would have just returned you to your wife."

"She doesn't love me. Give me a better reason."

The voice that wisped between the bars was as soft as summer twilight. "What if I told you I could give you the one object your enemies desire most? A glimmery-shimmery gewgaw that you could use to destroy everything they care about?"

"Would it make me rich?"

"Beyond measure."

"Powerful?"

"Extraordinarily."

"Tunnel boss for all of North America?"

"Tunnel boss for all the world."

Mr. Diggs's heart was small and leathery, like the rest of him. It didn't like to exert itself. But now it began to pound inside his chest like a pickax hammering for ore.

"What is this object?"

"Now, now," said the Calamand. "There's time enough for telling tales. First you must set us free."

⚜

That afternoon, following the Calamand's instructions, Mr. Diggs used the talons of his right foot to inscribe a series of symbols onto seven locks that hung at a convenient height. Then he set to work getting them open. They should have been simple enough for a man of his talents to pick, despite the fact that the only tools he had were rocks and sharpened sticks and a few thorns of varying sizes. He had spent his life working with mechanisms both large and small. Model trains. Clockwork figurines. Finicky machines for drilling, digging, and excavating. Certainly he could pick a lock.

But the locks that fastened the Gate of a Thousand Locks were the most irritating contraptions he'd ever encountered. They refused to respond to any of his usual gambits. Brute force did nothing. Neither did gentle tickling. It took several days for the first lock to succumb to his efforts. But then, at last, it popped open with a kind of groan and lay in his hands with its shackle exposed.

From somewhere nearby, there was a strange, sawing roar that ended mid-snarl, as if the mouth that made it had vanished into thin air. A moment later, the lock disappeared as well.

"Excellent," said the Calamand. "You won't have to worry about being eaten for a while. The spotty spotter has sprinted."

"Sprinted where?" said Mr. Diggs, who found the Calamand's verbal pyrotechnics almost as irritating as the brambles that had dotted his skin with welts.

"Off to find the one who locks the locks," the Calamand replied. "But don't worry. He won't find her. I have it on good authority. Back to work, my subterranean Pomeranian! Just six more locks to go."

"I don't get your math," Mr. Diggs said. "As I figure it, there are nine hundred ninety-nine locks to go before you're free."

"And that's why you need me to do your figuring for you," said the Calamand. "You're not unlocking locks to set me free. You're unlocking locks to send a message. After that, we simply wait."

"And what about the locks themselves?" asked Diggs. "Where do *they* go?"

"Ah," said the Calamand. "That's the question. Do you believe in entropy?"

"What's that in plain English?" Mr. Diggs did not like fancy language, nor did he like people who knew more than he did.

"The tendency of everything to fall into disorder," said the Calamand. "Castles become ruins. Gardens get overrun with weeds. Systems fall apart."

"Not goblin systems," said Mr. Diggs. "Not on my watch."

"That's what we're counting on," said the Calamand. "The first seven locks are meant to warn my captors that I'm in danger of escaping. But it was all so long ago." And there was the laugh again, far too musical for Mr. Diggs's taste. "Things change."

"Not goblin things," said Mr. Diggs.

"Exactly," agreed the Calamand.

⚬⚬⚬

The locks did as they'd been told to do.

One by one, they passed from the island of Imura and went to warn the Calamand's captors. But the Calamand was right. Things change. The arresting detectives had retired, or changed offices, or died. Buildings had been torn down and replaced. A long-dormant volcano had awakened and incinerated an entire city block.

The first lock landed in the soft dirt beside a bumper crop of bush beans.

The second lock sank into an emerald sea and was pocketed by an octopus.

The third lock was sent to a giant warehouse and unloaded by a helpful new intern who deliberated for several minutes before deciding to file it under *L*.

The fourth lock tumbled into a day-care center and was put to use as a teething ring for a very sharp-toothed infant.

The fifth lock landed in a novelty sock store that had recently gone out of business.

The sixth lock hissed into the flamingo-pink mouth of a dragon that had chosen a very inopportune moment to yawn.

The seventh lock rattled onto the desk of a goblin named Coquina Marl, who inspected it carefully. Coquina Marl inspected everything carefully—it was why she had risen so high in the Northwest Regional organization, despite her relative youth.

She picked up the phone.

"Mr. Gneiss," she said. "You have a message."

6

USELESS JUNK

For the past couple of weeks, Rufus's mom had been driving him to his various summer camps in the mornings, even when she'd just come in from a night shift and was probably dying to go to sleep. He liked being in the car with her almost as much as he hated camp—listening to music, watching the windshield wipers sway from side to side like two pointing fingers. It felt like being in a submarine, or wrapped in a blanket.

But today Rufus's mom turned down the music as soon as the car was moving.

"I guess Dad told you that someone's interested in seeing Feylawn."

"Yup."

"How are you feeling about that?"

Rufus studied his left knee. There was a scab on it, from when he'd slipped in the mud a few days before. "It was going to happen sometime."

"It's just one email." Rufus's mom looked over at him. Under her eyes were small crescent-shaped pillows. These days she was always short on sleep. "You're not losing Feylawn today."

Rufus watched the rain streaming onto the windshield. "I just wish I could spend more time there. While I still *can.*"

"I know," his mother said. "But given what happened to your dad, it's a tough sell."

"But how was that Feylawn's fault? He was too heavy for the rope, that's all!" Rufus had tried to explain to his father what had really caused the rope swing to break, but his father had insisted on the "scientific" explanation.

His mom leaned toward him, nudging his shoulder with hers. "I'll talk to him," she said. "See if we can make a little time for you to visit Grandpa Jack this weekend."

Make time. Rufus turned the phrase over in his mind. If only it were possible to actually do that—to *make* time the way you could make cookies or paper airplanes or tree forts. Then he'd have time to figure out how to stop his family from selling Feylawn.

∂⌒♥⌒∂

When Rufus walked into the BizBuzz classroom, Mark Trang was already at the front of the room wearing his bumblebee cap.

"Yesterday you brainstormed a list of business ideas based on your interests and hobbies. Today it's time to sharpen your stingers and turn those ideas into action! Who's ready to start writing a—drum roll, please!— BUSINESS PLAN?!?!"

Rufus had been dreading this moment: the moment when he would have to actively participate in Camp Biz-Buzz instead of staring out the window.

"Let's go up to Feylawn after camp," he whispered to Abigail after Mark had explained the elements of a business plan and handed them a worksheet to fill out. "We can talk to Grandpa Jack about the buyer, see if he has any ideas."

"I have to meet with my Mandarin tutor this afternoon." Abigail wrote her name in the upper right-hand corner of the worksheet. "I think you should talk to Nettle. Maybe there's some kind of feyling magic he can do to make the buyer go away."

"I told you: I don't trust him," Rufus said. "He's been hanging around my dad. He gave him a bottle cap and a peanut."

Abigail lifted her head. "Maybe he's trying to make up for what he did."

"With a *peanut*?" The last word came out a little too loud. The other BizBuzz campers looked over and grinned at each other in a way that Rufus knew all too well. At least he was used to it. Abigail clearly wasn't.

She narrowed her eyes at the closest cluster of kids and waited until they'd dropped their gaze back to their papers.

Then she opened her notebook to the rain-wrinkled page where she'd written down the prophecy. "They're like clues." She tapped the first line with the eraser end of her pencil. "'Read the book to unwrite the story,'" she said. "That *has* to be talking about one of the Glistening Glen books. They're *about* Feylawn."

"They're about a fictional place called Glistening Glen," Rufus corrected. "Which is loosely based on Feylawn. Also, Carson Sweete Collins was a terrible person who tried to kill all the feylings just because she was mad that her father died."

"It's still a place to start. And to answer whatever you're going to say next, let's talk more at lunch. I need to get started on my business plan before I fall behind."

"Fall behind?" Rufus repeated. "What does it matter? It's not like school. They can't *fail* us."

Abigail stared at him for a long moment.

"Technically, you're right," she said. "But I still want to win the Piranha Pitch Session."

"Why?" Rufus said. The future of Feylawn was at stake. How could she care about a stupid summer-camp contest?

"It's hard to explain," Abigail said. "It's just what I do."

⚬⟋⟍⟍⟋⚬

"Rufus! Come in out of the rain!" Grandpa Jack called when Rufus scraped open the barn door that afternoon. He was sitting in an imposing straight-backed chair surrounded by a scattering of cardboard boxes. The chair came from the jumble of furniture in the middle of the barn, the boxes from the floor-to-ceiling stack at the back.

"I can't stay long." Rufus stepped gingerly around the holes in the floorboards and wrapped his grandfather in a hug. "They still don't want me and Abigail coming here."

He didn't have to explain who "they" were.

Grandpa Jack pushed his khaki cap off his forehead. "If I had a working phone, I supposed I'd have to call your parents and tell them you're here."

"But you *don't* have a working phone," Rufus said. He selected a chair from the pile of furniture behind him and dragged it beside his grandfather's. "How are things going?"

"Aside from the unseasonable weather, it's as peaceful as a summer day," Grandpa Jack said. "I'm finally able to get started cleaning out the barn. Just wish we were doing it together."

Every summer Rufus and Grandpa Jack tried to make a dent in the barn's floor-to-ceiling stacks of cardboard boxes, digging through their contents to find the treasures and toss the trash. The only problem was that Grandpa Jack generally concluded that *everything* was a treasure, so the stack of boxes was never much smaller at the end of the summer than it had been at the start.

"Find anything interesting so far?" Rufus asked now.

"It's *all* interesting," Grandpa Jack said. "That's what makes it a challenge! But I'm sorting, Rufus. Organizing!"

He pointed to two open cartons by his feet. "I've got two categories: Keep and Throw Away."

The first box was filled to overflowing. The second one was empty aside from a tin cup without a handle.

Rufus lifted a rusted can of stewed pears from the Keep box. "These can't still be good. They look like they're a hundred years old."

"Fifty at the most," Grandpa Jack said. "Anyway, canned food lasts forever!" He sighed and began transferring cans of food from the Keep box to the Throw Away box. "I guess you're right. If I'm going to empty out this barn, I'm going to have to be more choosy." He picked up a tin of something called Dr. Dempsey's Hair Pomade. "I do think this one belongs in our Museum of Interesting Things. Hair pomade—can't find anything more interesting than that! And look at this pretty padlock!"

The padlock was round and jet-black, with a keyhole in its center. As soon as Rufus put his fingers on it, he felt its pulsing heat. It was unlocked, the open shackle curving outward like a question mark. Lying in Rufus's palm, it seemed to buzz with intention, with purpose. Rufus had felt something like it only once before—the first time he'd held the engine for the Roving Trees Railway.

"Where'd you find this?"

"In the garden, actually. Beside my bush beans. That's the beautiful thing about Feylawn, Ru. Treasures every-where you look!" He folded Rufus's fingers around the padlock. "You should take it. Use it to lock up your valuables!"

"But I don't have the key," Rufus said. "Or any valuables." He tried to press the shackle closed, but it resisted him, its inner springs determined to stay open.

"Keep it all the same," Grandpa Jack said. "I still have a lot of boxes to go through. Maybe one of them holds the key."

Rufus usually loved sorting through boxes with Grandpa Jack, every carton packed with possibility. But now he just felt sad.

"You don't have to let them sell it," he said. "Feylawn's your home."

Grandpa Jack shook his head. "I'm a stubborn old man, but that doesn't mean I can't see reason. Your dad nearly died here. Both my kids need money. And I'm getting too old to muck about with magical creatures nobody else can see and live in a place nobody else can find."

"*I* can see them," Rufus protested. "So can Abigail. And anyway, you're not old."

"I'm well past the age where people want to put candles on my birthday cake," Grandpa Jack said. "Old enough to learn from my mistakes. I always wanted Feylawn to stay in the family, but Chrissy's right—it's not the kind of gift you give to people you love."

"But everything's *fine* now!" Rufus was almost shouting. "You said so yourself."

"It's been fine before," Grandpa Jack said. "But it's always trouble sooner or later. I'm sorry, Rufus. It breaks my heart, but I know it's the right thing to do."

Rufus got to his feet. He'd never been mad at Grandpa Jack before, but then Grandpa Jack had never acted like a grown-up before.

"I've got to go," he said. "I have to check on a few things before I head home."

Then he pushed back through the barn door and headed for the creek. He needed to find Nettle.

7

CLAXONVINE

A Steller's jay squawked at Rufus as he walked toward the creek in the rain: "Rak! Rak! Rak! Rak!"

"There you are," Rufus said, struggling to control the fury he felt every time he saw Nettle. "I need to talk to you."

The bird twisted itself into the shape of a small man with a pinched face. "How can I assist you, Pledge Lord?"

"Just call me Rufus," Rufus said. "I've asked you a million times. It's not that hard."

"I beg your pardon, Pledge Lord, but the peony seed requires me to use the term to remind you that I'm at your service—"

"—until I say you've erased your debt." Rufus finished the sentence for him. "I know. You've told me. Which reminds me: stay away from my father."

Nettle's chin lifted. "Your father likes seeing me. He calls me Bluey."

"I don't *care* what he calls you. I don't want you close to him."

"I make him smile," Nettle said. "I bring him gifts."

"I don't care if you bring him gold coins. Leave him alone."

Nettle opened his mouth to speak, but then closed it and bowed his head. "As you wish, Pledge Lord. May I direct your attention to a more pressing matter?"

"In a minute. Something's come up—a person who wants to buy Feylawn. We have to stop them."

Nettle's face was impassive. "Glomper affairs are best solved by glompers, Pledge Lord. Only you can persuade your family not to sell."

"But *you're* the reason they *want* to! It's your fault!" Rufus shivered as the rain drummed against his jacket.

"And yet I can't undo the past." Nettle flew onto a branch over Rufus's head, unleashing a shower of water from its leaves. "In the meantime," he added, "we need to tendril the claxonvine. Getting all the anti-goblin measures in place will take time, and this will let us know about any incursions."

Rufus was not about to let on that he had no idea what Nettle was talking about. "Go ahead and um, tendril it then."

"Tendrilling the claxonvine requires *two* seed-speakers. Or, in our case, one seed-speaker and one glomper with a rudimentary understanding of seed speech."

➤ 48 ⬶

Rufus resisted the impulse to knock his feyling servant into the nearest puddle. "Just tell me what to do."

"Claxonvine must be told two things, Pledge Lord. Who to warn, and what to warn about. The plants communicate with each other through a system of tendrils—"

"Just. Tell. Me. What. To. Do," Rufus repeated. Rain gushed down his forehead and into his eyes. "I don't need a botany lesson."

Nettle looked insulted, but he drew a pebble-size yellow bulb from his pouch and tossed it to Rufus. "This is a claxonvine auraneme—you'll need to keep it with you at all times. Once you've opened it, it will tendril into the network. I will have done the same with mine. To activate the claxonvine tendrils, we must speak to each other *through* the tendrils about what we want it to be looking for. Which, if you've forgotten, is goblins. Ready?"

"Sure," Rufus said. He looked at the auraneme, which was whiskered with white roots.

SOUND THE HORN! I WARN! I WARN!

Rufus winced. Normally when seeds announced their powers, they did so in dulcet murmurs. But the auraneme's voice was a high, tinny squeal that felt like an ice pick in his inner ear.

Just open it, he told himself. He'd done this once before, so he knew the basics. He imagined the auraneme's root beard burrowing into the earth, a stalk rising out of its center.

SOUND THE HORN! the auraneme bleated. *I WARN!*
I WARN! I WAAAAAAAAAAARN!

The last word deepened into a chorus as the bulb erupted into a fountain of snaking tendrils. The green shoots wrapped around Rufus's wrists, gripping tight as the auraneme's runners unspooled.

"Whoa, what's it *doing?*"

The tendrils spread, slithered, snaked, and climbed in all directions, looping around trees, plants, rocks. They tapped, poked, and probed, into the earth, up to the sky. Dozens, maybe hundreds of tendrils, each tugging in a different direction.

"It's *tendrilling*," Nettle said, holding his own auraneme at arm's length.

"Does it ever *stop?*" Rufus asked.

"Just wait," Nettle said. "Watch. *There.*" He pointed with his chin.

Rushing toward them in a river of ripping green were more green tendrils, hundreds of them. They crept along the ground and twined through the trees like twisting green ropes, hurtling toward the auraneme tendrils with such force that Rufus braced himself for a crash as the two green armies met.

Instead the tendrils simply wove together, tangling and twisting until they had formed a dense mat of damp greenery.

"Now," Nettle grunted. "Call for the bloom that will learn to recognize our enemies."

"Can you be a little more specific?" Rufus said. "How exactly do I *call for the bloom*?"

"Just *call* for it," Nettle said impatiently. "Call the bloom out of the stem. Like *this*."

A claxonvine tendril stretched toward Nettle's face, shuddered, and then erupted into yellow, trumpet-shaped flowers.

"See?" Nettle asked.

Rufus felt the way he did when he and his father were playing chess. *Study the board, Rufus! You can put me in check in two moves.*

"I don't know *how to do it*," he said. "You're going to have to teach me."

"I can't *teach* you to be a feyling," Nettle snapped. "A feyling just *knows* these things."

"Well, I'm not a feyling, and I *don't* just know. Do you mean call like a phone call? Like a birdcall?"

"You *bloom* it!" Nettle snapped. "You—" His lips pressed together in frustration. "You use your mind to pull it out, but with pizzazz—like you're pulling a rabbit out of a hat."

"Right." Nettle might as well not have explained at all. But if Rufus didn't want to spend the rest of the day standing in the rain with his hands bound by claxonvine tendrils, he was going to have to figure it out. He shut his eyes, concentrated on one of the tendrils, and pulled—with pizzazz.

He opened his eyes. Two yellow-gold trumpet-shaped flowers quivered in front of him, alert and expectant.

"I did it!" Rufus exclaimed. As he did, the two flowers pressed themselves against his face, one at his mouth and the other at his ear.

"*Shh!*" Nettle's nasal voice hissed from the yellow-gold blossom pressed against Rufus's ear. "You're talking to me through the claxonvine tendril network now. Do so *quietly*, please—it amplifies sound quite a bit."

"Are we done?" Rufus hated the sensation of being connected to Nettle. It was like being trapped in an elevator with your least favorite song.

"This is the last step," Nettle said. "We each describe what we're looking for so the claxonvine will know when to warn us."

"That's easy," Rufus said. "Goblins. We want to know if goblins come to Feylawn."

"What are goblins?" Nettle said. "Describe them clearly."

"*You're* the expert," Rufus snapped. "They're *your* friends, aren't they?" He remembered Nettle and his All-Outers armed with metal spears, delivering him and Abigail and the others right into Mr. Diggs's hands.

"You slander me," Nettle said. "I am loyal to you, to Feylawn, and to my queen, may her memory never fade.

Goblins are my enemies. Now please describe them for the benefit of the claxonvine sentry system."

Rufus sighed. Magic was turning out to be a lot like school—a place where you had to explain things that were obvious. *Define* goblin, *giving three examples. Show your work.*

"They're short."

"Short from the perspective of a glomper," Nettle said. "We consider them tall."

An image rocketed into Rufus's brain of a giant goblin towering above him. He looked up at the creature, noticing its potbelly, swayed back, and furry legs. A warm wave of affection passed over him. The feeling sickened him.

"That's Dog Legs!" he exclaimed. "Diggs's henchman. The one who held Iris in his fist so she could be killed! You *like* him!"

"Goblins share certain characteristics," Nettle said, as if Rufus hadn't spoken. "For example, an underbite and large flapping ears. But there is also considerable variation, with some goblins having the limbs of dogs, goats, lizards, or birds, and others having horns, tails, or other animal characteristics." He paused expectantly. "Wouldn't you agree, Pledge Lord?"

"I agree that they're evil and destructive," Rufus said. He could see Mr. Diggs's hideous face hovering above him, his long nails trying to scratch out his eyes. "I agree that they want to destroy Feylawn and feylings and me and Abigail. Do *you*? Do *you* agree?"

"We're trying to train the claxonvine to recognize goblins," Nettle said testily. "A more neutral approach ensures accuracy. The pictures you're sending are too extreme."

"*Extreme?*" Rufus repeated. Images were bubbling across his brain like lava from a volcano vent: Diggs whistling at his window, Diggs's wooly sleeve pressed against his neck, Diggs ordering that they all be burned alive. Instantly, another set of images swamped them: Diggs smiling gently. Diggs listening with concern. Diggs looking regal and decisive. These were followed by other goblin faces: Dog Legs, Lizard Tail, Ram Horns, and dozens more, some male, some female, that Rufus didn't recognize.

"There are many types of goblins," Nettle was saying. "We are interested in rock goblins in particular. These goblins dig, tunnel, excavate, and extract. They are miners, metalworkers, and tunnelers."

"And killers!" Rufus said.

As he said the last word, a picture came into his mind, vivid and bright. But it wasn't a goblin that he saw—it was a boy. A dead boy, seen from a distance, as if you were looking down at him from a great height. Rufus gasped as the recognition hit him. That was his own body, lying flat and lifeless on the ground.

He wheeled to stare at Nettle and the image vanished. "What the hell was *that?*"

"Please stay focused, Pledge Lord." The feyling's face

was obscured by the yellow blossoms pressed around him. "Give the claxonvine the information without emotion so it can do its job. Then you can go home."

Rufus took a breath. "They live underground," he said. "In the Sunless World. They often wear a glamour to appear human."

A picture wobbled into his mind, of what must be a glamoured goblin: a short, amiable-looking fellow with a bald head and prominent ears. He sent back an answering image of the goblin undisguised: his piglike ears, his toothy underbite, his bird-like legs.

"Well done, Pledge Lord." Nettle's voice was soft. "I'll handle the rest."

The feyling raised his hands over his head, pulling the tendrils tighter around his wrists. "Claxonvine, you must guard the line," he cried. "If a goblin crosses into Feylawn, what will you do?"

All around them, the wet leaves of the claxonvine rustled and swayed, showering Rufus with rain. *Sound the horn! We warn! We warn!*

"Now disperse," Nettle said. With that, the tangled mesh of greenery unwove itself into distinct tendrils, which then slithered back the way they had come, like coiling spools of thread. As the green mass retreated, the auraneme in Rufus's hand shuddered, and the tendrils around his wrists went slack and then fell away. Within minutes, the only remaining sign of the great mass of claxonvine greenery were the sore creases on each of Rufus's wrists and the small yellow bulb in his hand.

"Put the auraneme in your pocket, Pledge Lord," Nettle said, rotating his own wrists to bring back the circulation. "It will alert you if there's been a goblin intrusion."

Rufus scowled at him. "You want me dead."

"I'm your loyal servant."

"I *saw* it, through the claxonvine. I saw the image in your head."

"I was reflecting on the danger the goblins pose to you, Pledge Lord."

"Stop calling me *lord*!" Rufus burst out in irritation. "I'm twelve years old!"

"Regardless of your age, you are my pledge lord, and I am bound to protect and serve you," Nettle said. His voice dripped with irony. "If you have no further instructions for me, I'll let you be on your way."

THE LEOPARD OF THE LOCKS

Head whirling, Rufus made his way back through the woods. The image of his own broken body throbbed in his mind like a scene from a horror movie. *Nettle wants me dead.* He clenched the padlock in his pocket, its strange warmth easing the chill in his fingertips. Yet another mystery. He wished, for roughly the thousandth time, that he could talk to Iris, even for a moment. He felt like he was running through a maze blindfolded. In the rain.

Then he heard a terrifying sound.

It seemed to come from everywhere at once, as if the woods had its own terrible voice. It began as a deep rumble and then opened into a scraping roar. Just as Rufus felt he might die of fear, the roar quieted into a throaty growl that managed to be the most menacing sound of all.

Moving as quietly as he could, Rufus pushed himself back against an oak tree and held as still as he could.

The beast gave a growling sigh. It was the wet click of its closing mouth that told Rufus where to look.

Up.

The leopard was almost directly above him, draped across a branch of the oak, perfectly camouflaged in the dappled shadows. Its head rested on one paw while the others dangled languorously.

Rufus didn't move. He barely breathed.

The leopard licked a paw. It shifted position and shut its eyes.

Sleep, Rufus commanded silently. If the beast slept, he might be able to sneak away.

The amber eyes blinked open again. They stared directly at Rufus.

"Are you the Locksmith?"

Rufus jumped backward, knocking his head on a low branch.

"Uh," he said. He rubbed the back of his skull.

The leopard's eyes narrowed. "Are you capable of speech?" he asked.

Rufus forced his lips and tongue into motion. "Flpth," he said. And then, after gulping air: "Who are you?"

The leopard leaped down from the branch and landed directly in front of Rufus. He sat back on his haunches with his tail curled in front of him. He was very large, with gold fur covered in perfectly round jet-black spots. His gums were black, his whiskers white. A splash of white frosted the point of his chin. He was simultaneously the most beautiful and the most terrifying creature Rufus had ever seen.

"Shamok," the leopard said. "The leopard of the locks."

"Locks," Rufus said. "You mean like this?"

He pulled the padlock from his pocket and held it out. The leopard's ears flattened. He gave a low growl.

Rufus froze, knowing he should put the offending lock back in his pocket but not wanting to make any sudden movement in case the leopard decided to pounce.

Shamok licked his right flank with his massive tongue.

"Is it very noticeable?" he asked.

"Is . . . ?"

"My lost spots." Shamok extended his hind leg to show Rufus a patch of spotless golden fur. He pushed his large black nose against the lock. "I've lost seven spots. That's seven locks."

Rufus was still looking at the leopard's spotted coat. Each spot, he saw, was shaped like a round padlock, with a keyhole at the center. Slowly, he shoved the lock back in his pocket. "Why are you losing them?"

"A trespasser is unlocking them," Shamok said. "When my spots are gone, the prisoner will be free and I will be dead."

"Prisoner?" Rufus said. "What prisoner? What are you talking about?"

"The Calamand. The Thief of the Eight Worlds. Safely

held behind the Gate of a Thousand Locks." The leopard glanced over his shoulder at his spotless right flank. "It's not a good look," he said. "It's not a good look at all."

The Crinnyeyes' words suddenly echoed in Rufus's head. *The leopard comes with his spots undone.*

"Where is this gate?" he asked. "The one with all the locks? If you don't mind me asking."

"On the island of Imura," Shamok said. "Where I have always lived."

"Which is where?"

"In the Lilac Sea."

Rufus had a familiar feeling of bewilderment so all-encompassing that he was unsure which question to ask first. "But how did you get *here*?" he asked after a moment.

The leopard lifted his amber eyes to meet Rufus's. "The island sent me. As it is written: *When the first lock is opened, the leopard will be sent to find the Locksmith.*"

"Sent you here *how*?"

"I was there. Now I'm here." The leopard licked his paw. "When I find the Locksmith, we will return to Imura to close the locks and keep the prisoner from getting out."

"How much time do you have?" Rufus asked. He shivered. Whatever the Calamand was, somebody had put a lot of effort into locking them up.

"I don't know," Shamok said. "It's never happened before. But the locks keep opening. One slowly. Two slowly. Three slowly. Then four-five-six quicker. Seven quickest of all."

"Maybe Nettle can go with you. I'll ask him."

"Is he the Locksmith?"

"No. He's just a feyling." The image of his own dead body flickered into his mind again. Perhaps if he sent Nettle to Imura, wherever that was, he'd be free of him for a while.

"Send him to me," Shamok said. "I'll be waiting."

"I will," Rufus said. "In the meantime, stay out of sight." His parents couldn't see feylings or cotters, but the leopard seemed too large and tangible to be invisible, even to people without clearsight.

"Nobody sees me unless I want to be seen," said Shamok, bounding up the side of the tree and settling back on his branch. "You can be certain of that."

9

DOLLARS TO DONUTS

I still can't picture it," Abigail said at camp the next day. "Like, an actual leopard? That talks?" Rufus had texted her the basics the night before, but he could tell Abigail was having trouble picturing Shamok as he actually was.

"Yes," he said. "With actual teeth. And actual claws."

Abigail made a swoony face. "I love cats."

"He's not a *cat*," Rufus said. "He's a problem. An *additional* problem. Didn't the well women talk about a leopard?"

"And locks," Abigail said. She frowned, as if trying to remember something. "I wonder if that's why the animals were so upset. They said something was coming to take them. Maybe they meant *hunt* them."

Rufus gave her a quizzical look. "'Said'? All I heard from the animals were some squeaks and heavy breathing."

Abigail shrugged. "All those squeaks and snorts have meanings. I've read a lot about animal communication."

"Of course you have."

He stared at the business plan he was supposed to be working on. So far, it was a sheet of paper that said *Business Plan* at the top. "I have literally no idea what to do with this," he added.

Abigail sighed. She had several pages of notes prepared for her own business plan, and was now generating a series of charts and spreadsheets on one of the BizBuzz laptops.

"You should just partner with me. My plan's almost finished."

"I'm fine." Rufus tapped his pen against his chin as if pondering an important detail.

"You just said you had 'literally no idea what to do.'"

"I was exaggerating."

"It makes sense to work together, anyway. My plan's about Carson Sweete Collins. It'll give us a new excuse to hang out at Feylawn."

Rufus looked up from his contemplation of his blank sheet of paper. "I thought you were starting a dog-walking business."

"That was my first idea, but it was kind of boring, and so I thought, 'What would Rufus do?'"

"Why would you think that?"

"Because you think outside the box," Abigail said. "You're creative. *And* practical."

Rufus rolled his eyes. "And what did this imaginary Rufus come up with?" he asked.

"Imaginary Rufus would try to do as little work as possible," Abigail said. "He'd try to figure out a shortcut, something that he was doing anyway."

Rufus nodded. This was true of Real Rufus as well.

"Then I remembered that we made that website about Carson Sweete Collins so our parents would allow us to go to Feylawn. And I thought, why not add a store to it and sell Carson Sweete Collins swag, like T-shirts and tote bags?"

Rufus wrinkled his nose. "I don't want to shoot down your—I mean *Rufus's*—idea or anything, but do you really think people would buy that stuff? I mean, I know she has that Glisteners fan club, but it probably has like fifteen members. All her books are out of print."

"But that's what's smart about it," Abigail said, pulling one of their great-grandmother's books from her backpack. "The quotes and illustrations are so cool that people will like them even if they don't know her books—and if the T-shirts get popular, then people might want to read the books and maybe we could publish them again."

Just for a moment, Rufus let himself imagine a mania for Glistening Glen books sweeping the nation. Glistening Glen lunch boxes and toys and video games. Money rolling in by the cartload. "That would be dope," he said. "Our parents might not sell Feylawn if they were getting rich from something else."

"Take a look," Abigail said. She opened a transparent purple folder and took out a stack of T-shirt designs.

Rufus scanned the pictures. Quotes from the Glistening Glen books in different fonts. Illustrations of fairies with bolder lines and brighter colors so that they looked more anime than fairy-tale. Not his style, exactly, but he could imagine some of the other kids in the room wearing them.

"Imaginary Rufus is smarter than I gave him credit for," he admitted.

"So?" Abigail had her eyes locked on him. "Want to be my business partner? We need to read her books anyway. For the prophecy."

Rufus hesitated. It was the easiest route. And yet. It still felt like admitting that he wasn't smart enough to come up with an idea of his own.

As if reading his mind, Abigail gestured at a group of three girls who'd teamed up to create a custom cookie-decorating business. "*Lots* of kids are working together," she said. "Look at them—their idea of being creative is using colored icing. We're going to be *way* better than they are."

"Are you always this competitive?" Rufus asked.

Abigail squinted at him. "I can't believe you're even asking me that," she said. "Of course I am. That's why you want to be on my team."

When Rufus came out of Camp BizBuzz that afternoon, Grandpa Jack's bottle-green pickup was idling at the curb, its windshield wipers beating chaotically against the steady downpour.

"I saw your mother at the hospital," he said when Rufus climbed into the cab. "She asked if I could pick you up. She feels bad about you taking the bus—said you came home soaking wet yesterday." His eyes crinkled at the corners. "I can't imagine why that would be, given that the bus picks you up right here at Stormweather Prep and drops you off at the end of your street."

Rufus gave a noncommittal shrug. He hated all the lying and sneaking, but at the moment the list of things he hated was so long that this one hardly made the top ten. "Why were you at the hospital?"

"Just checking on my progress," Grandpa Jack said, holding up the arm he'd broken in June. "They moved me to a soft cast—I'll be back to my old tricks in no time." He eased the truck onto the road. "Hope you don't mind if we make a quick stop at the dump before I take you home. I could use your help unloading if I'm going to get it done before sundown."

"The dump?" Rufus swiveled to look through the window of the cab at the flatbed of the truck, over which Grandpa Jack had secured a black tarp. "What's in there?"

"An assortment of junk nobody wants and I can't keep. Chrissy took me to see some apartments in town, and they don't offer much in the way of storage."

"Apartments? In town?" Rufus stared at Grandpa Jack. "You'd hate that."

"I didn't *always* live at Feylawn, you know. I'm more adaptable than you give me credit for." Grandpa Jack gave Rufus a pat on the knee and pulled over in front of Cloud Nine Donuts. "How about we grab a snack? Fortify ourselves for the work ahead."

"I'm okay," Rufus said. "We should probably just get going." The dump run would take a while, and he was hoping to introduce Nettle to Shamok before going home. Cross two problems off his list at once.

"Won't take but a minute," Grandpa Jack said, climbing out of the truck.

Unfortunately, there was no way to rush Grandpa Jack through an interaction at the donut shop. He and the woman behind the counter discussed the relative merits of the Snow Cloud (cake donut with powdered sugar and shaved coconut), the Thunder Cloud (chocolate sprinkles on a chocolate donut), and the Pigs in Heaven (glazed donut topped with maple icing and bacon bits) and then somehow segued from there into the story of how Grandpa Jack had broken his arm, the latest word from the doctors, and their planned trip to the dump, all while Rufus stood fidgeting at the counter, vainly hoping that another customer might walk in and pull the donut woman's attention away from Grandpa Jack, who had taken off his khaki cap and was obsessively smoothing his white hair.

"The dump just makes me sad," the donut woman was saying. "Down in the dumps, actually!" She laughed, a warm openmouthed laugh that made Grandpa Jack laugh, too. Her brown face was a series of circles—two wide-set brown eyes set above two round cheekbones with a scattering of round brown freckles on each one, a round nose with two perfectly round nostrils, and a round, laughing mouth.

"Never liked the place, myself," Grandpa Jack agreed. "Throwing something away just means you've run out of ideas."

"Old things are like stray dogs," agreed the donut-shop woman. "They might be missing teeth or ears or legs, but they still have so much love to give."

"That's it exactly," Grandpa Jack said. "I've got an old property on the edge of town that's filled with bits and pieces. It's the imperfections that give it character." He offered the donut-shop woman his uninjured hand. "I'm Jack Collins. And this is my grandson, Rufus."

"Robin-Ella LaFontaine." The donut-shop woman took Grandpa Jack's hand and held it, squeezing it as if they were old friends. "I own Old Soul Vintage next door, but I just open it up on weekends. We don't get much foot traffic during the week, so I fill in at the donut shop. Most of my business is online these days."

"Is that so?" Grandpa Jack said. "I've never bought anything online in my life. Don't even own a computer."

Robin-Ella patted his hand and released it, leaving a smudge of powdered sugar. "You're a look-and-feel person. So am I. Come on, I'll show you the shop."

"Doesn't the dump close at five?" Rufus said, grabbing his donut from the counter. "We should probably—"

But Robin-Ella was already turning the donut-shop sign to CLOSED.

⁓᠔᠕⁓

"I never display more than fifty objects at a time," Robin-Ella said as she unlocked the door to Old Soul Vintage. "The rest I keep in the back. People don't have the patience to hunt for treasures in a crowded shop the way they once did—they just want to type *treasure* into a search bar and have someone calculate the shipping."

The store was surprisingly light and airy, with an array of objects displayed in improbable clusters on white shelving and tables—a trio of cobalt-blue dishes with a set of blue Bakelite bracelets, a die-cast blue convertible, and a china doll in a blue dress. A stack of five different VHS movies that had *zebra* in the title alongside a zebra-printed pillow and a zebra-patterned pillbox hat. A tree branch painted crimson and hung with necklaces and bracelets. Somehow the store made even the most worn and ordinary objects look alluring and extraordinary.

➤ 69 ◄

"These days, it's all about display," Robin-Ella remarked. "You have to give your things some swagger or the browsers will pass you by. It's like dating. No one wants to get to know a person—they just want to see a flattering photo and a list of attributes. But I'll tell you, not everything is a 'priceless mint-condition example of mid-century design.' The important thing is to find how to let its true nature shine through. There's somebody out there who will treasure you for who you are, whether you're a crocheted pot holder or a direct-to-video Betamax movie."

Grandpa Jack grinned. "'Priceless mint-condition example of mid-century design,'" he repeated. "That's what I have on my dating profile." He winked at her and bit into his donut, instantly splattering the front of his shirt with a confetti of rainbow sprinkles and a red dollop of jelly filling. "Oopsy-daisy."

"I have paper towels in the back," Robin-Ella said. "Stay right there."

Rufus had eaten his own donut during Robin-Ella's monologue, and now he wiped his hands on his shorts. "I really think the dump is closing soon," he said. "Seriously—we should go."

But Grandpa Jack had stopped in front of a tall set of pale green shelves.

"Will you look at that!" he exclaimed.

Inside the cupboard were six antique cans, nearly identical to the cans of food in Grandpa Jack's discard box in the barn, except these were labeled COFFEE, CRACKERS, GREEN BEANS, MANDARIN ORANGE SEGMENTS, LIVER TONIC, and TOOTHPASTE.

"Those things sell like crazy," Robin-Ella said, returning with a wet paper towel. She dabbed at the jelly on Grandpa Jack's shirt. "Decorators snatch them up for putting in country houses. Lord knows what they use them for."

Rufus examined the price tag on the tin of liver tonic. "Thirty-four dollars and ninety-five cents," he said. "Grandpa Jack, do you still have the ones . . . ?"

Grandpa Jack was staring down at the bobbing pom-pom of Robin-Ella's hair. "In the truck," he said in a dream-like voice. "I was taking them to the dump."

"No!" exclaimed Robin-Ella. "Don't do it! I can sell them for you! Whatever you have, I can sell it!"

Rufus looked around the room. Old toys. Old books. Old dishes. Old shoes. It was like the contents of the barn at Feylawn, except that everything had a price tag.

"Grandpa Jack!" he said slowly. "I don't think we should go to the dump. I think we need to draw up a business plan."

10

THE AURANEME

"**R**oofaloof and Abby McTabby! How are the business plans coming?" Mark Trang pulled up a chair beside them and straddled it, leaning his elbows on the backrest.

"Great!" Abigail gave him a high-wattage smile. "I've found three vendors who can print my T-shirts and canvas bags, and I'm adding mugs to the list because my market research shows that people who read books drink a lot of herbal tea. This weekend I'm going up to my grandfather's house to find Carson Sweete Collins's original artwork, and right now I'm going through one of her books, looking for quotes to use." She held up *The Luminous Legends of Glistening Glen*. It bristled with brightly colored sticky notes.

Mark gave her a high five. "You're on fire, Abby McTabby! How about you, Roofaloof?"

Rufus found himself grinning as he handed Mark a stack of glossy pages, still warm from the BizBuzz printer. He and Grandpa Jack had worked out a financial arrangement with Robin-Ella in which they would bring her items from Feylawn and she would handle the sales and shipping in exchange for 40 percent of the profits. He'd stayed up late the night before writing what he hoped were a bunch of convincing sentences about his sales strategy (emphasize the connection to Carson Sweete Collins and Glistening Glen), the target market (decorators, collectors, and anyone who liked old stuff), and his vision (money raining down on him in sufficient quantities to save Feylawn). He'd taken some screenshots from Robin-Ella's online store to show the going rate for the antique food tins, and calculated what else might be in the barn, multiplying the number of cardboard cartons times the likelihood that there would be something of value in them. He and Grandpa Jack even came up with a name for their business: Geezer & Grandson Vintage Collectibles. His last-minute business plan was actually pretty impressive—*and* he'd done it himself, without any help from Abigail.

Mark flipped through the pages, his brow furrowed. "So you're going to be selling, uh, expired cans of food?"

"And other stuff, too," Rufus said. He wished he had some better examples. "There's all kinds of stuff in the barn. Dishes and old farming machines and—you know, collectibles."

"I read someone sold a half-eaten sandwich on eBay once," Mark said. "A fool and his money are soon parted, right? You have a great sense of humor, Roofaloof." He handed the pages back to Rufus and offered him a fist bump. "Looks awesome!"

Rufus's heart sank. *Awesome* was the lowest rank of Mark's praise, roughly equivalent to a C minus. He'd overheard enough of the exchanges between Mark and the Stormweather Prep kids to figure out that the top-tier business plans were either "fire" or "amazeballs."

"I guess I should have stuck with the T-shirt business you and Imaginary Rufus dreamed up," he said when Mark had moved to another table.

"Don't be discouraged," Abigail said. "A dream doesn't become reality through magic; it takes sweat, determination, and hard work." She was reading the inspirational quote Mark had written on the whiteboard that morning.

"Geezer and Grandson is not my *dream*," Rufus said. "My *dream* is to save Feylawn." He pushed the papers into a stack and stared out the window. It was raining again. He wondered if Shamok was staying dry in the woods.

"Rufus?" Abigail tapped his shoulder with *The Luminous Legends of Glistening Glen*. "There's something I think you should see."

He glanced at the chapter she had opened to: "The Story of the Calamand."

No one has seen the Calamand for years and years, it began.

> *But every fairy, big and small, sleeps inside a*
> *circle made of fern seed, so the Calamand won't*

find them and steal them in their sleep. Because what would the world's most notorious thief like better than a tiny creature who can talk to locks?

Luckily, the Calamand was imprisoned long ago, after stealing something dear to the fairies of Glistening Glen. The fair folk say that it was the first time in history the Thief of the Eight Worlds had ever been caught. Do you want to know what happened? It's quite an amazing tale!

Rufus thought, as he always did when he read one of his great-grandmother's books, that she had an uncanny knack for going on and on without ever getting to the point.

But first, the story continued,

I'd like you to picture the fearsome Calamand, the two-faced monster who terrorizes the eight worlds! I've never seen her, because she's locked behind a thousand locks. But I've heard she has two faces, one on each side of her head. Once she had a pretty little sister named Mandolyn, whom she loved with all her heart. Mandolyn was a quiet girl, a homebody. She didn't care to travel from world to world, stealing from everyone she met. But the Calamand couldn't bear to be parted from her. They argued, and in a fit of rage, the Calamand used her gold-handled scissors to steal her sister's face and arms. Now she wears them alongside her own, all that remains of her beloved baby sister.

Rufus was about to ask Abigail if she could give him the SparkNotes version when a blinding pain sliced through his skull. A horn blared at him from inside his own head at a volume he had never imagined was possible. He doubled over, wrapping his hands around his ears.

"Rufus?" Abigail pushed her chair aside and knelt beside him. Somehow he was on the floor in a fetal position, the unbearable sound still knifing through his brain. He screwed his eyes shut, trying to wrap his arms around his head.

"Make it stop," he pleaded. "Make it—"

And then the sound began to form into words.

GOBLIN! GOBLIN! GOBLIN!

It was the auraneme. He dug into his pocket. If he could just wrap his fist around the little bulb, maybe he could smother the sound.

GOBLIN! GOBLIN! GOBLIN!

Counselor Mark knelt beside him with his phone in hand. He was talking, but Rufus couldn't hear what he was saying. The only sound was the auraneme's screech.

GOBLIN! GOBLIN! GOBLIN!

His fingers found the auraneme in his pocket. The tiny bulb shivered in his hand and then tendrils began to wrap themselves around his wrist.

Uh-oh.

He rolled to his feet. "Bathroom," he murmured, sprinting through the door. Tendrils snaked up his forearm. He kept his hand in his pocket and his arm pressed against his side until he was safely locked in the restroom stall.

As soon as he drew his hand from his pocket, the vine shot up to his shoulder and sprouted a yellow-gold trumpet-shaped flower. The flower pushed against his face and then seemed to adhere to his forehead, like the mouth of a giant leech. As it did, a picture pushed into his mind. Two goblins he'd never seen before were driving across the meadow in ATVs, their tires etching muddy furrows in the grass. The bray of the alarm quieted. Now he heard the growl of the ATV engines, the patter of the rain, the terrified shrieks of small creatures as they galloped out of the way.

He tugged the flower from his face and the picture vanished. The flower, its petals ragged from his rough treatment, drooped. He began unwinding the tendrils from his arm.

The door to the bathroom opened. "Rufus?" Mark called. "Are you okay?"

"Yeah," Rufus said through the stall door as he dropped handfuls of leaves and flowers into the toilet. "I just get headaches sometimes."

"Can you come out?"

He flushed hastily, tucked the auraneme in his pocket, and opened the door of the stall.

Mark was leaning against the bank of sinks, brow furrowed.

"I called your parents," he said. "Your dad's coming to get you."

"My dad?" Rufus said, alarmed.

How on earth was he going to get to Feylawn now?

⚜

Rufus was sitting in the hallway outside the BizBuzz classroom with Abigail when he saw his dad striding down the hall with Aunt Chrissy. They were both dressed like TV reporters covering a hurricane: his father in khaki slacks and a black slicker, Aunt Chrissy in tight white jeans, a hot pink trench coat, and matching pink heels.

His father knelt in front of him. "You all right, buddy? Your counselor said you had a really bad headache."

"I'm okay now."

His dad lifted Rufus's chin with his thumb. "Is your head still hurting?"

Rufus shook his head. "It's fine—I'm just kind of tired. I think I need to go home and lie down."

He'd pretend to be napping and then sneak up to Feylawn. It would be risky, but it was the only way to find out what was going on.

Aunt Chrissy looked at her watch. "We don't have time to take him home, Adam. We're late as it is." She gave Rufus an appraising glance. "He'll be fine. His brain just isn't used to all the stimulation of a good summer camp. He can lie down at Feylawn."

"Why are you going to Feylawn?" Rufus asked. But he knew the answer even before his father spoke.

"To meet the buyer. Mr. Gneiss."

Abigail was already zipping up her backpack. "I'm coming, too," she said. "Counselor Mark says we should use every opportunity to study real-world businesses up close." She flashed her mother a politician's smile. "This is a really big deal you're putting together, isn't it?"

Aunt Chrissy cinched the belt of her trench coat a little tighter. "You bet your sweet bippy it is," she said. "Come along and see how your mother plans to make you rich."

THE DEES-TROY
PROPERTY GROUP

The two ATVs were parked in front of the farmhouse when they arrived. Two goblins stood beside them, talking to Grandpa Jack. One had a crocodile's leathery five-toed feet and long green tail. The other had shaggy cloven hooves like a reindeer. Rufus guessed that the goblins were glamoured to look human to anyone who didn't have clearsight, which was why his father and Aunt Chrissy were still smiling amiably even as Grandpa Jack rubbed the bridge of his nose with a puzzled expression.

The goblin with crocodile feet strode toward them with his hand extended.

"Chert Gneiss, project manager for the Dees-Troy Property Group," he said, shaking hands with each of them in turn. "And this is my chief surveyor, Ms. Rapakivi."

"Surveyor!" Aunt Chrissy repeated. "I didn't expect to see a surveyor on the first visit."

"It's an unusual property," the reindeer-hooved goblin

said crisply. "There are some things we need to get a good look at. There's a grassy spot on the far side of the creek, for example, that we'd like to inspect."

"Of course! Happy to show you anything you like!" Rufus's father bent at the waist, trying to reduce the height difference between himself and the two goblins. "I'm Adam Collins—we spoke on the phone. And this is my son, Rufus, and my niece, Abigail. They're here to learn more about real estate."

Aunt Chrissy flashed Mr. Gneiss a lipsticky smile. "They attend a *very* exclusive summer camp for young entrepreneurs."

"Honored to have you aboard," Mr. Gneiss said. "Why don't you kids join us on the tour? I bet you've never ridden in an ATV before!"

"We'd *love* to come!" Abigail widened her eyes in her most adult-pleasing fashion. "We're *very* interested in what you're proposing."

"You sure you feel up to it, Ru?" His father brushed the hair from Rufus's forehead. "How's your headache?"

"He's fine, Adam," Aunt Chrissy said. "He might as well learn a thing or two about Feylawn's *value*. Let's get going before the rain starts again." She strode over to the ATVs, the heels of her hot pink pumps punching holes in the wet grass.

Mr. Gneiss drove the ATV through Feylawn as if being chased by bandits, the tires spitting clods of dirt as he careened up the path toward the barn and then veered into the woods. Aunt Chrissy sat in the front seat beside him. Abigail and Rufus were in back. Rufus's dad was in the other ATV with Grandpa Jack and the goblin surveyor, Ms. Rapakivi.

It was hard to talk over the roar of the engine, but Aunt Chrissy was doing her valiant best, subjecting Mr. Gneiss to the kind of gale-force interrogation she usually saved for Rufus.

"ARE YOU MARRIED, MR. GNEISS?" she bellowed. "A HANDSOME MAN LIKE YOU OUGHT TO BE MARRIED!"

Birds and squirrels scattered in terror as the ATV barreled through the forest, tearing off tree branches and knocking aside stones and saplings. Rufus clenched his teeth, willing himself not to say anything about Mr. Gneiss's reckless driving. *Just find out what they're doing here*, he told himself. He scanned the air around them for some sign of Nettle, who must have been alerted to the goblins' presence by the auraneme, just as Rufus had been.

Then he realized where they were going. "Whoa, slow down," he yelled. "You're about to drive into the creek!"

Instead of slowing, Mr. Gneiss accelerated. "Top of the line all-terrain vehicle!" he shouted. "We want to inspect the other side!"

"What's on the other side of the creek?" Abigail whispered to Rufus.

Rufus shrugged, mystified. Behind them, Grandpa Jack was waving frantically from the front seat of Ms. Rapakivi's ATV.

"Hold up! The water's too high to cross!" he yelled. "Hold *up*!"

Mr. Gneiss didn't even slow down. The ATV burst through the leafy willow saplings that skirted the water's edge and plunged into the creek, tires spraying mud and stones.

"Careful!" Aunt Chrissy yelled as cold water rushed into the vehicle. "These are Louis Vuitton shoes, Mr. Gneiss!"

"Just a little water," Mr. Gneiss said. "Hang on, we'll be on the other side in a moment."

Above them, the skies opened, unleashing a torrent of fat raindrops. The roiling brown surface of the creek grew pocked and pebbled with the spatter of falling water. Mr. Gneiss gunned the engine, but the tires had already lost contact with the ground. They were floating . . . spinning . . .

Aunt Chrissy screamed as the ATV tipped over, spilling all four of them into the creek.

⚬⚭⚬

When Rufus surfaced, he saw the second ATV floating on its side beside him, spinning lazily as Ms. Rapakivi clung to the roll bar with one hand. Her other arm was wrapped around a glass vessel about the size and shape of a pickle jar.

"Mr. Gneiss," she shouted. "Help me! I have the container!"

"Hold on, Rapakivi!" Mr. Gneiss barked, pulling himself into the driver's seat of his sideways ATV. "If you value your life, do *not* let go." It sounded more like a threat than an encouragement.

Rain fell noisily around them. The ATVs drifted and swirled, banging against a cluster of boulders in the center of the creek. Rufus put his feet down and half waded, half swam back to shore. Abigail and the adults were all doing the same. The goblins, however, remained clinging to the ATVs.

"It's not that deep," Rufus called. "You don't have to swim far!"

"Swim diagonally!" Abigail instructed. "The current will carry you across!"

"Not much of a swimmer," Mr. Gneiss grunted. He looked queasy as well as terrified.

Grandpa Jack was already splashing toward the closest ATV with his good arm extended. "I've got you!" he shouted as the water reached his waist. "Just grab my hand."

Just then, there was a buzz of wings. Nettle Pampaspatch swooped down from overhead and tossed a long strand of ivy to each of the floundering goblins.

"Pull yourselves in," he called. "It's attached to a branch—it can hold your weight!"

Neither of the parents could hear or see him. But Grandpa Jack could. He looked up in surprise and lost his footing. For a moment he struggled for balance, his good arm waving. Then he slipped under the surface, and the churning current carried him out of sight.

12

THE GLASS JAR

Rufus and Abigail tore through the underbrush on the creek bank, slipping through mud and gravel, scraping over boulders.

"Grandpa Jack!" they shouted, scanning the water for any sign of movement. It was almost impossible to see through the downpour. "Grandpa Jack!"

A rustle overhead. They looked up. Abigail gave a muffled scream.

The leopard of the locks perched on a branch above the creek.

They didn't see him leap. What they saw was the long arrow of his body as he moved through the air with his tail stretched out behind him. Then his paws broke the surface of the creek, and he disappeared from view. When he surfaced, he had the collar of Grandpa Jack's shirt in his teeth.

Moments later, Shamok deposited Grandpa Jack on the

bank and stood over him, water drizzling from his whiskers.

"Are you the Locksmith?" he asked.

"Of course he's not the Locksmith," Abigail said. "Thank you for rescuing him, though." She reached out a tentative hand and stroked Shamok's forehead.

The leopard's ears flattened. He closed his eyes. "Are *you* the Locksmith?" he murmured.

Abigail shook her head. "No," she said. "But I'll help you figure out who is, I promise."

Grandpa Jack coughed and struggled to a sitting position. "I don't *think* I hit my head," he said. "On the other hand, this seems to be a talking jaguar."

Shamok growled. "Leopard."

Just then, Rufus's dad came running down the bank of the creek, followed by Aunt Chrissy, who was now barefoot.

"Pop!" Rufus's dad staggered over to Grandpa Jack and held him tight. "I thought you were this cursed place's next victim," he whispered. His chest heaved with a single sob.

Rufus looked around hastily. He could only imagine his father's reaction if he saw Shamok. But the leopard seemed to have vanished.

"Just a little dip in the creek. Could have been worse," Grandpa Jack said, squeezing his son. "Frankly, I prefer to swim when the sun's out and I have two working arms and a bathing suit, but sometimes life throws you a few curveballs."

"I was so scared, I ran right out of my four-hundred-dollar shoes!" Aunt Chrissy announced. She stared up at the downpour. "God, I hate the outdoors."

"Let's get you under a tree and out of the rain," Rufus's father said, draping his slicker over Grandpa Jack's shoulders. "Once we get the vehicles out of the creek, we'll run you back to the house for a hot shower."

Grandpa Jack got to his feet. "I'll be okay walking. It'll warm me up."

"Just *wait* a few minutes," Rufus's dad said. "You're dripping wet and surging with adrenaline. You might be more hurt than you know."

Grandpa Jack shook his head. "Nothing wrong with me a walk and a cup of tea can't fix. The kids will keep me company. I'll meet you back at the house."

Without waiting for a reply, he pushed into the woods.

⁖⁖⁖

Shamok joined them on the walk, pressing his body close to Grandpa Jack.

"You can warm your hands in my fur," he said. "I still have enough spots for *that*, at least."

"I don't think it's the spots that do the warming," Abigail said. "It's the fur."

Shamok gave her a haughty look. "I ought to know. They're *my* spots."

The rain had subsided into a steady drizzle, which pattered on the leaves around them. Rufus put his arm around Grandpa Jack, who was trying to conceal the fact that he was shivering.

"Do you notice how Nettle always shows up just as things go horribly wrong?" Rufus said to Abigail.

"It wasn't *Nettle's* fault the goblins drove into the creek," Abigail replied. "He came to help."

"Help who?" Rufus said. "He didn't help *us*. He helped *them*. If it wasn't for Shamok, Grandpa Jack might still be in the creek."

Abigail folded her arms around herself.

"You're right," she said at last. "I want to argue with you, but I can't. That's exactly what happened."

Grandpa Jack had hunched his chin into the collar of his borrowed slicker. Now he looked up. "Did you just say *goblins*? Is that what you call those short fellows with the funny feet and the dental issues?"

"They smell like poison." Shamok wrinkled his nose. "And the one with big feet had one of my spots in his pocket."

"You mean a padlock?" Rufus said. "How do you know?"

"You'd understand if you had spots," Shamok said.

"What I want to know," Abigail said, "is why they were

so interested in getting to the other side of the creek. What's over there?"

"No gold mines or oil wells, if that's what you're asking," Grandpa Jack said. "As far as I know it's just woods and meadow."

"But there's *something* over there they want," Rufus said.

Grandpa Jack tugged on the zipper of his raincoat. "The goblin with the deer feet, Ms. Rapakivi. The surveyor. She had a glass jar with her—what we used to call a specimen jar when I was a biology student. When the ATV filled with water, it was the first thing she reached for."

"I noticed that," Abigail said. "She was holding on to it in the water. I couldn't see what was in it, though."

"*I* could," Grandpa Jack said. "It was one of those fairy creatures."

"A *feyling*?" Rufus exclaimed. "But they've all gone to the Green World—all except Nettle anyway."

"Not *all*," Abigail said. "There's the one who married Mr. Diggs. Queen Queen-Anne's-Lace."

"But why would they have brought her with them?" Rufus asked.

Nobody could answer, so they continued on in silence. Walking from the creek to the farmhouse didn't take long when you were warm and dry, but when you were soaking wet it seemed to take forever.

"I wish we knew what they were up to," Abigail said.

"But there's no one to ask," Rufus said. Iris was gone. Nettle couldn't be trusted.

"We have the books," Abigail said. "'Read the tale to unwrite the story.'"

Rufus rolled his eyes. He hated to admit it, but Abigail was right.

A SCREAM IN THE NIGHT

The endpapers of *The Sparkling Stories of Glistening Glen* were a map of Glistening Glen, the terrain of which was almost identical to Feylawn's. Lying in bed that night, Rufus studied them carefully, hoping to find some clue about the far side of the creek. But there was nothing special noted on the map. That meant he would have to read the book itself, which seemed to be about the hunt for a missing magical hairbrush whose significance, if it was ever explained, Rufus had skimmed right over. By the third chapter, the hairbrush hunt had taken the fairies onto something called the Moving Meadow.

And the prettiest little meadow it was, too! his great-grandmother had written.

> *It was carpeted with red-violet blossoms like a sunset reflected in an evening lake. The seeds of these flowers were so rare and valuable that the*

fairies studied the movements of the meadow the
way an astronomer might study the movements of
a comet, waiting for the season of its return. Only
the wisest and the most scholarly of these flighty
flibbertigibbets knew when to expect it, or where
it might go next. That was the queen of the fairies,
of course: Lacy the Luminous. She kept the chart
of the meadow's movements tucked into the pouch
at her hip, worn and creased from all the times it
had been folded and unfolded . . .

Rufus's eyes fluttered shut. The book slipped out of his hands and landed on his chest.

He woke to the screech of the auraneme. It was even louder than it had been that afternoon, and it seemed to be concentrated in Rufus's right ear.

GOBLINS! it shrieked. *GOBLINS AT FEYLAWN!*

Rufus clapped a hand to his ear and grasped something warm that was beating against his palm.

He held it up to his face and found himself staring at Iris.

"All I asked was for you to keep Feylawn safe while we were gone!" she shrieked. "And yet I come back to find it soaking wet and stinking of goblins. You clearly haven't done one single thing I asked you to do, which I know because it's RAINING IN JULY!"

She twisted out of his hand and took a seat on his pillow.

She wasn't exactly like the Iris he remembered. Her hair was combed instead of tangled and her brown skin was no longer tinged with gray. Her injured wing was green and strong again, and she looked less scrawny and under-fed. She even had a new dress, of a deeper blue than the tattered one she was wearing when she left, with flowing sleeves and an embroidered hem. She almost looked like an illustration in one of his great-grandmother's Glisten-ing Glen books, except for the expression of annoyance on her face. More than anything else, it was her irritation that convinced him she wasn't a dream.

"How did you get here?" he asked. "You're supposed to be in the Green World."

"I took the train to Feylawn and then I flew here, which was tiring, but things were in such disarray that I had to make sure that you hadn't fallen off a cliff or been eaten by the troll while I was gone. And now it turns out that you're perfectly fine, which is even worse than I thought. Did you even *read* the list I left you? It said to *spetch the nimbolichen*! It said to *keep the goblins out*!"

Rufus grinned. He didn't mind being scolded—he didn't even mind having done a terrible job. The important thing was that Iris was back. Someone he could trust.

"How's Quercus? And Trillium?" he asked.

"They're fine. As am I. Fit as a fiddlehead fern. Strong as oxalis. Healthy as a horse chestnut."

"I didn't think you'd come back so soon," Rufus said. He

felt like dancing or jumping, or maybe both at once. "You said it would take a while to recover, and I figured that meant months, not weeks—" He broke off. "Did you just cough?"

Iris cleared her throat. "I'm much better than I was. Don't give me that look."

Rufus waited.

She coughed again and then tried to muffle it in her elbow.

"You're not supposed to be here, are you?" Rufus said. "You're supposed to be in the Green World still. Getting well." He bent over her, searching for signs of illness. There it was—a thin line of brown in one wing. "You need to go back. You can go over the list with me and explain what I need to do, and then you can go back—"

Iris shook her head. "There's something I need to take care of first. It won't take long. The train will be back to get me a week from Monday."

"But why can't someone else take care of whatever it is?" Rufus said. "You were so sick—you were sicker than anyone!"

"I have to clean up my own nest," Iris said.

"Mess," Rufus corrected. "It's clean up your own—"

"Nest," Iris said. "A bird won't lay an egg without a nice tidy nest. Which is why I brought some of the Green World feylings along to help with the chores—the ones who were trapped *there* when the train was stolen. They've been living in the present for seventy years, so their work ethic isn't what it was, plus they're a bit addled. The brain needs time as much as it needs oxygen. I have them spetching the nimbolichen now, although they keep stopping to sing. You do a lot of singing when you're in the present tense— I'd forgotten that. Forgot most of the songs, actually."

"What do you mean, *present tense?*" Rufus said.

Iris put her fingers to her temples. "I've been gone for *weeks*," she said. "Do you mean to tell me that you're still just as ignorant as you were when I left?"

"Yes!" Rufus said with more than a little annoyance. "It's not like you left me with *any* information! That list of yours, for example—it was just a bunch of words, with no instructions!"

"Go to sleep," Iris said. "I'm only going to explain everything once, and I might as well wait until your cousin's there to hear it. I've had a long journey, and the prospect of being peppered with pointless questions is more than I can stomach without a little rest."

"But I have things to tell you," Rufus protested. "Feylawn's in serious trouble. And there's a leopard—"

"Shh," Iris admonished. "Whatever it is you have to tell me can wait. Come to Feylawn tomorrow with Abigail. We can talk about it then."

14

A PORCELAIN CHICKEN

Getting to Feylawn turned out to be a lot more difficult than Rufus had anticipated. He had planned on going there on Friday, but Aunt Chrissy was waiting for them when they walked out of camp and insisted on dropping Rufus at home before taking Abigail to swim practice. Saturday was no better. The mishap in the creek had confirmed the adults' worst fears about the place, and they were adamant that Rufus and Abigail should stay away.

"Please," Rufus begged his dad. "I *have* to go to Feylawn or I'm not going to be able to do my BizBuzz project."

His father pinched the bridge of his nose. "Maybe you should choose a different project."

"My business plan's already written," Rufus said. "I have to follow through if I want to win the Piranha Pitch Session."

He had been hoping that the prospect of him winning something, as ludicrous as it sounded, might persuade his parents to yield. It didn't. His father didn't want him going into the barn, the floorboards of which hadn't been repaired since the fall that broke Grandpa Jack's arm. His mother didn't want him arguing with his father. Rufus and Abigail texted each other all day, refining their lobbying strategy. Nothing worked. At last Rufus resigned himself to spending Saturday afternoon on the couch, reading *The Sparkling Stories of Glistening Glen*.

He finished the book around five o'clock. It wasn't a satisfying ending. The fairies had recovered their magic hairbrush and thrown a party to celebrate, but Rufus hadn't learned a single useful fact about the far side of the creek, or repelling goblins, or deciphering prophesies from the Crinnyeyes. He texted as much to Abigail, then went outside and sat on his father's favorite chair on the patio, hoping that Iris might suddenly land on his shoulder and start scolding him for not showing up. It was raining again, and the drops made a comforting patter on the patio umbrella as he huddled into his sweatshirt.

A familiar indigo bird landed on the arm of the chair and cocked his crested head at Rufus. Rufus leaped to his feet.

"You have a lot of nerve coming here!" He swatted at Nettle, but the bird dodged him and fluttered to the glass-topped patio table.

"I'm aware that recent events may have appeared a certain way," Nettle said, examining his own reflection.

"*Appeared?*" Rufus sputtered. "I think it's pretty clear what happened. Instead of chasing the goblins out of Feylawn, you *rescued* them and left Grandpa Jack to drown!"

Nettle's black crest flattened against his head. "I know I failed you, Pledge Lord," he said, hopping closer to Rufus. "But if you'd let me explain—"

"You had *one* job," Rufus said. "Protect Feylawn and my family. But you don't want the job, and I hate the sight of you, so let's make it easy for both of us: *Stay away from me. Stay away from my whole family!*"

"But we're bound to each other!" the Steller's jay croaked. "Peony seed links our fates! And now you need my help. Mr. Diggs is up to something! Only a Pampas-patch can put it all to rights."

Rufus snorted. "We have Iris. We don't need you."

He shoved the table, hard enough to dislodge Nettle from his perch. The Steller's jay flapped into the air and circled his head, screeching. Then he flew into the trees and was gone.

Rufus went inside and texted Abigail.

I fired nettle

Abigail replied instantly: Good.

❧

On Sunday morning, Grandpa Jack showed up.

"Emi came by Feylawn this morning and helped me carry some boxes from the barn to the house," he announced to

Rufus's father. "I was hoping I could borrow Rufus for a few hours to help me sort through them."

Rufus looked at his mom, who was in her scrubs and heading for the door. What was she doing at Feylawn?

"I stopped in for a cup of coffee and a muffin while I was out for a run," she said, slinging a tote bag over her shoulder. "Needed to fuel up for the jog home."

"Which is a polite way of saying that she wanted to check up on me," Grandpa Jack said.

"*And* get out of the rain," Rufus's mother said. "I didn't realize you'd be putting me to work."

"And now I plan to put *Rufus* to work," Grandpa Jack said. "If you can spare him. Those boxes aren't going to empty themselves."

Rufus's father sighed. "Fine. But promise me you won't let him go wandering around outside. It's just not safe."

"It's raining out," Grandpa Jack said. "Who wants to wander around in weather like this anyway?"

Which, Rufus noted, was not a promise.

Instead of heading for Feylawn, Grandpa Jack stopped at Abigail's apartment and made a similar pitch to Aunt Chrissy. He had found a box of Carson Sweete Collins's drawings while cleaning out the attic, he said, and thought Abigail might want to see if any of them would be useful for her T-shirt business. "I have to start getting rid of things if I'm going to move to town," he said. "Figured the kids might give me a hand."

Which was how Rufus and Abigail found themselves spending the afternoon in the farmhouse with a fire blazing in the fireplace, a plate of sandwiches on the coffee table, and a stack of slightly damp crates and boxes stacked on the floor.

The first several boxes Rufus and Grandpa Jack unpacked were a complete disappointment—one was filled with well-worn winter socks and mittens, and another contained cans of paint and solvents. But then things began to improve.

"Look at this," Grandpa Jack said, pulling out a large porcelain hen perched atop a porcelain nest. "Pop Avery told me this was where he kept the money he bought Feylawn with." He lifted the chicken to reveal the compartment beneath.

"I thought he bought Feylawn with encyclopedias," Rufus said.

"A bit of both, I imagine," Grandpa Jack said. He stroked the chicken's painted head. "I always loved this chicken. When I was a kid, my mother kept her pens and paintbrushes in it. Seems like a good sign. Maybe this is where we'll keep the profits from our business."

The idea of there being actual profits seemed remote, but as they kept opening boxes, they began finding more things that Rufus could imagine seeing in Robin-Ella's shop: tiny china animal figurines wrapped in newspaper, a set of hand-embroidered napkins with a matching tablecloth, and two cartons of old board games with names like "Moon Mullins" and "Mystic Skull."

Meanwhile, Abigail was making a pile of drawings she wanted to use on her T-shirts and mugs, occasionally calling Grandpa Jack over to help identify what she'd found.

"What do you think this is?" she asked, holding up a square of translucent paper covered with swooping arrows and dozens of tiny icons. Each one was meticulously drawn in colored inks: a flower, a fish, a pickax, a storm cloud. "Some kind of chart, right? Or a calendar?"

Rufus looked over her shoulder. The top border of the chart was composed of months. The bottom border was made up of numbers from one to thirty-one. On the two sides were rows of clock faces marking the hours from one to twelve.

"Planting times, maybe? My mother loved her garden," Grandpa Jack suggested. "It's pretty, whatever it is."

"I think so, too," Abigail said, putting the chart in the pile of drawings she wanted to borrow. "I could sell copies on the website."

"I'd buy one myself," Grandpa Jack said. "I can hang it on the wall of my apartment in town."

Rufus got up and went onto the front porch to look for Iris. He'd been going out every half hour or so, expecting her to land on his shoulder and begin yelling at him for taking two days to get there, but there was no sign of her.

"Looks like the rain's stopping," Grandpa Jack said,

coming to stand behind him with his hands resting on Rufus's shoulders. It was true. Fingers of sunlight poked through the clouds, turning the wet grass into a field of diamonds.

Rufus tried to think of a plausible reason why he and Abigail should go out for a walk, despite his father's express instructions. But before he could come up with one, Grandpa Jack gave his shoulders a squeeze.

"I'm sorry, Ru—I hate to walk away from our work, but my garden's desperately in need of my attention, and I'm not sure how long the sunshine's going to last. Think you two can occupy yourselves for an hour or so?"

Rufus couldn't believe his good fortune. "Of course!" he said. "I mean, if you don't need any help . . ."

Grandpa Jack was pulling on the green rubber boots he kept by the front door. "You've been helpful all day. Why don't you relax for a bit."

Before Rufus could stammer his thanks, Grandpa Jack was already heading for the garden.

15

IRIS'S AGENDA

The meadow was still wet enough to soak their shoes, but as Abigail and Rufus walked toward the Boulder Dude, they could feel the warmth of the sun on their shoulders. The air smelled of grass and flowers and the peppery leaves of the bay trees in the woods.

"Wow, I've missed summer," Rufus remarked. "I wonder if the rain has *stopped*, or just paused."

"That depends on how much of the nimbolichen we can gather before the wind scatters more spores," Iris said, landing on Abigail's shoulder. "Did you even *read* the list I gave you? It said very clearly—"

"Spetch the nimbolichen, I know," Rufus said. "But I don't know what nimbolichen *is*, or where to find it, or what it does, or how to 'spetch' it!"

"Did it occur to you that it might be important to find out?" Iris asked. "Or were you just going to let it rain until all the diarnuts split open and the janati geese flew off without laying a single egg?"

As if to underscore her point, a flock of geese waddled across the meadow and fell in step behind them, honking irritably: "Tilting, robust, sprinkler, debonair."

"You have no idea what it's been like since you left," protested Abigail. "I mean, there's only two of us and so much to do and—"

"You mean it's been difficult to get all the chores done?" Iris asked, her voice dripping with sarcasm. "The chores that used to be spread among hundreds of feylings but then settled on just a few people because the others were too sick or too dead to do them? I wish I knew what that was like." She tapped her chin with one finger. "Oh, right. I do. That's what we've been dealing with for *decades*. I thought you'd be able to handle it for . . . however long it's been."

"Four weeks," Rufus said. "Plus a couple days. Sorry it took us so long to get here this weekend—we came as soon as we could. I was worried you'd think we weren't coming."

Iris frowned. "How long is 'so long'?"

Rufus and Abigail exchanged glances. "Three days," Rufus said. "You came to see me on Thursday, and now it's Sunday."

"It's Sunday already?" Iris slapped her palm to her forehead. "Well, I've been busy putting things to rights. Time must have gotten away from me."

They had reached the Boulder Dude. Iris fluttered up to the top of the giant's granite head and sat with her legs dangling over the side. The whir of her wings looked even more agitated than usual.

"A lot's happened since you left," Abigail said when she and Rufus had clambered up beside her. "Goblins are trying to buy Feylawn."

Iris's fluttering wings went very still. "Goblins?" she said. "But we sent Diggs to the Place Between! We found the train. It's safe in the Green World. Why would goblins . . . ?"

"That's what we're trying to figure out!" Rufus said. "They're super focused on the other side of the creek—but why?"

"That's the reason we need to rescue our queen," Iris said. "*She'll* know why, and she'll know what to do."

"Wait a sec," Rufus said. "Did you just say *rescue her*?"

"That's why I'm here." Iris seemed to think it should have been obvious. "Things in the Green World are a bit . . . chaotic. It's clear to me we need our queen. We never should have let her go."

"But isn't that how you got your train?" Rufus asked. "She married Diggs as payment for his help."

Iris nodded. "She sacrificed herself for us. And we let her do it. We *let her do it*, even though it meant that she'd be trapped with him in the tunnels until she died." She wiped her eyes on the embroidered hem of her dress. "We've never had another queen—we didn't have anyone smart enough or kind enough or as good at thinking about someone besides herself. We've just been running around hairy-scary ever since."

"Harum-scarum," Abigail corrected. "It means—"

"It means we have to rescue our queen before she dies!" Iris said. "*That's* what it means."

"You keep saying *rescue her*," Rufus said. "But *how*?" He held up a hand. "Don't tell me, actually, because no. I'm sorry about your queen, but right now we have to focus on saving Feylawn."

Iris stamped her foot. "But to save Feylawn we need Queen Queen-Anne's-Lace! You glompers performed far better than expected when it came to finding our train, but I can't expect you'll get lucky twice."

"*Lucky?*" protested Abigail. "It was a lot more than luck!"

"Is this where I'm supposed to make you feel good about yourselves?" Iris said. "Because I really don't have the temperament for that kind of thing. The point is, I left the Blue World with all our problems solved, and I came back a few weeks later and discovered that you haven't even managed to weed the wanderlust."

"We did our best," Abigail said.

"Yes, yes, we're all doing our best," Iris said. "But our best isn't good enough. That's the point. When I got back to the Green World, it was in shambles. Nothing's been taken care of—nothing at all. The Green World feylings didn't even remember us. They don't remember *anything*. It turns out that being trapped in the Green World for seventy years is almost as bad as being trapped in the Blue World. Except instead of dying, they just got very, very stupid."

"Why?" Abigail asked. "What makes them stupid?"

"There's no time!" Iris said.

"Look, we're in a hurry, too," Abigail snapped. "But if you want our help—"

"*In the Green World!*" Iris yelled. "In the Green World there isn't any time. It's just one continuous present. Turns out that without time, your brain turns to applesauce. You don't plan the future and you don't remember the past. I got out of there just at the knock of time."

"Nick," Rufus corrected.

"Knock," Iris said. "It's when the faint memory of what it was like to have time knocks at the door to say you better get going." She sighed heavily. "Queen Queen-Anne's-Lace used to give each of us a daily dose of time when we were there, just to keep us focused. But now she's gone and I don't know how to fix everything that's gone wrong. I just lost *two whole days* without even noticing."

"But you're in the Blue World now," Rufus said. "Aren't you getting time doses just by being here?"

"It takes a while for the time doses to take effect," Iris said. "You'll see when you meet the Green World feylings. They're like children."

"*We're* children," Rufus protested.

"Stop logicking me!" Iris yelled. "I'm not any good at

it!" She buried her face in her hands and began to cry. "We need our queen," she moaned. "We *need* her!"

Abigail was pulling on both her braids at once, as if they were the reins on a runaway horse. "The thing is," she said, "we saw your queen. Or Grandpa Jack did. The goblins had her in a jar."

"A jar?" Iris looked up. "Why would they put her in—"

A low rumble shook the granite beneath them. Iris flew over their heads in alarm.

"What in the eight worlds is *that?*"

Shamok slunk over the boulders, his body low to the ground and his ears pressed against his skull. His tail lashed from side to side as he tilted his head back and roared in short, sawing bursts, as if a lion's roar had been broken into pieces for ease of transport.

"I AM—THE LEOPARD—OF THE LOCKS!" he roared. "AND THE LOCKS—ARE OPENING!"

Nobody said anything for a moment. Then Abigail reached over and tugged the leopard's lashing tail. "Hey," she whispered. "Come here and talk to us."

Shamok lowered himself onto a stretch of granite below them. "I'm fine where I am. I don't like people to see my spotless parts."

Then he noticed Iris. "Are you the Locksmith?" he asked.

"I'm not anything. Who are you?"

"I am Shamok, the leopard of the locks. I've come to tell the Locksmith that someone is opening the locks that confine the Calamand. Seven locks have opened already. Seven of my spots have disappeared. Soon the Calamand will be free, and I will be dead. Not that anyone seems to care."

"*I* care," Abigail said. "I've told you I do. And I'll help you find the Locksmith. But you said there are a thousand locks and only seven of them have opened. We have a little time."

Shamok growled. "You *think* you have time. But that's only because you don't understand the Calamand. She was waiting, like a spider waits, for something to land in her web. And now it has, and it will free her." He lay down on the rock with his head between his paws. "I should have eaten that poisonous thing before it opened the first lock."

"You mean you *saw* the lock opener?" Rufus turned his gaze to Shamok. "Couldn't you have done something to stop it?"

The leopard suddenly became occupied with grooming his left foot.

"I stalked him," he said after carefully licking between his toes. "I stalked the half bird all around the island. He had a strong smell—like things that rot and make you sick. I didn't know what he was, so I followed him until he disappeared into a hole. And after a while he came out of his hole, and still I wasn't sure if he was safe to eat, so I watched him, until all at once he opened the lock and I found myself here."

"Perhaps you shouldn't be so particular about your meals," Iris observed.

"I can't do my job if I've been poisoned," Shamok said huffily. "There's only one leopard of the locks. And if the locks are opened, there won't be *any*."

"The lock opener," Rufus said. "You called him a half bird a minute ago. Why?"

"Legs," Shamok said. "Like a bird's legs, with talons. And the rest like a little man with floppy ears."

"Diggs!" Abigail said. Her eyes grew wide. "*Diggs* is the one opening the locks!"

"His name is Diggs?" Shamok's black lip curled to reveal a sharp fang. "I should have eaten him."

"Yes, you should have," Iris said. "You would have been doing us all a favor." She sniffed. "Since when are leopards fussy eaters?"

"I'm not fussy," Shamok growled. "I've eaten lots of *other* things. I could eat *you*, if I wanted to. You look like you might be tasty."

"She isn't!" Abigail said hastily. "Nothing that talks is tasty."

"Squirrels talk, and they're tasty," Shamok said. "Rabbits, too. Deer. Mice. Rats. Fish. Raccoons. Coyotes. Skunks. Porcupines—"

"Much as I'm sure we'd love to hear all about your dietary preferences," Iris interrupted, "we have other matters to discuss."

"Like stopping the half bird from freeing the Calamand," Shamok said.

Rufus dug the padlock out of his pocket. It still gave off that same shivery vibration he remembered from the train. It was a feeling of intention, he realized. The train had always seemed to *want* things—to be joined with its cars, to respond to Mr. Diggs's whistle, to travel between the worlds. The lock, on the other hand, seemed to want to be back on the gate where it came from. It wanted to join with the other locks like teeth in a long jawbone, biting down, holding fast. It hadn't liked opening. He turned it over in his hands, noticing as he did that there was a series of fine scratches on the padlock's round body. Chisel marks? Was that how the lock had been forced open?

But no, they were too regular for that. They were *symbols* of some sort.

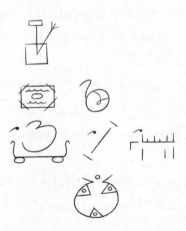

"Anyone know what these are?" he asked, holding up the lock.

Iris flew to his shoulder to look. "That's goblin writing,"

she said. "I tried to study it once. One of the Green World feylings who came back with me—Camellia Maplebranch—she's a goblin scholar, or *was*, when she was getting regular doses of time. She's still very present-tense, but she's *starting* to become temporally oriented now that she's here. Let's see if she can read it."

16

THE LANGUAGE OF THE LOCKS

They walked deep into the woods, to a grove of fat-needled spruce trees that Rufus had somehow never seen before. The clouds, which had been patchy over the rest of Feylawn, were gathered in a thick carpet overhead. A steady drizzle gave the grove a misty, distorted look, as if they were swimming through an underwater grotto. A dozen or more feylings were performing a complicated ballet among the trees, fluttering to the topmost branches, diving down to the tips of the boughs, pivoting back to the trees' peaks again, all the while singing to themselves like bees gathering pollen in a meadow.

"*This* is what *you* were supposed to be doing," Iris remarked as she directed Rufus, Abigail, and Shamok toward a tree in the center of the grove. "*If* you had been able to follow the simplest of instructions."

Rufus watched the zooming, humming feylings. They looked like circus performers swinging on invisible trapezes.

"If this is what spetching is, I feel like we might have had trouble pulling it off."

Iris harrumphed. "It's shortsighted of you glompers not to have any wings."

Shamok watched the flitting feylings intently, ears pricked. His tail twitched.

"You can't eat them," Abigail said to him. "No, not even *one*."

A feyling in a satiny pink suit sailed by, singing softly to herself. "Tiny clouds!" she murmured. "Tiny clouds. Fetch them, fetch them. Tiny clouds!"

"Camellia!" Iris called after her.

The feyling stopped and circled back, looking puzzled. Her long black hair was dusted with a latticework of blue-green powder that Rufus took to be nimbolichen spores. Her spore-stained pink suit was soaked through and clinging to her spindly limbs.

"Tiny clouds," she said. "Fetch them, fetch them."

"Yes, yes, you're spetching like a champ," Iris said. "We just need you to read something. In goblin script."

"Oh!" Camellia giggled. "Is that something I do? Am I doing it now?"

"Not yet," Iris said in the tone of someone whose patience had been severely tried. "It's something you *have done*, in the past. It's what you're *going to do* in the very near future. Show her, Rufus."

Rufus held out the padlock. "Can you read these symbols?"

"This is difficult." Camellia landed on his wrist and frowned. "The now of reading goblin script is far away."

"*Long ago*," Iris said. "You're trying to say it was *long ago*. For the love of all that is leafy, you were a *historian*, Camellia."

"Maybe try reading it out loud?" Abigail suggested.

"Okay." Camellia leaned so close to the symbols on the lock that Rufus feared she might topple forward. "This first one is a name icon that says who the writer is."

"Could it say Mr. Diggs?" Rufus said. He took a closer look at the symbol Camellia had said was a name.

"Maybe. Each name icon is unique. I only know a few from the important not-now."

"*History*," said Iris, fluttering over to stand behind Camellia. "The important not-now is called *history*."

Camellia smiled and looked up at the rain. "Am I doing history now?"

"You're looking at the sky now," Iris said with a deep sigh. She put a hand on Camellia's shoulder. "Look back at the goblin script. What does the rest of it say?"

Camellia refocused on the tiny scratchings on the padlock. "This one means *island* and then there's a symbol for *trapped* around it, so I suppose that means *trapped on an island*. And this one is two symbols combined, one for *world* and then a modifier that means that it isn't quite that. Like a world, but not a world."

"The Place Between!" Abigail exclaimed. "I think Diggs used the lock to send a message. Somehow he figured out that if he unlocks them *there*, they wind up *here*."

"Only the first seven," Shamok said. "Each lock goes to one of the seven detectives who arrested the Calamand." He sat down in the pine duff, ears back. "The Calamand wouldn't have known which lock would go where, so she had the half bird write on all of them."

Camellia was still squatting in front of the lock on Rufus's palm, her dripping pink suit puddling around her. "There's more," she said. "The next part is in the style that means it's a command. Telling the reader to do something in the next-now."

"*Future*," Iris said between gritted teeth. "Come on, it's a simple word. If you can read goblin, you can understand time."

"What's he telling them to do?" Abigail asked.

"These are two combined symbols that mean *bring* and *woman*—or, no, it's possessive, so here it would mean *bring wife*."

Iris's hand tightened on Camellia's shoulder. "Queen Queen-Anne's-Lace."

"Who?" asked Camellia.

"Never mind. Keep going."

"The next one means *take shortcut*, and then there's something that's kind of weird. The symbol for riding combined with the symbol for grass. Something like *ride grass.*"

"*Bring wife. Take shortcut. Ride grass,*" Abigail repeated. She huddled close to Rufus and peered at the padlock. "What's that last symbol?"

Camellia reached down and touched the final marking with her finger. "This is from their money alphabet—the special signs they have for talking about business."

"But what does it mean?" Rufus asked.

"It's very, very positive," Camellia said. "It's the sign they use for a bargain with no downside. Very lucrative and good for everyone."

"Maybe that's why the goblins were trying to cross the creek," Rufus said. "They're looking for the shortcut—some way of getting to Mr. Diggs." He frowned. A memory niggled at him, fleeting, like a piece of a dream.

Iris released her hand from Camellia's soggy pink shoulder. "Thank you, Camellia," she said. "Now you can go back to spetching."

Camellia looked at her blankly.

"Fetching the spores," Iris prompted. "The blue-green ones that make the rain. Gather them into your pouch. Don't let them drift away."

"Oh yes!" The feyling's face lit up. "Tiny clouds! Fetch them! Fetch them!" She smiled happily and lifted off from the padlock in Rufus's hand, singing to herself.

They walked back through the woods in silence, threading between the oaks and madrones on their way to the farmhouse.

"She doesn't even remember Queen Queen-Anne's-Lace," Iris burst out at last from her perch on Rufus's shoulder. "It's maddening!"

"I'm sorry," Abigail said. "I really am. But we need to focus. It won't be long before the goblins make another attempt to cross the creek."

"I suppose you'd better tell me exactly what happened last time," Iris said. "Everything."

So Rufus and Abigail explained about Mr. Gneiss's email and the ATV accident and the jar with a feyling in it and how Nettle had rescued the goblins instead of Grandpa Jack.

"Which is why I fired him," Rufus concluded. "Because he's *not* on our side, peony seed or no peony seed."

Iris pressed her fingers to her temples. "I should have just let the present wash over me and turn my brain to dandelion fluff. Feylings aren't meant to do so much thinking." She flew to Shamok and perched between his shoulder blades. "Tell me what you know about the Locksmith."

"The Locksmith can open and close the locks with a single word," said Shamok. "That's all I know."

"That's enough," said Iris. "The Locksmith must be Queen Queen-Anne's-Lace. That's why the goblins had her with them. They think she'll open the gate. But she won't do it. She helped put the Calamand behind bars in the first place. She knows what the Calamand can do. Nobody in their right mind would let her out."

Rufus hadn't spent a lot of time worrying about the Calamand—the bit he'd read in *The Luminous Legends of Glistening Glen* had been more boring than scary. But something about Iris's tone made him stop walking.

"What can she do?" he asked.

"She steals magical objects and she plays with them as if they're toys," Iris said. "She doesn't care what happens— it's fun for her to ruin things. She stole the Slicers, which can cut through anything, and used them to cut her sister into pieces so she could take her face and arms and make them her own. She used the Felling Ax to cut down every tree in a forest in a single afternoon. She's stolen the most beautiful songs, just so she could hear them forever. She stole a river once, the source of water for a whole country, and let everyone die of thirst. Who knows what she'd do if she got out."

"There's something she wants," Shamok said. "A magical object she left behind when she was arrested. I heard her talking about it with her sister."

"Her sister?" Abigail said. "The one she cut into pieces?"

"Mandolyn," said Shamok. "She lives on the back of the

Calamand's head. She's pretty angry about being locked up with the Calamand."

"Angrier about being *locked* up than about being *cut* up?" Rufus said.

"I don't know how angry she was then," Shamok said. "I only know how angry she is *now*."

"That settles it," Iris said. "We need to free Queen Queen-Anne's-Lace as soon as possible. She'll know what Mr. Diggs is up to and how to keep him from freeing the Calamand."

"Right," Rufus said. "We'll just march into the tunnels and demand your queen's freedom. What could go wrong?"

"Not into the tunnels!" Iris flew into the air and circled their heads excitedly. "To the island of Imura. We'll take the shortcut the goblins are looking for and get to Imura before they do. Then, when they arrive, we'll rescue her."

Abigail snorted. "The three of us? Against a bunch of goblins?"

Shamok's tail lashed. "I'll come, too. I'll devour them. No matter how poisonous they are."

"What if they have weapons?" Abigail kicked a stone out of the path. "Remember how Mr. Diggs tried to burn us alive?"

Rufus knew she was right. It felt like an impossible math problem. There was one goblin on Imura now and no Queen Queen-Anne's-Lace. Soon there would be three goblins and one Queen Queen-Anne's-Lace. But what they wanted was one Queen Queen-Anne's-Lace and zero goblins.

He clenched his teeth, trying to jolt his brain into spitting out an idea. It was there, he knew it was. A solution. A way through.

And then it came to him with such force that he almost shouted it. "We have to get there *before* the other goblins do! Then we'll capture Mr. Diggs and bring him back with us."

"But I don't want Mr. Diggs," Iris said. "I want my queen."

"But that's how we get her! We *trade* for her. Abigail, you know how Mark Trang says that every business should be a mutually beneficial exchange? If we get to the island first and capture Diggs ourselves, we can offer him *his* freedom in exchange for the queen's. Like a prisoner swap."

"And then she could relock the locks and give me back my spots," Shamok said.

"And help us figure out what to do next," Rufus said. He felt like his body was made of coiled springs.

Of the four of them, only Abigail seemed unimpressed by his plan.

"I have a better idea," she said. "It seems like the goblins and the Calamand and saving Feylawn are all connected somehow. So instead of rushing headlong into an incredibly dangerous situation, why don't we focus on the clues we got from the Crinnyeyes?"

"You can't be serious," Rufus said. "The Crinnyeyes

didn't give us *clues*. They told us to do a bunch of completely impossible and nonsensical things."

"They're riddles," Abigail said. "We can solve them. We just need a little time."

"But we don't *have* time," Rufus said. "Not if we want to get to Imura before the other goblins do."

"You really think we can capture Mr. Diggs? By ourselves?" Abigail folded her arms over her chest.

"He wouldn't be expecting us," Rufus argued. "We'd have surprise on our side. And Shamok."

"And he'd have being a goblin on *his* side," Abigail said.

Iris flew to her shoulder. "She who has a taste is last. Which, if you're not familiar with the expression, means that the person who keeps trying tastes of everything before making a decision about what to eat ends up being the last one to get fed. Sometimes you have to jump in and make a decision."

"That's *not* the expression," Abigail said. "It's *She who hesitates is lost*, and I'm not *hesitating*—I'm suggesting an alternative and much smarter plan so that we don't all end up dead."

"I don't like your plan," Iris said. "There's too much thinking in it. I say we go to Imura."

17

BEGUILUM

Rufus woke the next morning with Iris standing on the bridge of his nose.

"Are you ready to capture Diggs?" she asked.

"It's not that simple." Rufus blinked, his eyes crossing from the effort of getting her into focus. He brushed Iris off his face and sat up. "We still don't know how to get to Imura. And even if we did, Abigail and I have to be at camp until three."

"Rufus?"

The door opened and his father poked his head in. "Aunt Chrissy's taking you and Abigail to BizBuzz today. They'll be here in a few minutes."

"Why? Where's Mom?"

"Early shift. And I've got work to do!" His dad bounced on the balls of his feet.

"What kind of work?" Rufus asked. But he could guess the answer.

"Now that the sun's shining, Mr. Gneiss and his crew want to give their survey of the property another shot," he said. "I need to run some numbers before our meeting this afternoon." He drummed his fingers against the doorway. "I'm making pancakes—if you hurry, you'll have time to eat 'em before Abigail and Chrissy get here."

"I'll be down in five minutes," Rufus said. His heart was racing. If the goblins were going to make another attempt to cross the creek this afternoon, he and Abigail had to get there this morning.

"You're just going to have to talk your way out of camp," Iris said as Rufus pulled on clothes.

"*Talk* my way out?" Rufus said. "Believe me, if it were that easy, I'd have done it long ago."

"It *is* easy and you *should* have done it long ago," Iris said. "Then maybe you wouldn't have been so terrible at taking care of Feylawn."

Rufus sighed. "I'm putting myself in a lot of danger to help you," he pointed out. "So you might try being a little nicer."

"I *have* tried. I didn't like it." Iris ran her fingers through her hair, which was quickly returning to its familiar tangled state. "Listen carefully, and try not to repeat everything I say. When you get to camp, I'm going to give you a beguilum seed—I don't have many because they're hard to find, but I think one should do the trick. It'll make you *very* persuasive."

Just then, Abigail burst through the door. "I have something to tell you, but you have to promise to respond in a logical way."

"Not possible," Iris said. "Sorry."

"I didn't mean you," Abigail said. "I meant Rufus."

"Okay." Rufus was pretty sure he always responded to things in a logical way. Or mostly logical anyway. "Tell us."

"I figured out what Diggs meant when he said *ride the grass*." Abigail sat down on the bed. "It's in *The Sparkling Stories of Glistening Glen*. I was reading it last night and I realized—"

Suddenly Rufus remembered. "The Moving Meadow!" he exclaimed. "They go on it when they're hunting for the missing hairbrush!"

Abigail looked annoyed. "Yes," she said. "But that's not all—"

"It takes them somewhere," Rufus said. "Right? They travel around on it to different worlds!"

Iris had leaped to her feet and was doing a little victory dance on Rufus's pillow. "You two are really quite surprising," she exclaimed when she was done. "Almost everything you say is completely idiotic, and then every once in a while you blurt out something useful. It's like waiting for a janati goose to lay an egg—extreme irritation interrupted by a brief and glorious moment of exultation."

"Gee, thanks," Rufus said. "Let's just hope we can find this meadow before the goblins do."

"But that's what I'm trying to tell you!" Abigail was practically screaming. "If you two would stop *interrupting* me, I could explain—"

"BREAKFAST!" Rufus's dad yelled from downstairs.

Abigail unzipped her backpack and drew out her copy of *The Sparkling Stories of Glistening Glen*. "I'd better just show you. In the book, it says that it's really hard to know when the Moving Meadow's going to show up, or where it's going to be, but that Queen Lacy the Luminous had a chart. And I realized—I *found* a chart, in that file of Carson Collins's drawings." She extracted the chart from a manila envelope. "But I never asked myself: Why was it transparent?"

"If you're expecting me to answer a riddle, you really haven't learned anything at all about feylings," Iris said.

But Rufus saw what Abigail meant. "It's supposed to be placed on top of something else," he said. "It's only *half* a chart—the other half has to be a map."

"A map of Feylawn," Abigail said. She opened the book and placed the transparent chart over the map on its endpapers. As she did, the tiny drawings on the chart began to move, whirling around the map like spinning tops.

Rufus gasped. "What's it doing?"

"Just wait," Abigail said. The icons on the chart were already slowing and settling, like a compass needle landing on magnetic north. A tiny painted meadow, spangled with flowers, hovered on a point on the far side of the creek.

At the top of the chart, one of the twelve hand-lettered months seemed to rise from the page and hover, like a hologram. *July.* So did a number from the bottom of the chart: *23.* Finally a clock face joined them, with both hands clasped snugly together at twelve o' clock.

"July twenty-third is today," Rufus said. "So it's either coming at noon or midnight."

"Noon," Abigail said. "See that little sun beside the clock? I think that means it's during the day."

Iris flew to the book and landed beside it. "That's not Lacy's chart," she said. "But it's a pretty good copy of it." She bent low and traced one corner with her finger. "She must have given it to Carson as a gift."

"RUFUS! ABIGAIL! COME EAT!" Aunt Chrissy shouted from the bottom of the stairs. "WE'RE LEAVING FOR CAMP IN TEN MINUTES!"

"So that settles it," Rufus said. "We're going to Imura to capture Mr. Diggs. And we have to go today if we want to get there before Gneiss and Rapakivi."

"This is what I meant by being logical." Abigail's face was hidden as she replaced the book and chart in her backpack. "Just because we *can* go there doesn't mean we *should* go there. We should weigh the risks and the benefits."

"Absolutely," Rufus said. He tried to arrange his features into the expression of a person whose every decision was ruled by logic. "When we get to camp, we'll do it. We'll make a list. Two lists. Now let's go eat pancakes."

⚬⚬⚬

During Mark's morning speech, Abigail scribbled two lists in her notebook and slid it over to Rufus.

RISKS:
1. Moving Meadow (What is it? How do we get back?)
2. Imura (Dangerous?)
3. Mr. Diggs (injures or kills us)
4. Unknowns we haven't thought of

BENEFITS:
1. We stop Mr. Diggs from releasing the Calamand
2. Mr. Diggs agrees to release Queen Queen-Anne's-Lace

"You forgot the third benefit," Iris said from Rufus's shoulder. "Queen Queen-Anne's-Lace solves all our other problems and we live happily ever after, the end."

"Plus *Unknowns we haven't thought of*," Rufus said, adding the phrase to the Benefits column. "There could be unknown *benefits* as well as unknown risks. It's only logical. So that's four benefits and four risks."

Around them, campers were getting to their feet and gathering up their stuff. Today was the day they were supposed to make video commercials for their businesses and start practicing for the Piranha Pitch Session.

"Come on," Rufus said, elbowing Abigail. "We'll be okay. Let's go talk to Mark."

Abigail slid the notebook into her backpack and sighed. "Fine. But I still think this is a bad idea."

Iris pushed the pink, tongue-shaped beguilum seed between Rufus's lips. *With a smile, I beguile,* the seed sang.

Mark Trang was at his desk, looking over a spiral-bound business plan filled with glossy charts and illustrations.

"Hayley's pet-sitting plan is pretty impressive," he said when Rufus and Abigail approached. "Watch out for her at Thursday's pitch session—she's got that BizBuzz sting!" He made his hands into a point over his nose. "What's up with you two?"

"We've been working really hard on our businesses," Abigail said. "Plus all our other activities—sports, music, languages, volunteering,"

Rufus restrained himself from rolling his eyes. "Yeah," he said. "It's tough being overachievers."

"Not *over*achievers, just achievers!" Mark said. "Greatness isn't born, it's made!"

"So true," Rufus said. "Listen, we need to ask you . . ." He hesitated, searching for the right words. The beguilum didn't seem to be doing much to help. He tried again. "I mean, we wanted to know . . ."

"You good, Roofaloof?" Mark asked. "Your head hurting again? You look a little woozy."

"I'm *great*, Mark-in-the-park!" Rufus heard himself say. Something weird was happening to his face. It felt stretched, somehow. Widened. "I'm ready to conquer the world! Abigail and I are interested in making our pitches *next level*, if you know what I mean."

"I do know," Mark said. "Next level." He was smiling at Rufus in a way that Rufus had seen before—just not directed at him. It was the way adults usually smiled at Abigail.

"We don't just want to win in the piranha tank; we want to attract a solid round of financing," Rufus went on. The stretching sensation intensified. "And that's why we're going to have to miss the rest of camp today. We have a meeting planned with a venture capitalist who has previously expressed a high level of interest in monetizing our property."

Rufus wasn't even sure what he'd just said, but he knew it bore some relationship to the truth. They *were* planning to meet Mr. Diggs, who *had* wanted to make money on Feylawn.

"You have investor interest in literary T-shirts and expired canned goods?" Mark said. He gave Rufus a fist bump. "That's amazeballs."

"It is," Rufus said. "But *everything* depends on what happens at the meeting we have today."

"We have to go to the meeting now," Abigail said. "And we'll be gone all day."

Mark had been gazing at Rufus with a glassy smile. Now he turned to Abigail and gave a regretful shake of his head. "Sorry, Abby—you can't leave camp in the middle of the day. Liability—"

"It's not really leaving," Rufus interrupted. "We'll be *in* camp; we just won't be *at* camp. We're pursuing ventures related to our start-ups in a series of high-level meetings with hard-to-access decision-makers at an off-site location."

Mark turned back to Rufus. "That sounds awesome!" he said. "Great job pursuing your dreams! You two are such all-stars. I mean, canned goods and literary T-shirts! So brilliant! You're going to make *bank*!"

"We sure are," Rufus said. His teeth felt weirdly cold and dry. "We're the most incredible entrepreneurs you've ever seen. And we'll see you tomorrow—or whenever we feel like coming back to camp."

"No hurry!" Mark said as Rufus and Abigail sauntered toward the door. "You two could probably run this camp yourselves! You could teach *me* stuff."

"Well done!" Iris said when they were out on the street. "Such a lovely little seed—I wish it were easier to find."

Abigail shook her head. "I thought Rufus was going

to sprain his jaw with that smile," she said. "I didn't even know he *had* that many teeth."

"Is that what I was doing?" Rufus massaged his cheeks. The flush of power he'd felt from the beguilum was starting to fade. "I have no clue what I said in there."

"Me either," Abigail admitted. "But you were very persuasive."

"I was, wasn't I?" Rufus said. "It's because of how brilliant and good-looking I am."

"You *are* brilliant and good-looking," agreed Abigail.

"Probably the smartest, most accomplished, and best-looking person in the entire family," Rufus said.

Abigail nodded. Then she froze. "No way," she said. "It's not going to work on me."

"It *is* going to work on you," Rufus said. He tried to reproduce the wide smile he'd worn with Mark, but the muscles in his face weren't cooperating. "It's working now."

"Stop it," Abigail said. "And quit making that ridiculous face."

"Oh well," Rufus sighed. "It was fun while it lasted."

"I'm glad you enjoyed it," Iris said. "Now let's go capture a goblin and save my queen."

18

THE MOVING MEADOW

"Here's the first thing we should have planned," Abigail said. "How to cross the creek."

She, Rufus, and Shamok stood on the bank, watching the water rollick by. Iris rode on Shamok's back, perched between his shoulder blades. A pair of janati geese wandered the bank, plucking at tufts of grass.

"Do you think we can swim across?" Rufus could see the sandy bottom in places, but he knew from experience that the current was stronger than it looked. One wrong step and they'd be carried downstream like Grandpa Jack.

"The chart won't do us much good if it's wet," Abigail said. "And I have two of Carson's books in my backpack."

Iris climbed onto Shamok's head and surveyed the creek from there. "Have I mentioned how annoying it is that you can't fly?"

Abigail and Rufus both nodded.

"Luckily, I spent the whole night gathering seeds," Iris said. "Let me count how many jumpwort I have."

She dug through her pouch, coughing.

"You should have been sleeping," Rufus said. "You're not well enough to stay up all night." He had noticed a familiar gray tinge creeping into Iris's skin.

Iris ignored him. "I have six jumpwort seeds, but you only get one leap per seed, so don't waste it. You'll want to, trust me. Back when we were kids, we used to try to leap to the moon. Which isn't possible, it turns out, so don't bother trying. Jump *across*, not up."

She flew to Rufus and Abigail, holding a seed in each fist. Each was nut-brown with a feathery tip, like a dandelion seed.

"Back up a bit so you can get a running start," Iris said. "Hold the seed between your thumb and forefinger, and leap when I give you the word." She looked down at Shamok from her position between his ears. "Do you need one?"

"Don't be ridiculous," Shamok said. "I'm a leopard. I can leap just fine on my own." He turned and scampered up a nearby willow.

Iris waited for Rufus and Abigail to take a few steps back from the creek bank. "Good. Now *jump*."

Rufus didn't need to be told. The seed between his fingers was tugging skyward, babbling excitedly to itself. *Hop! Leap! Jump! Bound! Just one step, the whole world round!*

He bent his knees, certain that he could launch himself into the blue sky and—

"*Across*," Iris said in his ear.

He looked up in time to see Abigail leap like a ballet dancer, legs extended in an arabesque as she sailed across the creek.

He ran after her, pushed off with both feet, and felt the tiny seed tug him upward. For a moment he was in the air, the creek churning and chanting below him, and then his feet touched down on the gravel.

Above his head, tree limbs dipped and rustled as Shamok made his way across, leaping from branch to branch.

"Everyone accounted for?" Iris said. She settled on Shamok's back. "Now let's go find the Moving Meadow."

⚬⚬⚬

They wandered uphill for a while, through a boggy grassland that faded into sparse woods. Rufus scanned the edges of the trail nervously, certain that a goblin might leap out from behind a tree at any moment. But all he saw was a lone janati goose, pulling grass from the path ahead of them.

"This should be the spot," said Abigail, after consulting the chart.

Rufus glanced at his phone. "It's almost noon. Do you think that's when it arrives or when it departs?"

"Both, probably," Iris said. "I don't think it sticks around for very long."

And then the trees seemed to fade away, becoming less and less solid, until they were merely the suggestions of trees, a hurried sketch. Now the sun was beating down on them, and a carpet of purple flowers flowed under their feet. Bees mumbled around them, flitting from blossom to blossom.

"It's so pretty!" exclaimed Abigail. Shamok rolled onto his back and stretched his paws over his head. Abigail knelt beside him, stroking his chest with one hand and running the fingers of the other across the sun-warmed flowers.

Rufus looked across the meadow, trying to orient himself. Where were the trees? Where was the creek? Where was the ridgeline?

"Where *are* we right now?" he asked.

"Nowhere you've ever been," Iris said. "That's the point, isn't it?"

The ground under them trembled. Rufus could see the dark shapes of the forest trees shuddering into view, like stripes across his vision. The meadow was solid and the trees were transparent, or maybe it was the other way around. The carpet of flowers was sliding over—no, *through*—another landscape.

"Hang on," Iris said. "It'll toss you back into Feylawn if you let it."

"Hang on *how*?" Abigail asked. She dug her right hand deeper into the flowers and her left deeper into Shamok's fur.

A honk came from somewhere in the middle of the masses of flowers. "Brunette! Dishcloth! Fulminate!"

Iris groaned. "Shoo, goose! Stay at Feylawn! Go on!"

"Goose?" The leopard's ears cupped forward. In a single motion he rolled to his feet and crouched low.

"No!" Abigail shouted. "Do not hunt the geese! *Shamok!*"

But Shamok was already bounding through the flowers. Beyond him, Rufus could still see the landscape they had come from—the trees of Feylawn giving way to the paved streets of Galosh.

And then everything collapsed into itself. Rufus felt as if he were being snapped back and forth and then folded like a bedsheet.

Trees, no trees, streets, flowers, trees, nothing, flowers, no flowers, houses, clouds, sun, nothing, nothing . . .

He yelled through the blankness: "Iris? Abigail? Shamok?"

A sharp pinch on his left earlobe. He winced, and opened his eyes to find himself lying on his back in the meadow. Iris stood on his shoulder, twisting his earlobe. Abigail was still gripping the flowers with one hand. Shamok sprawled in the space between them, a goose between his paws.

"Monogram," the goose honked, rubbing her bill against the leopard's chin. "Squander. Atmosphere!"

Rufus brushed Iris from his shoulder and rubbed his smarting earlobe between his thumb and forefinger. "What just happened?"

"The meadow tried to toss you back," Iris said, landing

on Shamok's head. "Try not to look too hard at the landscapes beyond the meadow. If you look *at* them, you tend to end up *in* them."

She glanced down at the goose, who was staring up at the leopard with an expression of pure adoration. "Which is what would have happened to this goose if Shamok hadn't interfered."

Shamok licked the goose's head.

"If you eat her, I will push you off this meadow into the void," Iris told him. "Have I explained that she's valuable?"

"I *wasn't* eating her," Shamok said in a wounded tone. "I was cleaning her." He gave the goose another lick and buried his face in her feathers. "She smells amazing."

Iris rolled her eyes. "Well, you brought her, so you're responsible for her. We can't risk her getting left behind."

"Why not?" Rufus asked. "What's so important about these geese anyway?"

"*All* creatures are important," Abigail said. "This one has a name, which is Trinket, and she's important because she's a little bird who just wants to love and be loved."

Rufus looked at Iris. "No, really," he said. "What's the big deal about janati geese?"

"Let's just say their eggs have a lot of potential," Iris said. "I'd rather Mr. Diggs didn't know we have her."

Rufus didn't see why anyone would care about an egg's *potential*. Having been frequently told how much potential he himself possessed, he knew that it was one of those things that adults praised when they didn't have any other options. But he let it go. There were more important things to think about. The meadow was solid again, a humming expanse of bees and flowers. The sky was a strange sort of blue, almost lavender, and there was nothing in it—no clouds, no birds. It was like a cartoon sky, without any variation.

"This meadow," he said. "Where else does it go?"

Iris shrugged. "No idea. I've never stayed on it when it was in motion. Too dangerous. Especially after what happened to the Pampaspatches."

"Which Pampaspatches?"

"Nettle's sisters and parents. After Carson chopped down the Roving Tree, Queen Queen-Anne's-Lace sent scouts to look for another way home. First Nettle's parents and then his two sisters went off on the Moving Meadow. Unfortunately, they never came back."

"You might have told us this *before* we got on the meadow," Abigail said.

"But then you wouldn't have agreed to come." Iris stretched out her legs and pointed her toes. "I wouldn't worry too much about it. Haze makes ways, after all."

"That's not the expression," Abigail said. "The expression is *Haste makes waste*, which means that if you rush into things without preparing, you make mistakes."

"Not at all," Iris said. "It means that when you blunder

into something in a blind haze, you'll end up finding a way you didn't expect. Which is what we're doing now."

Abigail put her face in her hands. "That's the dumbest thing I've ever heard. What if we never get back?"

"I really have no idea why you're worrying about that now," Iris said. "We haven't even gotten where we're going yet."

19

THE ISLAND OF IMURA

It was hard to say how much time had gone by. Rufus and Abigail ate the lunches they had brought for camp. Iris went off to search the meadow for seeds. Shamok and Trinket slept. After a while, Abigail sprawled on her belly to read the Glistening Glen books. Rufus watched the shadows of the landscapes they traveled through: a rocky mountain pass, a frozen field, a highway of some sort, a cluster of small windswept cottages.

Sometimes a place they passed through seemed to merge momentarily with the one they were in. A mail carrier walked from a suburban neighborhood into the meadow, turned around slowly with her mail satchel pressed against her hip and her mouth opened in a small oval of surprise, and then vanished. A squirrel leaped right from a distant pine tree into the meadow, scampered through the grass, and was caught mid-stride by Shamok, who had somehow wakened from his doze in time to catch it and eat it. A dog wagged its tail, sniffed the air, barked, and faded. And then the meadow began to move over the sea, and all Rufus could see were waves, and, every once in a while, a solitary ship.

And still there was no sign of an island of any kind. If they lost their grip on the sunny meadow, this was where they would land: in a dark, restless, endless ocean, somewhere in another world.

"When do you think we'll get there?" he asked Abigail. She had put the books and chart back in her pack and was sitting with her arms wrapped around her knees, her brow knitted.

"I don't know. It's late. Really late."

She was right. It seemed to always be noon on the meadow, but the sea in the other landscape was silvered with moonlight. Rufus pulled out his phone, but of course it wasn't working.

"What time do you think it is back home?"

Rufus shook his head. "I don't know. Maybe it's still noon."

"I hope so," Abigail said. "Otherwise our parents are going to be really worried."

It was Shamok who saw it first. A silhouette of tall lines somewhere on the wavering horizon of that other place. He sat up and sniffed the air.

"We're here," he said. "Those are the bars of the gates."

Abigail and Rufus got to their feet, craning for a better look.

"Careful," Rufus said. "If we focus on the sea, we'll end up swimming."

"We're going to end up swimming anyway," Abigail said. "Look at the path we're taking—we're passing next to it, not over it." She shook her head and put on her backpack.

The gates were just ahead of them now, the bars striping the sky. But Abigail was right. The path of the meadow was taking them alongside the island, not across it. In a moment they'd be past it.

Iris landed on Rufus's shoulder, wings quivering with excitement. "Tell me you can swim," she said. "I know your cousin can."

Rufus tried to nod, but his head seemed frozen on his neck. He hated the idea of landing in that otherworldly ocean. He was an okay swimmer, but he'd never had to swim in the dark before. Who even knew what was *in* that water?

"*I* can swim," Shamok said. He crouched in the grass, his tail extended, the blank patch on his haunches tawny in the meadow sunshine.

"Elvin rattlesnake," Trinket honked. "Behemoth."

Abigail scooped up the goose. "You'll be all right," she murmured. "You can fly."

Rufus's body felt like it was inhabited by mice. He put his hand on Shamok's back, trying to draw strength from the warmth of his fur. The water looked cold. Dark. The island grew closer. He could hear the slur of waves mixing the stones on the pebbly shore.

"Now!" growled Shamok.

Rufus wasn't sure, afterward, exactly what they did—how it was that they leaped from the sunny meadow to the moonlit sea. All he knew was that there was a weightless moment of being suspended between the two, like when you're swinging on the monkey bars. Then the meadow was gone and the icy black water closed over his head.

⚬⚬⚬

He gasped. Where was the surface? In the dark it felt like it could be anywhere: up, down, sideways. His lungs burned. Cold water poked into his ears and sucked at his fingers, tugging at his clothes. Did he still have hands and feet? He kicked them to make sure and felt himself rise to the surface. There it was, air, blowing in his face. He gulped it as the waves jostled him, spinning and tugging him like an angry crowd. He swam toward the froth of the waves breaking on the shore and thought, *I'm not going anywhere; the sea is pulling me away; I'll get tired and I'll drown.* But Abigail and Shamok were swimming beside him, and there was Trinket, bobbing on the waves, and so he kept pulling, kept kicking.

The shore was an impossible distance, and an impossible distance, and an impossible distance, and then, all at once, he was close enough to put his feet down. He stood, feeling the waves shifting the stones beneath his feet, staggered forward, and landed on his hands and knees on a rocky beach. Abigail was beside him with Trinket at her feet. Iris darted in anxious zigzags through the air while Shamok shook the water from his fur and then licked his coat smooth.

"Everyone okay?" Rufus asked. A breeze blew across his dripping clothes. His teeth chattered.

"Fine," Abigail said, rubbing her own arms. She still wore her backpack, which drizzled streams of water. She didn't sound fine.

"Here." Iris dropped a seed in each of their palms. "Ragweed. Dry yourselves off."

Rufus inspected the seed, which had five prongs at the top like a crown. *Wipe tears. Don't cry*, it sang. *You drip. I dry!* He felt a tickle on the inside of his nose, and a sneeze nearly doubled him over. When he went to wipe his nose, he found he was holding a thick olive-green towel.

"Here," he said, handing it to Abigail. "Give me your seed."

One sneeze later, he had a towel wrapped around his shoulders. He dried himself off as best he could and then huddled inside the towel for warmth. A thin band of light was creeping over the edge of the horizon. Whatever time it was back home, it was almost dawn here. That would make it easier to see, but also easier to be seen.

"Cupcake. Inveigle. Hyena," Trinket honked. She plucked

pieces of seaweed from between the stones with her beak. "Estuary toothbrush, ambassador."

"Shh!" hissed Iris. "You'll give us away."

"Cursory," honked Trinket. "Nameplate."

Abigail scooped her up and stroked her white feathers, murmuring nonsense words in a tone that mimicked the bird's own goosey honks.

"Let's get off the beach," Rufus said. "Take cover in the trees until it gets lighter."

They crept up the shore until they were under the spreading branches of a stand of scrubby pines. Iris couldn't keep still, darting from shoulder to shoulder, zooming up into the trees and down again.

"Where's Shamok?" she said at last.

Rufus whirled around. The leopard had been with them a moment ago, crouched low among the pine needles. But now he was gone.

Dawn broke a moment later, and with it came an outpouring of song. Birds whistled and chirped, flocking from tree to tree. Rufus turned to Abigail, who sat on the ground with a drenched copy of *The Luminous Legends of Glistening Glen*.

"Everything okay?" Rufus asked again.

"Just wet," she said. "The books, the chart, everything." She spread out the chart and weighed down its corners with rocks. "I was hoping the chart would tell us when the meadow was going to come back. But now . . ." She let the sentence hang.

Rufus squatted down beside her. "The meadow will come back with or without the chart. We'll just have to watch for it."

Abigail shook her head as she laid out the books and her backpack to dry. "What if it doesn't come for days and days? What if we can't swim to it fast enough? What if we miss it?"

A twig snapped. They turned toward the noise in time to see Shamok pounce on a goblin in a tattered brown suit.

"Get off me!" Mr. Diggs shouted. His bird legs thrashed, but Shamok had him pinned. Rufus had almost forgotten how frightening Shamok had been the first time they met. He remembered now. The leopard's nose was wrinkled into a snarl, his jaw open to expose his long ivory teeth.

"Shall I eat you, half bird?" he growled. His hook-shaped claws dug into the goblin's chest. "Shall I chew up your lock-picking, spot-thieving fingers?"

Diggs didn't speak. Rufus felt a thrill of bright, giddy joy. Mr. Diggs was captured. Mr. Diggs, who had bullied and threatened him. Mr. Diggs, who was behind everything terrible that had happened. He looked over at Abigail to say, *See, it's all going to work out*, but she was still frowning, her face pale.

"Don't move!" Iris shrieked at the goblin. Not that Mr. Diggs had much choice. Three bindweed seeds from her pouch had sprouted thin green cords that bound him as tightly as a fly in a web.

"First you banish me; then you rescue me," Mr. Diggs croaked when he was trussed neck to toe. "You must have missed me, greenling, to go to all this trouble." He leered at Iris. "You look a bit healthier than you did when I saw you last. Would you like to be my second wife? My little lozenge won't last much longer, slender and weak as she is. I'll be looking for a strong new wife to take her place. Would you like that, Iris Birchbattle?"

"I'd *like* to make you drink snakeweed and hemlock," Iris said, her voice shrill with fury. "I'd *like* to feed you to the seagulls. But I have plans for you, Rance Diggs!"

"A feyling plan. What an amusing thought." Mr. Diggs opened his mouth and snapped his jaws at Iris, who was hovering just above his face. He chuckled when he saw her flinch.

A low rumble escaped from Shamok's throat.

"Careful now, pussycat," Mr. Diggs rasped. "The greenling says she has plans for me. I have plans for myself, actually. Plans for all of us." He smiled. "Aren't you curious to know what they are?"

Trinket extended her long neck toward the goblin. "So-so snicker wrist," she hissed. "Sassafras."

Mr. Diggs's eyes darted to the goose, and a small smile appeared at the corners of his mouth. "Friend of yours?" he asked.

Shamok placed a velvet paw on Mr. Diggs's lips and slowly extended his claws. "Quiet, half bird. Do you think you can be quiet?"

He waited, the sharp point of each claw making a small indentation on the goblin's skin, until Diggs nodded. Then he paced to the edge of the clearing. "I'll be back," he said. "I'm going to check on the prisoner."

"I'll come with you," Rufus said. "Maybe I can relock the locks and get you your spots back."

"Six locks are gone and my spots with them," Shamok said. "Only the Locksmith can replace them. But if you could replace the seventh—the lock in your pocket?" He turned his amber eyes on Rufus. "That spot belongs at the top of my head."

"You'll need latchthorn," Iris said, fishing around in her pouch. "You can't talk to locks without it. Just listen—it's not as hard as it seems."

The seed she handed him had an unusual way of speaking, with heavy consonants and throaty vowels.

Taste me once and forever talk
To latch and tumbler and lock.

Rufus hesitated. Forever was a long time, as Iris had told him once. It was weird enough to have seeds talking to him. Did he want to have locks whispering at him now, too?

"It's all right," Shamok said gruffly. "You don't have to. There's no one here to see the spotless patch anyway."

"No, I want to," Rufus said. He took the seed between his lips and swallowed. "I'll be back as soon as I can," he told Abigail.

She nodded. "I'll be watching for the return of the meadow." She held up a stainless-steel lifeguard's whistle that had been tucked underneath her shirt. "If you hear me blow on this, come back quick. We'll have to swim out to it, and we won't have much time."

"I'll make sure the goblin doesn't give us any trouble," Iris said. She landed on Diggs's forehead and shut her eyes for a moment, steeling herself. Then she grabbed hold of his nose and pinched the nostrils shut. When he gasped for breath she tossed a handful of seeds into his mouth and flew to Abigail's shoulder.

"That should do the trick," she said as Diggs coughed and sputtered, trying to spit out the seeds.

"What did you just do to him?" Abigail asked.

"That depends on which ones went down his gullet," Iris said. "But hopefully, I've made him buoyant. When the meadow comes, we ought to be able to float him out to it. Otherwise he'll sink like a stone."

Mr. Diggs's eyes widened. Then his tongue made a circuit around his lips, licking up the seeds he'd spat out. "I'm more valuable to you alive than dead," he croaked.

"We know," Iris said. "That's why we're here."

AN UNEXPECTED GUEST

Rufus and Shamok had only gotten as far as the edge of a bramble thicket when they heard the shrill of Abigail's whistle.

"We have to go back," Rufus said. "I'm sorry. Once we free Queen Queen-Anne's-Lace, she'll make sure you get your spots back."

Shamok's ears twitched. "When I'm sitting here in the grass, you can hardly see the bare patch, right?"

"You're still *very* spotted," Rufus assured him. "Come on, we don't want to miss the meadow."

Shamok didn't move. "I belong here," he said. "Guarding the locks."

A feeling like a wet sock lumped in Rufus's stomach. He hadn't considered the possibility that Shamok wouldn't return with them, but of course it made sense. He was the leopard of the locks. Sitting in the grass with his tail wrapped around him, he seemed both wilder and more distant than he had at Feylawn—like something that could be observed from afar but not approached. Rufus reached out to stroke his fur, but Shamok's ears flattened and his nose wrinkled with the beginning of a snarl.

"Go," he growled, and then he was gone, scampering up into the boughs of one of the scrubby wind-blown trees and disappearing into the foliage.

⚬⚭⚬

Rufus went. The beach wasn't far, and he was already preparing himself for the icy plunge and the swim when he saw that Abigail and Iris weren't waiting for him on the stony shore.

"Abigail?" he shouted. "Iris?"

"Hush!" Abigail motioned to him from behind a large driftwood stump. She was clutching Trinket, who had tucked her head under her wing. Beside her lay Mr. Diggs, still cocooned in bindweed. A long trail of dislodged stones showed the path she'd taken when dragging him down the beach.

"What are you doing?" Rufus asked. "Shouldn't we be swimming—?"

"Shh!" Abigail hissed. "Come here! Hide!"

Trinket pulled her head from under her wing and looked out at the horizon. "Pretzel!" she barked in alarm. "Corn! Effigy!"

"What are we hiding *from*?" Rufus whispered, darting

over to join them. But then he heard it: the whine of an engine. He peeked over the driftwood log. Out on the water, in the exact place where they hoped the Moving Meadow would appear, a gunmetal-gray speedboat sliced through the waves.

"What *is* that?" Rufus said.

Abigail stared at him, furious. "What *is* that?" she repeated. "What IS that? It's why we needed a better plan. It's why I shouldn't have let you and Iris talk me into this cockamamie scheme. It's the *goblins*, obviously, and since we have no way to overpower them, we'd better hide and hope they don't come looking for us." She glanced over his shoulder. "Where's Shamok?"

"We thought the meadow was here and he said he's staying."

"Pottery," clucked the goose. She looked up at Abigail beseechingly. "Emu."

"Stop fussing," Iris said, landing on Rufus's shoulder. "I brought plenty of seeds with me. They won't be able to land."

"Great," Abigail said in a tone that made it clear she did not, in fact, think that was great. "What happens if the meadow comes back while they're out there? How do we get past them?" She squeezed the goose against her chest. "We can't stay here forever."

Rufus looked down at Mr. Diggs, whose eyes were wide and staring. "What's up with him?"

"He's in a dream I made for him," Iris said. "He thinks it's the twenty-ninth feast day and he's watching the badger wrestling. It's a happy occasion for goblins, if not for badgers. He won't give us any trouble."

"Zither," wheezed the goose. She rubbed her beak against Abigail's chin, sounding doubtful. "Policy."

The speedboat slowed. It was only a hundred yards or so from shore, but it suddenly turned away from the island and motored alongside the cliffs.

"What's it doing?"

"Turntwist," Iris said. "Disorientallis. Scrimscram. I told you I had seeds."

"But how did those goblins *get* here?" Rufus asked. "I thought the Moving Meadow was the only passage from our world to here."

"Apparently not," Abigail said. "Apparently there were *unknown risks*."

"Not *unknown*. Just unlikely." Iris looked out at the speedboat. "From the look of it, that boat came from the Phantom Harbor. Not a place rock goblins usually frequent. They're not a nautical group, overall."

The boat had turned out to sea again. About two hundred yards from shore it cut the engine. Two goblins on the deck lowered an anchor.

"They're going to wait us out," Abigail said. "We're trapped."

Nobody spoke. The speedboat bobbed on the waves, its

bow drifting from side to side like a compass needle. Rufus felt suddenly aware of how sunburned he was, how hungry, thirsty, and tired. Abigail was right. This had been an extremely stupid plan.

Something was flying toward them: a small bird or large insect, its flight erratic as if it were being repeatedly blown off course by the breeze, which it probably was. As it came across the stony beach, Rufus saw that it was a feyling, and he felt his temper rising. Nettle, naturally. Come to gloat.

Except that it wasn't Nettle.

It was a feyling he'd never seen before. She wore a shimmering gold dress and her ruffled wings were green and white. A corona of moon-white curls haloed her head.

Iris gasped. "It's her! It's Queen Queen-Anne's-Lace!" She took wing, fluttering toward the windblown feyling.

"My queen!" she called. "My queen!"

Queen Queen-Anne's-Lace paused mid-flight. "Iris? What are you doing here?"

Iris bowed so low that she spun head over heels in midair. "I've captured Mr. Diggs," she said when she was upright again. "I have a plan! I'm going to trade him for your freedom. I'm here to save you, my queen. I'm here to fix things." She began to cry. "I'm so sorry for everything. But I'm going to make it right!"

The queen gave a short, bitter laugh. "You are going to make things complicated," she said. "You always did have a knack for it." She landed beside Mr. Diggs, breathing heavily. "He's alive?"

Now that she was closer, Rufus could see the telltale withering at the tips of her wings, the blotches of gray mixed into the brown of her skin.

Iris nodded. "Just dreaming. I gave him reverie and dancer's drop, plus some bladder wrack for buoyancy." She wiped her eyes. "What about you? Are you sick? You don't look as bad as I feared. The train will be back in a few days; we'll take you home and you'll get well. And then you can help us fix things, because we really—"

"I'm sorry, Iris," Queen Queen-Anne's-Lace said. Her breath came in little gasps. "There's no time to explain. No time for anything." She bent low, looking deep into Mr. Diggs's staring eyes. "I made my bargain. He's my husband. Nothing you can do will change that."

Then she flew over Iris's head, making straight for the gate of a thousand locks.

"Wait!" Iris called, flying after her. "Your Majesty! Queen Queen-Anne's-Lace! Laceeeeeeeey!"

Rufus and Abigail exchanged glances.

"Hacksaw," Trinket said. "Gravity!"

Abigail stroked Trinket's head. "She's right," she said. "We have to follow."

She set the goose down in the stones, beside Mr. Diggs.

"Guard him," she instructed. "And don't let anyone see you."

21

THE CALAMAND

Rufus and Abigail ran in the direction the two feylings had flown, until the bramble thicket blocked their path.

"Now what?" Abigail exclaimed as Iris and the queen disappeared from view.

"Hold on." Rufus had heard a familiar murmur. *Prickles have I, for those who pry.* It was the first seed he'd ever heard speak, back in his own bedroom, when they were protecting his house from Mr. Diggs. Wall of Thorns, Quercus had called it. Only then it had just been a seed, not a thorn-spiked thicket interwoven with stinging weeds. Still, these bloodred brambles must have started as seeds, so perhaps he could still speak to them.

He let himself slip into the place between sleep and waking. At first there was only silence. And then he heard it: the seed at the heart of the thicket. It breathed and sang, and its thorns flashed in the sun and its branches knit together, forming a trellis for stinging weeds.

Let us pass, Rufus begged it.

The thicket seemed to sigh, a wind rustling its crimson leaves. *Who are you to me?* it asked. *Let me taste the tang of your blood.* A barbed strand swung out and scraped across Rufus's cheek. He heard Abigail give a sharp cry of alarm.

"Are you okay?"

He met Abigail's eyes. She was frowning fiercely, holding her braids in each of her fists. Blood trickled down his face, hot and stinging.

The thicket shuddered. *You taste of the place where I was born*, it murmured. *Come, I will make you a path.* With creaks and rustles, the bramble strands leaned away from each other, opening a narrow corridor. Abigail stepped into it, her jaw set.

"We've come this far," she murmured. "Might as well see it through."

Creatures scurried in the pockets and shadows of the thicket.

"They're just watching us," Abigail said. "They won't hurt us as long as the brambles let us through."

She couldn't possibly have known the creatures' intentions, but Rufus was glad for the reassurance anyway. He could feel the animals' eyes on them, hear their squeaks and hisses. The path was so narrow that he had to keep his arms pressed tightly to his sides so they wouldn't scrape against the thorns.

At last they emerged at the base of the gates. The

brambles thronged so closely around the prison fence that he couldn't see how large it was, or even what lay on the other side. He could only see the gates themselves, bound tight with hundreds and hundreds of massive chains, each fastened with a round black padlock. At the foot of the gates were seven unlocked chains—the ones whose locks had been erased from Shamok's fur. Standing amid the chains with her head bowed was Queen Queen-Anne's-Lace. Iris lay on the ground beside her, unconscious.

Rufus ran to Iris and lifted her into his hands. She was breathing, but she didn't stir. "What have you done to her?" he shouted. "She came here to rescue *you*!"

The feyling ruler didn't answer. She took to the air and flew in a slow circle over their heads.

"Leopard," she called. "Come to me."

"Don't do it!" Abigail yelled. She looked around frantically for the leopard. "Shamok, stay where you are!"

There was a low growl and then Shamok shimmied out from the thicket. Crouching low, he crept to the base of the gates and lay down in the grass. Queen Queen-Anne's-Lace landed between his paws.

"You came at last," Shamok said, bowing his head. "I am your leopard."

Queen Queen-Anne's-Lace reached up and placed her hands on either side of the leopard's face.

"You have served nobly and well," she said. "And now it's over. Forgive me, but it must be done."

"No!" Abigail ran to Shamok and wrapped her arms around his neck. "Don't hurt him!" she commanded. She glared down at the feyling queen, her expression fierce.

"If I could find another path, I would," said Queen Queen-Anne's-Lace. "But the hard way is the only way."

Rufus could feel something building around them. A drone, like the buzzing of a hive. It came from the keyhole mouths of the nine hundred and ninety-three locks. They were talking, and thanks to the latchthorn he had swallowed, he could hear them.

Shut. Keep in. Closed. Keep out.

They were speaking to her, the Locksmith. Telling her they were doing what they were made to do. They were watchdogs wagging their tails. Soldiers marching in formation. *Shut. Keep in. Closed. Keep out.*

And then the locks went silent.

"Don't!" Rufus yelled, understanding what was about to happen. "Don't do it!"

But that wasn't the way to talk to them. He knew it as soon as the words left his lips.

The click, when it came, rang out like a gunshot. Together, nine hundred and ninety-three locks fell open, their chains slithering to the ground in a metallic clatter.

Shamok sank into the dirt, his amber eyes fixed on Queen Queen-Anne's-Lace. His fur was pale gold. Spotless. Open padlocks lay strewn around him, their shackles curved like question marks.

"Shamok!" Abigail shouted as the leopard fell onto his side. "Shamok!"

But the leopard's eyes had already closed.

⁂

With a squeal of metal hinges, the giant gates swung open. Queen Queen-Anne's-Lace took to the air, making graceful swoops and circles. She reminded Rufus of a courting hummingbird the way she darted high and low, showing off her aeronautic abilities.

Rufus couldn't believe they'd come all this way to rescue her.

"Come on!" he hissed at Abigail. "Let's get out of here!"

Whatever was behind those gates, he did not want to meet it here, alone, without Iris or Shamok to help defend them.

But Abigail didn't move. Tears streamed down her face as she bent over the leopard's motionless body. "You're still here," she murmured. "You're not dead. You're not."

Rufus tucked Iris into the side pocket of his shorts and tugged on Abigail's arm. "We have to go," he whispered. "Before the Calamand gets out."

Abigail got to her feet, wiping her face with the back of her hand.

"Where's the path?" she asked.

Rufus looked at the place where they had emerged from

the brambles. The path they'd followed had closed. They were surrounded in all directions by a dense wall of thorns.

"I'll open it," he said. But even as he spoke, the Calamand walked through the gates.

She was a tall figure with flaming red hair dressed in billowing maroon trousers and a long maroon jacket popping with gold buttons. Her feet were bare. She wore a white scarf wrapped around her head and knotted under her chin, and she carried a blanket tied up in a bundle, like a cartoon burglar.

"Oh dear," she said when she saw Shamok's body. "Poor leopard. How niketty-naked you look without your spots." She giggled.

"It's not funny!" Abigail yelled, leaping to her feet. She swung her leg back, and Rufus thought she was going to kick the prisoner.

He gripped her arm. "Don't." Assaulting the world's most notorious criminal while armed only with a scuffed tennis shoe, a dead leopard, and an unconscious feyling didn't seem like the smartest move.

The Calamand stared at them, blinking rapidly against the sunlight. "Well, hello!" she said wonderingly. "This island is more populated than I'd imagined. I'd thought I was all alone, but apparently it's poppled and pimpled with peepers and people."

"They just got here." Queen Queen-Anne's-Lace

plummeted down to hover before the prisoner like a spider lowering itself on a thread.

"I remember you," the prisoner said, watching the feyling the way a cat watches a bird. "I stole something from you once, and then you stole something from me—my freedom, which is quite a cruel thing to steal. Are *you* the goblin's wife? The Missus with No Kisses? We've had some time to talk, Mr. Diggs and I. He tells me you don't love him. Not that I blame you, lovely and lacy as you are. You could do better and probably have. Still, you honor a bargain, and that's the goblin way, and by *way*, I mean way, way underground."

Queen Queen-Anne's-Lace smiled. "We'll talk as we go. My husband's waiting for us, and he's never patient, particularly not when he's tied up."

"Hold on there, teeny-tiny!" The prisoner dropped her bundle and spread her arms wide. "Let's take our time, shall we?" She laughed. "Oh, I *like* the sound of that. When you're *doing* time, your time isn't your own, do you follow me, itsy-bitsy? You can forget yourself. Yet here I am!"

She undid her scarf with a flourish and draped it around her neck. As she did, her head swiveled 180 degrees, revealing a second face on the other side. This one was younger and rounder, and her bottom lip protruded peevishly.

"And here *I* am," the new face said. "Where she goes, I go, not that I have any choice in the matter. I'm Mandolyn, the tagalong younger sister, slap-dashed on the back of her head because that's how *Calamandra* likes it, and that means *I've* done the time for *her* crimes, even though *I'm* the injured party. But I guess you know all that since you helped slap the cuffs on us in the first place. Who'd have guessed you'd be the one to take them off?"

"Things change," Queen Queen-Anne's-Lace said. Her tone was light. "I had no use for you then. I do now. And you for me, I think."

Rufus stared, still unable to move. He knew he needed to open a passage through the thicket and get away, but he couldn't get his mind to settle into the place where seed speech happened. He pushed against the brambles, hoping they might open on their own, and was rewarded by an immediate outbreak of itching welts on his left calf.

Calamandra's face spun to the front and winked at him. "Did you lose your way?" she said. "Or did I take it? What else do you have that I might like?"

Rufus felt the grip of her interest as she scanned him, first with her own face and then with Mandolyn's. He tried to focus on the brambles, but the Calamand was talking again.

"You wouldn't be the first boy unable to concentrate when I'm around," she said laughing. "We'll keep you daz-zled and dizzy, Mandolyn and me. I wouldn't trust a word that comes out of our mouths."

Mandolyn rolled her eyes at Rufus as she circled past. "Don't listen to her—all she does is lie," she whispered.

The neck spun again and Calamandra crossed her eyes. "Sisters," she sighed. "Can't live with them, can't live without them. But that one always has my back, so to speak, even if she is a bit light-fingered. Steals anything that isn't nailed down. You didn't need this, did you?" she added, blowing a blast through a stainless-steel whistle. "It makes me feel so important, like a lifeguard at a pool. She who wears the whistle makes the rules!"

"Hey!" Abigail said. "That's mine! My coach gave that to me . . ."

"So I see," said the Calamand. She squinted to read the writing engraved on the side of the whistle. "'For Abigail Vasquez, who scored the highest on the 2019 Lifeguarding' yadda yadda yadda . . ."

The head spun in circles, issuing whistling snores as it did. "Talk of scores makes us snore, Abigail," Mandolyn said. "Unless you count the ones we plan to settle."

"I like her name, though," said the Calamand. "Shall I take it?"

She took a step toward Abigail, who flinched and crossed her arms over her chest. "I like my name," she said, her voice unsteady. A look of horror crossed her face. "I just can't remember what it is. I know *your* name," she said, looking at the Calamand. "It's Abigail. But who am I?" She turned to Rufus. "What do *you* call me?"

Rufus opened his mouth to answer, but the name he

was about to use didn't seem to fit. "I guess I just call you Cousin," he said.

"Come along," Queen Queen-Anne's-Lace said to the Calamand. "Give the child back her name. You'll have plenty of time to pick pockets when we get to the Blue World."

The Calamand laughed with both her faces. "Time to pocket pocket watches and watch where the time goes!" she chortled. "You're right, Mini-Miney-Mo. Plus, we need a name with a bit more sizzle. Here you go, *Abigail*—here's a lesson, given free. Never let a stranger have your name!"

Abigail scowled at her. "I didn't let you have it—you took it!" she said. "You can't just take everything you want. That's why the feylings locked you up in the first place."

"Oh, but I can, and I do!" said the Calamand. "And that's why they've *un*locked me in the second place." She shouldered her blanket bundle again. "I've cleared out the prison, for example. I've always loved the Horn of Plenty. People complain about prison food, but this little gadget put the refinement in our confinement." The head spun, laughing from both of its mouths.

"We're quit of this place at last!" Mandolyn exclaimed. "Soon I'll have new toys to play with!"

"Time to grab our future with both hands!" agreed the Calamand.

"All four hands, even!" Mandolyn added, extending a second pair of arms and waggling them in the air.

"Follow me, then," said Queen Queen-Anne's-Lace, fluttering over to the bramble thicket. A path opened beneath her.

The Calamand sashayed into the gap, grinning from ear to ear and ear to ear. "Time to fetch my gobbling goblin," she sang. "Time to take the world by storm—or else to simply take the storm!"

The bramble thicket closed up behind them, leaving Rufus and Abigail alone with Shamok's motionless body.

22

LONG JUMP

Rufus tried again and again to open a passage through the Wall of Thorns, but it refused to speak to him.

"It's ignoring me on purpose," he fumed. In frustration he lowered his shoulder and tried to shove his way through, but the brambles thrashed back at him, ripping a hole in his T-shirt and raising welts on his arm and forehead. A chorus of shrieks came from inside the thicket.

"They'll attack if you try that again," Abigail said. She squatted at the base of the thicket and peered into the shadows. "There are snakes in there. And rats. And some kind of bird with a very pointy beak."

"We have to get out of here somehow," Rufus said. He lifted Iris from the side pocket of his shorts, hoping she might be able to help, but she was still unconscious. "Let's walk around the back of the prison. Maybe there's another path."

"We can't leave Shamok!" Abigail stroked the leopard's limp spotless body.

"We have to," Rufus said, tucking Iris back into his pocket. "I'm sorry. But we can't help him now. He's dead."

"He isn't!" Abigail protested. "He's just—"

"Depressed," Shamok said, lifting his head. "What's a leopard without spots? I'm like a bird without wings or a fish without fins."

Rufus stared. "But the locks—I thought opening them would kill you!"

"So did I," Shamok said. He looked over his shoulder at his tawny body. "Maybe it should have. Look at me. I'm hideous."

"You're beautiful," Abigail said fiercely. "You're pure gold."

"Can we discuss this later?" Rufus asked.

"I'll make a path for us," Shamok said. He crawled on his belly into the thicket, giving one of his sawing roars as he did. "I AM—THE LEOPARD! AND THESE ARE—MY GUESTS!"

A low passage opened in the brambles. As Rufus and Abigail crawled behind Shamok, the thicket rustled with small beasts. Black vipers flicked their tongues at them. Crabs and scorpions scuttled sideways, clicking their claws.

Their eyes followed them all the way to the end of the thicket.

Trinket waddled across the beach to greet them, dragging Abigail's backpack by one strap. "Rotund!" she cackled joyously, dropping the backpack at Abigail's feet and raising her bill to the sky. "Armory!"

"Hello, you!" Abigail said. She picked up the goose and nuzzled her face into her feathers. "I'm glad you're safe!"

"Not safe yet," Rufus said. On the horizon, a purple glint wavered into view. It could have been a streak of sunset, or a trick of the light, but Rufus knew it wasn't. It was their only way home, and it was moving swiftly. So was the goblin speedboat, which had pulled up anchor and was headed straight for the island.

"I can't swim fast enough to get to the meadow before it leaves," he said. He lifted Iris from his pocket and removed the tiny pouch from her waist before tucking her back in. His fingers were too big to reach inside, so he had to dump the contents into his palm, shielding them from the wind. When he'd located what he was looking for, he brushed the remaining seeds into the plastic baggie he kept in his pocket to hold the seeds he gathered at Feylawn. He and Iris could sort them out later. Assuming she ever woke up.

He handed Abigail a feathery jumpwort seed. "We'll have to jump to the meadow. Quickly, before it's gone and the goblins get here."

Shamok growled. "Even if I were a *proper* leopard,

I couldn't leap that far." He lay down among the stones. "Doesn't matter. I have no purpose anyway."

"Stop it," Abigail said, tucking Trinket under one arm. "Give him one of the jumpwort seeds, Rufus. He *has* to come with us."

Rufus sighed and dangled the feathery seed in front of the leopard's nose. Shamok snatched it in his teeth. With his eyes half closed, Rufus silently spoke to the seeds, telling them what to do.

"Jump *across*, not up," he reminded Abigail and Shamok. Then he ran down the beach. Just as the waves lapped the toe of his sneaker, he jumped.

Up.

❧❦❧

Too up, he thought as the waves shrank to distant wrinkles below him. *Whoops*. He was in the bright blue, a wingless boy flying too close to the sun. There was Abigail, legs outstretched, braids streaming behind her. There was Trinket, flapping and honking. And there was Shamok, paws wide, tail arrowing out. A gull screeched indignantly at them, demanding to know what kind of motley flock was wandering through her airspace. Below them was the purple of the Moving Meadow.

Rufus tucked his legs into a cannonball, willing gravity to do its work. He plummeted past Abigail and Shamok, the ground coming at him a whole lot faster than he'd hoped. He stretched his legs out again, clinging tight to the feathery seed between his fingers, pressing his other hand against the warm lump that was Iris in his pocket. The meadow was below him, but so were the waves, both at once, occupying the same space. He didn't know which one he would land in.

"Keep looking at the meadow!" he yelled to Abigail, because what if *he* landed in the meadow but she went straight through the grass and into the waves?

"What?" Abigail yelled, cupping her hands to her ears.

"The meadow!" Rufus shouted. "The meadow!" And then he was tumbling, head over heels, into the grass.

When he finally came to a rest, he was only wearing one sneaker and Abigail was standing over him, her expression all too familiar. "Remind me to teach you how to land properly," she said. "Assuming I ever speak to you again."

Rufus sat up and looked around for his missing sneaker. "What did I do now?"

"You didn't *listen* to me," Abigail said. She tossed her backpack onto the grass and sat down. Shamok and Trinket settled down beside her, the goose resting her bill on Shamok's shoulder. Abigail stroked them in turns, her mouth tugging at the corners. "I *knew* something bad was going to happen on this trip. I *felt* it in the pit of my stomach. But somehow we always do what *you* want to do, because *you* have magic powers and can talk to seeds." She opened her backpack, blinking back tears. "And I know you and that two-faced monster think prizes are stupid, but I worked hard for that whistle and it meant something to me and now it's gone, and I know it's not the worst thing that happened today, but it's not *nothing*, either."

"It's definitely *not* the worst thing," Rufus retorted, feeling around in the grass for his missing shoe. "The worst thing is a four-way tie between the Calamand getting released, Mr. Diggs getting away, Queen Queen-Anne's-Lace not being on our side, and whatever Queen Queen-Anne's-Lace did to Iris."

He lifted the unconscious feyling from his pocket and laid her in the purple flowers, yanking up handfuls of grass and showering them over her head. In the past, when Iris would pass out, covering her with a leaf was usually enough to rouse her. But now she didn't stir.

Abigail scooted over to look at Iris. "You're right," she said. "I'm sorry. I just *hate* it when I don't know what to do."

Rufus located his missing sneaker in the tall grass and crawled over to get it. "I'm sorry too," he said. "About your whistle. And about not listening to you when you said it was a stupid plan." He met her eyes. "You said it was about *logic*, though. Risks and benefits. You didn't say it was a feeling in your stomach."

"Because I'm 'the smart one,'" Abigail said, making quote marks in the air. "I'm not the magic one."

"It's not like I *actually* have magic powers," Rufus said. "Magic powers are like *shazam* or *abracadabra*! I just have a thing that I can sort of do, sometimes, but it's like feeling around in the dark. I don't even know *why* I can do it at all. It just *happened*, like getting clearsight." His lips twisted. "I couldn't talk to the locks today—I *tried* to keep them from opening, but I couldn't."

"You got us to leap over the water using a seed," Abigail said. "That's magic powers."

She pulled the Glistening Glen books from her backpack. They were still damp, pages curling.

"Trinket packed everything up so we wouldn't leave them behind," she said. "She's a very clever goose."

Trinket nosed the book with her beak. "Wrinkle," she cackled. "Bric-a-brac."

"That's what I think." Abigail handed Rufus *The Luminous Legends of Glistening Glen*. "Now it's time to do things my way," she said. "How about we solve the clues the Crinny-eyes gave us?"

23

IRIS THE INCOMPETENT

It seemed to Rufus that they had been gone for hours, possibly days, but when they returned to Feylawn the sun was high overhead, just as it had been when they left. He checked his phone, which had somehow survived the swim to Imura. Still noon.

He and Abigail managed to clean themselves up enough to return to camp, although they were both so exhausted they could barely stay awake through the afternoon. And all the while, Iris remained unconscious in Rufus's pocket.

It wasn't until evening that she finally woke, clutching her head and moaning.

"Thwack," she groaned. "Of all the seeds to hit me with, she had to use thwack. I feel like a bomb went off inside my head."

"What exactly is thwack?" Rufus asked. He was sitting on his bed with Iris stretched out on his pillow beside him.

"What it sounds like. When you use it right, it's like hitting someone over the head with a frying pan." She pressed her palms against her eyes and began to cry. "You'd better fill me in on what happened afterward. She freed the Calamand, didn't she?"

Rufus nodded. He told her about the Calamand's release and Shamok's near-death.

"The Calamand can offer Diggs anything he wants," Iris said when he was finished. Her voice was soggy with tears and snot. "And my queen is going to help him get it. My queen, who I wanted to rescue. My queen, who was going to s-s-save us!"

She collapsed into a fresh round of weeping.

"Iris," Rufus said. "You're not helping."

"No, I'm not!" Iris agreed, wiping her nose on her sleeve. "I never help, no matter how hard I try. All I do is *ruin* things. I took a perfectly good queen and I made her into an evil goblin wife who f-f-f-frees the Ca-ca-CALAMAAAAAND!"

"Maybe she wasn't that great to begin with," he said. "I mean, I know you *think* she was awesome and everything. But she hit you with thwack and helped Diggs escape and nearly killed Shamok and made it so we were trapped by the brambles. She kind of seems like a jerk."

Iris shook her head so hard her hair wrapped around her neck. "But she isn't! If she was, she would have given in to Diggs years ago. Helped him build a second train like he

wanted. How could she betray us now? After all this time?"
She put her face in her hands and began to sob again.

Rufus's cell phone dinged. Abigail had sent a photo of
Shamok asleep on her bed.

What is he doing there?! Rufus texted back.

He must have followed me He had a
rough day

He's a wild animal! Rufus replied. Your mom will flip
out!

In reply, Abigail texted a photo of Shamok hiding under
the bed. Stealthy, she wrote.

Then another picture: three cans of clam chowder.

He likes these Was very hungry

Rufus sent back an eye-roll emoji.

Abigail sent a photo of the sleeping Shamok with a copy
of *The Luminous Legends of Glistening Glen* balanced on his
golden belly.

Are you reading the books right now?

Because you need to!

Sighing, Rufus lay down on his bed and opened up *The
Luminous Legends of Glistening Glen* to the chapter on the
Calamand.

*Perhaps you know someone like the Calamand.
She's like a magpie, always wanting another shiny
thing to stash in the nest. All the magical beings in
all the eight worlds once knew to lock their doors*

lest the Calamand steal their precious treasures.
She's pilfered enchanted clocks, carpets, lamps,
bread boxes, and the seven-league boots of fairy
legend. She's stolen enough magical coins, amu-
lets, rings, and swords for a dragon hoard, and
of course she's stolen her share of dragons, too.
She's taken a stable full of enchanted horses, and
more than her share of unicorns. But these are just
misdemeanors in the Calamand's lists of crimes.
Some magical objects are so dangerous that they
have the power to destroy whole kingdoms and
turn them into desolate wastelands. They say that
the Calamand stole the worst of these, and that
that is why there are now eight worlds instead of
nine.

There was a knock on the door and Rufus's dad poked
his head in.

"It's late," he said. "Time to switch off the light."

"I will," Rufus said. "Just finishing this chapter."

His dad came into the room and sat down on the edge of
the bed. "You and Abigail can't get enough of those Glistening Glen books," he observed. "Most kids like books
that are a little more up-to-date."

"We're not *most kids*," Rufus said, a familiar frustration
rising in his chest.

"Of course you aren't," his father said, brushing Rufus's

hair out of his eyes. "I'm proud of how you're really making the most of Camp BizBuzz," he said. "Grandpa Jack says he's been selling a lot of junk—I mean *stuff*—from the barn to that lady in town. I can't wait to see your pitch on Thursday."

Rufus looked up. "You're coming?"

"Of course! Wouldn't miss it!" his father said, kissing Rufus's forehead. "So get some sleep. I know you've been working hard."

Rufus picked up the book again.

But however much the Calamand takes, she's never satisfied. What she wants most is whatever she doesn't have. Some say the Calamand wants to build a world of her own, furnished with all the treasures she has stolen from the other eight. But these days, the Calamand has only one treasure in her possession: the Horn of Plenty, which serves you any food you desire at the moment you imagine it. When the fairies locked her away forever, they put it in her prison so that she would always have something to eat and no one would have to cook for her. If it weren't for the face of her little sister, she'd be completely alone.

What did she do to make the fairies so stern and angry?

"Please tell me you're about to get to the point," Rufus said to the book. Beside him, Iris's eyes blinked open, then drifted shut again. He read on.

As I was told, the Calamand had always eluded capture, despite her many crimes. Then, not so long ago, she heard about the fairies' most prized possession: the locket that the fairy ruler wears. Fairies have no use for things like heavy, cumbersome crowns and scepters, for how can you dance and frolic with a chunk of metal on your head? But since the beginning of time, the fairy queen has worn a plain silver locket that is steeped in the strongest magic, the magic that binds a ruler to her kingdom. The ruler who wears it can feel her kingdom's beating heart and master its many passions. She can protect its borders and ward off intruders—but herein lies the tale.

"Does it?" Rufus said to the book. "Because you've been promising to tell this tale for like three pages now." Iris gave a small snore and rolled over, groaning. Rufus kept reading.

Fairies, as you know, travel back and forth between the worlds in order to do their work of caring for the magical plants and animals that dwell within their sanctuaries. Sometimes these responsibilities require them to travel outside the borders of Glistening Glen and into the world of humans. And so it happened that after a particularly pleasant night of song and dance, a young fairy overslept. Slumbering on her downy pillow all the way until afternoon, she neglected to do her daily chores. On this particular day, the fairy, whose name was Iris—

"*Iris!*" sputtered Rufus.

Iris sat up, pressing her fingers to her temples. "What are you yelling about? My head is splitting already without you trumpeting like an elephant."

"You're in this book!" Rufus said. "In the story about the Calamand!"

"Of course I'm in that book," Iris said. "I'm in all the books. Or some version of me, anyway." She narrowed her eyes at him. "Do you mean to tell me you're just reading Carson's books now?"

"You told me they were full of lies," Rufus said.

"So?" Iris said. She fluttered from the pillow to the book, landing with her feet dangling onto the page. "That doesn't mean they don't also contain a few truths. You just have to read *between* the lies."

"It's *Read between the lines*, actually," Rufus said, knowing as he did that he was wasting his breath. "It means to look for the hidden meaning."

"Exactly," Iris agreed. "Find the truth between the lies. For example, Carson put the entire blame on me for that whole troll incident, when there were a dozen of us who were supposed to be weeding the wanderlust and *all* of us overslept."

Rufus lay the book flat on his lap, sending Iris up in the air. "Maybe you should just *tell* me the true parts. Carson Sweete Collins is taking forever to get to the point anyway."

Iris landed on the book's spine and pushed her hair out of her face. "There's not much to it, really. The wanderlust was growing around the base of the bridge, and we waited a bit too long to weed it, and it bloomed, and the troll—"

"Hold on—what troll?"

"The troll who lives under the bridge," Iris said. "The one you were *supposed* to have lunch with."

"You can deliver my apologies when *you* have lunch with him," Rufus said.

Iris made a face. "Maybe I can get one of the Green World feylings to do it. Have you ever seen a troll eat?"

"Anyway," Rufus said, "you were going to tell me about the Calamand."

"Right. The long and the short of it is that the troll stumbled through the blooming wanderlust, and you can guess what happened next."

"I can't, actually," Rufus said.

"He *wandered*, of course. Right into downtown Galosh, which was hardly a town at all back then, more like a railroad stop with a few shops and a tavern, and after the troll came along, there were just the shops."

"What happened to the tavern?"

"Trolls are mean drunks," Iris said. "They're not all that nice when they're sober, to be frank, but alcohol really doesn't agree with them."

"Good to know," Rufus said, vastly relieved that lunching with the troll was no longer his responsibility. "But what does this have to do with the Calamand?"

"Apparently the Calamand was in the tavern. In those days she freely roamed the worlds, looking for things to steal. Naturally, she bought the troll a few drinks. Got him talking about his own little bridge, which he was already homesick for by the end of his first beer. Trolls are homebodies by nature. So it probably wasn't too hard for the Calamand to quiz him about Feylawn, although he was never able to remember exactly what he told her. All we know is that by the time Queen Queen-Anne's-Lace went into Galosh to round up the troll and bring him back to Feylawn, the Calamand must have known exactly what she was looking for."

"Which was?"

"The ruler's locket. She stole it right from our queen's neck while the queen was busy trying to extract the troll from the rubble of the tavern."

Rufus gaped at her. "So then—did the *Calamand* become the ruler of Feylawn?"

"It's not that simple. You have to be a feyling to even put it on." She sniffled. "We don't know what she did with it. We just know we never got it back."

"But you caught the Calamand!"

"She insisted she didn't have it. Said she must have lost it. Which is why your great-great-grandfather was able to find Feylawn in the first place. Once the locket was gone, Feylawn was unprotected. Over time we learned to smuckle the border, but it took practice to do it properly, and whenever there were gaps, some glomper would wander in and decide he owned the place. Then we'd have to spend weeks scaring him off. Except that Avery Sweete wouldn't scare, and eventually we decided he could stay."

"I know that part of the story," Rufus said. "Grandpa Jack's told me."

"Well, now you know the rest of it. How not weeding the wanderlust led to the loss of the ruler's locket, and how the loss of the ruler's locket led to glompers coming to Feylawn, and how glompers coming to Feylawn led to the entire string of unbroken disasters in which I am always involved, no matter what I do."

Iris rolled over onto her stomach and sobbed onto the spine of *The Luminous Legends of Glistening Glen* until a large dark splotch covered the binding.

Rufus sank a little deeper into his pillows. A wave of

sleepiness passed over him. He switched off the light and rolled onto his side, the book landing on the blanket beside him.

"How did you catch the Calamand?" he asked.

"We had to bait the trap with a magical object. So we used one of our own."

Rufus could feel the doors of sleep closing around him. He struggled to keep them open. "Which one?" he murmured.

But by the time Iris answered, he was already asleep.

24

THE RULER'S LOCKET

Rufus spent the next day at camp in a kind of daze. He felt more tired than he ever had in his life, and his head whirled with Feylawn-related problems—the sale of Feylawn, the Calamand, Mr. Diggs, Queen Queen-Anne's-Lace, Nettle.

"Do you think the goblins will still want to buy Feylawn now that they've rescued Diggs and freed the Calamand?" he asked Abigail. "Maybe they just wanted access to the Moving Meadow."

The two of them were in their customary lunch spot, halfway up Stormweather Prep's main staircase. There was a window seat with a panoramic view of Galosh, where they could sit and eat in relative privacy.

"I don't know," Abigail said. "But our parents still want to sell it, so they'll keep looking for a buyer even if the goblins back out."

"What if they *couldn't* sell it?" Rufus asked. "Like, even

if they had a buyer." He had been turning this idea over in his mind since Iris had told him the story of the Calamand the night before.

"What do you mean?" Abigail asked.

Rufus stuffed the remainder of his salami sandwich into his backpack and retrieved *The Luminous Legends of Glistening Glen*. "Remember how the Calamand stole the ruler's locket? In the book, Carson says that the ruler who wears the locket can protect Feylawn's borders and ward off intruders. Wouldn't that mean that the ruler could keep it from being sold?"

"'Read the tale to unwrite the story'!" Abigail exclaimed. "That *has* to be what the first clue means—we're supposed to find the ruler's locket! In the story, the locket is stolen, and then we *unwrite* it by finding it." She grinned at him, as triumphant as if the locket were in their hands already. "I *knew* we should be focusing on the prophecy."

"So do you think that's why Queen Queen-Anne's-Lace freed the Calamand?" Rufus said. "To get the locket back?"

"Maybe." Abigail took a thoughtful bite of her peanut butter and jelly sandwich. "But she's married to Diggs. So if she got it back, then *he'd* control Feylawn. Do you think she'd do that? After refusing to help him with the train for all those years?"

"I don't know!" Rufus groaned. "Why do the goblins even *care* about Feylawn? Don't they have their own territory?" He flipped through *The Luminous Legends of*

Glistening Glen for probably the hundredth time that day, looking for some kind of answer.

A familiar face caught his eye. She had large pointed ears and a fanged underbite, and was covered in a patchwork of multicolored fur. In Carson Sweete Collins's illustration, her eyes were large and winsome, and she was wearing a pink-and-orange striped gown with puffy shoulders.

"Garnet," he said. "That's who we can ask."

Abigail looked over his shoulder and wrinkled her nose. "Why would we ask *her*?"

"She's Mr. Diggs's sister. She'll know what he's up to."

"But why would she tell *us*?"

"Remember that day by the creek, with Mump? She told us that if we ever needed her help, we'd find her on the other end of that ball of yarn. I still have it." He dug around in his backpack until he found the ball of red yarn, the fibers of which had acquired a layer of sandwich crumbs, mud, and pencil shavings in the weeks since he'd first put it there.

"You're not serious."

"I *am* serious. What do we have to lose?"

Abigail didn't answer. Instead she unzipped her backpack and pulled out her folder of Carson Collins's papers. "That knitting fanatic doesn't do anything for free," she said. "If we want her help, we're going to have to bring her a present."

༄

"How is this supposed to work again?" Abigail asked as they walked across the meadow the next afternoon. It hadn't been easy, but they had managed to persuade their parents that they needed to spend a couple of hours at Feylawn to take last-minute photographs for Thursday's Piranha Pitch Session.

"I'm not sure, exactly," Rufus admitted. "Garnet's supposed to be on the other end of the yarn, so I guess that means we have to unravel it." He took the ball of yarn from his backpack and threw it as hard as he could into the woods. It sailed into the trees, uncoiling as it went.

"Now what?" Abigail asked as the ball disappeared from sight.

Rufus scanned the underbrush. "I guess we see where it ended up."

They walked in the direction the ball had flown until they found a dangling end wrapped around some branches. The rest of the yarn extended further into the trees. They followed the strand, winding it up as they went, and emerged into a clearing. A furry goblin in a turquoise cardigan sat on a fallen log. A striped cable-knit scarf was wrapped around her neck, and a pillbox hat topped with a veil and a clump of silk violets rested precariously between her ears.

"I was wondering when you'd call," said Garnet, tossing Rufus the ball of yarn. "Run out of people to turn to, have you?"

"We thought you might have some answers," Rufus admitted.

"*You* thought." Garnet cackled. "Your cousin doesn't seem to share your thinking." She gave Abigail an up-and-down inspection. "Such a sour expression, missy—it's not at all pretty."

Abigail glared. "We didn't come here for beauty tips."

"What *did* you come here for, then? Surely not just to glower at me." Garnet reached into the bag at her feet and drew out her knitting. "Now, it seems to me that if anyone were to hold a grudge, it would be me, seeing as it was *my* brother you hit with a train and knocked into the next world."

"Sorry about that," Rufus said. He juggled the ball of red yarn from hand to hand, not meeting Garnet's eyes. "It wasn't on purpose."

Garnet burst into shrieks of laughter. "Not on purpose! Not. On. *Purpose!*" She leaned forward, gasping for breath. "Take my advice, son: don't apologize if you're not sorry."

"You're the one who doesn't seem sorry," Abigail said. "I don't think you *care* what happened to your brother."

"You're a sharp one, I'll give you that," Garnet said. "I have more brothers than I can keep track of—one more or less makes no difference to me. And that *particular* one has a way of showing up when you're least in the mood for him. I assume that's why you're here. I understand you tried to kidnap him the other day." She sucked her teeth.

"If you'd asked me, I'd have advised you not to pick a fight with my brother if you weren't certain you would win. Not that he liked you much before."

The ball of red yarn dropped from Rufus's hands and rolled a few feet away. "We weren't expecting Queen Queen-Anne's-Lace to be on his side," he said as he retrieved it. "You told us she refused to help him build a second train. You brought us a message from her, even. So why would she help Diggs free the Calamand?"

"Why indeed," Garnet said. "Once upon a time, Lacy would tell me what was on her mind. But she's been peculiar lately. Stays in her chamber without even a candle to brighten the room."

"But you must have a guess," Abigail persisted. "Why do you *think* she agreed to free the Calamand?"

"She's running out of time," said Garnet. "She needs to get back to the Green World or she'll die. Perhaps she's decided she'd rather live on my brother's terms than die on her own."

"She should just leave!" Abigail looked outraged. "We'd help her!"

"It's not so simple, missy. After she first married my brother, she tried to leave, over and over. But a goblin's wife belongs to her husband—*he* decides where she goes and when. All he needs to do is call for her and she's compelled to return to him. She can't even kill him, which might seem like the obvious choice. The enchantment prevents her from laying a hand on him. All of which explains why *I* never married." Garnet looked up from her knitting and batted her eyelashes. "I'm sure you've been wondering."

Rufus wasn't sure what to say to this, so he changed the subject. "I still don't understand what Mr. Diggs is up to. What does freeing the Calamand have to do with Mr. Gneiss's plan to buy Feylawn?"

"Mr. Gneiss works for my brother," Garnet said. "So you should be asking, *What does freeing the Calamand have to do with Mr. Diggs's plan to buy Feylawn?*"

"Okay," Rufus said. "What's Mr. Diggs planning to do with Feylawn? And why did he release the Calamand?"

"Excellent questions," Garnet observed, needles clicking. "Unfortunately, I don't think I owe you any answers." She sighed dramatically. "Such a shame. It's always so much more interesting if somebody owes somebody something."

Abigail drew a rolled-up sheet of paper from the pocket of her hoodie. "I found something in our great-grandmother's papers," she said as she handed it to Garnet.

The goblin unrolled the paper. It was a charcoal sketch of Garnet clutching a nosegay of flowers and gazing at the viewer with dewy eyes. "Oh my," Garnet said, mirroring the pose. "How very flattering." She sighed. "I was just a squenk, back then. Sixty-seven if I was a day. Your great-grandmother really was a fine artist."

She tucked the drawing into her bag and picked up her knitting needles again. "My brother freed the Calamand.

The Calamand plans to repay him by retrieving a little knickknack that belonged to Lacy once—one that will give him the power he's always craved."

"The ruler's locket!" Rufus said. "That's what we thought! But what does he want with it?"

"Whatever he can chop up, cut down, and sell for parts." Garnet held up her knitting and inspected it. "If my brother's feyling wife has the ruler's locket, my brother will control all of Feylawn through her. And if I know my brother, he's figured out a way to turn Feylawn into something he can sell for profit." She looked up suddenly and met Rufus's eyes. "*And* it's a chance to get revenge. You've embarrassed him, Rufus Takada Collins, several times now. Traditionally, that means he'll seek your death *plus* the destruction of all you hold dear, although the order varies. He might go for destruction first, then death, or he might opt for death, then destruction. Or possibly both at once."

Rufus was suddenly very cold and very hot at the exact same time. He folded his arms across his chest, trying to prevent his heart from breaking through the bars of his rib cage. "Does the Calamand know where it is?" he asked through numb lips. "The ruler's locket, I mean."

"Ah, that's the question isn't it? The Calamand has treasures squirreled away across the eight worlds—she's already retrieved her famous Slicers, the ones she used to cut up her sister. But I suspect she doesn't remember where she stowed the locket, judging from the runaround she gave my brother over dinner." Garnet smirked. "I don't imagine those two will stay friends for long. Neither one of them plays well with others."

Abigail squinted at her. "I don't get why you're telling us this. Mr. Diggs is your brother. Whose side are you on, exactly?"

"Who says I'm on anyone's side?" Garnet tucked her knitting into her bag. "Perhaps I'm just a sweet little goblin who enjoys knitting and caring for my nephew Mump and gawking at pretty pictures from times gone by." She flashed a smile filled with pointed teeth. "Which reminds me—Mump needs his lunch." She pushed herself off the fallen log. "If I were you, I'd ask that spotless cat of yours to tell you more about the Calamand. She didn't come to Galosh solely to do favors for my brother, I'll wager. She'll have plans of her own. I'd be very interested to know what they are."

⁂

His parents were in a good mood when Rufus sat down to dinner that night. His dad leaned back in his chair with his long legs extended, the stem of his wineglass dangling from his fingers. His mom wasn't wearing her scrubs for once, and she had let her hair out of its ponytail. She still had tired pouches under her eyes, but she was smiling as she ate.

"What happened?" Rufus asked. "Why do you both look so happy?"

"No reason," Rufus's mom said. "I have the night off. The shrimp is perfectly done. Your dad doesn't have a headache."

"In fact, I'm getting *rid* of a headache," Rufus's dad said.

Rufus's mom made a noise in the back of her throat—the one that meant *let's change the subject.* "Are you excited for the pitch session tomorrow?" she asked Rufus. "We hear you and Grandpa Jack are doing well with your business. He said he's starting a college fund for you with the profits."

"College?" Rufus said. "I won't be going to college for ages. I was thinking Geezer and Grandson could help pay for some of the regular stuff. So you don't have to work so much and so"—he knew he shouldn't say it, but he couldn't help it—"you wouldn't have to sell Feylawn."

Rufus's mom's eyes grew pink at the corners. "You shouldn't be worrying about me working or us having money," she said. "We're going to be fine."

"You're not fine, though," Rufus said. "You're always tired."

Rufus's father put down his fork. "It's true," he said. "You *are* always tired, Emi. Too many extra shifts." He rested his hand on Rufus's arm. "I appreciate you wanting to help out—it says a lot about your character."

Rufus heard the *but* coming even before his father said it. He lifted his arm out from under his father's hand and used it to spear a shrimp with his fork, keeping his eyes fixed on his plate.

"But," his father said, "we are going to be fine, because Aunt Chrissy and I have negotiated a terrific deal with Mr. Gneiss, and Mr. Gneiss has been *nice* enough to accept our terms. Once the papers are signed, our money worries will be over."

"When will that be?" Rufus could barely draw enough air into his lungs to ask the question. *Destruction first, then death.*

"Monday," his dad said. "We have a big stack of documents to go over between now and then."

Five days. Rufus bit into the shrimp that was dangling on his fork and forced himself not to say anything, because he was not going to fight with his father, he was not going to ruin dinner, he was not going to make his mother sad. Instead he chewed the shrimp, which seemed to be made out of old bubble gum. Chew. Chew. Chew.

At last he swallowed. He took a bite of rice. He smiled across the table at his mother, who was watching him with a worried crease between her eyebrows. Soon the crease relaxed, and the conversation resumed. His parents started telling stories about commercials and TV shows from their childhood, laughing as they sang the songs from candy-bar ads. He chewed his food, and with every bite he told himself:

I won't let them sell Feylawn.

I won't let them sell Feylawn.

I won't let them sell Feylawn.

He and Abigail were going to have to find the ruler's locket. Quickly, or it would be too late.

PIRANHA PITCH DAY

"Horizon shine!" Iris said.

Rufus blinked awake to find her perched on his chin.

"Why are you so chipper this morning?" he asked, sitting up. "For days, all you've done is cry."

"Got it out of my system," Iris said. "Now I'm ready to plan."

"Maybe not a good idea," Rufus pointed out. "The last plan didn't go so well."

Iris looked hurt. "It was my first time," she said. "It takes practice. Although," she admitted, "I'm not exactly sure how to start."

"I'll help you. We need to find the ruler's locket."

"Impossible," Iris said. "We've looked for it and we didn't find it. Also, we don't"—her lip trembled—"*have* a ruler anymore!" A large tear slid down the side of her face.

"That's exactly why we need to find it! Queen

Queen-Anne's-Lace is working with the goblins now. If she gets the ruler's locket, she could give *them* power over Feylawn. Abigail and I think that's why she freed the Calamand. To get her help finding the locket."

Iris flew at his face and pulled his hair. Hard.

"*Ow!* What was that for?"

"I was just starting to feel better and now I feel worse again."

Rufus knew how she felt. He'd lain awake most of the night watching the window, certain that Mr. Diggs was about to break in and murder him.

"We have to find the locket before Diggs does," he said. "Where would the Calamand have put it?"

Iris put two fingers to her temples. "Thinking," she said, her face furrowing with effort. "Thinking, thinking, *thinking.*"

Rufus began putting on the "business casual" khaki pants and button-up shirt he had to wear for the pitch session. He was so tired, he felt like his head was filled with sweaters.

There was a knock on the door and then it flew open.

"Happy Pitch Day!" his dad sang. "I heard you talking— were you rehearsing your pitch?"

Rufus's cheeks grew hot. He needed to be more careful about talking to Iris. "Yeah," he said. "Practice makes perfect, right?"

"Right you are!" his Dad said. "Preparation is the key to

success! Are you bringing props? Examples of your products?"

"I told you, my presentation's a surprise," Rufus said. He wasn't about to tell his dad that the only prop he needed was the pink beguilum seed he'd found in Iris's pouch and placed in the pocket of his khakis. It would be more than enough to make his pitch sound like pure genius.

"Well, I'm pretty excited about seeing it," his Dad said. He patted Rufus on the shoulder. "Come on down for breakfast. We're leaving in twenty minutes."

"Be right there," Rufus said. "Just need a few minutes to concentrate."

He waited until he'd heard his father's footsteps going down the stairs before he turned to Iris. "Camp ends after lunch today. Let's meet at Feylawn this afternoon. We'll come up with a plan then."

⁂

"Ready?" Abigail whispered. They were standing backstage in Stormweather Prep's theater. The murmur of excited parents drifted in from the auditorium.

"I guess," Rufus said. "You?"

"I was born ready." This was probably true, Rufus thought. Abigail's jaw was set; her braids were neat. She wore a dusty-rose skirt with a matching blazer and a crisp white button-down.

All around them, BizBuzz campers in suits and dresses were pacing, their faces scrunched as they rehearsed their pitches in low whispers. Abigail scanned them with a practiced air of assessment.

"Jelani Madu has the best business idea, but he gets nervous when he's talking. Aside from him, the only one I'm worried about is Taylor L. She's a good speaker, but I bet she hasn't prepped for the judges' questions the way I have."

"The judges ask questions?" Rufus said.

Abigail narrowed her eyes at him. "Mark went over this like fifteen times. Haven't you been listening?"

"Not really," Rufus admitted. "I've been kind of preoccupied with trying to save Feylawn. Speaking of which, I talked to Iris and—"

"Ready, BizBuzzers?" called Mark. "Leeeeeeeeeeeet's *do* this!"

Abigail grabbed his hand and shook it. "Good luck. May the best person win."

"Don't be stupid," Rufus said. "We both know that's you."

❧⟟☙

When it was time for Abigail's pitch, she climbed onto the stage carrying a copy of Carson Sweete Collins's book of poetry, *The Mermaid's Song and Other Poems*. Then she recited, from memory, the first poem in the book.

I was a girl in a bridal veil,
but I took it off and made a sail
and sailed away on a salty breeze
to tour the world and scout the seas.
When I grew tired of my galleon,
I traded the ship for a milk-white stallion.
I cantered all night by the silvery moon,
then exchanged my horse for a blue balloon
and soared aloft through sun and cloud,
singing my giddy thoughts aloud.
The song I sang was clear and brave.
It reached the folk beneath the wave.
And that's how I earned my mermaid's
   tail:
Just by taking off my veil.

Rufus had never really liked poetry, but Abigail made this poem sound like regular language, only better. She spoke in a strong, clear voice, and when it was over, she let the words hang in the silence for a moment, until the parents in the audience started to applaud. Then she smiled and held up a hand to stop them.

"That poem was written by my great-grandmother, Carson Sweete Collins, a famous children's book author who lived here in Galosh," she said. "And it's always meant a lot to me, because it showed me that you can take whatever misfortunes life gives you and turn them into opportunities. Like the girl in the poem, my great-grandmother had a marriage that didn't work out. But then she became a famous author and illustrator. Like the girl in the poem, she turned her bridal veil into a sailing ship."

She smiled and took a few steps downstage, and a slide came up behind her that showed the illustration from the poem—a mermaid floating in the waves.

"The girl in the poem is a pretty smart businesswoman," Abigail went on. "She trades her sailing ship for a horse, exchanges her horse for a balloon, and eventually, through smart bargains and hard work, she earns a *mermaid's tail*. And that's why my business is called Mermaid's Tail Productions. My product? T-shirts and other memorabilia that celebrate the wit and wisdom of my great-grandmother, Carson Sweete Collins."

She clicked to the next slide, a photo of Aunt Chrissy modeling a T-shirt that said *That's how I earned my mermaid's tail* on the front and *Just by taking off my veil* on the back.

Rufus was transfixed. He'd met the ghost of Carson Sweete Collins, and she'd been awful. But Abigail made her sound cool—like somebody who'd had some tough breaks and then bounced back. Abigail showed slides of T-shirts, mugs, and hoodies with fairy illustrations and quotes from the Glistening Glen books on them, sweet ones and funny ones and mysterious ones. When the judges asked her about the market for these products, she showed a bunch of charts and graphs that explained how the Glisteners—the Carson Sweete Collins fan club—would be "brand ambassadors" who would help her reach people who had never heard of the children's book author but just liked the sayings on the T-shirts. When she was done speaking, all three judges looked as if they wanted to leap onto the stage and hand Abigail a check then and there.

"You were amazing," Rufus whispered when Abigail came backstage. His own presentation was next. He clutched the beguilum seed in his right palm while his stomach did a series of backflips and cartwheels.

"Thanks," Abigail whispered back. She glanced down. "Why are you clenching your fist like that?"

"Just nervous, I guess," Rufus said.

Abigail grabbed his wrist. "No, really. What's in your hand?"

Reluctantly, Rufus opened his fist. Abigail snatched the beguilum seed from his palm. "That's cheating!"

"No it isn't," Rufus protested. "It's—"

"Let's give a hand to our next BizBuzz entrepreneur," Mark shouted from the stage. "Our very own Rufus! Takada! Colliiiiiiiiiiins!"

"Give it back," Rufus pleaded. He made one last attempt to grab the beguilum seed from Abigail, but she eluded his reach, tucking the hand with the seed into her armpit.

Cheater, she mouthed.

"Rufus!" Mark whispered. "You're up!"

Rufus stepped onto the stage. Without the comfort of the beguilum seed, his hands felt like blocks of ice. He wasn't even sure he knew how to work his fingers. Mark fastened a small cordless mic to his lapel and clipped the receiver to his belt.

"Go get 'em, Roofaloof!" he whispered, clapping Rufus on the back. He handed Rufus the clicker for advancing his slides. *Slides, right*, Rufus thought. He did have slides, although he hadn't spent much time on them.

He looked out at the audience. The auditorium was half empty, so it was easy to pick out the familiar faces. His parents and Aunt Chrissy in one row. Grandpa Jack in the row in front of them. Beside him was Robin-Ella LaFontaine, who was inexplicably holding the ceramic chicken that used to belong to Carson Sweete Collins. When he caught her eye, Robin-Ella raised it over her head as if to give it a better view.

Rufus tried to say something, but his mouth felt like someone had dried it with paper towels. He stared at the chicken. The chicken stared back.

Rufus jumped down from the stage and walked into the audience.

"Can I borrow this?" he asked Robin-Ella, lifting the chicken from her hands.

26

HEN ON NEST

Back on the stage, Rufus saw his father shifting uncomfortably in his seat. His expression was hard to read from across the auditorium, but there was so much expectation in it, so much hope, that Rufus thought, *I've done it again; I've disappointed him*, and then remembered that he was still up on the stage, holding a ceramic chicken, and so he opened the Sonoran Desert of his mouth and began to speak.

"This is a ceramic chicken," he said.

Next to his father, his mother was beaming him the most brilliant of her emergency-room smiles, the one that practically screamed, *You are likely to die in the next ten minutes, but I don't want you to panic.*

"It's a chicken that my great-great-grandfather, Avery Sweete, had in his horse-drawn wagon when he first came to Galosh," Rufus continued. "I mean, I don't know that for sure, but that's what my grandpa always told me, and he has no reason to lie."

Grandpa Jack guffawed, which made a few other people in the audience chuckle, mostly out of relief, Rufus guessed. At least words were coming out of his mouth. All he needed to do now was survive the next fifteen minutes, and even if his presentation was terrible, which it would be, at least it would be over.

"The story is that Avery Sweete came to town to sell encyclopedias, and stumbled onto a beautiful piece of property at the edge of town. He had this ceramic chicken stowed under the seat, and in it was his life savings, which wasn't nearly enough to buy land of any kind, so he threw in some encyclopedias—"

"Volumes A through R," called out Grandpa Jack helpfully.

"Volumes A through R," Rufus repeated. "And he bought the property and grew apricots on it, and it's been in my family ever since."

He seemed to have run out of things to say, so he tried swallowing a few times, in the hope that he might moisten his mouth. Then he remembered that he was holding the chicken.

"And that's why this chicken is important to my family," he added. "Because it's a reminder of our history, and this piece of land that I love more than any place in the world." He looked out at his father, whose expression was impossible to read.

"For most people, of course, this chicken is just, like, a

chicken," he continued. "And if you don't care about my family's story, then you probably wouldn't pay anything to have this chicken. Unless you collect porcelain chickens. Which some people do. The point is," he continued, knowing he was rambling, "every old object has a story. And if you like that particular story, that object will be meaningful to you, and if it's meaningful, then it's valuable. Sometimes something will look like old junk. But if you look beyond the surface, you discover that one person's old junk is another person's treasure. And that's what we do at my business, Geezer and Grandson Vintage Collectibles. We look beyond the surface."

The chicken was kind of heavy, so he set it down at the foot of the stage and reached into the pocket of his khakis, half hoping he might find a beguilum seed he'd forgotten about. Instead he found the remote for the projector, and hit it, praying the next slide would give him some inspiration.

The slide showed the pile of old cans he'd found in the barn.

"Take these cans," he said. "Vintage canned food from different periods, 1910 to 1960. Not good for eating, but people use them for decoration. They go for about thirty-five dollars each, so that's three hundred fifty dollars, minus the forty percent commission we pay to the store that sells them. So we made two hundred and ten dollars on those ten cans."

One of the judges nodded. Rufus hit the button to advance to the next slide, which was another photo of items from the barn. So he explained how the barn was filled with junk, how the junk had turned out to be valuable, and how he and his grandfather had partnered with Robin-Ella LaFontaine of Old Soul Vintage to sell it—here Robin-Ella stood up and took a bow. After a while it seemed like he'd been talking for a long time, so he tried to figure out how to stop, which was harder than he'd expected.

"Not everybody can see beyond the surface of things," he said. "Some people are only going to see what's ugly, or what's dirty, or what's imperfect, or what's old or dangerous or inconvenient. But some people can see beyond what's obvious, and appreciate things for whatever they are, even if those things are unusual or even weird. And that's the kind of person we're trying to reach with Geezer and Grandson."

He looked out at the auditorium. There was a woman sitting by herself near the back. She wore a maroon jacket with gold buttons and a white scarf wrapped around her head that almost entirely covered her flaming red hair. She smiled at him, and applauded, and Rufus realized simultaneously that he had somehow come to the end of his presentation and that he was staring at the Calamand.

"Bravo! Bravo!" Grandpa Jack shouted, leaping to his feet and clapping wildly.

Mark Trang made a silencing gesture and Grandpa Jack sat back down.

"Now we'll have questions from the judges," Mark said.

There were three judges. One was the head of Stormweather Prep, and the other two were executives from local companies: Christian Sardo from Sardo Brothers Roadside Revelries and Patricia Martinez from DeLouge Plumbing Supply. In retrospect, he was pretty sure he answered questions from all three of them, but the only thing he remembered doing was trying to watch the Calamand. With her extra face and arms covered, she looked fairly ordinary— except for the way she kept smiling, as if she were watching the most entertaining performance of her life.

And then the judges were thanking him and Mark was shaking his hand and announcing that they were going to take a break for lunch. Just after he left the stage, Rufus remembered the porcelain chicken. But when he turned around to get it, it was gone.

⚬⚬⚬⚬

He found Abigail backstage.

"Not bad," she said, arching her eyebrows at him. "I guess you didn't need to cheat after all."

"The Calamand's here," Rufus said. "And she just stole my chicken."

Abigail crept to the side of the stage and peeked around the curtains. "Where?"

Rufus peered over her shoulder.

"She *was* there," he said. "I swear."

"I'll find her," Abigail whispered. She slipped down the aisle on the side of the auditorium, smiling politely and staring straight ahead in a way that made it seem like she was on an official mission.

Rufus tried to follow, but suddenly, every adult in the auditorium was streaming toward the stage. Rufus found himself engulfed in one of Grandpa Jack's massive hugs. Then his father was hugging him, and his mother, and even Aunt Chrissy, who bellowed, "I should have known my nephew would have the weirdest business of anyone in the whole camp!"

After everyone else had congratulated him, Robin-Ella stepped forward and took his hands in her warm ones and said, "You spoke it just the way I feel it."

Then she dropped something into his palm. "I found this wedged in the lid of that chicken. It's pretty, isn't it?"

It was a seed of some kind—red-orange and half-moon-shaped. Rufus tried to listen for its properties but too many people were talking to him. He shoved it in the plastic baggie of seeds he kept in his pocket and began moving toward the exit in search of Abigail.

He found her on the steps where they usually ate lunch.

"I caught up with the Calamand," Abigail said. "She was talking to one of the judges, Christian Sardo. But she didn't have the chicken with her—at least not that I could see. Why would she be here? Is she following us?"

"I don't know," Rufus said. "Where is she now?"

"I think she left. I started to follow her and then she turned around and saw me and I guess I kind of chickened out." She tugged on one braid anxiously. "Speaking of which—why would she take your chicken?"

"Maybe she thought there was money in it?"

Abigail shook her head. "She steals magical things, not valuable things. Is it magic?"

"I don't think so." He thought of the way the train and the lock had felt in his hands. Like they wanted something. The chicken just felt like a chicken.

"Robin-Ella found a seed in it," he said, remembering the one in his pocket. "But why would the Calamand care about a seed?"

"Show it to Iris," Abigail said. "Maybe she'll know." She stood and straightened her skirt. The crowd of adults was now spilling from the doors of the auditorium. "Here come our parents."

Rufus's father and Aunt Chrissy had stopped to talk with one of the judges.

"Rufus! Abigail!" his father called, waving them over. "This is Gail Silverman, head of school here at Stormweather Prep." He rested a hand on Rufus's shoulder. "My son Rufus has really flourished here at Camp BizBuzz! Just being in this beautiful building is—"

"My daughter Abigail has *also* flourished here," Aunt Chrissy interrupted, putting an arm around Abigail. "You remember Abigail—she's the one who gave the winning presentation."

"Mom," Abigail said. "They haven't even *chosen* a winner yet."

"But you will!" Aunt Chrissy said to Ms. Silverman with a broad wink. "And not to brag, but just speaking objectively, Abigail's the kind of girl who is driven to excel— which I know is what you look for in your Stormweather Prep students."

Ms. Silverman gave a noncommittal smile and glanced over Aunt Chrissy's shoulder. "Excuse me, I need to sit down with the other judges. Nice job today, Abigail, Rufus. I'll look forward to seeing your applications."

"Applications for what?" Rufus said when the headmistress had walked away.

"I wouldn't worry about it, Rufus," Aunt Chrissy said. "It's not your type of thing."

The surge of parents was now moving toward the dining hall. Rufus and Abigail let themselves be carried toward the table where a buffet lunch had been set out for the families.

There was a soft throat-clearing behind them.

"Excuse me—I think this is yours?"

Rufus turned to find a disheveled-looking man standing behind him with a porcelain chicken. *His* porcelain chicken. It was Christian Sardo, the judge Abigail said had been talking with the Calamand.

"Oh, wow!" Rufus said, taking the chicken. "Where did you find it?"

"Backstage. I was looking for my briefcase. I have a tendency to lose things. Looks like you do too." Mr. Sardo's expression was friendly but vague, as if he was thinking about several things at once. He had pale skin and light brown eyes magnified by thick black-framed glasses. He wore wrinkled suit pants, a red-checkered button-down shirt, and a dark green fleece vest with a noticeable stain on the front.

"That's Victorian Staffordshire Hen on Nest, as you probably already know," he continued. "You ought to put it somewhere safe."

"I will—thanks." Rufus lifted the chicken from her nest and peered inside. How had it gotten backstage?

"I have an interest in antiques myself, actually." Mr. Sardo reached out to stroke the head of the chicken. "I opened a little museum across the street from my office. You might want to check it out, since you like old what-nots. We've got plenty of stuff for kids."

Rufus tried to look interested, but he was still preoccupied by the Calamand. What was she doing there? What if Diggs had sent her to slice him to pieces the way she'd sliced up her sister?

Abigail stepped forward, her please-the-adults smile at

medium wattage. "I'm Abigail Vasquez," she said, extending her hand to Mr. Sardo.

"I remember you, of course," Mr. Sardo said. "Terrific presentation."

"Thanks." Abigail studied his name tag. "I saw you were talking to a friend of ours. The one with the red hair?"

"Another antiques lover," Mr. Sardo said. "She's interested in my museum as well. Maybe she can bring you with her when she visits."

"What kind of museum is it?" Abigail increased the intensity of her smile.

Mr. Sardo reached into his pocket and handed her a crumpled brochure.

"Memorabilia from America's carnivals, circuses, funfairs, and midways. The Sardo family business is *fun*." He gave them a melancholy smile.

"Your carnival's in one of our great-grandmother's books!" Abigail exclaimed. "It's one of my favorite chapters."

"Is that right?" Mr. Sardo said. "I don't read much myself. I was in a magazine article once, though. They called me the mayor of Fun Town, which is a load of baloney. I might be the paper pusher of Fun Town, but that doesn't make as good a headline." He laughed, and then seemed to forget he was laughing and patted his pants pockets as if looking for something. "Now if you'll excuse me, I'm supposed to meet with the judges and I lost my keys for the fourteenth time today."

As Mr. Sardo wandered away, Abigail studied the brochure he'd given her. "Look at this," she said, pointing to one of the photographs. "There, in the background—that's an illustration from *The Luminous Legends of Glistening Glen*." She frowned. "So why did he just pretend he'd never heard of it?"

27

AUNT CHRISSY'S ADVICE

"My jaw dropped to the floor when they gave you that honorable mention," Aunt Chrissy announced on the drive home, looking at Rufus through the rearview mirror. She had volunteered to take both kids home since Rufus's mom had to work and Rufus's dad wanted to prepare for a meeting with their attorney. "You've come a long way since the start of the summer. It just goes to show that if you listen to your Aunt Chrissy's advice, you can turn things around a hundred and eighty degrees."

"Mom," Abigail said, sitting beside Rufus with the Piranha Pitch Competition trophy wedged between her knees. "Please stop."

"I'm not telling him anything he doesn't already know!" Aunt Chrissy said, waving a heavily ringed hand in the air. "You're kind of an oddball, Rufus; you know it and I know it. It's nothing to be ashamed of! It's just that most people don't like you when you're too weird. I've said as much to your parents, who were very proud of you today, especially your dad. He looked like the cat who ate the canary when you walked up on that stage to get your little certificate."

"Abigail's the one who won the whole—" Rufus started, but Aunt Chrissy interrupted.

"Oh, Abigail's used to winning; it's nothing special for *her*. But since it's *your* first time, I'll give you some free advice. Try to be less weird. You're not as weird as you used to be, now that you have some summer camps under your belt, but let's be honest: that proposal of yours was still kind of bizarre. I'm not sure why the judges encouraged either one of you to go on and on about that old albatross we call Feylawn, frankly."

"Because they love the Glistening Glen books," Abigail said. "Ms. Silverman said she read them as a child."

"Books, schmooks! They loved *you*, Abigail. That's what you're selling when you're an entrepreneur—*yourself*. You're a terrific product, and yes, I'm taking credit for that since I paid for all your camps and classes. Bottom line: people like you. Whereas you, Rufus, you don't say much, and that's not a winning strategy. Right now, for instance. I'm talking to you and you're not saying a thing."

"Sorry," Rufus said. "I just—"

"Let me finish." Chrissy wagged a finger at him. "The point I'm making is that you were a bit too quiet and odd to do well in life when Abigail and I arrived in June, but we're whipping you into shape, aren't we, Abigail?" She smoothed her hair. "I like a man with a head for business, kids; I always have. Mr. Gneiss and I were chatting the other day—he's been *very* successful in the underground development arena—and I told him that it was his talent for business that I admired most. 'Mr. Gneiss,' I told him, 'if I've said it once, I've said it twice: I like a man who knows his price.'" She giggled in a most un-Chrissy-like way. "Mr. Gneiss who knows his price! I'm a poet and I didn't know it! Do you like poetry, Rufus?"

"It depends—"

Aunt Chrissy slapped her hands on the steering wheel and bellowed, "Mr. Gneiss! I've told you twice! He's so precise! He adds some spice! Like cream with ice." She looked over her shoulder at Rufus. "Now *that's* poetry for you."

A silence fell over the car. Abigail's face was mostly hidden behind the enormous gold piranha at the top of her trophy, but Rufus could see her chest rise and fall with the weight of a heavy sigh.

"Mom," she said suddenly. "I'm quitting the swim team."

Aunt Chrissy looked up. "But you love swimming," she said. "You have so many medals!"

"I *know*." Abigail flooded the words with regret. "But now that I have this enormous trophy, I don't really have space for any more."

"We can get a bigger house," Aunt Chrissy said. "Once we sell Feylawn—"

"Anyway," Abigail pressed on, "my business has to come first. If I'm going to make the most of this five hundred dollars in seed money, I have to prioritize." She paused. "I can't go to camp next week, either."

"You can work on your business in your free time, Abigail."

"I don't *have* any free time," Abigail said with sudden fierceness. "All I *do* is lessons and camps and projects!" She took another breath and her voice turned sweet again. "And now I have a business that will look *amazing* on my college applications, and I really need to focus exclusively on this opportunity."

Rufus gave his cousin a sidelong glance. As often happened when his cousin was talking with adults, he couldn't quite tell whether he was listening to Real Abigail or Fake Abigail. Maybe it was a mixture.

"Perhaps it *is* time for you to specialize," Aunt Chrissy said thoughtfully. "They tell me colleges want depth as well as breadth."

She was silent for the rest of the drive. It wasn't until she'd pulled into the parking lot of the condo complex where she and Abigail lived that she turned to face the back seat.

"You can have two weeks off from camp and swim team," she announced. "*You* tell your coach."

Rufus stared at Abigail. Had she somehow learned how to use beguilum? Or was she just born knowing how to get what she wanted? However she did it, she was now free.

He, on the other hand, was still supposed to go to Banking Camp next week. Alone.

⚬ɕⵔⵔɕⵔ

After dropping them off, Aunt Chrissy went to join Rufus's father at a meeting with their attorney. That left Rufus and Abigail on their own, supposedly to spend the afternoon watching educational videos about famous entrepreneurs.

"I told Iris we'd meet her at Feylawn," Rufus said. "We can see if she has any ideas about where to find the ruler's locket. We'll take Shamok."

He glanced over at the leopard, who was lying under Abigail's desk with his face to the wall.

"I can't get up," Shamok said. "I should be dead."

"But you're *not* dead," Rufus said. "You're fine."

"Weak," murmured Shamok. "Can't walk. Need . . . ice cream."

"Ice cream?" Rufus looked at Abigail. "This is *your* doing, isn't it?"

"He needed nourishment," she said. "I'll be right back."

"She understands me," Shamok whispered when Abigail left the room.

"She *babies* you," Rufus said. "You're not dying. You're just—"

"Spotless," growled Shamok. "Go ahead. You can say it."

Abigail came back in carrying an open pint of salted caramel. The leopard licked at it lazily while she stroked his ears.

"Tell me about Mr. Sardo," Rufus said as he watched the leopard's tongue at work. "What's his connection to *The Luminous Legends of Glistening Glen?*"

Abigail gave Rufus a stern look. "I thought you'd read it."

"I *did*. Part of it, anyway."

"Not the important part, or you'd have recognized the name. It's in the chapter where detectives from each of the different worlds that had something important stolen by the Calamand team up to catch her. And guess where they set their trap?"

"Mars?"

"Sardo Brothers Roadside Revelries!" Abigail said, loud enough that one of Shamok's ears twitched. "It's one of the *best* parts of the books!"

Rufus gave her a skeptical look.

"It is! The carnival has a carousel, and a giant swing, and the Five Fighting Princes of Marrakesh, who will box with anyone who volunteers, and a Corridor of Curiosities with a bearded baby, a mermaid named Palimsa, and this guy they call the Canary-Voiced Man Who Can Sing Any Song."

"And why did they set the trap there? Does the Calamand like bumper cars or something?"

"It explains in the book." Abigail reached over her head and felt around on the surface of her desk for *The Luminous Legends of Glistening Glen*. "Listen: 'The Calamand was fond of carnivals, for amid all the hokum and fakery, fairs and carnivals often attract bits of genuine magic. And so from time to time she hitched a ride with the colorful wagons of a traveling circus, allowing herself to be exhibited as the Four-Armed Girl while keeping watch for magicians whose tricks were better than average, fortune-tellers who could actually tell the future, and fairgoers whose carnival finery might include a family jewel whose remarkable powers had gone unnoticed.'"

"You can give me the abbreviated version," Rufus reminded her. "I don't need the whole encyclopedia."

"The point is"—Abigail rotated the ice cream carton so Shamok could lick the bottom—"the detectives knew she'd be there. And what they did was, they set a trap with a magical object as the bait, and when she came looking for it, all seven detectives were there to capture her."

"What was the magical object?" Rufus said, trying to remember his conversation with Iris.

Abigail frowned. "In the book it's called the Soothsayer Cabinet. There was a fortune-telling booth at the carnival, and the Calamand went to it because she wanted to know if she would ever get caught. And then she *did* get caught, precisely because she wanted to know the answer!" She stroked the book with her free hand. "It's a really good chapter."

Rufus went to the door. "Let's go find Iris," he said. "I feel like there's something we're not seeing. You, me, and Shamok each have a piece of it, but we need all four of us to put it together."

28

THE MISSING MINUTES

Grandpa Jack's truck was gone when they arrived, but Feylawn was humming with activity. The Green World feylings were everywhere, chattering among themselves as they pulled up weeds and gathered seeds. They were different from the Feylawn feylings in appearance, wearing exquisitely tailored clothes made of leaves and bark instead of slapped-together outfits made from litter and household objects.

Rufus, Abigail, and Shamok found Iris issuing instructions to a group of surly-looking feylings by the barn. Compared to the others, she was a tangle of trash and temper. Her new blue dress was already snagged and stained, and her wild black hair was badly snarled.

"Have any of you seen Nettle?" she asked. "I thought he was in charge of the smuckle."

The three feylings shrugged. "Here and there. Not recently," said one.

"Then I'll need you to fly down to the northwest corner, Atropa. The smuckle's come undone over there, and you'll have to tuck it back in." She turned to Rufus, Abigail, and Shamok. "You three come with me. We have a situation." With that, she took off toward the creek.

"What do you mean by a *situation*?" Rufus asked as they followed her.

"Nests," Iris called back over her shoulder. "The janati geese are getting ready to lay, and I can't find the nests."

"Why does it matter?" Abigail said, running to catch up. "You've been obsessed with the geese ever since you came back, but you've never told us why."

"A janati goose lays a janati egg," Iris said. "And there are times when a janati egg is *exactly* what you need."

"What times are those?" Abigail asked.

"You'll know it when you come to it," Iris said. "Assuming we can find the nests."

"I thought we were trying to find the ruler's locket," Rufus said.

Iris made a midair U-turn and settled on Abigail's shoulder.

"Nests," she said. "They'll be by the creek."

They walked in silence for a bit. Shamok stayed close to Abigail, his massive body pressed against her leg.

"You need to snap out of it," she scolded him. "Try thinking about something other than your missing spots for one minute."

"I didn't say a word," Shamok said reproachfully.

"You didn't have to," Abigail retorted. "I can hear your thoughts and they're extremely boring."

"You *can?*" Rufus asked.

Abigail flushed. "Kind of," she said.

Iris snorted. "It's always hard to choose which of you two glompers is the most irritating, but right now you're winning," she said to Abigail. "Every five minutes you announce some utterly uninteresting thing you know how to do, and when you finally develop a skill that other people might want to hear about, you decide to keep quiet about it."

Rufus looked from one to the other. "What are you talking about?" he said. "*What* skill?"

For some inexplicable reason, Abigail was staring at the ground in front of her, looking as if she'd like to disappear.

"Sometimes," she said softly. "It's like I can hear . . . or understand, I guess—"

"Animals!" Iris interrupted. "She can communicate with animals. I'm surprised you didn't notice it yourself."

"I thought it was just me," Shamok said. He sounded hurt.

Abigail shook her head. "It's *more* you. I can't do it all the time. Just sometimes, partly. A little. It's like speaking Mandarin."

"Which you can *also* do," Rufus said. He felt unexpectedly annoyed. The *one* thing that made him special was seed speech, and now Abigail was announcing that she could do something way cooler.

"Which I can do *a tiny bit*. It's not like I could go to China and have conversations with people. I just know some phrases. And I can't understand most animals. Just sometimes, recently . . ." She trailed off. "I know it sounds weird."

"Of course it sounds weird!" Rufus exclaimed. "Everything we do here is weird! How long has this been going on?"

Abigail shrugged. "I guess it started with the umbrals," she said. "And then it's happened a few other times since then. Like when the animals were scared by the scrygrass. I could understand what they were saying."

"Which was?" Rufus asked.

"It didn't really make sense. That something was coming to steal them. Take them somewhere." She shrugged. "I could have gotten it wrong—it's not like I've taken a class in it or anything. I can't control it, and I'm not good at it, and until right now I wasn't even sure it was real."

"You'll get better at it," Iris said. "Rufus has. He was a bit quicker on the uptake than you, though. And *you're* supposed to be the smart one." She lifted off from Abigail's shoulder. "Now can we get going? We have nests to find."

They spent the next hour walking up and down the banks of the creek searching for nests, without any success. The creek was still swollen from the rain, but the waters had receded enough to reveal the gravelly shore.

"Peculiar," Iris said at last. "Yesterday I saw the geese gathering bits of grass and moss. I *know* they're nesting, or thinking about nesting anyway. But now I don't see them."

"Can we talk about how we find the ruler's locket?" Rufus sat down on a boulder and rested his arms on his knees. The anxious feeling he'd had ever since yesterday's conversation with Garnet swarmed over him like a colony of ants. "If we don't get it first, none of this small stuff matters."

"We should focus on the next clue," Abigail said. She took a seat in the gravel with Shamok beside her. "We know we're supposed to unwrite the story by finding the ruler's locket. Now we need to figure out how to find the moment that was lost."

Iris landed on Shamok's shoulder. "Time cabinet," she said. "When Queen Queen-Anne's-Lace trapped the Cala-mand, she baited the trap with a time cabinet."

"You mean the Soothsayer Cabinet," Abigail corrected. "In the book they bait the trap with a cabinet that tells the future."

"But it didn't *really* tell the future," Iris said. "That was just a story to get the Calamand's attention. Palimsa—"

"She's the mermaid detective," Abigail interjected.

"Correct," agreed Iris, stretching out on Shamok's golden fur. "She said if we wanted to trap the Calamand, we had to use a real magical object. The Calamand would only be attracted to something powerful. So we used our own time cabinet. We set up a fortune-telling caravan. The witch detective played the role of the fortune-teller, and Hornfels—he's a goblin, before you interrupt again—was the money-taker."

"There was a goblin detective as well?" Rufus asked, opting not to ask about the witch.

Iris sat up. "Are you incapable of closing your mouth for more than five seconds at a time? Because I literally just told you that."

"I just thought that goblins and feylings—"

"Sometimes you have to work with people you don't like," Iris said. "The Calamand had stolen from all of us. We needed it to stop. So Hornfels stood outside the booth and took the money, and he told each customer that if they gave us five minutes of their time, we could tell them ten years of their future. Then Lacy and another kronkel-wander took five minutes from each customer—"

"How do you *take* five minutes?" Abigail asked. "Don't roll your eyes. I just need an explanation."

Iris blew the hair out of her face. "This is what I was trying to avoid," she said. "If there's one thing that humans are greedy about, it's time. But I suppose you won't understand the rest of it if I don't explain." She stared up at the sky for a moment. "I hope I don't regret it."

"We're not our great-grandmother," Abigail said. "You should know that by now."

"The only thing I know is that whenever I open my mouth, trouble falls out," Iris said. "But here goes. We don't have time in the Green World, as I've told you. But here, in the Blue World, every glomper is unspooling it, like a spider unspools its web. Feylings have always stolen bits of human time to bring home with us, back to the Green World. The time cabinet has the tools for taking it, and drawers for holding it, and cases for carrying it."

"But why?" Rufus asked. The idea of someone stealing his time made him feel woozy, like thinking about donating blood. "What do you need our time for?"

"I thought I explained this already," Iris said. "Time allows our children to grow into adults, for one thing, and we need small doses of it to keep our minds clear, because when you live entirely in the present, you don't learn things, or remember things, or plan things. The Green World feylings are a perfect example of what happens when you marinate in the present for seventy years."

"Can we get back to the day of the carnival?" Abigail asked.

"Hornfels took the money and two of our kronkelwanders took the time," Iris said. "It's easy to do when someone's waiting in line. They tend not to be paying attention, so you just sort of wind it up with the kronkelwand and what you get is almost perfectly clean, so you don't have to spend much time washing out the memories. People look up and say, 'What did I miss?' and shrug, never suspecting that the minutes they're missing went into our cabinet."

"That's me in every math class," Rufus said.

"Classrooms used to be a great place for time-gathering," Iris said. "Waiting rooms, too."

"Anyway," Abigail said. "Go on with the story."

"While she was waiting in line to get her fortune told, we took five minutes from the Calamand. The hope was that when we got it back to Feylawn, the spoolers would go through the memories and see if there was anything that would tell us where she'd stashed the magical objects she'd stolen."

"What are spoolers?" Rufus asked.

Iris sighed. "You can't just reuse someone else's time— you have to clean it first," Iris said. "Otherwise it's all snagged with memories, like a sheep that's been walking through a field of burrs. The spoolers are the feylings on the time crew whose job it is to wash the time and comb it and spin it into skeins so we can transport it to the Green World."

"But none of that's in the book," Abigail objected. "The book just says that Queen Lacy the Luminous and the other detectives lured the Calamand to the fortune-telling caravan and arrested her."

"I believe we've discussed the accuracy of Carson's books," Iris said. "Anyway, it wasn't important to the story. The time cabinet disappeared before we ever had a chance to look at what we'd taken."

"What do you mean, *disappeared*?" Rufus said. "Did the Calamand take it?"

Iris shook her head. "Impossible. As soon as she went into the caravan, she was arrested. The detectives clapped her in cuffs and took her to Imura."

"So what happened to the time cabinet?"

Iris pushed herself into a sitting position. "If I *knew* what happened to the time cabinet, we'd still *have* the time cabinet. And if we *had* the time cabinet, I wouldn't have arrived in the Green World to discover a bunch of addle-brained feylings singing the ten thousandth verse of "I See a Pine Cone in a Tree," holding babies who hadn't grown into children and children who hadn't grown into adults."

"Garnet said the Calamand didn't seem to remember where she'd left the ruler's locket," Rufus said thoughtfully. "Does that mean the memory is in the time cabinet?"

Iris nodded. "It's possible. We don't usually see the only copy of a memory caught up in a strand of time, unless it's a brand-new one—something that was just floating around loose. But if the Calamand was thinking about what she'd done with the ruler's locket when Lacy wound up her time, and if it was a fresh memory, the memory could have gotten caught in the strands."

"So if we find the time cabinet, we might find the lost moment!" Abigail exclaimed. "And if we find the lost moment, we find the ruler's locket." She turned to Iris. "When did you discover the time cabinet was gone?"

"The next day." Iris's lip trembled. "Queen Queen-Anne's-Lace sent me and a few others to collect the cabinet, but when we got there, the whole fair was already packed up and ready to move on to the next town. The fortune-telling caravan was there, but the time cabinet was gone." She wiped her eyes with the back of her hand. "Everyone blamed me, of course, just like they blamed me for not weeding the wanderlust. But I swear, it vanished before we got there."

"Anyone could have taken it," Rufus sighed. "Someone who worked at the carnival, or someone who went to the carnival and saw the cabinet when they got their fortune told."

"Or"—Abigail pulled a piece of paper from her pocket— "someone who *owned* the carnival." She held up the brochure they'd gotten from Christian Sardo at that morning's pitch session. "Christian Sardo's family owns Sardo Brothers Roadside Revelries *and* the Circus and Carnival Museum. That must be why the Calamand wanted to talk to him."

"She must think *he* has the time cabinet," Rufus said. "And she wants those five minutes back."

"She's no fool," Iris said. "She'd have figured out what the time cabinet really was as soon as she got close to it."

Shamok lifted his head from his paws. "She and Mandolyn used to talk about time," he said. "I could hear their conversations from outside the gate."

Rufus remembered what Garnet had said about finding out the Calamand's plans. "What did they say?" he asked. "Do you remember?"

"Of course," Shamok said. "I'm the leopard of the locks. It's my business to remember."

They waited expectantly while he cleaned one of his golden paws.

"Mandolyn was always complaining about being locked away," he said when he was done. "*She* wasn't the master criminal, she kept saying. She never *asked* to be attached to the Calamand's head. Why did *she* have to waste years of *her* life being bored in prison?"

"I see her point," Abigail said.

"So did the Calamand," Shamok said. He began grooming his other paw. "She promised Mandolyn that she'd make it up to her. 'Once we get out,' she said, 'I'll give you all the time we've lost and then some.'"

Iris's wings trembled. "We need to find the time cabinet before she does," she said. "Feylings only take tiny bits of time. But the Calamand? She'll take it all."

SHAREHOLDERS' MEETING

Mr. Diggs didn't like meetings. Meetings required sitting, which he disliked, and talking, which he disliked even more, and listening, which he disliked most of all. Perhaps it was the meeting that had put him in a foul temper, or perhaps it was the presence of the Calamand, whose constantly spinning head had begun to fray his nerves. Or maybe it was the ceaseless coughing of his wife, Queen Queen-Anne's-Lace, who was slumped on a tiny stone throne Diggs had fashioned for her and placed in the center of the table. *Cough, cough, cough.*

"Take a seat," Diggs snapped at the Calamand, who was pacing by the door. "We have work to do."

"Only if I can open the door a crack," the Calamand said. At the back of her head, Mandolyn clawed at her throat in an elaborate pantomime of choking. "My sister doesn't like confined spaces. Probably because she spent a hundred years in prison."

"You're in the tunnels," pointed out Mr. Gneiss, who sat at the opposite end of the large conference table with documents stacked in front of him in neat piles. "*All* our spaces are confined." He smiled as he said it, which Mr. Diggs found irritating. Gneiss had been educated aboveground, among humans, and he had adopted too many of their mannerisms for Mr. Diggs's taste. When Mr. Diggs became North American tunnel boss, maybe he'd send Mr. Gneiss on a long journey somewhere far away. That was almost as pleasant to contemplate as the title itself. *North American tunnel boss.* Once he acquired Feylawn and the ruler's locket, the job would be as good as his.

The Calamand left the door ajar and sat down on a bench. One set of hands reached into her pockets and withdrew a pair of gold-handled scissors, which they used to trim the fingernails of the other set.

"Here's where things stand, my hair-trigger digger," she said. "Mandolyn and I lost track of time a few years back. The location of the locket slipped my mind and landed in a little box the feylings call the time cabinet. Your mini-miney-mo had the cabinet, but she lost it right around the time she locked me up. When I find the cabinet, I'll find the time. When I find the time, I'll locate that locket."

"How soon can you have it?"

"Patience, Digg-Dawg," said the Calamand. She tossed her hair and winked at Mr. Diggs's wife, a liberty he found infuriating. "Give me a day or two and we'll both have what we came here for."

Mr. Diggs's eyes narrowed. "I thought you *came here* to repay your debt to me by retrieving the ruler's locket."

"Among other things," the Calamand said. Her two pairs of hands exchanged roles—now it was Mandolyn's hands that received the manicure and the Calamand's hands that wielded the scissors. "I know you won't mind if I add the feylings' time cabinet to my collection of treasures while I'm in the neighborhood."

"I'll decide what I do and don't mind!" Mr. Diggs snapped. He'd have to find out more about this time cabinet. His wife would tell him. Although she was looking, he had to admit, none too healthy.

"Gneiss," he barked, because it was always pleasant to bark at someone less powerful when he was in a temper. "Where are we with the purchase of the property?"

Mr. Gneiss smiled again. "The Collins family is extremely motivated," he said. "They believe they're going to get rich. We should have a contract signed within days."

Mr. Diggs drummed his long nails on the table. "You were not authorized to make them rich. You were authorized to take possession of Feylawn."

"They won't *get* rich," Mr. Gneiss said. "*We* will, though. The contract I've written has enough loopholes to string a belt through. We'll get the property, and when all the fine print is finalized, we won't have paid a cent for it. If anything, the Collins family will end up owing *us* money." He leaned back in his seat with his crocodile legs splayed and his crocodile tail wrapped around his chair. "I've also given them samples of some of our products. One variety of pill per family member, for better tracking."

"And?" Mr. Diggs leaned forward.

"Initial results are in line with our projections."

Mr. Diggs nodded. "Good. Then all we need is that locket." He reached over and stroked the wilted wing of his feyling bride. "A locket for my lozenge," he said. "And then we'll take back my train and send you to the Green World for a little pick-me-up."

Queen Queen-Anne's-Lace gave him a wan smile. "You're the only one who cares about me, Rance. The only one in all the world."

"Not true! Not true!" Wings whirred through the crack in the open door. "I care, Your Majesty. I remain your most humble and obedient servant!"

Diggs's lip curled as the feyling landed on the table in front of Queen Queen-Anne's-Lace and bowed low.

"You remember Nettle Pampaspatch, Mr. Gneiss?" he said. "I believe he helped rescue you after an unfortunate mishap involving an ATV?"

"Of course." Mr. Gneiss's cheeks creased with one of the bland smiles he'd copied from the humans. "Glad to have you back on the team."

"Never left it, sir," Nettle said. "I'm a simple fellow, but I can tell winners from losers. And I like winners." He swaggered across the conference table until he stood directly in front of Mr. Diggs. "I'm here for my instructions."

Mr. Diggs glanced at the Calamand, whose head was now spinning like a weathercock as her two faces took turns studying Nettle.

"My associate here is searching for a certain time cabinet," he said, gesturing at the Calamand. "See if the children and their pet greenling have any idea where it is."

30

SARDO BROTHERS ROADSIDE REVELRIES

Mr. Sardo's office was on the seventh floor of a downtown building behind a small sign that read SARDO BROS. ROADSIDE REVELRIES in faded lettering. A receptionist whose hair was the same shade of gray as the carpet and walls looked at them sternly as they came in.

"This is a corporate office," he said. "No arcade games, no rides, no ring toss, no clowns. The closest Sardo Brothers carnival is currently seventy-five minutes down the highway, and the museum is across the street."

"Actually," Abigail said. "We have an appointment with Mr. Sardo."

"Send them in, Norman, send them in," called Mr. Sardo, standing on the threshold of an office behind her. "Abigail Vasquez and Rufus Collins, am I right? I was so happy when you called yesterday. Very entrepreneurial of you. Plus it's a break from the paperwork. So much darn paperwork in this job, you can't believe it." Indeed, his desk was covered with such a thick layer of paper that no wood was visible. Drifts of paper carpeted the floor around him as if blown there in a windstorm.

Mr. Sardo grabbed their hands and gave them an enthusiastic squeeze before sitting back at his desk and motioning at two chairs. "Sit down! Welcome to Fun Town," he said. "Would you like a balloon? Norman can get balloons and clown noses from the supply cabinet."

"That's okay—" Rufus began, but Mr. Sardo was still talking.

"Honestly, nobody wants a clown nose, not even a clown. The squirt guns are a bit more popular. Speaking for myself, I wouldn't be opposed to filling up the squirt guns and chasing each other around the building. Or we could drop water balloons off the roof. Not on passersby, of course. Liability issues, unfortunately." He gave them a regretful smile and rubbed his hands together as if warming them. He was wearing a shirt with purple and blue checks, a yellow blazer, and a tie with orange and green stripes, a combination that seemed like it might be seizure-inducing if you looked at it too long.

"We actually had a couple questions for you," Rufus began, but Mr. Sardo wasn't finished.

"Paper airplanes wouldn't hurt anybody!" he said with sudden enthusiasm. "Do you want to throw paper airplanes off the roof? No liability issues there!"

"Ask him about the time cabinet!" Iris instructed from

Rufus's shoulder. "Otherwise he's just going to keep suggesting things until we all die of exhaustion."

Abigail unzipped her backpack. "I'm really eager to show you my T-shirt designs," she said. "Can we do that first?" She pulled out a folder and spread several sheets of paper across his desk.

Mr. Sardo's smile collapsed like a folded umbrella. "Of course," he said. "Business before pleasure. As always." He sighed heavily and scanned the three designs Abigail placed before him, which were all based on illustrations from *The Luminous Legends of Glistening Glen*. "I like them!" he said, sweeping up the designs and handing them back to Abigail. "Send me three of each one in every size you can think of. Make them in circus colors—I'll let you figure out what that means. Shall we go to the roof?"

Abigail was so startled she forgot to smile. "Thank you! I'll start on them right away."

"THE TIME CABINET!" Iris was practically screaming. "What are you *waiting* for?"

"Mr. Sardo," Rufus said quickly. "We had a question about one of the illustrations." He took the folder of designs from Abigail. "This one." He put his finger on an illustration of the mermaid detective beside the time cabinet. "It's in one of our great-grandmother's books, actually—"

"We saw the same illustration in the brochure for your

museum," Abigail interjected. "It shows the Soothsayer Cabinet."

Christian Sardo's pleasant, absentminded face grew wary. "It's not for sale," he said. "As I told your friend at the pitch session yesterday." He dropped his eyes and began folding a paper airplane out of one of the documents on his desk.

Iris landed in front of Mr. Sardo, her wings trembling. "Where is it?" she demanded. "Give it back at once!"

Unable to hear her, Mr. Sardo continued folding.

"What friend?" Rufus asked. He had a feeling he already knew.

"The redhead. Ms. Calamand. I assume you're working together? Using my fondness for children to sweet-talk me into making a sale?" Mr. Sardo tapped the point of his folded airplane with his index finger. "I may work with clowns, but I'm not one myself. See that diploma on the wall? Stanford Business School."

"We're not working with her!" Abigail protested. "We just met her—"

"Not that she's the first," Mr. Sardo continued. "At least once a year I get a call from some Carson Sweete Collins enthusiast interested in purchasing the Soothsayer Cabinet from, what is it, *The Luminous Legends of Glistening Glen?*"

"Is that why you pretended not to have heard of the book?" Rufus asked.

Mr. Sardo turned his watery eyes on them and laughed. "Did I?" he said. "Truth is, I hate that stupid cabinet—it used to sit in my father's office and it always gave me the creeps. I like antiques, but objects have their own personalities, and I swear that thing doesn't like me."

"Of course it doesn't," Iris snapped. "You stole it! It wants to go back home."

"We'd be happy to take it off your hands," Abigail said. "I won five hundred dollars in the pitch session. I could buy it from you."

"I'd *give* it to you if I could," Mr. Sardo said. "Unfortunately, my father's will specifies that if I get rid of even *one item* from his collection of circus memorabilia, I'll be banished from the company and disinherited." He stood up. "Shall we throw some paper airplanes from the roof?"

Abigail widened her eyes to the point where Rufus worried her eyeballs might actually come loose and fall out of their sockets. "Could we just see it? It would be *super amazing* if I could take a picture with it for my social-media accounts. To generate interest in the T-shirts." She leaned forward. "I really want to go to Stanford Business School someday," she said shyly. "I was hoping a successful T-shirt business might help get me in."

Mr. Sardo sighed and got up from his desk. "Very well,"

he said. "I suppose we can throw paper airplanes another time. Now, let me see where I put my keys."

⚬ʃ◌◌ʅ⚬

The Sardo Brothers Circus and Carnival Museum was across the street, in an old brick warehouse papered with circus and carnival posters that featured dancing elephants and acrobats on horseback and strongmen in tiny shorts. There was a popcorn cart next to the admissions counter, sandwiched between two painted carousel animals: a zebra and an ostrich. A number of sticky-looking children were darting around the cramped lobby waving ice pops and spilling bags of popcorn while their adult chaperones bleated their names in a tone of growing despair. At the admissions counter, a short line of people waited to buy tokens for the carnival games.

"These two are with me!" Mr. Sardo called, flashing an ID badge as he ushered Rufus and Abigail past the line. He plowed across the lobby, nearly knocking over a little girl in a princess dress.

"I'll take you to see the Soothsayer Cabinet, and then you can explore the rest of the museum on your own," he called over his shoulder. "Got to work at some point today, not that I want to. The gift shop's to your right—that's where we'll sell your T-shirts—and the painted circus wagons are to the left."

He pushed open the door to a dim stairwell. "Can't be bothered with the elevator," he murmured as he huffed up the stairs, continuing his narrative over his shoulder.

"I'm afraid when you see the cabinet you're gonna be disappointed. It's just a painted wooden box with a few drawers that don't open and some weird-looking tools of unknown purpose."

Iris, fluttering ahead of them, snorted. "*Unknown purpose*," she repeated disdainfully. "That's glomper arrogance for you. If *you* don't know it, then it's *unknown*."

Rufus was barely listening. He was trying to think of some way that they could walk out of the museum holding the time cabinet. Nothing came to mind. Even if Mr. Sardo hadn't been right beside them, the museum was filled with patrons. He looked over at Abigail. Judging from her frown, her thoughts seemed to be running along the same lines.

They had reached the third-floor landing. Mr. Sardo pushed open the door and led them down another narrow hallway until they reached a lurid circus-style poster advertising the exhibit.

The Hall of Prophecy
Fortune-tellers, Seers, and Soothsayers
Come inside and pierce the veil of time!
Consult the oracles to learn what lies ahead!

Iris sped past it into a narrow room with wooden floors and dark velvet curtains cloaking the windows. Fortune-telling tools of every description were arrayed in display cases, while women in flowered headscarves peered at them from paintings and photographs on the walls.

"This way, this way," urged Mr. Sardo, hustling into an enormous room whose walls were lined with mechanical fortune-telling machines. Some looked like old radios or grandfather clocks and promised to read your palm or decipher your horoscope. Others had glass cases containing a mysterious-looking figure—a bearded genie, a one-eyed pirate, a donkey in a billowing dress, a cat in a red jacket.

"These are the real attraction," Mr. Sardo said as Rufus and Abigail watched the mechanical figures nod and blink. "Over a hundred years old, some of them. Most spit out a printed card, but two of them have recorded voices—actual wax records! Compared to those, the little box from your great-grandmother's book is kind of a dud."

"Where is it?" Rufus said. He had the sensation that the mechanical figures inside the old machines were watching him. Waiting to see what he would do.

"It's here," Iris said. Her voice was hushed. "It's here."

It was far smaller than Rufus had imagined, no bigger than a dictionary. It sat unnoticed in a small glass display case in a corner of the room, a blue painted box embellished with gold symbols: the phases of the moon, an hourglass, a snake eating its own tail. One end of it had a drawer that had been opened to reveal the tools inside.

Iris landed on the display case and stretched out on her stomach, peering down at the cabinet until her breath fogged the glass.

"Could I hold it?" Abigail asked. "I think the photo might be more interesting if I'm in it." She did the eye-widening thing again.

Mr. Sardo gave her the kind of defeated look you give a begging puppy. "The things I do for kids," he said as he fumbled in his pockets for a key, pulling out business cards, a billfold, a cell phone, two packs of gum, a roll of Life Savers, a ballpoint pen, and a pair of sunglasses, a good portion of which ended up scattered on the floor by his feet.

"Ah, here it is!" he said at last, holding up a ring of keys. He unlocked the case and handed the box to Abigail, who motioned for Rufus to snap some pictures with his phone. She tried to open one of the drawers, but it was stuck fast.

"They don't open, as I said," Mr. Sardo said. "Merely decorative, I'm guessing."

A moment later, he was replacing the cabinet in the display case. "Please feel free to enjoy the rest of the museum at your leisure," he said as he turned his key in the lock. "Are you sure I can't interest you in paper airplanes?"

31

THE HALL OF PROPHECY

"Stop! Go back! What are you doing?" Iris protested as Rufus and Abigail left the museum a short time later. "That was the time cabinet!"

"We can't just walk out with it," Abigail said. "We'd get arrested."

"Why? *We're* not the one who stole it," Iris said. "He was!"

"Let's get some pizza," Rufus said. "Then we can sit in the park and come up with a plan while we're eating."

"I don't need pizza." Iris landed on Rufus's shoulder with her arms folded. "I need my time cabinet."

"Well, *I* need pizza," Abigail said. "I'm ravenous."

Iris's complaints continued through the purchasing of pizza slices and the selection of a bench under a weeping cedar tree that was far enough away from passersby for them to be able to talk freely.

"We could go in tonight when the museum's closed,"

Abigail said slowly. "Iris opens the locks. We go in, take the cabinet, and leave."

"What about a burglar alarm?" Rufus said. "You know they'll have one." He turned to Iris. "Can you talk to burglar alarms?"

Iris shook her head. "You'll need to handle that."

Rufus laughed grimly. "That should be easy."

"It might be," Abigail said. She reached into her pocket and pulled out a card with a bar code at the bottom.

"That's Mr. Sardo's ID badge!" Rufus exclaimed. "Where'd you get it?"

"He dropped it when he was trying to find keys to the display case," Abigail said. "I just thought it might be useful."

Rufus gave her a long look. "Did you go to Burglary Camp or something?"

"Of course not," Abigail said. "I'm just quick-thinking."

Iris coughed. "Let's get back to the topic at hand. Is that badge that Abigail found enough to get us into the museum without setting off the alarm?"

"I think so," Abigail said. "As long as Mr. Sardo doesn't discover that it's missing."

A rustling sound came from a branch overhead. Then something blue plummeted into the grass in front of them.

Rufus and Abigail bolted over to it, both of them knowing what it was before they got there. A Steller's jay lay on its side, eyes closed, feet in the air.

"Is he dead?" Rufus asked. He realized he hadn't seen Nettle since the day he fired him.

"He's breathing." Abigail put one finger on the bird's trembling chest. "What do you think happened?"

"He was eavesdropping on us," Rufus said. "That's what happened."

He didn't like how Nettle's motionless form made him feel. Relief, if he was to be honest, but also pity.

Iris draped a maple leaf over the bird's chest. "He's sick," she said. "Like I was."

The jay quivered and extended his wings. "Let me go home," he murmured. He opened one eye. "I can—help—you." He coughed, and then coughed again, one cough breaking over another like waves. "I've been watching"—he coughed again—"the Calamand. She's searching for the time cabinet. She told Mr. Diggs she'd have it by morning."

A shiver snaked up Rufus's spine. Mr. Diggs always seemed to be one step ahead of him.

"We have to get there first," he said. "If we want to get the time cabinet before the Calamand, we'll have to go in as soon as the museum closes."

Nettle's crest quivered. "It's in that museum? Is that where it ended up?"

A look of consternation passed over Iris's face, followed quickly by indignation. "Don't try your tricks on me, Nettle Pampaspatch," she said. "You're supposed to be giving us information."

"I've told you what I know!" Nettle protested. "I just want to help!" He rolled to his feet, his feathers ruffled and untidy, and began to transform into his feyling form. Halfway through he seemed to get stuck: he had the jay's crest instead of his own black topknot, and a rather impressive feathery blue tail.

Rufus snorted. "Help your goblin friends, you mean." He met Abigail's eyes. "What do we do now? We can't risk him telling Diggs what we're up to."

It was Iris who answered. "You're staying here," she said to Nettle. "Hand over your pouch." When Nettle didn't move, she unfastened the pouch from his waist and wrapped it around her own. Then she studied him a moment, hands on her hips. "Better safe than sorry," she said to herself. In a moment, Nettle was trussed head to toe in bindweed and fastened to a branch above their heads.

"He'll be here when we return," she said to Rufus and Abigail. "Let's go."

⁂

"The Sardo Brothers Circus and Carnival Museum is now closing. We ask all patrons to please make their way to the exit at this time."

From the first-floor exhibit hall, Rufus and Abigail watched the final patrons meander toward the gift shop. They were both smuckled, but they'd taken the precaution of hiding behind a red-and-purple painted wagon ornamented with silver scrollwork and topped with an enormous carved dragon.

"Closing time, folks," a security guard repeated as she motioned the last patrons toward the door. "Come back and see us tomorrow. Thank you. This way. Closing time."

Rufus felt as if his entire body were made of bees. His head, his hands, his chest, his legs, everything was buzzing with fear and anticipation. Inside his sneakers, his toes clenched. The museum seemed vast and silent now that the patrons were gone. His nose itched. His eyes itched. He needed to clear his throat.

At last he heard the security guard lumbering across the hall, breathing heavily.

"That's it," she said. "All clear."

Rufus poked his head around the edge of the caravan in time to see the guard pull out her ID badge.

"Now!" he hissed to Iris, who was perched on his shoulder. "She's about to set the alarm. Watch carefully."

Iris hovered just behind the security guard's shoulder as she held her ID card to a sensor and punched in a series of numbers. There was a two-note beep. The security guard patted the heads of the ostrich and the zebra by the front entrance.

"You two keep an eye on things until I get back," she told them. "See you in twenty minutes."

Then she walked through the door, locking it behind her.

"Did you get the code?" Abigail whispered when Iris returned to them.

"Some sevens," Iris said. "And a three, and maybe a two. Plus a couple of others."

Rufus struck his forehead with his palm.

"We need the *exact* numbers, in order," Abigail said. "I *told* you that."

Iris smirked. "Just having a little fun," she said. "Seven-eight-two-four-three-seven, and then the key that looks like a box."

"The pound key." The smuckle kept Rufus from looking at Abigail directly, but he heard the scratch of her pen as she wrote down the numbers in her notebook. "Okay. Let's try it."

He listened intently to the sounds of her moving across the floor, crawling in spots to avoid triggering the motion detectors. There was a beep as she waved Mr. Sardo's ID in front of the sensor and punched in the code. Then two more beeps as the burglar alarm turned off.

"Got it!" Abigail's voice seemed to be moving away from them, rather than toward. "Hold on, there's one more thing we need."

Silence. Then a rummaging sound.

"What are you *doing*?" Rufus hissed. "The security guard said she'll be back in twenty minutes!"

"Just a quick trip to the gift shop." Abigail's voice was moving back toward them. She dropped something onto the floor in front of him. When he knelt down, he saw that it was a pair of polyester clown gloves, red and yellow, adorned with pom-poms and a shiny white ruffle.

"Put them on," Abigail said. "I'm wearing them, too. So we don't leave fingerprints."

Feeling ridiculous, Rufus pulled the gloves over his hands.

"Let's go," he said. "Third floor."

⚬⚬⚬

The Hall of Prophecy was as stuffy and dry as a cotton ball. The heavy black curtains cloaking the windows made it feel like the middle of the night, even though they could hear the faint sounds of late-afternoon traffic drifting up from the street. Rufus and Abigail used the flashlights on their phones to make their way through the dark hall. In the phone's blue-white glow, the faces in the fortune-telling machines were pale and ghostly. Beneath a sign saying TEA LEAF READINGS, a turbaned mannequin grinned at them, holding out a cup of tea. Ouija boards, tarot cards, crystal balls and palmistry charts lay silently in their glass cases, offering to reveal how the whole escapade might turn out.

"Glomper playthings," Iris sniffed as she circled the room. "Why your kind cares so much about prophecy is beyond my understanding. The future will show up soon enough. It's the past you'll never see again."

"Can we focus?" Rufus said. "Iris, we need you to unlock the case."

"You're not going to try?" Iris asked. "You took the latch-thorn. You can speak to locks."

"Not really," Rufus said. He could hear the locks as they chanted: *Safe. Keep in. Secure. Keep out.* But he couldn't find a way to speak to them.

"Just try it," Iris said, landing on the display case that held the time cabinet. "You have a key inside you now. Use it."

As she said the words, Rufus saw a flash. Not in the room but inside his head—a glint or a glimpse of something gold behind his eyes.

"That's it," Iris said. "Now take it."

The key took shape in his mind: a looped bow at the top, a ridged bit at the base, a slender stem between. But how was he to take it? He reached with his hands first, snatching foolishly at nothing.

"We don't have time for me to learn how to do this," he said. "Just open it. I'll try another time."

"As you like," Iris said. He heard her whisper to the locks in a language of turns and clicks. He reached for the key again, yearned for it, and it was there, not in his hands but in the back of his throat—a press of cold metal, like the root of a brass tongue.

Open. He said it silently, in that strange tongue of twists and clicks. *Open!* he said again, elated. *Open!*

"That's enough," Iris said. "Close them up now. You can play later."

But something was happening behind him.

The Puss in Boots fortune-teller creaked to life, nodding his carved wooden head. Across from him, a mannequin named Madame Zasha began to write a fortune with a quill pen, earrings dangling. One by one, every machine in the room whirred into action. Wheels of fortune spun. Bells rang. Levers pulled of their own accord, sending pointers this way and that. "You will embark on a journey," a deep voice intoned. "You will discover a hidden secret," warned another.

"What did you *do?*" Abigail squeaked. "Somebody's going to hear!"

"The machines must have some form of lock inside them," Iris said, watching the whirring machines in horror. "Maybe it wasn't the best time for Rufus to learn to talk to locks." She flew to his shoulder. "Lock them up again. You have the key. Just tell them."

Rufus tried to find the words in that mysterious tongue, but fear had closed his throat. Why did all these machines have to make so much noise?

"You do it," he said. "I can't."

The machines had begun spitting out squares of white cardboard, one after another. If he didn't try to look directly at her, Rufus could glimpse Abigail through the smuckle.

She was kneeling on the floor, gathering up the squares of cardboard as quickly as they came. "Stop it!" she hissed as the cards flew from the machines. "Enough already!"

Iris circled the room, silently speaking to each of the open locks. One by one, the machines began to quiet. The mechanical fortune-tellers nodded a final time and went still. At last, the room was silent again.

"What a mess." From the sound of it, Abigail was still gathering up the cards that had scattered across the floor. "If the security guard sees all these, she'll know something's up."

"What *are* they?" Rufus asked as he knelt down to help.

"They're supposed to be your fortune—like in a cookie. They always say things like 'You will cross a body of water' or 'You will meet a mysterious stranger.' Stuff that can be true for anyone."

Rufus squinted to read one in the dark. GIVE UP ALL THAT YOU LOVE FOR ALL THAT YOU ARE.

His heart skittered like a kicked pebble. He'd heard that phrase once before. From the Crinnyeyes. But what did it mean?

He flipped to the next card.

GIVE UP ALL THAT YOU LOVE FOR ALL THAT YOU ARE.

He shuffled through the rest.

GIVE UP ALL THAT YOU LOVE FOR ALL THAT YOU ARE.

GIVE UP ALL THAT YOU LOVE FOR ALL THAT YOU ARE.

GIVE UP ALL THAT YOU LOVE FOR ALL THAT YOU ARE.

"Are we here to take the time cabinet or to get our fortunes told?" Iris demanded as she landed on his shoulder. "Because if we're here to take the time cabinet, maybe we should get going."

Quickly, Rufus shoved the fortune cards into his pocket. Then he went to the display case and lifted out the time cabinet.

"Now let's get out of here," Abigail said. "We have eight minutes."

32

THE VIEW FROM THE FERRIS WHEEL

It was almost six o' clock, but the park was still full of people riding bicycles and skateboards or eating picnic dinners on the grass. Rufus and Abigail sat under the drooping branches of the old cedar, still out of breath from running. Iris landed on the ground between them and did a little dance.

"We did it!" she cried. "We got it! We took it! We have it!"

Rufus took a gulp of air. It seemed impossible that they had pulled it off. No one was chasing them. And even though Iris had lifted the smuckle, no one was even looking at them. He peeled off the clown gloves and tossed them in a nearby trash can. Abigail did the same. Then she knelt in the grass, unzipped her backpack, and, after looking over both shoulders, drew out the time cabinet. Its colors were rich and bright in the late-afternoon light. The gold image of the snake eating its own tail shimmered and seemed to spin. She tugged at the cabinet's drawers. None of them budged.

"How do I open them?" she asked.

Iris flew over. She tugged at the drawers, bracing her feet against the cabinet for leverage.

"I'm not—*entirely*—sure," she grunted.

"Trace the shape of the snake, then touch each of the four quarters of the moon."

Rufus jumped. He'd forgotten about Nettle, who was still bound to the branch where they'd left him.

"New moon, waxing crescent, full moon, waning crescent," Nettle said.

Abigail did as he instructed and pulled at the drawer. This time it opened. She sucked in a breath. "What is all that stuff? Is that time?"

Iris landed on her shoulder. Her eyes widened. "There's so much of it! There must be a time bundle from every single person who stood in that line!"

The bundles looked like clumps of matted yellow-white fur. They were dingy, and bristled with brightly colored burrs, like a dog that had walked through a briar bush.

"How do we know which of the bundles is the one we're looking for?" Abigail asked.

"Maybe I can help." Nettle squirmed in his bindings. "One of my sisters was a spooler. I used to help her when she was down at the creek, washing the memories out of the time the kronkelwanders gathered. She showed me how to use the poke-pick and the hook and the borstel-brush and chandercomb. Sometimes I'd look through the memories we combed out." He met Rufus's eye. "If you tell me what you're looking for, perhaps I can—"

"You can *leave*," Rufus said.

"I'll untie you," Iris said. "Then you can be on your way."

"As you wish." Nettle bowed his head as she undid the bindweed. He fluttered to the ground beside the cabinet. "Perhaps you could return my pouch to me before I leave? If it isn't too much trouble."

Iris unbuckled Nettle's pouch from her waist and inspected its contents. "I don't see you doing much harm with these," she said as she handed it back to him. "Off you go."

Nettle fastened the pouch around his own waist. He still looked pale and his hands trembled slightly, but he was able to complete the transformation into feyling form. Once the jay crest had melted into his own black top-knot, he flew to the time cabinet and pulled open the tool drawer.

"You'll need the snaghook to grab a memory from each one, so you can see who each bundle belongs to," he said, holding up a long wooden tool that looked like something a dentist would use. "Once you find the time bundle you're looking for, use the poke-pick to separate the fibers. Be careful or the whole thing will fly apart, and you'll lose the memories *and* the time. Next, use this borstelbrush, brushing always in the same direction. The memories will snag in the bristles, and then you can comb them out with the larger of the two chandercombs. When you do—"

Abigail turned to Rufus. "We're going to need his help."

"No," Rufus said. "Absolutely not."

"Yes," Iris said. "Abigail's right. We have one chance to get this right. If we mess it up, we lose the memories and any hope of finding—"

"I don't trust him," Rufus said quickly, before she could finish the sentence. "He's loyal to the goblins, not to us."

"You misjudge me, Pledge Lord," he said. "I am bound by peony seed to serve you and your cousin."

Rufus peered into the drawer that Abigail had opened. "These burrlike things—they're memories?" He took the hook from Nettle's hand and tried to lift one from the topmost time bundle.

The burr clung and wriggled, flexing its barbed spikes. As Rufus tried to tug it free, the whole time bundle began to crumble. Bits of white fluff peeled off and floated above his head. It had a funny smell, like a mixture of fireworks and eucalyptus. Suddenly he felt as if he were moving at regular speed in a slow-motion world. He could see the burr tumbling over his head, its spikes stretching and flexing until they formed a kind of latticework of blue fibers that domed over their heads. The noises of the park hushed as if under a blanket of snow. Iris flew to Rufus's shoulder.

"What did I just—" Rufus began, and then stopped as the

scene filled in around them. A carnival, tinkling with lights and laughter and music. He was standing in line in front of a painted caravan beside two young women he'd never seen before. The women wore old-fashioned calf-length frocks with pleated skirts and funny bell-shaped hats.

"You don't even like ginger cake, I told him!" exclaimed one. "Why would you help yourself to the ginger cake I made for Mother's birthday before it's even frosted?"

"He did it out of spite," said the other. "My brother's the same way."

"Spite and malice," the first woman agreed. She gestured toward the caravan ahead of them. "I can't wait to have a house of my own. Maybe that fortune-telling machine can find a handsome stranger in my future—one who doesn't eat somebody else's birthday cake!"

As the two women erupted into giggles, Nettle took the snaghook from Rufus's hand and broke up the latticework of memory the way you might brush aside a spider's web. The figures wavered, folded, vanished.

"I presume that's not the memory you were seeking, Pledge Lord?" he asked.

Rufus shook his head, his mouth half open. He'd just seen someone's *memory*—someone who had lived a hundred years ago. He looked at the drawer of time bundles again, each one flecked with memory burrs. How could they possibly look through them all?

Nettle twirled the snaghook as if it were a baton. "I

assume it's the Calamand's memories you're looking for? Give me five minutes and I'll tell you which time clump is hers."

ৎ৶৩৴৹

The memories fell around them like autumn leaves, a whirl of mundane moments from random strangers: walking the dog, counting change, losing at the milk-bottle toss, stealing kisses behind a caravan, stubbing toes, buying root beer, laughing at jokes, arguing over politics.

"No. No. That's not her," Nettle murmured to himself as he snagged one memory after another. Rufus wasn't sure how the feyling could be so certain, but he was grateful not to have to make the determination himself.

But then he saw something familiar. A face in a mirror, combing a short flaming-red bob. The neck spun.

"Our hair was our crowning glory!" a voice wailed. "Whyyyyyyyy did you cut it off?"

"That's it!" Abigail cried. "That's the Calamand!"

Nettle waved the memory aside with the snaghook. "In that case, this is the time bundle you're looking for." He gave a low bow and tossed the time bundle in the dirt. It seemed thicker and fluffier than the others, and it was so peppered with memories that the snowy time fibers were almost invisible.

Iris groaned. "Why does *her* time bundle have so many more memories than the others?"

"Two faces—so two sets of memories," Abigail said. "The Calamand's *and* her sister's."

"Now we sort them," Nettle said. He was already working over the time bundle, picking, brushing, combing, stopping periodically to sweep the clean tufts of time into a drawer on the right side of the cabinet. He swept the memories into a flat tray where they glinted in the late-afternoon light: red, yellow, blue.

Rufus took a tool that Nettle had set aside and poked at them gently, watching their barbed spines stretch, eager to attach themselves. It was funny how every object seemed to want something. Locks wanted to close. Seeds wanted to grow. Even old board games wanted to be played. What did memories want? To tell their story, he guessed. He let himself slip to the place between sleep and waking, wondering if he could hear them speak.

Such delicious cherry pie . . . She was ignoring me, as usual . . . Imagine what it would be like to . . . Ow, calf cramp! . . . Why is he staring at me? . . . What a funny dog! . . . She promised . . .

"The yellow ones are sensations," he said, opening his eyes. "Like loud, or hot, or yummy. The red ones are feelings. But the blue ones are different—they're like little stories."

"Very good, Pledge Lord," Nettle said, sweeping the last of the clean, brushed time into a drawer. "The brighter ones are the stories that have been told before—the memories that have been polished by being thought about again and again."

"So that means we're looking for a duller one," Rufus said. "Right?" He looked at Iris. "You said it would have to have been a new memory for her to lose it completely. Something that had just happened. Because she doesn't remember what she did with the—" He interrupted himself, remembering Nettle's presence.

"Time for you to go," he said for the second time that afternoon. "We can take it from here."

Nettle had been replacing the tools in the cabinet. He hovered in midair with his back to them, his shoulders hunched. "But you haven't found what you're looking for."

"I *said* we can take it from here," Rufus said. He could see the burr that he wanted. Pale blue, like an early morning sky.

Nettle shut the tool drawer. "As you wish, Pledge Lord." In a moment he had taken wing, fluttering out of the canopy of branches that kept them hidden and into the summer evening.

Rufus watched him until he was out of sight. Then he lifted the pale blue burr from the tray and flung it into the air.

⚬⚬⚬⚬

The barbs stretched and spread, weaving an intricate dome of fibers above their heads. The dome grew thicker, more solid, until it was a cloudless blue sky. Snatches of tinkling music and stray laughter wafted their way, as if from a distance. Beneath them, the ground rocked. Rufus looked around frantically, but he could only see a suffocating white that closed over his nose and mouth.

"Can I take it off yet? I hate this thing!" It was Mandolyn's voice, he realized, and then he understood. Her face was covered with the white scarf that was normally on the back of the Calamand's head. It was *her* memory they were inside.

"Just a moment, my music box." That was the Calamand's voice, with its ever-present note of merriment. "A second face might look out of place, and we're trying to be inconspicuous."

"You should have thought of that before you sliced me to pieces and stuck me on the back of your head," Mandolyn groused. "I never asked for any of this! But since I'm here, the least you could do is let me see the view!"

"You'll have a look when the time is right, and when I say right, I mean right about . . . now! Let's go for a spin, my little grin!"

The scarf lifted from his face just as Rufus felt himself lifted from the ground with a sudden lurch. A breeze ruffled his hair, one that smelled of popcorn and spun sugar. They were on a Ferris wheel, looking down on the Sardo Brothers carnival.

"Well, this is a panorama with panache!" the Calamand cried. "I spy, with my little eye, a busy-buzzy feyling queen. Do you see her? There, by the mermaid's wagon." She leaned forward, tipping the gondola and giving Mandolyn a glimpse of the swinging legs in the gondola above them. "Now why would a feyling go to a fair? Could she be looking for the locket in my pocket?"

The head spun on the Calamand's neck, and now Mandolyn faced front. She squinted over the side of the gondola. "How can you possibly see something so tiny from way up here?"

"I have a hawk's eyes, my sister, as you ought to know. Not like those blurry blue peepers *you* peer through. Plus I like eeny-weeny wittle playthings. I should catch her and make her my pet. Feylings can talk to locks, did you know that? We could keep her under our hat and take her out when things need unlocking."

"We don't wear a hat and there's no room under that horrible scarf for anyone but me." Mandolyn scanned the scene below. Rufus could feel her eagerness, her envy, an all-encompassing craving for a world that would always be out of reach. An organ-grinder played a tinny song, and a little dog danced on its hind legs. Children squealed as two puppets chased each other around a tiny stage. A crowd gathered to watch a man trying to knock down a pyramid of milk bottles with a baseball, and a line formed in front of the Corridor of Curiosities, which featured the Mermaid of the Distant Sea, the Bearded Baby, and the Canary-Voiced Man Who Can Sing Any Song.

"There's something interesting in the fortune-teller's caravan," the Calamand said, her face spinning forward again. "It sings to me like a little lark—it's the real deal, whatever it is. That sign says it's a Soothsayer Cabinet. I'd like to know what the future holds, wouldn't you?"

"Only if it tells me that I'll be free of you one day," retorted Mandolyn.

"Nonsense, baby boots. You're more precious to me than all the goods I've ever nicked. I'd never leave you behind—never-ever-ever! But a Soothsaying Cabinet might tell us where to find more loot, and whether anyone is on our trail. Let's just nip in and nab it, what do you say?"

Mandolyn shook her head, which meant shaking the Calamand's head as well. "You're too reckless," she chided. "You're going to get us caught. You said yourself there's a detective who wants to arrest us."

Calamandra laughed a long trilling laugh. "So nervy-nervous and anky-wankshus. Poor, sweet Mandolyn—not cut out for a life of crime. I'd kiss your cheek if it wasn't on the other side of my head." She kicked her feet out, rocking their floating basket. "I do love a carnival, don't you?" She threw her head back and sang a snatch of song.

A blue-sky day
and a starlight night.

We'll walk away
with our pants too tight.

"That's not my fault," grumbled Mandolyn. "*You're* the one who has to sample all the pies."

"And you're the one with the taste for hot dogs and fairy floss. That's what comes of having two mouths and one waist." The Calamand's hands grasped Mandolyn's and gave them a squeeze. "I'll tell you what, my shivery sister, one more heist and we'll be on our way to another world."

She stood up on her seat, causing the gondola to rock wildly. Mandolyn's face spun forward. "Stop!" she cried. "We're too high for your high jinks."

"Siddown before you break your neck!" the ride operator shouted from below. "Are you nuts, lady? Siddown!"

The Calamand laughed. "Wheeee!" she cried, doing a can-can kick. "Let's see what the future has in store for us!"

Something silver slipped from her pocket and tumbled through the air, but the Calamand didn't seem to notice.

"Catch it!" Iris shouted, but of course they weren't actually there. They could only watch as the ruler's locket sailed over the crowd and then landed with a splash in the sea-green tank of Palimsa, the Mermaid of the Distant Sea.

∼⟋⟋∽

The latticework of threads broke apart into a swirl of blue stars. *Ha-ha-ha!* laughed the Calamand, still dancing in her Ferris wheel seat. Or, no, she was dancing under a tree, clutching a blue box to her chest. *Ha-ha-ha!*

The stars spun and scattered and faded.

The Calamand's laughter drifted away.

Rufus blinked and looked around. His surroundings suddenly came into sharp focus: Abigail, pushing wisps of hair from her forehead as if waking from a dream. Iris, on his shoulder, weeping.

"It's okay," he said, lifting her from his shoulder so he could see her. "Don't cry. It's a clue, at least. More than we had before. We just have to find Palimsa the mermaid. She's one of the detectives, right?"

But Iris was wailing now, the sobs coming in angry croaks. "How could we have been so stupid?" she moaned. "Nettle led her right to us!"

Abigail rubbed her eyes. "Led who?"

Iris lifted her head and took a ragged breath. "Isn't it obvious? The Calamand was here, watching the whole thing. She knows where the locket is. And she's *taken* the time cabinet."

⚬⚬⚬

"How was the movie?" Rufus's father asked when Rufus came in. He was sitting on the living room couch surrounded by documents and papers.

"It was okay. The ending was a little too predictable," Rufus said. Iris had fallen asleep on the way home, and he gently set her down at the base of a potted plant, hoping he wouldn't wake her. He couldn't handle any more sobbing.

Rufus's mother came in, holding two mugs of tea. "Do you want one?" she asked. "The water's still hot."

Rufus nodded, a lump rising in his throat. He did want tea. A lot.

His mother handed him one of the mugs and put the other on the coffee table next to a stack of documents. "Are you feeling okay?" she asked, touching a hand to his cheeks. "You look flushed."

I lost the time cabinet, Rufus wanted to say. *I let my guard down and another terrible thing happened and now the Calamand knows where to find the ruler's locket.*

Instead, he swallowed until he'd cleared his throat of lumps. "Just tired. Abigail and I walked all over the place. She sold some T-shirts to the Carnival Museum."

"Well done, Abigail!" Rufus's father smiled at Rufus as his mother went back into the kitchen. "You both have turned out to be very enterprising."

Rufus shrugged and took a sip of tea. It was chamomile, with honey. *I'm so tired,* he wanted to say to his father. *I'm so tired of trying to be good at things that I'm not good at and trying to fix things I don't know how to fix. I'm so tired of everything going wrong.*

His father put down the papers he had been reading and rubbed his eyes with his thumb and forefinger. They sat like that for a few minutes, not talking.

Rufus's mother came in from the kitchen carrying her own mug of tea. "Aunt Chrissy didn't want to come in? I thought she picked you up at the movies."

"She was in a hurry to get home," Rufus said. "She said she had a bunch of important papers to read." He stared into his mug, letting the steam dampen his face.

"I hear Abigail's taking a couple weeks off from camp," his mom said. "Chrissy says she was feeling stressed out."

Rufus looked up from his mug. "Abigail doesn't really get stressed," he said. "She just wants to focus on her business."

"Abigail doesn't *say* she's stressed," his mother corrected. "That doesn't mean she isn't."

Rufus didn't say anything. Of course everyone was worried about *Abigail's* stress levels. She was the one with the awards and the accomplishments. People didn't worry about kids like him getting stressed out. They worried about kids like him not being "enterprising" enough.

"You've been working hard, too," his mother said. "Are you looking forward to Banking Camp next week?"

"Yeah," Rufus said, because he'd made a bargain with the universe.

His father studied him. "You don't sound excited."

"I am, though." Rufus looked into his mug of tea again, as if he might find a more convincing tone of voice inside its depths. "I'm just tired. Camp has turned out to be a really good experience."

His father leaned back, resting his long legs on the coffee table beside the stacks of papers. "I don't know if I've told you how proud I am of you. Not *just* because you excelled in the piranha tank. The most important thing is that you took advantage of the opportunity. You showed passion, Ru. Grit. Determination."

"Thanks," Rufus said. He smiled at his dad from across the tea mug even though tears were pricking his eyes. *Don't give up. Stick it out. Fall seven times and stand up eight. Blah blah blah.* But what if you *did* see something through, and then it got taken from you? What if you kept falling down, no matter how many times you got to your feet?

"We were thinking," his mother said. "Maybe you could postpone going to Banking Camp. If you wanted. There's another session later in the summer. We thought you might want to focus on Geezer and Grandson for a bit."

"Really?" Rufus looked from his mother to his father.

His father nodded. "Grandpa Jack said he patched the floorboards in the barn. He assures me it's safe to walk on. I inspected it myself and it seems pretty solid."

"Of course it is!" Rufus said. "Grandpa Jack can fix anything."

"He told me he's going to need your help if you're going to get the barn emptied out before the sale. We sign the papers on Monday. Thirty days after that, we'll be handing over the keys. Not that Feylawn *has* keys, but you get the idea."

"Thirty days!" Rufus said. "But what about Grandpa Jack? Where's he going to live?" The tears he'd been holding back filled his eyes. He looked down at his mug again. Stared right through to the bottom of the cup. *Don't cry,* he told himself. *Don't make a scene.*

"Grandpa Jack will be fine," his father said. "Maybe he'll stay with us for a while. You'd see more of him that way."

Rufus tried to smile. At least they weren't talking about Grandpa Jack moving to a retirement community like Orchard Meadows.

"I'd like you to come with us to meet with Mr. Gneiss," his father continued. "We have some last details to go over on Sunday. I want you to come along and see what we're going to be part of."

"*We?*" Rufus said. "*We're* not going to be part of anything. Feylawn will be gone."

"Not gone," his father said. "Reimagined. Trust me, Ru. You're going to be proud of what we've come up with."

33

A GLOMPER THING

Rufus had barely crossed the threshold of the barn on Saturday when Grandpa Jack wrapped him in a hug. He was out of his soft cast now, and able to give Rufus a good strong squeeze with both arms. "I've missed you," he said when he released him. "And now your dad tells me you can come by as much as you want."

"For a week, anyway," Rufus said. "And then, in a month . . ." He couldn't even say it.

"I know," Grandpa Jack said. He took off his khaki cap and ran a hand through his hair. "Could be worse, I suppose. They could be turning the place into one of those big box stores. I hate those things. You go in looking for a roll of tape and you walk out with seventeen bags of Lord knows what. I bought myself a beard trimmer the other day. Why do I need a beard trimmer—I don't even have a beard!"

"You could grow one," Rufus suggested.

"Robin-Ella said the same thing," Grandpa Jack said.

"She said she liked beards, which is probably what put the thought in my head. But I can't blame her for the muffin tins. That was my own foolishness."

"That doesn't sound foolish to me. You bake muffins all the time."

"In muffin tins!" Grandpa Jack said. "That I already own!" He shook his head. "And here I am trying to get rid of things. Speaking of which . . ."

He gestured at the stacks of crates and boxes at the back of the barn. For as long as Rufus had been alive, the stacks had reached from floor to ceiling and taken up most of the right half of the barn. Now they were hardly taller than Rufus, and there were places where he could see the dusty corners that had long been hidden from view. *When the boxes are gone*, Rufus thought, *that'll be the end.*

Now that the holes in the floorboards were patched, Grandpa Jack had moved some tables from the barn's assortment of mismatched furniture to the front of the barn so they could sort through the cartons without moving them to the house. There was a stack of newspaper for wrapping up fragile items, and another stack of empty boxes to fill with the sorted and labeled items they wanted to sell.

They worked for a while without saying much of anything besides "What do you think Robin-Ella will make of this?" and "Customers always like these!" and, very rarely, "Some things really are trash, no matter how you look at them."

Finally Rufus asked the question he'd been avoiding

asking, because asking it would be admitting that it might actually happen. "What are they going to do here? Mr. Gneiss and Dad, I mean."

"And Aunt Chrissy," Grandpa Jack said. "It'll be a partnership." He reached into a box and pulled out an old-fashioned telephone, the kind with a dial that you stuck your finger in to make a call.

"But what will they be *doing* here?" Rufus asked. He swallowed, almost unable to bear hearing the answer.

"Science," Grandpa Jack said at last. "Some sort of pharmaceutical laboratory. I admit my attention seems to wander whenever they try to explain it to me."

"Pharmaceutical? You mean like pills?" Rufus asked. Alastair Gruen and Mr. Diggs had told him they wanted the train so they could turn the Seeds of Life into pills that allowed people to live forever. But as far as he knew, the goblins couldn't travel to the Green World to get the Seeds of Life without the train. So why would Mr. Gneiss be talking about pills?

"They're starting out with vitamins, supplements, things like that. I've been trying to look on the bright side," Grandpa Jack said. "We'll be helping heal sick people, right?"

Rufus scowled. "I can't imagine that goblins care about sick people."

"Don't be that way, Rufus," Grandpa Jack said. "This Mr. Gneiss fellow seems like a perfectly decent guy, goblin or no." He placed the heavy black telephone in the box marked *Old Soul Vintage*. "Still," he admitted. "I haven't been able to bring myself to take the pills he gave me."

Rufus put down the set of drinking glasses he'd been packing in newsprint. "He gave you pills?" A phrase floated into his mind—something the Crinnyeyes had said. *Little pills for every ill.*

"Herbal supplements to improve my vision," Grandpa Jack said. "Chrissy mentioned how I stopped wearing glasses. She thinks I'm refusing to admit I have eyesight troubles. Mr. Gneiss said he had just the thing."

"But you didn't take them?" Rufus tried to keep his voice casual.

Grandpa Jack shook his head. "Told the others I advised against it. So did your mother, incidentally. Said she didn't believe in vitamins and the like. Chrissy swears by hers, though."

"Can you show them to me?" Rufus asked. "When we get back to the house?"

"If you like. Not much to see." Grandpa Jack gave Rufus's shoulder a squeeze. "I never was one for popping pills, but it makes your dad happy to think Feylawn will be helping folks stay healthy. And it seems to me that having a lab here won't interfere too much with the critters."

"Feylawn wasn't *meant* to be a lab," Rufus protested. "It's meant to be what it is. Wild."

"Well, we got to see it," Grandpa Jack said. "That's something, isn't it? I'm grateful I took my glasses off and had a good look before I had to go."

⚬๏๛๏๛๏⚬

The pill bottle Grandpa Jack handed Rufus had a flowery label that said FEYLAWN PHARMACEUTICAL BRIGHT-EYES BLEND ALL-NATURAL HERBAL SUPPLEMENT.

"That Gneiss fellow said they're plant extracts that help you see better," Grandpa Jack said.

They were sitting on the wraparound porch with a pitcher of lemonade and a plate of blueberry muffins between them.

Rufus opened the cap and poured a pill into his hand. The pills were pale orange and had a soft glow to them. He listened to see if they would speak, but they didn't.

"I want to show these to Iris. Can I borrow them?"

"Be my guest." Grandpa Jack handed Rufus a muffin. "Wasn't planning on taking them anyway. I like how I see just fine." He squinted over Rufus's shoulder. "Looks like Abigail's here. I'll go get another lemonade glass."

"Where have you been?" Rufus asked when Abigail came up the steps of the porch. "I thought we were going to figure out our next move."

"Sorry." Abigail settled in one of the porch's wicker chairs. "I ran into Loubella on my way here. She can't find Bobalo. He's been missing since yesterday. And she said another cotter's missing, too. Oolissa."

"Sounds like Bobalo's met somebody new," Rufus said. "You know how cotters are."

"But Bobalo said a badness was coming." Abigail helped herself to a muffin. "The day the scrygrass bloomed. He said it would separate him from Loubella. And it's not just him. The geese had their feathers ruffled by something. The umbrals were circling. Everyone's anxious. Unsettled."

"Of *course* they're anxious," Rufus said. "They're about to lose their home. Let's focus on finding Palimsa, the mermaid detective. The ruler's locket dropped in her tank. Assuming she went back to her world after the Calamand's arrest, she could very well still have it."

"I did some reading today," Abigail said. "According to *Luminous Legends*, Palimsa comes from a place called the Realms—I think it's a kind of aquatic world. And if I'm reading the chart right, the Moving Meadow goes there. Tomorrow, at two fourteen in the afternoon. It'll be on the ridge this time. Not far from where the graveyard is."

"Good," Rufus said. That was something, at least.

Abigail still hadn't taken a bite of her muffin. "There's one problem."

Rufus waited. Abigail examined the muffin. He was just about to ask her if she'd recently gotten a job at a baked-goods appraisal service when she finally spoke.

"I have an admission interview tomorrow afternoon. At Stormweather Prep. At two."

"Who cares?" Rufus couldn't believe what he was hearing. "The future of Feylawn is at stake!"

"I have to go, Rufus. My mom will kill me if I don't show up. The school's not even officially accepting applications. They scheduled the interview especially for me, on a *weekend*."

"But—" Rufus couldn't even find words. "It's our only chance. The Calamand saw exactly what we saw. If we don't go tomorrow, she'll get there first."

"You have to go without me. I'm sorry."

"But we *need* you! You're the one with a brain!"

"You'll be fine." Abigail bit into her muffin at last. "You're the one with seed speech, and you'll have Iris."

Rufus tried to answer, but the words snagged in his throat. He got up and ran down the steps. "Tell Grandpa Jack I'll be back in a bit," he said over his shoulder.

"Rufus," Abigail said. "Wait!"

But Rufus was already walking down the path toward the barn, refusing to look back.

⸙

He walked blindly at first, the emotions of the past twenty-four hours rushing over him in waves. Then his stride lengthened and soon he was running through the trees, shoving aside the low branches that blocked his path, scattering birds and squirrels. He ran for a long time, until his breaths came in gasps that felt like sobs. Then he slowed and stood in a clearing with his hands on his knees, panting. The air was warm and filled with the peppery smells of bay and oak. He could hear the chatter of seeds, mixed with the whisper of the summer wind and the trills of songbirds. It was all so beautiful he thought his heart might shatter into pieces. There *had* to be some way to save it.

Something wet grazed his elbow. He turned to find Shamok nudging him with his nose.

"What were you hunting?" the leopard asked.

Rufus squatted in the leaf litter and stroked the leopard's forehead. "Nothing. I was just running."

Shamok's ears flickered. "Why?"

"I don't know. Feels good to do when you're mad."

"Like roaring." Shamok rubbed his cheek against Rufus's hand. "You've lost something important and nobody cares."

"I guess you could say that."

"And without it, you're not yourself."

Rufus wrapped his arms around Shamok's neck. "Exactly."

"You think you might die." The leopard's breath was warm on his back.

Rufus nodded. The memory of Garnet's warning prickled his skin.

"We are the same," Shamok said. "You too have lost your spots. Come, we will sit in the sun and listen for rabbits."

They moved through the woods side by side until they came to the bank of the creek. The water rollicked along as it always did, swirling and shimmering, green-gold with reflected trees. Rufus sat in the gravel and settled into the quiet that had always come to him at Feylawn. Shamok lay beside him, white chin resting on his golden paws.

Iris landed on the gravel beside them.

"See any sign of one?"

"Sign of what?"

"A janati goose nest. I thought Trinket was on the verge of building one, but I haven't seen her for days."

Rufus shook his head. "I was just—"

"Saying goodbye to it? Before the goblin bulldozers roll in?"

"No! I'm not giving up. The meadow goes to the Realms tomorrow afternoon at two fourteen. We're going to find Palimsa and get the locket."

Iris cocked her head to one side. "It's a glomper thing, isn't it?"

"What?"

"Optimism. Never giving up. Thinking there's lint at the end of the toenail. That sort of thing."

"Light at the end of the tunnel," Rufus corrected. "And that's not usually my attitude. My dad says I need more grit."

"If that's what *grit* is, you and your cousin could do with quite a bit *less*."

Shamok lifted his head from his paws. "You've lost *your* spots, too," he observed.

"I never *had* spots," Iris snapped. "I was just dumb enough to think it was better to try to *do* something than to watch everything fall apart. But I'm not the queen, and I've done all I can." She coughed into her fist. "The Green World feylings are on the edge of outright rebellion about having to do so many chores. The train comes in two days and they can't wait to be on it."

Rufus looked at the line of brown on Iris's left wing. It had thickened and spread. Her time in the Blue World was taking its toll. "Two more days is just enough time to find the mermaid," he said. "All we have to do is figure out how to locate her when we get to the Realms."

Iris struck her forehead with the heel of her hand. "You really don't get it, do you? The Calamand has the time cabinet, and she knows where the locket is. It's over. We've lost."

"No, we haven't!" Rufus protested. "We just have to get there before she does. The Moving Meadow will take us there *tomorrow*."

"The Calamand doesn't have to wait for the Moving Meadow. She knows more ways between the worlds than we ever will—you don't become Thief of the Eight Worlds without knowing every back door and secret passage."

"It's true," Shamok said in a low growl. "Now that she's out of her prison, she comes and goes as she pleases. She was here this morning. I stalked her, but by the time I drew close, she was gone."

Iris slumped. "We need to face facts, Rufus. Feylawn is finished. If we're lucky, the Green World feylings and I can escape before Diggs can get the train." She ran her hands through her tangled hair. "I'm sorry. I shouldn't have gotten your hopes up."

"My *hopes* up?" Rufus felt like pitching her into the creek. "You make me sound like a kid who wanted to go to Six Flags. I'm trying to save Feylawn. What will happen to all the creatures here if the goblins get it?"

Iris wouldn't look at him. "Things die in your world, Rufus. We've been over this."

"*Individual* things die. And then new ones are supposed to be born. The things that live here don't have anywhere to go. The umbrals. The cotters. Those weird women from the well. All the magical plants—"

"Don't forget the janati geese," Iris said. "This is the only place they can lay their eggs. And there are quite a few more creatures you haven't encountered yet. You'd have liked the vallomills."

"You sound as if you don't care."

Iris got to her feet. "I *do* care. I care more than anything. I care about Feylawn and I care about the Blue World, which we're supposed to protect from the goblins and their mania for destroying everything that's quiet and beautiful. But I don't like the way caring about all those things makes me feel, particularly when there's absolutely nothing I can do to change what's going to happen. I'd rather go back to the

Green World and get lost in the present than watch every-thing be destroyed." She rose into the air and then turned back to circle Shamok's head.

"You'll need to find somewhere else to go," she said. "Try to find your way back to Imura. It's all that's left."

And then she was gone.

34

SACRIFICES

"W here *is* this place?" Rufus asked from the back seat of the car. He and his parents were on their way to meet Mr. Gneiss at the offices of the Dees-Troy Property Group.

"Not much farther," his dad said from the passenger seat. "This project—what we're going to be part of—it needs to be somewhere out of the way. That's what makes Feylawn so perfect." He turned around to squeeze Rufus's knee. "You'll be excited when you learn about it, Ru. Sometimes you get to be part of something that's bigger than yourself."

His mother was behind the wheel, her hair still pulled back in its night-shift ponytail. She hadn't been to sleep since getting off work that morning, and the pillows under her eyes looked like they were resting on pillows of their own. She met Rufus's eyes in the rearview mirror, her gaze steady. She'd moved beyond the reassuring-smile stage of things. Her face simply said, *I'm sorry.*

The Dees-Troy office was in an unremarkable prefab concrete building that could have held anything—a veterinary clinic, a government office, a janitorial company. Aunt Chrissy and Abigail were waiting for them inside the front door, in a sparse anteroom with a few plastic chairs and a plastic table covered with old magazines. Abigail sat on one of the chairs with her hands folded in her lap. She was wearing a blue-and-white dress with a navy blazer, and white sandals with a wedge heel. Her hair was loose and neatly brushed. She looked like someone he'd never met. Abigail's older sister, maybe. She smiled at Rufus but he turned away. If she thought getting into Stormweather Prep was more important than saving Feylawn, he had nothing to say to her.

There were a few awkward minutes while the adults told Abigail how nice she looked, and then Mr. Gneiss ushered them into a windowless conference room furnished with a conference table and an assortment of chairs. Rufus looked around the room for signs of Mr. Diggs, but Mr. Gneiss seemed to be the only goblin present.

"So glad the whole family could come. Help yourself to refreshments!" He gestured to a carafe of coffee and a box of pastries in the center of the table and waited for everyone to take their seats.

"Rufus and Abigail, you're the guests of honor here. Your parents told me that you're not entirely on board with our project. I understand that completely. Who wouldn't be attached to a place as pretty as Grandpa's estate? Mom and Dad may feel one way, but kids know things grown-ups don't, am I right?" He winked at them, and Rufus felt the hairs on the back of his neck prickle. Gneiss must have known Rufus and Abigail could see his crocodile feet and tail, his fanged underbite. What was the purpose of this whole display?

"Depends on the kid," Abigail said. "Depends on the grown-up."

"I see why you say she's the smart one!" Mr. Gneiss said, grinning at Aunt Chrissy.

"They're both smart," Rufus's mom said. She poured herself a cup of coffee, looking exhausted and out of patience.

"Well, the first thing you need to know, Rufus and Abigail, is that the place you love so much—the place we'll be calling Feylawn Pharmaceutical—is hardly going to change at all. We'll be preserving a good portion of the grounds exactly as they are today. Grandpa insisted on that, and he holds the deed, so his word is law!"

"Are you related to us?" Rufus asked.

Mr. Gneiss blinked.

"Because you keep calling him *Grandpa*, like he's *your* grandpa, too, and I figured if he isn't your grandpa, you'd call him Mr. Collins." Rufus looked around the table. "But what do I know? I'm not 'the smart one.'"

Mr. Gneiss laughed. "Fair enough! Fair enough! Sometimes we Californians can get a little too informal. Thank you for the reminder, Rufus. As I was saying, we respect

Mr. Collins's wishes." He pushed a key on his laptop to begin a PowerPoint presentation. The first slide showed a map. Rufus recognized it at once—Feylawn, as if seen from the air.

"In this map you can see that we're able to save the orchard, a portion of the forest, and of course the creek."

"What about the rest of it?" Rufus asked. "And why does it say 'breeding lab' next to the orchard?" On the map Feylawn was covered by square lines meant to represent buildings, roads, and parking lots. The "portion" of the forest being saved was tiny, and the meadow was completely gone. Even the Boulder Dude had disappeared.

Mr. Gneiss clicked to the next slide, which showed a group of happy children of different races frolicking in a field of flowers. "Let me ask *you* a question, Rufus. What if you could improve the well-being of humans around the world? Wouldn't you think a small personal sacrifice was worth it?"

"Improve their well-being how?" Abigail interjected. She was eating a frosted donut in small, careful bites so as not to get crumbs on her dress.

"With science and technology!" Mr. Gneiss said, flipping to a slide of scientists in lab coats looking through microscopes. "By using genetic engineering to create compounds that not only cure diseases, but cure aspects of humanity itself. What if we could help compatible people fall in love? What if we could force criminals to tell the truth? What if we could extend the human life span? While we're not there yet, we are discovering amazing new chemicals all the time. Many of them may even reside among the rare and unusual species you have at Feylawn! Our researchers have focused on the problems that have plagued humans for millennia. Busy executives who don't have enough hours in the day will be interested in our formula for increasing productivity, for example."

"TIME IS MONEY!" Aunt Chrissy boomed. "And we'll be minting it—thanks to Mr. Gneiss!" She fluttered her eyelashes at the goblin.

Mr. Gneiss had clicked to a new slide. This one showed the forest at Feylawn, a plant that Rufus had never seen before, a molecule, and a pill, each connected to the next by an arrow.

"I thought you'd like this part, Rufus," Rufus's father said. "It turns out that Feylawn may have plant species that science doesn't even know about yet. Maybe that's why you couldn't find those seeds of yours in a field guide. They're unknown species!"

"*Valuable* unknown species!" Aunt Chrissy added.

"Quite true," Mr. Gneiss said. "You know it firsthand, right, Chrissy? How are you all enjoying the vitamins I gave you? Chrissy? Adam? Want to tell the kids about your experience with our all-natural herbal remedies?"

Rufus looked around in alarm. "I don't think people should be taking pills without a prescription," he blurted.

"I agree," Rufus's mom said. "Just because something comes from nature doesn't mean it's safe."

"Of course, of course," Mr. Gneiss said. He never disagreed with anyone, Rufus noticed. "You're right to be cautious, Emi! But the supplements we provide are absolutely harmless, and rigorously tested to the highest standards. And I think they might help with your fatigue! Adam, are you finding them useful?"

"I find them *extremely* useful," Aunt Chrissy interrupted, holding up a bottle labeled VITAMIN C+. "They make me *youthful*. And I'm being truthful." She giggled. "I can't be neutral!"

"They've worked for me as well," Rufus's father said. "I was kind of low after my accident, but these Smile-A-Day vitamins have really helped me stay positive."

Mr. Gneiss smiled at Rufus and Abigail. "I know you kids love Grandpa's farm, but your loss is going to be the world's gain. We're going to take Feylawn's natural wealth and spread it around. Don't you think that's worth the small sacrifice of your personal playground?"

"What kind of sacrifice are *you* making?" Rufus asked. "Are you going to be giving these pills away for free?" He saw his father frown and mentally kicked himself. He had sworn to himself that he wouldn't do this.

"It's a fair question," Rufus's mom said. "Prescription drugs are often too expensive to help the people who need them most."

Mr. Gneiss's crocodile tail twitched from side to side like an irritated cat's, but he gave a pleasant chuckle. "So true. So true! And in an ideal world, all medications, vitamins, and supplements *would* be free. But in the *real* world, the research we do is extraordinarily expensive. We have to pay money to our researchers and our investors! So *our* sacrifice is in the form of hard work!"

Rufus's father nodded. "Feylawn is going to be a top-tier laboratory that develops innovative solutions to all kinds of problems. It's the kind of thing I always dreamed of being part of."

"Adam's joining our team," Mr. Gneiss said, clapping Rufus's father on the back. "He'll be on the board of Feylawn Pharmaceutical, helping guide our corporate vision."

Rufus's father beamed. "It's a dream come true."

Rufus looked around the table. Everyone was smiling except his mother, who was contemplating her cup of coffee as if there were a bug floating in it, and Abigail, who looked as if she'd earned a ninth-degree black belt in unreadable facial expressions.

He took a breath. "Congratulations on the new job, Dad," he said. "This looks like a really worthwhile project."

Rufus's father reached over to ruffle his hair. "Thanks, Ru. Thanks for being so mature."

Abigail flashed her politician's smile. "Congratulations, Uncle Adam," she said. "And congratulations to you, too,

Mom." She turned to smile at Aunt Chrissy. "I know you worked hard on this deal."

"YOU BET I DID!" Aunt Chrissy bellowed. "Now you kids can go wait for us in the hall. We've got some papers to look at. Here." She shoved the bakery box at them. "Take the pastries."

⚬⚬⚬

"What do you *really* think?" Abigail said. They were in the waiting area. Rufus had slumped into one of the plastic chairs. Abigail put the bakery box on the plastic table and picked out a raspberry Danish.

"You *know* what I think," Rufus said, helping himself to a chocolate croissant. "And I know what *you* think." He took a bite and found he could barely swallow it. "But the profits from selling Feylawn will cover the tuition of your fancy new school, so maybe that's all that matters."

"You don't have to be like that." Abigail bit into the Danish, showering her blazer with powdered sugar. "I'm just as upset as you are. That whole presentation looked like they just grabbed a bunch of sciencey images from the Internet and threw them into a slideshow. That molecule on the slide? That was plain old aspirin. I made one with marshmallows for the science fair in fourth grade. I mean, yes, it comes from a plant, but it was discovered in the 1800s. It's not exactly an unknown species or whatever Mr. Gneiss said."

Rufus looked at the croissant, which was easier than

looking at Abigail. "The point isn't to be *upset*. The point is to *do* something about it."

He tossed his half-eaten croissant back in the pastry box and walked down the narrow, industrial-looking hallway. The doors were bare and unmarked and—Rufus found after jiggling the handles—locked. He tried each one of them, not even sure what he was looking for. Information? Evidence? A way to convince his parents to change their minds? He just knew that he had to do *something*, and that he was going to have to do it alone, because nobody else cared about Feylawn as much as he did.

"Rufus," Abigail hissed from behind him. "What are you looking for?"

"What do you care?" Rufus jiggled another doorknob.

"I care a lot! But what am I supposed to do? I can't just *not go*. It's a huge opportunity."

Rufus turned to look at her. "Do you *want* to go to Stormweather Prep?"

"That's not the point!" Abigail said. "She's my mom. I have to do what she says."

Rufus kept walking. It *was* the point. He had thought Abigail was his actual friend. They'd go to the same school in the fall, maybe even find other kids to hang out with who didn't think he was weird just because he liked nature. But Abigail was always going to be Abigail, doing special Abigail things, and he was always going to be Rufus, marching to the beat of a different drummer.

In front of him was a door marked LABORATORY. He shook the handle. Locked.

"I wish Iris was here," he said.

Abigail gave him a sideways look. "I thought *you* could talk to locks."

Rufus shrugged. "It didn't go that well the last time I tried."

"It was your first time. Try again."

If he listened, Rufus could hear the locks' dreary chant, spoken in their guttural language of clicks and twists. *Keep in. Keep out. Keep in. Keep out.*

There was a cold spot at the back of his throat. A metal taste on the tip of his tongue.

Open, he said silently, and the lock obeyed.

VALUABLE UNKNOWN SPECIES

Cages. At first that was all Rufus could take in. Cages and cages and cages, in stacks and rows, large and small. In the center of the room was an operating table, with a tray of tools and powerful lamps set up beside it. A long counter along the wall held microscopes and more tools and tubes. The room was white and sterile.

"What *is* this?" Abigail asked.

There was a rattle from one of the cages. "Knuckleball. Emissary? Goggle!"

"Trinket?" Abigail looked wildly about. "Where are you?"

"Shoehorn?" honked the goose. "Wistful! Gorge!"

Abigail followed the honks to a cage at the top of the last row. Trinket sat with her bill pressed against the wire squares of the cage, surrounded by leaves and branches.

"Looks like they wanted her to build a nest," she observed. She lifted Trinket from the cage and held her close to her chest. The goose's white feathers were dirty. She tucked her head under Abigail's chin and shut her eyes.

"She says the person who took her had two faces," Abigail's eyes were shut, her expression rapt, as if listening to far-off music.

"The Calamand!" Rufus squinted at Abigail. "Wait—are you *talking* to Trinket right now?" He'd imagined she did it by making animal noises, the way she'd done with the umbrals.

Abigail opened her eyes. "I guess I am. It's not words, though. It's more like . . . feelings."

Rufus walked around the room, looking at the various scientific instruments, many still in boxes. "Diggs and Gruen talked about synthesizing the Seeds of Life in a lab," he said, examining the label on one of the boxes. "But if that's what they're doing, why do they need all these cages?"

He picked up a clipboard from one of the counters. Someone had been making notes on it, under the heading *FEYLAWN FAUNA: POTENTIAL USES/MARKETS.*

"Fauna is animals, right?" he asked Abigail.

She nodded and came over to look, still holding Trinket. The handwriting was hard to make out, and some of the writing used symbols similar to the goblin writing they'd seen scratched on the lock. But the few English words told them plenty.

> JANATI—known to be temperamental and
> unpredictable. Will need hatchery to
> determine how to influence egg-laying.
> UMBRAL—large, destructive. Will need
> special equipment due to electrical
> disruptions. Many military applications.
> Initial attempts to extract dimpsy
> smoke unsuccessful—specimen
> refrigerated.
> COTTERS—distillation of sample
> specimens produced effective "love
> potion" lasting 24–36 hours on human
> subject. Side effect: rhyming.

Abigail gasped. "Those vitamins my mom's taking! Do you think that's why she's been flirting with Mr. Gneiss?" She took the clipboard from Rufus's hands and read aloud. "'Wide potential consumer market. Suggest begin with five hundred breeding pairs, harvest babies at fourteen weeks. Sample breeding pair under observation.'"

"Harvest!" Rufus said. "Does that mean *kill?*" He felt a swell of nausea.

Abigail's eyes filled with tears. "That's exactly what it means. They're making pills from dead cotters." She kicked the tray of operating tools and sent them clattering to the floor. "No wonder all the animals have been so frightened.

They saw what was coming. The goblins are planning to kill every animal in Feylawn, or lock it in a lab."

Half strangled in Abigail's grip, Trinket clucked anxiously. "Slug primp. Riddance."

Rufus looked at the notes again. *Specimen refrigerated.* There were stainless-steel refrigerator drawers on one wall of the lab. He pulled open one of the drawers and quickly shut it again.

"What is it?" Abigail asked, coming to stand beside him.

"You don't want to see."

"Show me."

Abigail's jaw was set as Rufus pulled open the drawer. A baby umbral lay on its back on a stainless-steel tray, surrounded by dissection tools. It had lost the inky luster it had when it was alive and was now just a faded black scrap with a tiny pointed tail. Its white eyes were open and staring, its tiny mouth closed in a breathless gash. The squirmy creatures had given him the creeps when they were alive, but now Rufus remembered their tiny piping cries, the violet tongues lapping up reflections, the way they'd come to his and Abigail's rescue and saved them from the goblins. A sob rose in his chest, a storm of fury and sorrow.

Abigail slammed the refrigerator drawer closed.

"It was just a *baby,*" she cried. "It never hurt *anyone!*" She looked around wildly. "Trinket said there are others here. Other animals. We have to check every one of the cages."

They started at opposite ends of the lab, peering through the mesh of one cage after another, flinging open drawers and cabinets. Trinket waddled behind them, sticking her beak into cages and honking inquisitively. Slowly the creatures began to accumulate: eight mice with enormous eyes and orange whiskers. A pair of large rose-colored toads. A dozen pale white bees.

"*This* is what our parents think is so amazing," Rufus burst out. "Putting wild creatures in a lab and—" He yanked at the wire mesh of an open cage, wanting to pull the whole thing to the floor, obliterate it. His parents were part of this. His *dad*.

"That's only because the goblins made it sound different from what it is," Abigail said, trying to fit the toads into blazer pockets that were already overflowing with mice and bees. "We'll tell them the truth and—"

She stopped suddenly and yanked open the door of a cage near the back. "Oh no. Rufus—come here."

She drew out two small, limp orange bodies. "It's Bobalo. And this must be Oolissa."

"Are they . . . ?" Rufus asked. He couldn't bring himself to say the word.

Bobalo's green eyes fluttered open. "Abby-gell," he said weakly. "You were always . . . one of . . . my fav . . ." His eyes drooped shut.

Abigail's eyes filled with tears. "Oh, Bobalo! What happened to you?"

"Cally-mand . . ." The cotter trembled violently. "Then gobby-lin . . ." He hauled himself up to her shoulder with his suction-cup paws and hid behind the curtain of her hair. "Bobalo isn't liking knives and cages," he murmured.

Oolissa lay limp in Abigail's hands. She moaned and rubbed her eyes with her paws. "Where is Wassapite?" she whispered. "Of Wassapite I must . . . recite . . . morning . . . afternoon . . . and—"

"Night," Abigail finished hastily. "It's okay, don't recite right now. You're too weak."

"Wassapite . . . makes me . . . weak," the cotter moaned. "Of Wassapite . . . I . . . must always . . . sp . . . sp . . . sp . . ."

"Speak!" Abigail said. "It's okay. We'll get you back to him." She looked at Rufus. "Wassapite must be her mate. We need to get them out of here. Can you take Trinket and the bees? They've promised to be good."

"Great," Rufus said as the bees flew to him and burrowed into the button pocket of his shorts. He lifted the goose awkwardly and made for the door.

But the door was already opening.

"Why is it," rasped a familiar voice, "that you children always seem to be taking things that belong to me?"

⚶⚶

Mr. Diggs had gained some weight since leaving the island of Imura, and he had acquired a new mustard-yellow suit.

He stepped into the room, his talons clicking on the linoleum floor.

"I don't like children," he said. "But I'm beginning to understand why people say they bring joy to hardened hearts. The look of horror on your childish faces is something I'll always savor."

Rufus stepped backward, trying to put as much distance between himself and Mr. Diggs as he could. Garnet's words echoed in his head. *You've embarrassed him, Rufus Takada Collins. Traditionally, that means he'll seek your death.*

"You can't hurt us!" he said, hoping it was true. "Our parents are right down the hall."

"Your parents," Mr. Diggs said. "My good friends and business partners. They won't be happy to learn that you've tried to steal my pet goose."

"She's *not* yours!" Abigail said. She'd somehow managed to conceal both cotters beneath her hair, which she'd fanned over her shoulders.

"Relish!" hissed Trinket from Rufus's arms. "Sepia!"

Diggs clicked closer, his eyes locked on theirs.

"How wrong you are," Diggs said. "Every part of Feylawn is mine. Mine to use. Mine to destroy. My trees to fell for timber. My rocks to shatter into gravel. My plants. My animals. My feylings, to labor in my factories. And soon, oh so soon, my *train*."

Rufus was backing up as Mr. Diggs advanced. He clutched Trinket close to his chest, unsure if he was protecting her or hoping that she would protect him. What would Iris do in this situation? Pull out a seed of some sort, he guessed. His baggie of seeds was in the pocket of his shorts, but he had no idea which one to use and no time to slip into the place where he could ask the seeds themselves.

His heel hit the back wall, then his shoulder. As he pressed against it, a steel lever dug into his kidneys.

A door. He reached a hand behind him to push the lever but it didn't budge. The door was locked.

"You don't own them yet!" Abigail said. "And you never will. We'll tell our parents what you're *really* planning to do."

"They may find your story a bit hard to believe," Mr. Diggs replied. "Invisible imps who live in the apricots. Talking geese with valuable eggs. Shadowy creatures that blow purple smoke. Storybook stuff."

"My grandfather knows about Feylawn," Rufus said. "And *he* has to sign the papers." Grandpa Jack would never sign, not when he and Abigail explained what Diggs and Gneiss were planning.

"But he *has* signed the papers," said Mr. Diggs. He pulled a document from the breast pocket of his suit and held it out for them to see.

And there it was. The fountain-pen flourish of Grandpa Jack's signature.

"It's just paper," Abigail said. "It doesn't mean anything. Feylawn belongs to the feylings."

Mr. Diggs raised a fist in the air in a mocking power salute. "Feylawn for the feylings!" he chanted. "All-out war until the glompers are all out!" He smiled, revealing the pointed teeth of his lower jaw. "I encouraged that nonsense when it was useful to me. But now you glompers *are* all out, and it's time to put away childish things. Nettle Pampaspatch and his All-Outers always worked for me. As will the rest of the feylings, once my plans are in place."

Rufus didn't say a word. He was listening, but not to Mr. Diggs. He was listening to the guttural chant of the locked door behind him.

Shut. Keep out. Locked. Keep in.

He tasted the key at the back of his throat. *Open,* he said silently, and felt the click.

He had no idea what was on the other side, but he pushed the door open anyway.

"Abigail!" he yelled. "RUN!"

36

THE WHOLE PACKAGE

The door opened onto some kind of loading dock. Rufus had a vague impression of parked trucks and forklifts as he sprinted through with Abigail behind him. Mr. Diggs clattered after them, the click of his talons echoing through the desolate parking lot.

"I'm not fast!" the goblin called. "But I don't get tired."

"This way," Abigail called, sprinting past Rufus. "The cars—"

And there they were. Aunt Chrissy's red SUV and his family's old green Toyota, parked near the entrance to the building. Aunt Chrissy was leaning against the driver's-side door, punching something into her phone.

Trinket wriggled in his arms.

"Let her go. She says she's strong enough to fly back to Feylawn on her own," Abigail said. "She'll take the bees."

"Scooter vacate," Trinket honked. She plucked at Rufus's collar with her beak. "Marshmallow."

Rufus tossed her into the air. The goose stretched her neck and flapped into the sky. The bees lifted from his pocket and followed her in a swarm.

Aunt Chrissy looked up. "There you are!" she shouted. "Where have you been? We've been looking for you!" Then she caught sight of Mr. Diggs and her face gentled into a smile. "Mr. Diggs! How nice to see you! We missed you at today's meeting."

"I found your children poking around the building," Mr. Diggs said. "You need to keep an eye on them, Ms. Vasquez. We have some dangerous compounds in our laboratories. Not safe for kids." He gave Rufus and Abigail a long look.

"I'm so sorry they gave you trouble," Aunt Chrissy said as Mr. Diggs turned to go. "Get in the car, Abigail." She turned back to her phone.

Abigail nodded and made her way to the side of the SUV, cradling the two cotters under her chin. Rufus followed her.

"Here," Abigail whispered, holding them out to him. "You can take them back to Feylawn."

Rufus had never held one before. They were surprisingly soft. Bobalo scampered up his shoulder, but Oolissa wrapped her arms around his finger and squeezed it tight.

"What is your name?" she asked weakly.

"Ru—" he began, and then thought better of it. "It doesn't matter."

The little cotter gazed up at him with her wide green eyes.

"I thought I'd die without my Wassapite," she murmured. "But you will do, Boy Called Ru. Shall we be bonded?"

"Uh, thanks," Rufus said. "But you should hold out for What's-a-pie. I'll get you to him soon."

"I'll get *you* the moon," whispered Oolissa. "I'll get it soon. And then you'll swoon."

Abigail opened the door of the SUV, her face troubled. "It helps keep them quiet if you rub their armpits."

Rufus watched his parents come out of the Dees-Troy office building and make their way across the parking lot, caught up in their own conversation.

"Iris isn't coming with me to the Realms," he blurted.

"What?" Abigail stared at him.

"She's given up," he said. "She thinks we should too."

"You can't go alone," Abigail said, keeping her voice low. "You're not thinking of it, are you?"

"What choice do I have?" Rufus said. "You've seen what Diggs is planning. We have to get the ruler's locket before the Calamand does."

"I—" Abigail started to say, but then Rufus's parents were upon them.

"We're going to grab some lunch," Rufus's father announced. "Abigail's interview isn't until two, and she should have a full stomach before she goes." He winked at Abigail, who flashed a brief smile and then shoved her hands into the mouse-and-toad-filled pockets of her blazer.

One of the toads trilled.

⚬⚭⚭⚬

The adults had settled on a Chinese restaurant called the Silver Pagoda. Usually it was one of Rufus's favorite places to eat, but now he found himself toying with his food, unable to manage more than a few bites. The cotters had begun to recover from their ordeal and were chattering on his shoulders, occasionally venturing down to the table to help themselves to a morsel from his plate.

Abigail looked almost as ill as Rufus felt. She slumped in her seat with her hair falling over her face, the rose-colored toads and orange-whiskered mice squirming in her pockets. But at least *she* wasn't about to ride the Moving Meadow to a strange world in search of a mermaid. What if he drowned? What if he couldn't get back? He snuck a peek at his phone. One fifteen.

"I have to go soon," he said to his mom. "I told Grandpa Jack I'd help him get some stuff packed up for Geezer and Grandson."

"We'll drop you," his mom said. "Let's just enjoy being out together as a family."

"I hope you kids were impressed by what you saw," his dad interjected. "We've found a way to do well by doing good. Feylawn won't stay in the family, but it's going to be put to its best and highest use. I think that's something we can all be proud of."

Abigail snorted.

"What's the matter, Abigail?" Aunt Chrissy asked, wiping black bean sauce from the corners of her mouth. "You're not nervous about your interview, are you? Because all they need is a good look at you, and if they don't have room for you in their school, they're gonna kick out some other kid who doesn't have your brains. You're what they're looking for—the whole package!"

"I'm not a package," Abigail said. "I'm a person."

"A person who excels!" Aunt Chrissy said. She turned to Rufus. "If you keep at it, you might be able to apply to Stormweather Prep for high school. You've already come a long way!"

"Rufus is doing *fine*." Rufus's mother put down her chopsticks. "He's fine, Chrissy."

"No, I'm not," Rufus said. "I'm not fine." He could feel it rising in him like a storm—an error, a mistake, a complete catastrophe.

There was a sudden silence. Each of the adults was watching him, trying to figure out what to say. His dad spoke first, reaching across the table to stroke his arm. "I know this is hard. You've been great about it—"

"I'm not being great now. In fact, I'm being un-great."

"*Ungrateful*, you mean," Aunt Chrissy said. "Everything your parents and I do is for you kids. We're creating opportunities, Rufus. Opportunities for you to have a successful future!"

"But what about the present?" Rufus said. "Why are kids always supposed to be thinking about the future when we still have to live in the present?" He tried to keep his voice steady, but he could hear it quavering as the memories of the laboratory flooded his body. "Feylawn Pharmaceutical isn't what you think it is. It's not going to be like it was in that presentation. Once they own Feylawn, they'll destroy it, every piece of it! We found the lab, where they're experimenting on animals—rare animals that they only have at Feylawn."

Rufus's mother reached a hand across the table. "Animal experiments are part of science," she said. "I'm sorry you had to see it, but sometimes it's necessary. You have to test new drugs to make sure they're safe."

"But that's not what they're doing!" Rufus said. The two cotters trembled against the sides of his neck. "They're taking wild animals and breeding them so they can use them. These sweet little creatures that live inside apricots and these big things called umbrals that look kind of like manta rays and—"

"Those aren't real," Rufus's father interrupted. "Those are made-up things from Carson Sweete Collins's storybooks. You're too old for imaginary games, Rufus. I know it's been a tough summer, but just for today, I need you to *act your age.*"

Abigail stood up. "Of course you don't believe us," she said, looking hard at her mother. "Because you only think I'm smart when it's *convenient* for me to be smart, and you never give Rufus any credit for *anything*. But we saw what we saw! We saw the cages where they're going to put all the Feylawn creatures and the laboratory where they're going to experiment on them! We even found some of the animals!" As if to underscore her point, an orange-whiskered mouse peeked from her pocket.

Aunt Chrissy shrieked. The other adults exchanged glances.

"That's a lab mouse," Rufus's father said. "It didn't come from Feylawn. It came from a breeder."

The mouse chittered angrily. A spark flew from one of its tiny claws, singeing a hole in the tablecloth.

"I know what I saw," Abigail said. "Once they own Feylawn, they can do whatever they want! It doesn't matter what they promise you!"

Her voice was loud enough that other people in the restaurant were starting to stare.

"Sit down, Abigail!" Aunt Chrissy bellowed. "I expected better from you."

"Why?" Abigail said. Her lip trembled. "Because I always do whatever you want me to do? Because my room is full of stupid trophies that I don't even care about?" She slammed her hand down on the table so hard that one of the water glasses tipped over. "I don't even *want* to go to Stormweather Prep. I want to go to school with Rufus."

Rufus gaped at her. She did?

Aunt Chrissy leaped up as the spilled water trickled toward her lap. "Oh no, young lady! You're supposed to be raising *Rufus's* standards. I am *not* going to allow him to bring *yours* down."

"HE'S MY ONLY FRIEND!" Abigail shouted, and ran out of the restaurant.

Rufus ran after her. He had a pretty good idea where she was headed.

CRACK THE NUT

Rufus finally caught up with Abigail a few blocks from Feylawn. It was a long walk from the restaurant, and her blazer was now tied around her waist by the arms. Her face was streaked with tears and sweat, and she'd pulled her hair back into a knot at the nape of her neck. She was stroking one of the rose-colored toads.

"That was awful," she said. "I don't know why I thought they'd believe us. What we saw barely even makes sense to *me*."

"Abby-gell always makes sense," Bobalo asserted, scampering down Rufus's legs and up to Abigail's shoulder. "Abby-gell was loud and sensible! And her words were comprehensible!" He stroked her cheek with one paw. "You are tired from being so good at speaking. Bobalo can get you a nice spider or cricket for snacking."

"No thanks, Bobalo." Abigail wiped her nose on the back of her hand. She shoved the toad back into the pocket of her blazer. "We need to hurry. The meadow's due in fifteen minutes."

They took off at a jog, but slowed when they got to the stand of seven oaks at the end of the gravel road. Their parents' cars were parked behind Grandpa Jack's pickup.

"Of course," Abigail said. "They knew we'd come here."

"So what do you want to do?"

"I don't know. I've never yelled at my mom before."

"Never?"

She shook her head. "It always seemed easier to do what she wanted. I know she wants what's best for me."

"Stormweather Prep's a good school," Rufus admitted. "You'd probably like it there."

"But at Galosh Middle I can be *anybody*! At Stormweather Prep I'll have to be exactly who I am now."

"I like who you are now," Rufus said. "Most of the time."

"Everybody likes Abby-gell!" interjected Bobalo. "She is as deep as a water well! Of every ball, she is the belle!"

"You like who I *actually* am," Abigail told Rufus, reaching for Bobalo and stroking his armpits until he quieted. "But you didn't like the person you *thought* I was at the start of the summer. That's the person who would go to Stormweather Prep. The person who has to win everything."

"Losing isn't all it's cracked up to be," Rufus said. "Take it from someone who knows."

Abigail looked at the parked cars. "You'd better smuckle

us," she said. "And we should say goodbye to the cotters." She was already taking the mice and toads from her blazer pockets and depositing them in the grass.

Rufus lifted Oolissa from his shoulder and gave her a kiss on the head. "Bye, Oolissa. Stay safe."

"You love me, Boy Called Ru!" Oolissa squealed, clinging to his hand. "Let us be bonded!"

"You already *have* a mate," Rufus said, placing her on the ground. "Remember?"

Oolissa's green eyes grew very large. "In Wassapite I will delight! His eyes are green and his fur is bright!" she sang. Then she tucked herself into a ball and rolled away.

Rufus was getting faster at seed speech, but smuckling still took time, and they had none to spare. "We're going to have to run," he said as Abigail slid out of sight. "Those shoes don't look very comfortable."

"Let's go," Abigail said. "We've got eight minutes."

The path through the woods was longer and twistier than Rufus remembered, and the path up to the ridge was steeper and dustier. The sun beat down on them as they slogged up the trail. He wanted to check the time, but that would only slow them down. Instead he scanned the ridge for signs of the meadow.

He saw it just as they reached the crest of the ridge. Not purple this time, but a muddle of colors: orange, blue, and green. It was the shimmer, the way it was there and not there that made him recognize it. He felt for Abigail's hand. "Come on," he urged, and they ran.

⚬⚭⚬

The honey-sweet smell of blossoms rose up around them.

Rufus whooped. "We made it!"

"Ouch! That was in my ear," Abigail said. "Can you lift the smuckle, please? I hate trying to talk to you when I can't see you."

He did, then looked around. This version of the meadow was tall grass with orange poppies and blue lupines. A stream ambled through it, no more than six feet from bank to bank, its flow far gentler than the creek at Feylawn.

Abigail took off her sandals and stepped into the stream to soothe her blistered feet. A delighted honking greeted them. "Ceramics! Coronate!"

"Trinket!"

The goose paddled toward them, her feathers a snow-bright reflection in the stream. "What are you doing here?"

"Fondue," Trinket honked, extending her neck to receive an embrace from Abigail. "Monitor."

Abigail swiveled. "He is? Shamok, are you here?"

The leopard rose from the tall grass and extended his front paws in a massive stretch. His gold fur seemed to glow in the meadow sun. "I'm returning to Imura," Shamok said. "As Iris commanded."

"Blight and mildew!" Iris flew up from the grass. "I didn't *command*. I made a suggestion." She settled on a smooth stone in the middle of the stream. "Stop gaping at me, Rufus. We agreed to meet here yesterday."

"No, we didn't!" Rufus protested. "You said you were giving up."

"Yes, well. As the saying goes, if at first you don't suck seeds, try tarragon."

"Tarragon?" Rufus said. "Suck seeds? That makes even less sense than most of your expressions. It's *If at first you don't succeed—*"

"It means," Iris interrupted, "that if you're having trouble sucking one kind of seed, you should try another. Like tarragon."

"But yesterday you were telling me to *stop* trying and give up," said Rufus, thoroughly exasperated. "You said I should 'face facts.'"

"I did," said Iris. "But the facts continue to move around, much like this meadow. I suggested, quite sensibly, that you stop trying to do what you were doing, and try something else, which was to give up. Now I'm suggesting that you stop giving up and try something else, like tarragon, the seeds of which are useful in protecting against dragons, venomous snakes, and mad dogs."

"None of which are the problem right now," Abigail said. "Although who knows what we'll run into in the Realms." She splashed to the side of the stream and sat down in the grass. "We need a plan for finding Palimsa. I don't know how long any of us can swim—aside from Trinket."

Iris stretched on the rock, her wings fanned out on either side of her. "I don't see how you can plan for something you don't know anything about. Better just to grow with the flower."

"It's *go with the flow*, and no, it's not better," Abigail said. "But fine, I'll do the thinking for all of us." She rested her chin on her hands and stared into the stream, brow furrowed.

Rufus was inclined to agree with Iris. He stroked Shamok's soft fur and watched the bees and the dragonflies as they flitted over the meadow, each one on its own quest. After a while he took off his shoes and began to empty his overstuffed pockets. Soon he had arranged a small pile of items in the grass.

One round black padlock, its shackle open like a hook.

Five identical fortunes from the Hall of Prophecy.

His phone and the plastic pouch he'd brought to protect it from the waters of the Realms.

One plastic baggie full of miscellaneous seeds, collected at Feylawn over the course of the summer.

One auraneme, whiskered with roots.

Twenty dollars of Geezer & Grandson profits, in case of emergency.

Seventy-eight cents in loose change.

He pulled a seed from the bag and turned it over in his hands. It was a red-orange half-moon, the size of a quarter.

Oddly, he had no memory of gathering it. Was it one of the ones from Iris's pouch? He was pretty sure she'd reclaimed them all. He shut his eyes, waiting for it to introduce itself.

In my shell, time will tell.

He opened his eyes and squinted at it. It was dense and hard and smooth, like a horse chestnut or a buckeye. Where had it come from?

Then he remembered: Robin-Ella had pressed it into his palm at the end of the Piranha Pitch Session.

"Iris?" he said. "What kind of seed is this?"

Iris sat up. "For the love of all that is leafy," she said. "Why do you insist on asking questions you already know the answer to?"

"But I *don't* know. Otherwise I wouldn't be asking."

"You *should* know," Iris sniffed. "*If* you'd read the list I left you. It's a diarnut. The kind you were *supposed* to have dailied while I was gone." She flew to his knee and peered at the seed in his hand. "It looks like it's already been used."

"Used how?"

"*Dailied.*" Iris rolled her eyes. "Obviously."

Abigail scooted over to look. "Isn't that what was inside the lid of the porcelain chicken?"

Rufus nodded. "Which might be why the Calamand took the chicken. Except how would she have known about it?"

"She can sense magic," Shamok growled. "It's like when

you see something move and you have to pounce on it to see if it's good to eat."

"Diarnuts aren't for eating," Iris said. "It's not that kind of nut. When it drops off the tree, the inside is just light and vapor."

"'Crack the nut that has no meat,'" Abigail said. "Rufus, that's one of the tasks from the prophecy!"

Iris took the diarnut from Rufus. It was almost the same size as her torso. "Tell me again where you found it."

"I didn't—it was Robin-Ella, our business partner. She found it in a porcelain chicken that Carson Sweete Collins used to keep her pens and paintbrushes in."

"Queen Queen-Anne's-Lace must have given it to her. It's a tradition to give one to someone if you've had a nice day together. To remember it by." She saw Rufus about to open his mouth and dropped the nut on the ground. "I can see this is going to be one of those glomper question sessions, so let me just explain. Diarnuts are how we keep records. Back when we had a queen, she was the one who recorded each day's events. After she left, nobody dailied a diarnut for years and years. After a while, I started doing it myself." She pulled a snagged thread from the hem of her dress. "Just so there would be a record, when we all died."

She picked up the diarnut again and flew over to the stream. Then she dropped it in. Rufus dashed after it.

"What are you doing?" he demanded as he plunged his arms into the water, trying to grab the sunset-colored nut. "We *need* that!"

But just then, Queen Queen-Anne's-Lace stepped out of the stream.

38

A BRIGHT SPOT

Rufus took a step backward. The feyling queen looked so different from the one he'd seen on the island of Imura. Her wings were bright green, her skin deep brown, her body round and strong. She wore a pale green dress that was fitted at the waist, and her hair was braided and coiled above her head.

Iris gave a heavy sigh. "That's how I remember her," she said. "Brave and strong, and always laughing."

Queen Queen-Anne's-Lace was indeed laughing, her eyes closed, one hand over her heart, gasping for breath.

"Okay, okay," she said. "I'm going to be serious. *Serious*." She tried to compose her face and then burst out laughing again. "*Serious*, Carson Sweete Collins. I told you I wouldn't waste a diarnut on something foolish."

She settled into a cross-legged position and stretched. "Frankly, I think it's foolish to get so excited over one day with a mermaid's tail, but you told me that when you were an old lady this was going to be your fondest memory, so here it is: your very own diarnut to remember it by. You had a mermaid's tail today, Carson. It was red and purple and turquoise, and it looked *ridiculous*, if you ask me, but you stared at your own reflection in the water as if it was the prettiest thing you ever saw. Why this made you so pleased is beyond my understanding. I can make you into a *whole* fish anytime you like; I have trout lily in my pouch. But for some reason you glompers think being *half* a fish is the absolute pinnacle. When Palimsa was at the carnival working to catch the Calamand, she got the same kind of treatment. Nobody cared that she was the head detective for the Realms, or that she could wrestle a great white shark. Nope. It was all about that pretty tail.

"Anyway, we had a fine time of it today, you, me, and Palimsa. I haven't laughed so hard in a long time, and I thought that conversation we had about systems of government was interesting, too. Palimsa told us the merfolk don't have leaders at all—they just move together like a school of fish, first one person leading, then another. Imagine if we feylings tried that! We'd just fly in a hundred different directions."

She leaned her head back and laughed. It was a full-throated, openmouthed laugh, and it made Rufus remember the queen he'd met on Imura, so weary and bitter. Was there any of that laughter left in her?

"It's something to think about," Queen Queen-Anne's-

Lace continued. "Maybe we've been doing everything the wrong way around here and we should all trade off ruling the way the merfolk do. Even little Iris would get a chance to be in charge—not for long, of course, given her penchant for trouble."

Rufus glanced at Iris, whose cheeks flamed. But Queen Queen-Anne's-Lace was still talking.

"It was the first time I'd seen Palimsa in years and years, and the most astonishing thing happened. She gave me back something I thought I'd lost forever. The ruler's locket. You know the story—you put it in one of your books. But now it turns out *Palimsa* had it all this time, never knowing it was the very thing I'd been looking for when she and I first met. She had it wrapped around one of her braids, a little bauble to tie her hair. The funny thing was, I'd given up searching for it. And after that conversation we had today, I wonder if I've been better off without it. Maybe a ruler should earn her powers, not get them from a necklace." She frowned, seeming to lose herself in thought, before laughing again.

"*You're* certainly better off without that ridiculous tail. I hope you think this was worth wasting a diarnut on, my friend. Good night."

ᗏᑎᑎᗍ

Nobody spoke as Queen Queen-Anne's-Lace turned around and stepped back into the stream. After a moment, Trinket dove underwater, her white tail flashing in the sun, and came up with the diarnut in her beak. She waddled out of the water and deposited it at Abigail's feet.

"Cotton," she honked. "Invigorate."

"She's right," Abigail said, putting the diarnut in the pocket of her blazer. "I guess we don't need to go to the Realms after all."

Iris put her face in her hands. "It doesn't make sense! If Queen Queen-Anne's-Lace had the ruler's locket, she would have worn it, and if she'd worn it, she could have banished Carson Sweete Collins and we'd never have lost our Roving Tree or our train, and nobody would have died, and she wouldn't have had to marry Mr. Diggs!"

"But she didn't know all that was going to happen," Rufus said. "How could she? Back then, she and Carson were still friends!"

Iris took her hands from her face long enough to glare at him. "That doesn't help," she said, and covered her face again.

Rufus began returning things to his pockets as he tried to think what to do next. They'd followed the trail to the end, and now it was dead. The ruler's locket was still missing. Feylawn was still going to be sold. The Calamand was still at large. Nothing he had tried had done any good—not even telling his parents the truth, or something close to the truth. He wasn't ready to give up, but he was out of ideas.

"Did you know," Iris said suddenly. "It was Queen Queen-Anne's-Lace who gave Carson clearsight."

"What?" Rufus said. "I thought she was just born with it."

"Well," Iris said, "it was given to her as soon as she was born. That's almost the same thing, isn't it?"

"But why?" Abigail said.

"She had hope," Iris said. "Even after the ruler's locket was lost and Feylawn became visible to glompers. Even after Avery Sweete moved into Feylawn and built himself a house. Even after we had to start working all the time to protect Feylawn's borders and keep the goblins out. Queen Queen-Anne's-Lace thought there might be a way for humans and feylings to coexist. If one of them could see us and hear us, she said, then we could work together, the way she and the other six detectives had worked together to capture the Calamand. So when Carson was born, Lacy gave her clearsight."

A breeze ruffled through Rufus's hair. Thinking about the feyling queen's optimism made everything that much sadder. "I didn't know you could do that," he said. "Give the power of clearsight."

"It's in the last book of the series," Abigail said. "*The Gifts of Glistening Glen.* 'Circle once to clear the sight / Circle twice and they'll hear right. / But if you circle them again / You give fairy gifts to mortal men.'" She glanced at Iris. "Is that what happened to us? To me and Rufus? Did someone circle us three times? Is that why he can speak to seeds and I can—"

Iris suddenly seemed very interested in the patch of brown on her left wing.

"Iris?" Rufus prompted. "Answer the question!"

"I needed help," Iris said at last. "I didn't know who else to turn to. We didn't have a queen and I knew I couldn't find the train by myself. I was never meant to be in charge, but nobody else would do anything and we were all dying. I thought maybe if I gave you some abilities"—she wiped her eyes with the back of her hand—"you could help me, and I wouldn't be so alone."

"I used to like being alone." Shamok rolled onto his side so that Rufus could scratch his tawny belly. "But that was before I discovered belly rubs."

Rufus scratched Shamok's golden fur. It was warm from the sun and it smelled like the meadow: grassy and sweet.

"Very nice," Shamok said, and licked Rufus's hand appreciatively.

"Shamok," Rufus laughed. "You still have a spot."

The leopard sat up. "I do? Where?"

"On your tongue. Right in the middle. Show Abigail."

Abigail leaned over to look. "That does look like a spot!"

Shamok dangled his tongue from his mouth and crossed his eyes in a futile attempt to get a good look at it. "Are you thure? A real thpot? Round? Like a padlock?"

"Rhombus!" Trinket flapped her wings ineffectively as she hurried over to look. "Jigsaw!"

Shamok put his tongue back in his mouth. "A spot," he murmured. "A spot! I'm still a leopard after all!"

"That's probably why you didn't die," Iris said. "Queen Queen-Anne's-Lace must have forgotten to open one of the locks."

"But if one of the locks was still locked," Rufus pointed out, "the gates wouldn't have been able to open."

"Unless it wasn't on the gate," Abigail said. "Rufus— what if she didn't open one of the locks on purpose?"

"What do you mean?"

"Let's say you wanted to hide something where no one would think to look for it. Where would you put it?"

Rufus stared at her, understanding slowly dawning. "Right under the nose of the person most likely to steal it! Beside a thousand things that looked exactly like it!"

"Oh my God," Abigail said, clapping a hand to her own mouth. "Do you think it's been there the whole time?"

"It could be," Rufus said. "We have to look!"

Iris gave a shriek of frustration.

"You know I'm no good at puzzles," she said. "So will you *please* explain to me what you're talking about?"

"We think we know where the ruler's locket is," Rufus said. "We just have to get back to the Gate of a Thousand Locks."

39

THE STORM

It was afternoon when Imura first came into view, judging from the shadows the chiseled cliffs cast over the Lilac Sea. As Rufus stared at them, he felt the meadow growing spongy and indistinct. "Not yet!" Abigail said. "We have to get closer."

He returned his gaze to the meadow's blue and orange flowers. He and Abigail were on their feet, ready to jump. Iris hovered between them. Shamok crouched with his ears flattened against his head. Trinket flapped her wings against the breeze, her neck extended like a striking snake.

"What's that?" Abigail said suddenly.

Rufus let his eyes focus on the fuzzy scrawl of the lilac waves. A gray speedboat with a razor-sharp prow sliced toward the island.

"How did they find us?" he cried. "It's like they know

where we're going before we do." He turned to Iris. "Is there some way to turn them back?"

She shook her head. "We're not actually *there*. We're too far away for any seed to work on them."

"You have to have *something*!" Abigail said. "We can't let them get there before we do."

With a sigh, Iris plunged both hands into her pouch. When she drew them out, her fists bulged with powdery blue-green spores.

"I'll release the nimbolichen when we jump," she said. "It won't be pleasant, but we should have a few minutes to get to shore before the storm really gets going."

They were already passing close to the island.

"Ready?" Abigail said. "Let's go."

Rufus let his gaze fasten on the rolling sea. It grew sharper, more vivid, and then he was falling, out of the meadow and into the waves. As he hit the water, the first drops of rain landed beside him.

He swam as hard as he could, trying to stay close to Abigail and Shamok without getting clawed by Shamok's paddling paws. The raindrops spattered around him. Having done it once, he knew he could make it to shore, but he wasn't sure how he would fare once the wind kicked up. Already the swells were slapping him from side to side. Each time he went into a trough, Abigail and Shamok disappeared from view, and his heart constricted. By the time they drew close to shore, the water was dark and flecked with fringes of spray. Somehow they had missed the beach. In front of them was a cluster of flat rocks and then the sheer face of a cliff.

"We have to climb," Abigail said, scrambling onto the closest of the rocks. She took off her sandals and shoved them into the pockets of her blazer. "Remember: maintain three points of contact at all times."

"Trinket and I will fly," Iris called. "Meet you at the top."

Abigail was already scaling the rock wall, her hands and feet nimbly finding holds and crevices even as the waves battered them with spray. Shamok followed, emitting a low whine as he pulled himself upward, his claws scraping against the rock.

Rufus couldn't keep up with either of them. He was half blinded by the rain, and his feet kept slipping as he wedged them into one crevice after another. The only thing that kept him moving was the certainty that if he stopped, he would fall, and that if he fell, he would die. Every rock he gripped felt like it might give way. Every foothold felt like it was being washed out from under him. And yet somehow he came to the top of the cliff, and Abigail was there, hoisting him by the armpits onto solid ground.

"Let me guess," he said, lying flat on his belly with his face in the mud. "Rock-Climbing Camp."

"Rock-Climbing *Club*, actually," Abigail said, refastening her sandals.

"I think I overdid it with the nimbolichen," Iris said. "The wind nearly blew us straight into the cliffs."

Rufus got to his feet and looked back the way they'd come. Waves battered the goblin speedboat. A streak of lightning sizzled across the sky.

"Let's go," he said. "We still have a chance to get to the gates before they do."

⚬⚭⚬

They ran toward the interior of the island, hunching against the onslaught of rain and wind. Soon the Wall of Thorns was before them. The brambles thrashed with the wind.

"I am the leopard of the locks!" Shamok snarled. "Lie down before me! Let me pass!"

Rufus heard the whispering inside his head: *The leopard of the locks! He lives! He lives!*

"Lie down!" Shamok roared.

The brambles rustled. *No one shall pass this way again,* they protested. *The Locksmith said. No one shall pass.*

Rufus tried to speak to them, sliding into the place between sleeping and waking even as icy rain trickled down the back of his neck and the wind moaned in his ears. But the Wall of Thorns only hissed and rustled, spikes slicing the air. *Now you have angered us,* it shouted. *Come*

➤ 337 ➤

snakes, come birds, come stinging biting things! No one shall pass this way again!

With a whir and hiss, the creatures came flying and crawling from the bramble thicket.

Rufus and Abigail turned and ran. The birds cheeped and dove, pecking at their necks and heads. The insects swarmed around them, stinging their arms and legs.

"Follow me!" Shamok called. He crawled into a hole at the base of a tree and disappeared. Rufus and Abigail scrambled after him.

It was quiet in the dirt burrow, and dry. There was no light. Rufus wormed blindly forward, following the twitch of Shamok's tail.

"What *is* this?" he said at last.

"The half bird's hidey-hole," Shamok growled. "It smells of his poison."

"Are you here, Trinket?" Abigail called.

"Stasis!" Trinket honked. "Connection! Altitude!"

"I'm here, too," Iris said. "But I wish I wasn't. It reeks of goblin."

"It beats being pecked, stung, scratched, and drenched," Rufus said. He was bleeding from the brambles and bird beaks, and his skin was yelping from a dozen or more stings. He was also wet in every place that it was possible to be wet, and crawling through the goblin's tunnel meant that he was covered with a thin layer of mud.

Abigail sneezed. "Where do you think this ends?"

"*When* do you think it ends, that's what I'd like to know," Iris said. "Poor Queen Queen-Anne's-Lace, having to live like this for years and years."

"'Poor Queen Queen-Anne's-Lace' is the reason we're in this predicament," Rufus reminded her. "She's the one who freed the Calamand, and she's the one who turned the whole island against us. So I'm not really that sorry for her."

Behind him, Iris sniffled. "She was the best of us," she murmured. "Once upon a time."

"She took my spots," Shamok said. "And now she returns to take the last of them."

Rufus stopped in his tracks, causing Abigail to collide with his backside.

"How do you know?" he asked.

"I feel her," Shamok said. "The Locksmith. She's somewhere close."

⚜

The tunnel had already begun to rise. Soon there was enough light coming in for Rufus to see Shamok creeping ahead of him. Then he was pulling himself over a lip of earth into the rain.

In front of them were the enormous open gates of the prison, festooned with hundreds of open padlocks. Hundreds more were strewn on the ground, which was swiftly turning into a muddy lake.

"My spots! My beautiful spots!" Shamok cried and flopped

onto his side, rolling back and forth over the locks as if he could push them back onto his coat. When he rolled to his feet, he was covered in streaks and clots of mud.

Rufus touched the cold place in his throat and listened for the voice of a closed lock. Thunder boomed overhead. Rain pelted and pummeled the ground. It felt impossible to think or hear. He stared up at the gates, rain running into his eyes and nose, his teeth chattering. Abigail stood beside him, the wind whipping her hair around her face. She put on her blazer and turned up its collar, looking miserable.

"You're too cold," Iris said, landing on Rufus's shoulder. "You both are." She pressed a warm ember into each of their hands. At least, it felt like a warm ember. When Rufus examined it, it turned out to be a peppercorn. *I bring heat from head to feet*, it promised. He closed his fingers around it and the warmth spread through his body. His jaw unclenched. His teeth stopped chattering.

"Do you see the lock?" Abigail asked, fist knotted around a peppercorn of her own.

Rufus shook his head. "Not yet. Do you, Iris?"

"I'm not looking," Iris said. "I'm more concerned about preventing Diggs from finding us. You find the lock—I'm going to see where he is."

"Wait!" Rufus said. "What if I need your help with the lock?"

"Sticks and weeds! I can't do *everything*," Iris said. "You know how to do this. You just refuse to believe it for some reason." Then she lifted off from his shoulder and was gone.

Rufus stared at the gates, listening. He touched the spot in his throat again and tasted metal. The locks around him lay silent, their open shackles sighing. He could feel the intensity of their desire to be closed again, but they were silent, as if holding their breaths. Where was the closed one, the one that should be chanting proudly?

I know you're here, he said aloud, his tongue and throat forming the words in the language of clicks and twists. *It's time to open.*

Silence.

Let go, he said. *I've come to find you.*

She said to stay quiet, a small voice said. *She said, Don't speak.*

Rufus was about to reply when he felt something tugging on the hem of his shorts. He looked down to find Trinket with the cuff in her bill, staring up at him intently. "Speck," she honked. "Speck speck speck. Hanky."

"It's all right," Shamok said. He lay down in the mud with his head between his paws. "I should be dead anyway."

"Blankness," Trinket honked. "Reduction! Shingle!"

Shamok's ear twitched. He shut his eyes.

Abigail knelt beside him, rubbing her hands over his damp fur. "Rufus, she's saying he'll die! If you open the last lock, it'll kill him!"

Trinket bowed her head and waddled over to Shamok. She settled beside him in the mud, wrapping her long neck around his shoulders.

"What if I close one of the other locks?" Rufus said. "Then you'd be safe, right?"

"Yes," Shamok said in a low voice. "If you wouldn't mind."

Rufus shoved the peppercorn into a pocket and picked up a chain from the mud. Once he'd slung it through the bars of the gates, he pulled the padlock from his pocket.

Close, he told it.

The lock seemed unimpressed by his rudimentary command of its language. *Tell me how*, it replied. *Show me you know. Tell me what you know of closing.*

Rufus could feel the cold returning to his body. The rain streamed down his face and arms. But he let the lock language take over his tongue and spoke of fastening, of linking, of completion and impenetrability, of doors that held fast when pounded and kicked, of safety.

Ah, said the lock as its shackle swiveled and slid into place. *You know.*

Then it began to chant. *Closed. Keep out. Shut. Keep in.*

Abigail stroked Shamok's wet forehead. "Look at that. A nice black spot."

"Are you sure?" Shamok said, rolling his eyes up in a vain attempt to see.

But Rufus was no longer watching. He was staring up at the gates and talking as if his tongue and throat were made of metal. He spoke of release and relief, of freedom and letting go. He talked of water flowing out of faucets and wind blowing from place to place and boats drifting from the dock and knots untying. And just when he felt that he had said everything he could possibly say about the opening of things, he heard a tiny sigh and a minuscule click.

A lock dropped from somewhere above his head and landed between Shamok's muddy gold paws.

40

FOUR QUESTIONS

Rufus picked up the lock. Instead of a keyhole, its center was a raised oval, like a closed eyelid.

All the way, he coaxed, still speaking in the language of locks. *Open, all the way.*

The lock gave a croaking kind of sob, and the lid retracted.

Inside was a tiny silver locket, strung on a woven chain just long enough for a feyling's neck. Rufus pulled it out. A scrap of paper was wrapped around the chain. He read it aloud even as the rain smeared the ink.

> *"You cannot take me.*
> *I must be given.*
> *Open my clasp.*
> *Four questions, I'll ask.*
> *Answer me right*
> *and answer me true.*
> *Only then can I*

be given to you.
Answer me wrong
or tell me a lie,
my gift will be swift
as you sicken and die."

The locket shimmered in his hand, now green, now blue, now silver again. Rufus could feel its power. It came to him in waves, like the tones of a bell. But this bell sang in deep bass tones that made his whole body vibrate. Like every magical object he'd encountered, it wanted something. But the locket's desire was more urgent than anything he'd encountered. It hungered. It longed. It was desperate.

Shamok's nose wrinkled. "It smells of strong magic."

"Backbone," Trinket agreed. "Epiphany."

Rufus found his knees buckling. "It's heavy," he said. "A lot heavier than it looks."

Shamok nudged him with his nose. "Give it to Abigail, for now," he said.

"I'm okay." Rufus shoved the locket into his shorts pocket and dropped the empty padlock in the mud. The locket's hunger washed over him, a desire so sharp he felt tears sparking behind his eyes. He'd expected to feel triumphant, but instead he felt hollow. The little necklace had eaten up the warmth from the peppercorn. He shivered.

Abigail was watching him. "We need to give the locket to Iris. Where is she?"

Rufus stole a glance at the dripping sky. Iris had been gone a long time. "Let's get back to the rocks," he said. "She's probably there, making sure Diggs can't land."

"He's landed," Shamok said. He had opened his mouth as if tasting the air. "I smell his poison."

"Then we need to get off this island," Abigail said. "I wish we knew when the meadow was coming back."

⟋⟍⟍

They had no choice but to return through Mr. Diggs's tunnel. Shamok led the way, slinking low. Abigail went next, with Trinket behind her. Rufus was last. His legs felt leaden, especially the one closest to the locket. The necklace was tiny—the size of a paper clip. Yet it pressed against his thigh like an iron ball, its hunger sharp and insatiable. What did it *want*? But even as he asked, he could sense the response. *You cannot take me. I must be given. Let me ask you my questions.*

The tunnel rose slightly. He was crawling on his belly now, pulling himself forward with his arms.

Abigail's face appeared in the mouth of the tunnel. "Are you hurt?"

Rufus could only shake his head. "The locket's heavy," he said, but Abigail was already back in the tunnel, grabbing him by the arms to pull him the last few feet of the way.

"Give it to me," she said. Rufus rolled onto his back and looked up at the sky. He knew he needed to get to his feet, find Iris, get back home. But he was so tired.

"Give it to me!" Abigail said again, reaching into his pocket.

"It's just going to have the same effect on you," Rufus protested. But the necklace seemed to lighten as he handed it to her. "It wants to be given to someone," he said. "Maybe if we keep giving it to each other, it'll stop doing whatever it's doing."

"Come on," Abigail said, dropping the locket into the pocket of her blazer.

Without the necklace, Rufus immediately felt lighter. The feeling came back into his legs, and he was able to push himself to a standing position. Shamok and Trinket were perched at his feet, looking at him with concern.

"You three find a place to hide. I'll hunt for Iris," Shamok said. "If I find the Calamand and the half bird, I'll eat them both."

✦

But where could they hide? Mr. Diggs had dug the tunnel, so it would probably be the first place he'd look. The brambles were impenetrable. The shoreline was exposed. Rufus and Abigail trudged along the rocks, battered by the downpour. Anyone who'd grown up in Galosh was used to rain, but Rufus thought he had never been quite as damp and miserable as he was right at that moment.

At last they came to a shallow cave in the rocks, just deep enough for them to shelter in. They huddled there with Trinket between them, pressing her feathers against their legs as if to keep them warm. Abigail was very pale.

"Give it back to me," he said, holding out a hand. "We'll pass it back and forth."

Abigail didn't argue. "If this is the way it feels to wear it, I understand why Queen Queen-Anne's-Lace didn't want to."

"I don't think it felt like this when she had it. In the memory we saw, the one from the time cabinet, the Calamand didn't seem sickened by having it in her pocket. I think Queen Queen-Anne's-Lace did something to it before she hid it, to protect it. She must have created the four questions. I think the locket will do this to anyone who doesn't answer them."

Abigail frowned. "She must have hidden it just before she married Diggs. Which makes sense—she didn't want him to gain control over Feylawn."

"So what's she up to now?" Rufus braced his hand against his knee as the locket grew heavier. "She clearly doesn't want to give Diggs the locket, or she would have given it to him when she freed the Calamand. But if she *didn't* want to give it to him, why *would* she free the Calamand?"

"And why did she free *Diggs*? We had him tied up!" Abigail stroked Trinket's feathers. Outside their alcove, the rain was starting to let up. A glint of light peeked through the heavy gray clouds. Rufus tried to think, but the locket drowned out his thoughts. *You cannot keep me until you answer my questions!*

Abigail reached out and caught him by the shoulder. "Whoa, are you okay?"

He realized he'd sunk to his side on the rocks. The locket sickness seemed to come faster each time.

"It's kind of insisting that we answer its questions," Rufus said. "Let's just hear what they are."

"But the note said if we can't answer them, we sicken and die!"

Rufus put his head between his knees, glad for the salt spray on the back of his neck.

"The note said we'd sicken and die if we answered wrong or answered with lies. It didn't say anything about what happens if we don't say anything at all."

"All right," Abigail said. "Let's just hear the first question."

She took the locket from Rufus's fingers and opened the clasp.

⬥⬥⬥

Somehow they were in a tree, but not an ordinary tree. A tree like a house, with smooth, orange-gold limbs thick enough to hold hundreds of people. Enormous leaves whispered over their heads, each one the size of a dinner plate.

> *What enemy became your friend?*
> *What friend became your enemy?*
> *What sacrifice did you make for your*
> *   fellow fey?*
> *Once bound, how did you become free?*

Abigail snapped the locket shut.

"She made it so that only a feyling can answer." Her knuckles were white as she clenched the locket. Her face was slowly losing its color.

Rufus nodded. "One who isn't married to Mr. Diggs. If she's still bound to him, she can't wear it. And if she says she's free when she isn't, she'll die."

"Remember the Crinnyeyes' prophecy?" Abigail said. She slid into a sitting position like a marionette with a broken string. "There were four impossible tasks. And we did three of them."

Rufus took the locket from Abigail. "Not that they did us much good," he reminded her.

"They got us here, didn't they?" She ticked them off on her fingers. "We read the tale to unwrite the story—that was the story of the Calamand stealing the ruler's locket. We recovered the moment that was lost—that was the memory in the time cabinet of the locket falling into the mermaid's tank. We cracked the nut no one can eat—that was the diarnut that told us Queen Queen-Anne's-Lace had gotten the locket back. There's just one left."

"'Sunder the bond that cannot break,'" Rufus said, shoving the necklace in his pocket. "Do you think that means the bond between Queen Queen-Anne's-Lace and Mr. Diggs?"

"Yup," Abigail said. "I just don't know how we do it. Garnet said one of them would have to die."

Suddenly Rufus saw figures moving over the rocks: the long lean strides of the Calamand, the hunched hops of Mr. Diggs. "They're coming," he said. "Run!"

Abigail tossed Trinket into the air. "Fly! As far as you can!"

They had no plan except to get away, but there was nowhere to go. On the right: a wall of brambles. On the left: the sea. Behind them, Mr. Diggs's talons clicked, surefooted, relentless.

"A chase, Mandolyn! Not a steeplechase but a peoplechase!" the Calamand shouted.

The rocks were slippery from the rain and matted with slick green seaweed. Rufus staggered after Abigail, his thoughts slowing. Just ahead of them, something whirred and fluttered.

"Iris!" he shouted. "Where's Shamok?"

But Shamok was nowhere to be found. And the fluttering shape had a black topknot.

"Slow down, Pledge Lord," Nettle said. "You too, Pledge Lady. I wouldn't want you to twist an ankle." Then he smiled and gave a midair bow to each of them. "Your safety is always my most important consideration."

41

FACE-TO-FACE

Rufus's legs buckled. Abigail reached for his hand. He gave her the locket. Thirty seconds, then he'd take it back.

Behind them, there was the click of talons. They turned to find Mr. Diggs, breathing heavily. "I ran into a friend of yours just now," he said. "She seems remarkably well *preserved.*" He chuckled and held up a glass jam jar. Iris was trapped inside. She screamed something inaudible and beat against the side of the jar with her fists.

Nettle landed on the lid of the jar. He looked down at Iris with a satisfied smirk and cupped his ear to indicate he couldn't hear her screams.

"What's that you say, Birchbattle?" he mocked. "Sorry, can't hear!"

Rufus had never hated anyone so much in his life. "She gave you a second chance," he yelled. "And that's how you repay her?"

"My loyalty is to my queen, Pledge Lord," Nettle said. "And my queen is married to Mr. Diggs."

"That she is!" Mr. Diggs puffed out his chest. "And together we'll rule two worlds!"

Rufus saw then that Queen Queen-Anne's-Lace rested on the goblin's shoulder. She looked very weak and ill: her hair matted, her skin ashy and dull. She clung to the collar of Mr. Diggs's mustard-colored suit as if afraid she might fall.

Nettle was still talking. "Iris *says* how much she loves our queen, but *I'm* the one who serves her. *I* saved my queen on the day of the ATV accident. She would have died if it wasn't for me." He fixed Rufus with an unblinking stare. "*You* didn't know that, of course. *You* didn't ask. *You* always assumed the worst of me."

"Because you've been working against us the whole time!" Abigail's fingers clenched Rufus's. He took the locket from her, feeling its icy pull almost immediately. "How can you serve a man like Mr. Diggs? A man who wants to destroy your people?"

"Mr. Diggs doesn't want to destroy *me*," Nettle said. "He *trusts* me."

Rufus tried to think of some response, but the locket made him woozy and dim. His legs felt like sponge cake, his brain like pudding. The only thing that kept him upright was the hot fury burning in his chest.

"You made a vow!" he said. "You pledged to protect us!"

"Perhaps peony seed has an antidote," Nettle said coolly. "Iris Birchbattle never was the sharpest thorn on the rose." He did a little tap dance on the lid of the jar and then flew up to circle Rufus's head.

The Calamand made a clownish sad face, her lower lip jutting out. "Aw! I thought children were supposed to enjoy playing games!" She had been carrying the time cabinet under one of her four arms, but now she set it on the rocks and grabbed Rufus's wrist, holding it in an iron grip. "What was the name of the game we just played together, Rufus? Follow-the-leader or hide-and-seek?" She stretched another arm around Abigail and squeezed her close. "You don't play games, do you, Abigail? You prefer to be the referee." She used one of her remaining arms to lift a silver whistle from around her neck and blow a sharp blast.

"That's mine!" Abigail spat, trying to twist out of her grasp. "You stole it from me!"

"Did I?" laughed the Calamand. She made a show of inspecting the whistle. "Do you know—I think you're right! It has your name inscribed on it. *Abigail Vasquez*. Sometimes I say, 'Where are you right now, Abigail Vasquez?' And my little silver whistle always answers me, because her name is the same as yours. 'I'm in the school on the hill,' she says. 'I'm in the park with the time cabinet,' she says. 'I'm headed to the island of Imura. I'm hiding in a little cave.'" The Calamand laughed and her head twirled like a spinning top. "How easy it is to find you when I want you!"

One hand held Rufus. One hand held Abigail. One held the whistle. The fourth tipped an imaginary hat to Mr. Diggs.

"And so our partnership comes to an end, Digg-Dawg. I have my freedom, and you have your locket. I'm expecting a meadow in a minute or two that should take me where I want to go. There's just one thing I need."

She released the whistle and snatched up the time cabinet. "I want the time I lost when I was imprisoned here. So does my poor innocent sister, locked up for a crime she didn't commit!" She opened the drawer of the cabinet and pulled out a thin tool with a flattened end like a paddle. "We're each owed a hundred years, but we'll take what we can get. Tell one of your flittery minions to use this kronkel-wand to gather all the years these little ones have left and pack them up to go."

Rufus tried to understand what she was saying, but his mind couldn't seem to make sense of it. Take all the years? Abigail took his hand, prying the locket from his fingers.

Mandolyn's face swung to the front and looked at them curiously. "What does it look like when you take their time?" she asked. "Will they grow old before our eyes?"

Understanding flooded Rufus's brain all at once. They were planning to use the time cabinet to steal their future.

All of it.

He struggled against the Calamand's hold, but she held him fast.

"The way I always heard it," she said into his ear, "the time comes out in one long strand, like a long cord pulled from deep inside your bones. The strand only breaks when your heart gives out."

Rufus could feel Abigail's breath coming in nervous gasps. He took her hand. They would find a way out of this, he promised her silently. They had to.

"Let's do this, Mini-Miney-Mo!" cried the Calamand. "Mandolyn and I have no time to waste—not yet anyway!"

Queen Queen-Anne's-Lace didn't move. Neither did Nettle.

"That wasn't our deal," Mr. Diggs rasped. He set the jar that held Iris on the ground and moved toward the Calamand in a succession of quick bird-like hops. "Your payment was your freedom. You got the time cabinet while working for me. That makes it mine. As is the time *I* plan to take from these two children. Every year they lose is one I plan to sell. Busy humans will pay good money for it. I'm afraid I can't be giving it away."

The Calamand pulled Rufus and Abigail closer. "Don't be a greedy goblin, Diggsy," she said. "*I* took the time cabinet—not you. I set my sights on it long ago." She threw back her head and laughed. "Imagine the mischief Mandolyn and I can make with it!"

Mandolyn's head spun to the front. "I've been bored for so long without a new toy to play with," she sighed.

Diggs hopped forward, his talons scraping the rocks. "Goblins always honor a bargain, Calamand. But we don't renegotiate the terms."

The Calamand's laughter had both music and discord in it, like a cat walking across a piano. "Never bargain with a thief, Mr. Diggs. I take what I like. And I like your wife. I'm afraid I can't operate the time cabinet without her."

She moved so fast that Rufus didn't even feel her release him. But a moment later, the Calamand was dashing toward the water with the time cabinet under her arm and Queen Queen-Anne's-Lace clenched in one fist. Glimmering on the horizon was the blue-gold of the moving meadow. Diggs bolted after her. So did Nettle.

Abigail tugged Rufus's arm. "Let's go!"

He grabbed the jar that held Iris and they ran along the cliffs, searching for some place to hide. Then Abigail staggered, the locket dragging her to her knees. Rufus stooped to take it from her, dropping the jar in his haste. It rolled, bounced over a rock, and shattered. Iris flew out, cursing.

"Took you long enough!" she fumed, circling over Rufus's head. "How long were you going to keep me trapped in that thing?"

Rufus ignored her and yanked Abigail to her feet. "Come on! We have to get out of here."

Then he heard the thrum of wings. Nettle was above

them, sprinkling seeds. In an instant they were surrounded by four skeletal dragons, each one the size of a horse. The dragons were bone-white, their eye sockets empty. They marched in a slow and deliberate circle, swiveling their heads to stare at Rufus and Abigail through vacant eyes. When Iris tried to fly past them, they opened their jaws and exhaled flowery plumes of red and yellow fire that sent her tumbling backward.

"It's for your own protection," Nettle said. "We need to talk."

"I have nothing to say to you, traitor! Thief!" Iris shrieked. She collapsed onto Rufus's shoulder, her hair and dress singed and smoking. "You took those snapdragon seeds when you took my pouch."

Rufus looked around. The dragons' fiery exhalations drew spirals of steam from his wet shorts and T-shirt. The locket he'd taken from Abigail was heavy in his fist. He blinked, trying to keep the darkness from closing over his vision.

A few feet away, Mr. Diggs and the Calamand wrestled on the rocks, first Diggs on top, then the Calamand, then Diggs again. Mr. Diggs slashed with his talons, trying to pin the Calamand in place and pry Queen Queen-Anne's-Lace from her grip, but it was the Calamand who had the upper hand. She had dropped the time cabinet and was straddling him, punching with three of her four fists. Queen Queen-Anne's-Lace drooped in her remaining hand, coughing.

"Pledge Lord!" Nettle hovered in front of Rufus's face, trying to get his attention. "We don't have much time. Any moment, the Calamand will kill Diggs. Once she does, the queen will be free. She'll need the locket—if she puts it on, she'll be transported back to Feylawn, safe from the Calamand. Give it to me so I can give it to her. I'll make sure the Calamand can't hurt you."

The reflection of the dragons' flames flashed in Abigail's eyes. "Why the heck would we trust you?"

"You have no reason to, Pledge Lady. But—"

A furious scream interrupted him.

The Calamand had Mr. Diggs pinned on the rocks with two of her hands. A third wielded a pair of gold-handled scissors. "I'll cut the life from you or I'll cut the wife from you—one way or another, she's mine," she said as she straddled him.

"We'll take all the little mini minions!" sang Mandolyn from the other side of her head. "A pocket army of flitterbugs to open locks and gather time! In no time at all we'll have all the time in the world!"

The Calamand leaned back, raising her gold-handled scissors. But at that moment, Mr. Diggs lifted one of his bird-like legs. In a single sweeping motion, the talons of his feet sliced Mandolyn's face from the back of the Calamand's head.

The Calamand screamed in pain and fury. Diggs rolled

out of her grip, grabbed the fallen face by its long red hair, and ran for the cliffs.

"Calamandra!" shrieked Mandolyn as she swung in his hand. "Help me! I'm nothing without you!"

"GIVE HER BACK TO ME!" The Calamand roared with fury and launched herself at Diggs, her scissors aimed for his heart. Mr. Diggs stepped aside like a matador evading a bull.

The Calamand stumbled, flailed, and tumbled headfirst over the cliff.

"Calamandra!" shouted Mandolyn. "Don't leave me! Wait!"

But the Calamand lay unmoving on the wave-beaten rocks below. Mr. Diggs flipped the wailing face of her sister after her. "More trouble than you were worth," he grunted, and wiped his hands on his mustard-colored trousers.

Nettle landed on his shoulder, his face white. "Where's the queen? Is she all right?"

Diggs shrugged. "The Calamand released her when she fell," he said. "She'll come back as soon as I call for her. She has no choice." He lifted his chin. "Come to me, my little lozenge," he sang. "Come to your husband, as you must."

Trapped inside the snapdragons' ring of fire, Iris gave a sob of frustration. "Why can't he just let her be?"

Rufus tried to speak but found he had forgotten how.

Then the locket pulled him to the ground.

42

TRUTH OR
CONSEQUENCES

Rufus opened his eyes. Abigail stood over him, the locket in her hand. Iris was perched on her shoulder, her wings drooping. The skeletal dragons were still marching in a slow circle, their flaming breath arching over their heads.

"Nettle took my pouch," Iris said. "I've got nothing to work with."

Rufus scrambled to his feet. "What do we do?"

"What indeed?" said Mr. Diggs. He had a wet and bedraggled Queen Queen-Anne's-Lace in one hand. She slumped, water dripping from her hair and dress. Nettle flew above them, one hand on his pouch. His eyes were bright with tears.

"We let them answer the questions," Abigail said, and opened the locket.

༄༅

They were in the tree again, but this time Mr. Diggs stood beside them, his lip curling to expose his upper fangs. Nettle and Iris knelt beside Queen Queen-Anne's-Lace, who lay on her side, her eyes half closed. The feylings were now human-size—or else Rufus, Abigail, and Diggs were feyling-size.

"I am here to claim the ruler's locket!" Mr. Diggs bellowed.

Leaves rustled above their heads.

Then answer us this, they breathed.

> *What enemy became your friend?*
> *What friend became your enemy?*
> *What sacrifice did you make for your*
>   *fellow fey?*
> *Once bound, how did you become free?*

Nobody spoke. Rufus met Abigail's eyes. *Answer me wrong / or tell me a lie, / my gift will be swift / as you sicken and die.*

Their only hope was to keep their mouths shut and hope that either Nettle or Mr. Diggs would be stupid enough to answer the questions.

Mr. Diggs poked Queen Queen-Anne's-Lace with one finger, then tilted her ashen face toward his. "This is the moment we've been waiting for, lozenge," he rasped. "The moment I take possession of your kingdom."

Queen Queen-Anne's-Lace's breath came in shallow spurts. "You must . . . first . . . answer . . . the questions," she wheezed.

Answer! echoed the rustling leaves.

> *What enemy became your friend?*
> *What friend became your enemy?*
> *What sacrifice did you make for your*
>   *fellow fey?*
> *Once bound, how did you become free?*

Mr. Diggs tried to shake the feyling queen awake, but her head lolled to one side. "Not . . . free," she murmured. "Cannot answer." Beside her, Iris wept noisily.

Diggs grabbed Nettle by one arm and pulled him to his feet. "Answer them!"

"Those questions were intended for your wife, sir," Nettle said. It was strange to see him as he must have looked to other feylings: a pale young man, perhaps twenty years old, his black hair pulled into a feathery crest.

"My wife can't do it," Mr. Diggs said. "And I need a feyling to wear the locket. I reward loyalty, Nettle. Would you like to be king of the feylings?" He grinned. "I'll make you my second-in-command. You'll be like the son I never had."

"I'm just a servant," Nettle protested. "Your servant, sir. I—"

Answer! the leaves thundered. *What enemy became your friend?*

Nettle swallowed. "Rance Diggs," he said at last. "I met him when I was searching for my family. He told me that my feyling friends laughed at me for being weaker than my brave sisters. He promised to return me to the Green World when we found the missing train. He said he'd put me in charge."

"A heartwarming recollection," Mr. Diggs said as the leaves rustled appreciatively.

True, they murmured. *True, true.*

Nettle breathed a sigh of relief.

Answer! the leaves commanded. *What friend became your enemy?*

Nettle looked around as if hoping to see the answer carved in the trunk of the tree. His eyes landed on Iris as she knelt beside the half-conscious feyling queen.

"Iris Birchbattle," he said. "She and I were childhood playmates. Before I lost my family and formed the All-Outers. Then she fought against me and kept me from returning to the Green World."

The leaves trembled, whisking together like clapping hands.

True, they breathed. *True, true.*

Mr. Diggs smiled.

Rufus met Abigail's eyes, which were wide and serious. This wasn't going the way he'd expected. What if Nettle could answer all four questions without telling a lie? Abigail folded her hands in front of her lips, scarcely breathing.

Answer! the leaves intoned. *What sacrifice did you make for your fellow fey?*

Nettle stared at the ground, his wings trembling.

Mr. Diggs hopped closer to him. "Go ahead," he urged. "Tell them."

"I sacrificed my mother, my father, and my two sisters," Nettle said. "They went to find a new way home to the Green World, and none of them returned."

The leaves grew still. *Was this your only sacrifice?* they asked.

Nettle swallowed. "I have played the role of spy," he said. "I sacrificed my pride and pretended to serve those I despised and who despised me. By doing so I was able to serve the queen of the feylings, Queen Queen-Anne's-Lace."

Above them, branches lashed back and forth as if in a storm. Their leaves whipped across Nettle's body until he fell to his knees.

You served Rance Diggs! the leaves hissed. *Enemy of the fey!*

"I did it for my queen!" Nettle cried.

The leaves pressed against his face and arms, holding him in place. *Enemy!* they murmured. *Traitor!*

This was it, Rufus thought. He would see Nettle die. The thing he'd imagined so many times would happen now. He shut his eyes.

Silence. And then the leaves gave a long sigh. *For the queen*, they breathed. *It's true. It's true.*

Rufus opened his eyes as the leaves drew back, leaving Nettle alone on his knees. Mr. Diggs was smiling. "True," he repeated. "She's my wife. He serves her by serving me."

Answer! The voice of the leaves was gentler now. *Once bound, how did you become free?*

Nettle looked at Rufus.

Answer! the leaves intoned, sterner now.

Nettle bowed his head.

"Answer!" shouted Mr. Diggs. "You were bound by whatsit seed! You found the antidote and became free!"

"I was bound by peony seed," Nettle whispered, and faltered.

Rufus shut his eyes again as memories assaulted him, demanding clarification. Nettle helping them sort through the memories in the time bundles. Nettle begging them to give him the locket to save Queen Queen-Anne's-Lace. Nettle calling him Pledge Lord, no matter how many times Rufus told him to stop. Maybe peony seed had an antidote, Nettle had said. But maybe it *didn't*.

Whose side was Nettle on?

The great tree's branches had begun to sway and shake.

If you lie, you will die, the leaves warned. *Once bound, how did you become free?*

"Tell them!" Mr. Diggs commanded. "Tell them and be king!"

Rufus let his mind drift to the place between sleep and waking, searching for something he had never tried to see. But there it was. A blue-black cord extending from Nettle to Rufus. It was a beautiful thing, strong and sleek as a water snake.

He gulped for air. "Abigail," he whispered. "Follow my lead."

She looked at him questioningly, but nodded. If he was wrong, this would be the biggest mistake of his life.

"Nettle Pampaspatch," Rufus said.

The feyling's wings opened slightly, like lips about to speak.

From the corner of his eye, Rufus saw Iris stiffen. "Don't," she said. "Whatever you're thinking, don't do it."

But Rufus kept going, fumbling for the right words. He'd tried to fire Nettle once before, unsuccessfully. Now he had to do it right. "I free you from your pledge. You've erased your debt. You're not bound to me."

With a tug to his heart, the cord snapped.

Abigail bit her lip. Then she took a careful breath. "Not to me, either," she said. "I free you from your pledge."

Nettle stood with his wings spread, his expression stunned. He put his hands to his chest.

"I was bound by peony seed," he said softly. "Until Rufus Takada Collins and Abigail Vasquez set me free."

There was a roar as the tree shook from side to side, its branches lashing the sky.

Leaves cascaded down on their heads, spinning in circles like endless drifts of snow.

True! they sang. *True! True! True!*

The branch below them was gone. They were on the rocks again. A hail of leaves blackened the sky like an endless flock of migrating birds. The dragons had withered into dry husks, which the wind scattered over the rocks. Mr. Diggs stood with his fists raised, his mouth open in a scream of triumph. "We are kings, Nettle! *Kings!*" he shouted.

But Nettle Pampaspatch was nowhere to be found.

43

KING OF THE FEYLINGS

Abigail lurched forward and grabbed the time cabinet, then bolted across the rocks, veering away from the sea. Rufus followed, pausing only to lift up the unconscious queen and stuff her in his pocket. Iris flew ahead of them, zigzagging in wide arcs as she searched for some place to hide. "Down here!" Abigail whispered, and disappeared into a gap in the cliffs.

The drop was both steep and narrow, the gap barely wide enough to fit into. Abigail moved down the cliff, clutching the time cabinet with one hand and feeling for handholds with the other. Rufus lowered himself after her, his sneakers slippery on the wet rocks. As he did, Iris landed on his shoulder and twisted his earlobe, apparently unconcerned with the fact that he was in the midst of a precarious climb down the face of a cliff.

"King Nettle Pampaspatch!" she screeched. "King. Nettle. Pampaspatch. What were you *thinking?*"

Rufus didn't answer. He was listening for the sound of Diggs's talons clicking on the stone above. But all he could hear was the crash of the waves below.

At last they dropped down into a rocky cove surrounded by steep cliffs. The Lilac Sea swirled onto the shore, kicking up flecks of purple foam.

"Can you see him? Is he coming?" Abigail asked as Rufus looked back the way they came.

"Of course he's coming," Iris said, alighting on the time cabinet in Abigail's arms. "He's just taking his time. It's not as if we can go anywhere. The Moving Meadow's long gone, and we have no idea when it's coming back." She put her face in her hands. "We're doomed."

There was a loud honk and flurry of feathers, and a white goose came flapping toward them with her neck outstretched. "Cotton socks," she honked as she hurled herself at Abigail's shins and wrapped her wings around them. "Yogurt!"

"Really?" Abigail looked around. "Where?"

"Carpentry bathrobe," Trinket said proudly, waddling across the beach to a cluster of flat rocks that nuzzled the side of the cliff. Perched atop the tallest rock was Shamok. And between Shamok's paws was something that looked like a basket made of twigs and seaweed.

Iris gave a shriek and clapped her arms around the goose's neck. "Oh, Trinket! A nest! I *knew* you had potential!"

Inside the nest was a single yellow egg. Shamok gazed at it proudly.

"I'm keeping it safe," he said as they approached. "It's very important."

Abigail snorted. "You were supposed to keep *us* safe. What happened to eating Diggs and the Calamand?"

Shamok refused to meet her eye. "Trinket needed me," he said. "And the half bird smells like poison."

"We can discuss this later," Iris said, landing in the nest beside the egg. "Abigail, ask Trinket for permission to use the egg. Don't be too specific about what it's for. When you get specific, somehow it always turns out badly."

"Use the egg?" Abigail said. "How?"

"I told you there are times when a janati goose egg is exactly what you need, didn't I? Well, this is one of those times. Hurry!"

As Abigail took the egg from its nest, Rufus felt a fluttering in his pocket. He lifted out the feyling queen and stroked her small forehead. Her eyes fluttered open. "My husband is calling me," she said, pushing herself into a sitting position. "I have to go to him."

"No," Rufus said. "Come with us—"

"It's not over yet," the feyling queen said. She wobbled to her feet, her white-and-green wings opening and closing like a beating heart. "Here he is."

Mr. Diggs was climbing down the rocks, his talons loosening a hail of stones. "Ah," he called to them. "Everything

I need in one place. My wife. The time cabinet. That goose. The feisty little greenling." He grinned as he landed on the beach. "And my revenge."

"Crack the egg!" cried Iris. "Quickly!"

Abigail bit her lip. "Sorry," she whispered to the egg.

Then she smashed it against the rock.

∽⌒♈⌒∾

The egg didn't shatter the way Rufus had expected. Its shell became veined with forked cracks, each one lightning-bright. The light grew brighter and then burst through, sending bits of shell flying in every direction. For a moment there was nothing on the rock but a pool of light and a spatter of shell, and then the light began to shape itself into something solid. A long glowing oval that gradually faded into a marbled yellow-white door.

Iris flew to Queen Queen-Anne's-Lace. "Come with us! Quickly, before he can follow."

The feyling queen shook her off. "I can't," she said. "You know I can't."

"Please!" Iris begged. Tears streamed down her face.

But the feyling queen was already flying toward Mr. Diggs.

"Go through the door, Iris," she said in a voice that expected to be obeyed. "All of you. Go."

Diggs ran toward them, his talons clattering and sliding on the stones. Abigail grabbed the time cabinet and ran through, disappearing into a frothy yellow-white mist. Trinket flew after her with Iris close behind. Rufus followed. From inside the mist, he could see Diggs's furious expression as he reached for them. The beach was already fading from view. He could just see Shamok's golden shape, still crouched on the rock beside the empty nest.

"Shamok!" Rufus called. "Hurry!"

But Shamok's eyes were focused on Mr. Diggs.

⚬⚬⚬

Rufus felt the crunch of stones under his feet, heard the rush of moving water. For a moment he thought they were still on Imura, still on the same beach. Then the smell filled his nose. The peppery scent of bay laurel trees. The earthy smell of oak. Hot stones, green grass. Clover wafting from the meadow. They were at Feylawn. Standing by the banks of the creek.

Rufus sank down onto the gravel, too tired to speak. Abigail sat beside him, the time cabinet on her lap. Trinket waddled into the creek.

"Well, would you look at that," Iris said, landing on Rufus's shoulder. "If it isn't the king of the feylings."

Nettle fluttered toward them in an oddly indirect fashion. He spun, then twirled and darted, swaggered and zigzagged, his progress constantly interrupted by fits of exuberance.

"Look at him gloat," Iris said bitterly. "I hope you're pleased with yourself, Rufus."

Nettle landed at their feet, the ruler's locket dangling from his neck.

"I felt your presence," he said. "Do you know, I can feel everything that happens here? I feel the trees and the insects and the birds and the fish and the foxes. I feel where the edges of Feylawn meet the road. I feel the grass grow. It's the most delightful and delirious experience—" He broke off. "Am I making any sense?"

"What doesn't make sense is the idea of *you* wearing the ruler's locket." Iris's expression was steely. "After everything you've done. How is it that the cruelest, the least qualified, the most selfish of all the feylings would end up with it?" Her lip trembled, but she didn't look away. "How is that fair?"

Nettle met her eyes. "You're afraid," he said. "You were always the rudest when you were afraid."

"Of course I'm afraid, you strutting popinjay!" Iris shrieked. "I don't have to wear a necklace to feel the trees and the insects and the birds and the fish and the foxes! I can just look around me and see how beautiful it all is and how little you care about anything besides yourself and how heartbreaking it will be when it's all gone!"

"Gone?" Nettle said. "I guess I should explain. It's hard to think clearly with this thing on. Maybe you get used to it?" He took a seat in the dirt. "The thing about wearing the locket is that I don't feel alone anymore. I felt so alone after my family was gone. And then, when everyone left for the Green World without me, I was the most alone I've ever been. I didn't even want to be a feyling anymore. I stayed in my jay form as much as I could." He leaned forward. "I was angry at you, Rufus, and you, Abigail, and especially at you, Iris, who did everything right when I did everything wrong."

Iris snorted. "Not exactly."

"But do you know who I liked?" Nettle continued. "I liked Rufus's father. He didn't know who I was or what I'd done, but he let me give him presents. Everything I brought him made him happy. Marbles. Peanuts. Bottle caps. Just the *sight* of me made him happy."

"But I made you leave him alone," Rufus said. He wasn't sure what to make of this version of Nettle Pampaspatch. A Nettle who didn't swagger or preen.

"You did," Nettle said. "I hated you for that. I hated you for everything—especially for being the one who saved the feylings instead of me. I wished you dead . . . as you saw through the claxonvine. But I was pledged to serve you in word and deed, so I tried to do so without sacrificing my pride. Until." He gazed out at the chattering creek.

"Until what?" Abigail prompted.

"Until the day the goblins came to Feylawn in their ATVs with Queen Queen-Anne's-Lace sealed in a jar. I couldn't bear seeing how they treated her. I wanted to help. So I rescued the goblins from the creek."

"How did that *help?*" Iris said.

"It allowed me to regain the goblins' trust," Nettle said. "And it gave me a chance to talk to Queen Queen-Anne's-Lace. She told me I would be most useful to her if I pretended to be their spy. So that's what I did."

"But if you were just pretending, why didn't you *tell* us what you were doing?" Rufus asked.

"We thought *you* were the one telling the Calamand where we were," added Abigail. "But it was the whistle, wasn't it? The whistle she took from me."

"You already didn't trust me," Nettle said. "I couldn't imagine why you would. And after a while, it stopped mattering what you thought of me. What anybody thought of me. I just wanted to be somebody I wasn't ashamed of. So I gave Diggs enough information to fool him into thinking I was on his side, and I did what I could to keep you safe and serve my queen."

He reached behind his head and unfastened the clasp on the ruler's locket. "Until our queen is freed from her marriage bond, this belongs to you, Iris. You're the one who thought about all of us when we were too defeated and angry to do it ourselves."

Iris shook her head. "No."

"Don't be ridiculous," Rufus told her. "Nettle's right—you're the reason the feylings got their train back. And if you put on the necklace, you'll be the reason Feylawn gets saved."

"No," Iris said. "We did it together. You, me, and Abigail. And you need to understand what will happen if I—if *anyone*—wears this locket."

44

ALL THAT YOU LOVE

They found Grandpa Jack in the garden, picking beans.

"Look at these beauties," he said, holding out a basket filled with purple, green, and scarlet beans. He peered at them from under the brim of a straw sun hat. "Your parents were just here looking for you two. Said there was a disagreement over lunch and Abigail missed her interview at Stormweather Prep."

"Where are they now?" Rufus asked. He glanced at his phone: 2:48. It was almost as if they'd never left.

"Checking to see if you went home. I'm supposed to walk down to the road and call them the second I see you. Unless you'd like some lemonade first." He gestured to the wooden table under the grape arbor. There was a pitcher of lemonade on it, and three glasses, and a basket of muffins.

Abigail sat down at the table with a grateful sigh. "I don't think I've ever been so hungry and thirsty in my life."

Grandpa Jack filled the glasses and handed them

around. "Do you feel like telling me what you four have been up to?" He looked at Iris, perched on Abigail's shoulder, and Nettle, sitting on Rufus's. "You're Iris, the moth who helped cure my son," he added. "And you're the little fellow who spent weeks throwing marbles at me and breaking my crockery."

"Sorry about that," Nettle said. "I've been trying to do better."

Rufus attempted to speak, found that his throat was too dry to make anything more than a croak, and took a long, quenching swallow of lemonade.

"I think we did it," he said. "I think we saved Feylawn." Saying it out loud made it almost seem real.

"We *did* do it," Iris said, swooping from Abigail's shoulder to hover in front of Grandpa Jack. "It's just a question of whether it's saved for now, or for always."

Grandpa Jack stared at Iris. He looked at Rufus, and Abigail, and Nettle. "Are you saying they won't be turning it into a laboratory?" he asked. "No little men with loud motors zooming across my creek?"

"It's not actually *your* creek," Iris said. "It's ours. All of Feylawn is. You humans were never supposed to know it existed." She landed on the table and folded her hands in front of her. "Glompers like Avery Sweete were only able to find it because we lost the ruler's locket, which was how we'd kept Feylawn hidden."

"It's pretty well hidden now," Grandpa Jack said. "Just ask the postal service. They've been trying to find this place for seventy years."

"All that took a lot of work," Iris said. "And overall, it hasn't gone that well. We've been in danger all the time. From goblins *and* from glompers. And so now we're at a crossroads." She pulled the tiny locket from her pouch and held it out. "If I put this on, Feylawn disappears."

"What?" Rufus exclaimed. "What do you mean?"

"She means that you three will be the only non-feylings who can find it," Nettle said.

"Why us?" Abigail asked between bites of muffin.

"You have clearsight," Iris said. "And other gifts. You'll find your way. It won't be as easy as it was, but it won't be impossible."

The lemonade, so cold and sweet a moment ago, suddenly felt like it was dissolving Rufus's tongue. He didn't want to "find his way," whatever that meant. He wanted things to be like they always were.

"But—" he began.

A terrifying sound made it impossible to continue. It was something like thunder that had been pureed in a blender.

"Shamok!" Abigail cried.

The leopard galloped toward them, his tail arrowed behind him as he threaded among rows of carrots, beets, lettuce, and tomatoes. From tail to whiskers, his golden coat was once again dappled and decorated with round black spots. He slowed down at last and then plunged his head into a bucket filled with mossy rainwater.

"I've been poisoned!" he panted, slurping noisily. "I'm going to die."

"You won't die," said Queen Queen-Anne's-Lace, who sat astride the leopard's back. "I've told you that several times. You have a bad taste in your mouth, that's all."

Iris gasped and flew to embrace her. "How did you escape?"

The queen's hair was matted and bedraggled. Her dress was marbled with saltwater stains. Her wings were brown and curling at the edges. But for all that, she seemed to be doing much better than she had been just a short time before. She met Iris's eyes and smiled.

Shamok lifted his dripping muzzle from the bucket. "I ate the poisonous half bird and now I'm going to die."

"You *ate* Mr. Diggs?" Rufus gasped.

"And now I must die." Shamok lay down on his side and shut his eyes.

Iris had begun to weep. "You're free, Lacy," she said, holding out the locket. "Now you can rule us again. We've done a terrible job without you. We need you to fix everything. We've been running around like chicks with our hens cut off."

"Heads," Rufus said.

"Actually," Abigail said, "she means *hens*, I think."

"Of course," said Iris. "The hens are the ones who take care of the chicks. We feylings need a hen to take care of us because we're too selfish and scatterbrained and bad at thinking to manage on our own."

Instead of taking the locket, Queen Queen-Anne's-Lace grasped Iris's hands, leaving the necklace to dangle between them.

"The locket is yours, Iris," she said. "If I had been more like you, none of this would have happened."

"How can you say that?" Iris said. Tears trickled down her face and poured off the end of her nose. "Everything's been my fault, from the moment you lost the locket to the Calamand."

"I got the locket back," the queen said gently. "But putting it on was harder than I expected. Things had changed. Glompers lived here now, and they'd become my friends. And when Carson betrayed us and cut down our Roving Tree, I felt responsible. So I tried to fix the situation on my own. I accepted Mr. Diggs's marriage proposal without consulting anyone—not even Garnet, who could have told me what I was agreeing to. It was only the night before our wedding that I understood what I had done. If I married him with the ruler's locket, he'd have control over Feylawn. So I hid it, using a riddle-fern spell that I hoped would keep him from forcing me to retrieve it."

"That was clever," Iris said. "You always put us first."

"Did I? I wonder. Because in the end, it was you who

saved us, Iris. You did it by asking for help. Something I never did."

"But so many things went wrong!" Iris cried. "I've been a nervous wreck! My stomach hurts all the time!"

"Mine too," Shamok said. "Because I've been poisoned."

Iris sniffled. "All I ever wanted was to be like you," she said to Queen Queen-Anne's-Lace. "When you freed the Calamand, I thought my heart was going to break."

Queen Queen-Anne's-Lace coughed, a dry rattling cough that Rufus remembered from when Iris was at her sickest. "It broke my own heart to do it," she said. "But I was desperate to get out of the tunnels before I died and terrified by what Rance and Garnet were telling me about Feylawn's future. I wanted the Calamand to steal me from Diggs and sever our marriage bond with her gold-handled Slicers. She'd agreed to do it, but Diggs got in the way. And the scissors, alas, went to the bottom of the sea." She flew over to Shamok and stroked his ears. "Luckily, I had another option."

Grandpa Jack had been listening to their conversation with an expression of profound bewilderment. He took off his straw hat, rubbed his head, took a sip of lemonade, and then finally spoke. "I'm having a bit of trouble following all the ins and outs of this conversation," he said. "But I'm gathering we have a choice to make that has to do with that little necklace."

"If one of us wears the locket," Iris said, "Feylawn vanishes. It happened once today already—maybe you noticed?"

"I've just been working in my garden," Grandpa Jack said. "Felt like a beautiful afternoon."

"Nothing much changes when you're here—it's getting here that would be the problem. You wouldn't be able to come and go the way you do now. Feylawn would exist in its own time and place, here but not here."

"I wouldn't be able to live here is what you mean." Grandpa Jack turned his glass of lemonade in circles on the table. He turned to Rufus and Abigail. "What do you think?"

Abigail knelt beside Shamok and rubbed his belly. "I don't know," she said. "It's your home. I hate for you to give up your home. But it's *their* home, too."

"Rufus?"

Tears poked behind Rufus's eyes. "I want it to be like it was before," he said. "I want us to just be able to come here whenever we want to. And I want *you* to be here when we do." He took a breath, trying to keep his voice from breaking. "But I also want it to be protected. We came so close to seeing it destroyed."

The afternoon was already cooling down. The beans on their tripod trellises sent tall witch-hat-shaped shadows across the garden.

"The truth is, I'd gotten used to the idea of moving,"

Grandpa Jack said. "It's occurred to me that I'm getting a bit old to live so far out of the way of things. And then Robin-Ella and I . . . well, we're enjoying each other's company. She's asked me to move in with her, and I said I would."

"You did?" Rufus felt like the grass beneath the table was tilting, twisting. He had never imagined Grandpa Jack leaving Feylawn voluntarily. He tried to imagine the farmhouse without Grandpa Jack's things in it. Grandpa Jack's things living in someone else's house. "But why wouldn't she move in with you at Feylawn?"

"Robin-Ella likes Feylawn quite a bit, but she likes having a telephone and Internet and the like, too." He paused. "Would I be able to bring her with me? If I found my way back here?"

Queen-Anne's-Lace nodded. "Just hold on to her hand."

"I do that anyway," Grandpa Jack said. "Can't help myself."

"Then it's up to you," Iris said, looking first at Rufus and then at Abigail.

Rufus shut his eyes and felt Feylawn all around him, its rustles and birdcalls, its smells and breezes, its soil and sky and trees and grasses.

What do I do? he asked it. He didn't know how he expected it to answer.

But an answer came to him anyway. It was the voice of the Crinnyeye who had whispered in his ear two weeks before. The fortune that had kept spitting out of the machines in the Hall of Prophecy.

Give up all that you love for all that you are.

Who was he?

He was Rufus. And Feylawn was a part of him.

He'd always be able to find it.

He opened his eyes and met Abigail's. She nodded.

"I think you should wear the locket," he said. "But not yet. We'll need to pack Grandpa Jack's things. Empty out the barn."

Grandpa Jack got up and put his hand on Rufus's shoulders.

"It won't be easy," he said. "But that doesn't mean it's not the right thing to do."

45

A GIFT FROM BLUEY

Rufus had set his alarm to go off at midnight. His mother was at work and his father was asleep. He crept into his parents' bedroom and gently shook his father's arm.

"Dad," he whispered. "I need you to see something."

His father blinked at him through a haze of sleep. "It's the middle of the night, Ru."

"It's important."

His father rolled to a sitting position. "What's wrong? Are you sick?"

Rufus shook his head. The only thing that was wrong was that his father had gone to bed angry at him. Again.

"Just come. I promise it's for a good reason," he said.

Nettle was waiting for them in the backyard. He perched on the patio table in his Steller's jay form, his crest fanned to full elegance. When he saw Rufus's father he cawed a greeting and then dropped a shiny penny on the table.

"Bluey!" Rufus's father said. "Where have you been?" He picked up the coin. "Is that a present?"

"A small token," Nettle said. "I'm deeply sorry for hurting you. I was a vain, spiteful feyling, and I'll never forgive myself for the way I behaved."

Rufus's father gaped at the bird in front of him. "It's almost like he's speaking," he said to Rufus.

"He *is* speaking," Rufus said. "He's apologizing. He's the one who caused your accident."

"A broken rope caused my accident," his father said. "I know you've felt responsible, Ru, but you shouldn't." He turned the coin over in his hand. "I'm sorry I got mad at you today. You had every right to be upset about losing Feylawn."

"I'm sorry, too," Rufus said, because he knew that it was his father who had ended up losing Feylawn, even if he didn't know it yet. "I wanted you to have a job that made you proud."

His father slung an arm around his shoulder. "I *have* a job that makes me proud," he said. "I'm your dad. It's the best and the hardest job I'll ever have."

"I know I don't make it easy," Rufus said. "I'm not like—"

"You're not like *anyone*," his father said. "You're just who you are, which is exactly who you should be." He sat down on one of the patio chairs and looked up at the night sky. "You probably won't understand this until you have kids of your own, but sometimes I look at you and I forget that you're not me. But you're somebody else, somebody new, and my job is just to help you be that person."

"I *am* that person," Rufus said. "You're doing fine."

His father sat up. "I'm trying," he said. "How 'bout we go back to sleep?" He held the coin between his fingers and looked over at Nettle, who was busy preening the feathers of his chest. "Thanks, Bluey. I'll treasure it always."

Rufus let his father walk him back to bed and tuck him under the covers.

He waited until his dad had returned to his own room, and then a little longer to make sure he was asleep. Then he got dressed and went back downstairs to the backyard, where Nettle was waiting for him.

"Let's go," Rufus said. "I don't want you to miss your train."

⁓⦿⦿⦿⁓

Dawn was pinking the sky by the time they'd loaded Grandpa Jack's truck with the last of the furniture. The Green World feylings had helped more than Rufus had thought possible, using a whole herd of green horses to carry bags and boxes to Robin-Ella's along the Wind's Road. In the end, both the farmhouse and the barn were bare and empty, and Rufus felt as though his insides had been emptied, too.

At last they went to sit by the stump of the Roving Tree to wait for the train. It felt so different from the last time it had come, just five weeks earlier. Then, there had been a mood of celebration and euphoria. Now the feylings wore the somber expressions of people at a funeral.

"Are you sad?" Abigail asked.

"Of course," Rufus said. "But relieved, too. I'm so tired of worrying about everything."

"Me too," Abigail said. Shamok was asleep at her feet, and she rubbed her bare toes in his fur. "There's no prisoner on Imura anymore. I guess he'll stay here."

Grandpa Jack sat in the grass beside them, looking up at the stars. For a while, none of them spoke.

"What's that?" Grandpa Jack asked suddenly. A small figure was tramping across the grass.

Rufus squinted into the darkness. "Garnet?"

"I was hoping for an invitation to the party," Garnet said. She wore her turquoise cardigan and a yellow cable-knit scarf.

"It's not exactly a party," Rufus said.

"I'm afraid we have some bad news for you," Abigail said. "About your brother."

"I ate him," Shamok said, lifting his head.

"So I heard." Garnet scratched her colorful belly. "I suppose that means you won't be returning to the tunnels, Lacy. It's too bad. I enjoyed our chats."

"You won't have much time for chatting now," Queen-Anne's-Lace said, swooping over to hover in front of Garnet. "If I'm right about your plans."

Garnet smiled. "We'll see. Gneiss will make a run for it."

"A run for what?" Rufus asked. He had hoped his troubles with Mr. Gneiss were over.

"Now that Mr. Diggs is dead, the goblins will have to choose a new tunnel boss for the Northwest Region," said Queen-Anne's-Lace. "Garnet's got quite a following down below."

"Tunnel boss?" Abigail said. "You mean like—leader of the goblins?"

Garnet looked up at her from under her eyelashes. "It's up to the voters, of course."

"Is that why you helped us?" Rufus said. "You wanted Diggs out of the way?"

"I never do anything for just one reason. But I won't deny that this turn of events has been useful for my career." She gave a small bow. "It's been a pleasure doing business with you both."

Just then, two thin strands of tracks glided over the grass like quicksilver. A cloud of white steam appeared. Then the train came rocketing out of nowhere, its green cars emerging one by one as if from an invisible tunnel. Grandpa Jack's mouth fell open.

"Feylawn never runs out of wonders," he murmured.

As the train huffed to a halt, Trillium stuck her head from the window of the cab. "Sticks and weeds! Is that Queen Queen-Anne's-Lace?"

"Just Queen-Anne's-Lace. You have a new queen now."

Queen-Anne's-Lace fluttered close to Iris. "Are you ready?"

Iris nodded. "If you'll help me."

"We'll all help you," Queen-Anne's-Lace said.

Then she fastened the ruler's locket around Iris's neck.

46

DISAPPEARANCES

Rufus and Abigail sat at the patio table in Rufus's backyard, doing nothing.

It had been a very long time since Rufus had done nothing. He found it slightly uncomfortable, like a favorite shirt that had somehow grown too small. Still, he was determined to enjoy it, since immediately after the nothing there was likely to be something, and chances were high that the something would be unpleasant.

A door slammed somewhere inside the house.

"Here we go," Abigail said. "You talk first."

"*You* talk first," Rufus countered. "They'll listen to you."

"Not after yesterday," Abigail said. "My mom's still mad about me missing my interview."

At that moment the back door flew open.

"Well, I hope you're satisfied!" Aunt Chrissy tromped down the back steps and flung herself into a metal patio chair. "We've been swindled!"

"We haven't been *swindled*," Rufus's father said, sitting down beside her "We didn't sign anything. No money has changed hands. Which is a big relief, given everything that's gone on this morning."

"What happened?" Abigail asked. Her eyes widened with concern even as she gave Rufus a small nudge with her elbow.

"Dees-Troy has *disappeared*!" Aunt Chrissy said. "We went to their office to discuss the contract and the place was empty. Stripped! As if it was never there! I tried to call Mr. Gneiss, but his phone's disconnected. Tried to email, but it bounced back. Even the website's gone!"

"And that's not all." Rufus's father ran a hand over the waves of his hair. "We're having trouble locating Feylawn."

Rufus tried to make his face look confused. "Feylawn's always been hard to find," he said.

"Well, now it's IMPOSSIBLE!" Aunt Chrissy shrieked. "We've been looking for *hours*. Even your grandpa Jack can't find it."

Grandpa Jack came through the back door carrying a pink bakery box of Cloud Nine donuts. "It's my fault, I suppose," he said, placing the box on the glass-topped patio table. "I got it into my head to move my things down to Robin-Ella's yesterday. Without all my stuff weighing the place down, it must have floated off."

"It's not a joking matter." Aunt Chrissy helped herself to a Thunder Cloud donut and bit into it as if it had claimed personal responsibility for Feylawn's disappearance. "Feylawn was supposed to make us rich. Now we have nothing! Everything we've worked for is gone!"

Rufus's father leaned forward and rested his elbows on his knees. "Maybe it's for the best," he said after a moment.

"*What?*" Aunt Chrissy stared at him. "In what way is it *for the best?*"

"Feylawn's never brought us anything but misfortune. We wanted to be rid of it and we are. The most important thing is that we got Pop out of there. Imagine if it had disappeared and taken him with it."

"But we wanted to be rid of it *and* get rich," Aunt Chrissy said. "We were *this close* to selling it."

"I don't think we were, actually," Rufus's father said. "The more I read through that contract with Dees-Troy, the worse it looked to me. It was too good to be true, Chris. They were taking us for a ride." He pulled a jar of pills from the pocket of his blazer. "I'm afraid the Smile-A-Day vitamins they gave me might have clouded my judgment."

Aunt Chrissy ran her hands through her frizzy blond mane. "I can't *believe* Mr. Gneiss would do this to me," she sighed. "I really thought we had a bond."

⚬⚬⚬

Two weeks later, Rufus stood in the parking lot of Floodtown Burrito, drinking a watermelon agua fresca from a paper cup and looking through the trees at the place that used to be Feylawn. It wasn't much to look at—just a sliver of weedy ground behind a barbed-wire fence. The rest of Galosh had knitted together in its absence, like the skin closing over a wound. The one time he'd walked up the old gravel road, he'd found himself wandering through residential streets, past a playground and a Pilates studio and a fire station.

The family had come to terms with Feylawn's disappearance sooner than he'd expected, even Rufus's father, who he thought would take it the hardest. A few days afterward, his father had come down to breakfast one morning with the fidgety expression of someone who had an announcement to make.

"I flipped a coin," he told Rufus, "and I've decided I'm going to get my teaching credential. I've always wanted to teach math—share my passion for numbers! Shape young minds! Nurture the next Steve Wozniak!"

"Flipped a coin?" Rufus repeated. That wasn't the way his father usually made decisions. Usually there were lists involved. Pros and cons.

"The coin Bluey gave me, actually," his father said. "I did a little research. Turns out it's a 1944 steel wheat penny. Worth enough to pay off our debts *and* let me go back to school."

With that, things in the Takada-Collins household had begun to shift. His mother was working regular hours again. His father was busy with his applications for teaching programs. No one was worrying about how Rufus spent his time. So today he'd texted Abigail and suggested they meet at the burrito shop.

"Do you have a plan?" she asked when she arrived.

"Nope," Rufus said. "I just figured, haze makes ways."

As they walked up the gravel road, he could almost smell the sweetness of the meadow grass and the peppery scent of the woods. Feylawn was there, just out of sight, like a door waiting to be opened. The two of them would find it, if not today, then tomorrow, or the next day.

Summer wasn't over yet.

ACKNOWLEDGMENTS

My deepest and milkiest thanks to the Pigeons, whose wings lifted this book from the ground when it was struggling to take off and who were always beside me, sometimes literally, while I wrote it. Bushels of gratitude to my editors, Joy Peskin and Elizabeth Lee, whose guidance improved this book at every turn. Heartfelt thanks to my agent and lodestar Erin Murphy, whose vision got me here back when Rufus and Abigail were still at the start of their journey. All the love in the eight worlds to Cliff, who helped me tease through the tangled plotlines, and to Milo, who is always willing to answer my oddball questions. Спасибо to the Northeastern University Russian-Speaking Club for helping me name Shamok. A special shout-out to all the folks at FSG BYR and MacKids who work to make beautiful books and connect them to readers—without you, I'd just be talking to myself. A tip of the hat to the real Christian Sardo, and his mother, Meredith Momoda, for winning the chance to name a character in the Kidlit Against Anti-AAPI Racism Auction. And to any reader who finds what they're looking for in these pages: I wrote them just for you.